Romantic Times BOOKreviews loves

ELIZABETH
LOWELL

"It is not hard to see why Lowell's novels have enjoyed their
superior success over the years."
—on *This Time Love*

"The masterful storytelling skills of perennial favorite
Elizabeth Lowell place her in a rarefied class of authors
who never disappoint."
—on *Running Scared*

"The powerful storytelling that is a hallmark
of Elizabeth Lowell's work makes each of her books
a riveting journey."
—on *Moving Target*

"An emotionally driven and sensually charged book
that is vintage Lowell."
—on *Eden Burning*

"When it comes to delivering epic romance and suspense,
Ms. Lowell is in a class by herself."
—on *Midnight in Ruby Bayou*

ELIZABETH LOWELL

GRANITE MAN & WARRIOR

HQN™

HQN™

ISBN-13: 978-0-373-77254-4
ISBN-10:   0-373-77254-8

GRANITE MAN & WARRIOR

Copyright © 2007 by Harlequin Books S.A.

The publisher acknowledges the copyright holder of the individual works as follows:

GRANITE MAN
Copyright © 1991 by Two of a Kind Inc.

WARRIOR
Copyright © 1991 by Two of a Kind Inc.

This edition published by arrangement with Harlequin Books S.A.

® and TM are trademarks of the publisher. Trademarks indicated with ® are registered in the United States Patent and Trademark Office, the Canadian Trade Marks Office and in other countries.

www.HQNBooks.com

Printed in U.S.A.

CONTENTS

GRANITE MAN

CHAPTER ONE

FORCING HERSELF TO LET OUT THE BREATH she had been holding, Mariah MacKenzie fumbled with the brass door knocker, failed to hang on to it, and curled her trembling fingers into a fist.

Fifteen years is a long time. I should have telephoned. What if my brother doesn't remember me? What if he throws me off the ranch? Where will I go then?

Using her knuckles, Mariah rapped lightly on the door frame of the ranch house. The sound echoed like thunder, but there was no response. She lifted her hand again. This time she managed to hold on to the horseshoe-shaped knocker long enough to deliver several staccato raps.

"Keep your shirt on! I'm coming!"

The voice was deep, impatient, unmistakably masculine. Mariah's heartbeat doubled even as she nervously took a backward step away from the door. A few instants later she was glad she had retreated.

The man who appeared filled the doorway. Literally. Mariah started to say her brother's name, only to find that her mouth was too dry to speak. She retreated again, unable to think, unable to breathe.

Cash McQueen frowned as he stared down at the slender girl who was backing away from him so quickly he was afraid she would fall off the porch. That would be a pity. It had been years since he had seen such an appealing female. Long legs, elegant breasts, big golden eyes, tousled hair that was the color of bittersweet chocolate, and an aura of vulnerability that slid past his hard-earned defenses.

"Can I help you?" Cash asked, trying to soften the edges of his deep voice. There was nothing he could do to gentle the rest of his appearance. He was big and he was strong and no amount of smiling could change those facts. Women usually didn't mind, but this one looked on the edge of bolting.

"My car b-boiled," Mariah said, the only thing she could think of.

"The whole thing?"

Cash's gentle voice and wry question drew a hesitant smile from Mariah. She stopped inching backward and shook her head. "Just the part that held water."

A smile changed Cash's face from forbidding to handsome. He walked out of the house and onto the front porch. Clenching her hands together, Mariah looked up at the big man who must be her brother. He had unruly, thick hair that was a gleaming chestnut brown where it wasn't streaked pale gold by the sun. He was muscular rather than soft. He looked like a man who was accustomed to using his body for hard physical work. His eyebrows were wickedly arched, darker than his hair, and his eyes were—

"The wrong color."

"I beg your pardon?" Cash asked, frowning.

Mariah flushed, realizing that she had spoken aloud.

"I'm—that is—I thought this was the Rocking M," she managed to stammer.

"It is."

All other emotions gave way to dismay as Mariah understood that the unthinkable had happened: the MacKenzie ranch had been sold to strangers.

Of the many possibilities she had imagined, this had not been among them. All her plans for coming back to the lost home of her dreams, all her half-formed hopes of pursuing a lost mine over the landscape of her ancestors, all her anticipation of being reunited with the older brother whose love had been the bright core of her childhood; all that was gone. And there was nothing to take its place except a new understanding of just how alone she was.

"Are you all right?" Cash asked, concerned by her sudden pallor, wanting to fold her into his arms and give her comfort.

Comfort? he asked himself sardonically. *Well, that too, I suppose. God, but that is one sexy woman looking like she is about to faint at my feet.*

A big, callused hand closed around Mariah's upper arm, both steadying her and making her tremble. She looked up—way up—into eyes that were a dark, smoky blue, yet as clear as a mountain lake in twilight. And, like a lake, the luminous surface concealed depths of shadow.

"Sit down, honey. You look a little pale around the edges," Cash said, urging her toward the old-fashioned porch swing. He seated her with a restrained strength that allowed no opposition. "I'll get you some water. Unless you'd like something with more kick?"

"No. I'm fine," Mariah said, but she made no move to stand up again. Her legs wouldn't have cooperated. Without thinking, she wrapped her fingers around a powerful, hairy wrist. "Did Luke MacKenzie—did the former owner leave a forwarding address?"

"Last time I checked, Luke was still the owner of the Rocking M, along with Tennessee Blackthorn."

Relief swept through Mariah. She smiled with blinding brilliance. "Are you Mr. Blackthorn?"

"No, I'm Cash McQueen," he said, smiling in return, wondering what she would do if he sat next to her and pulled her into his lap. "Sure you don't want some water or brandy?"

"I don't understand. Do you work here?"

"No. I'm visiting my sister, Luke's wife."

"Luke is married?"

Until Cash's eyes narrowed, Mariah didn't realize how dismayed she sounded. He looked at her with cool speculation in his eyes, a coolness that made her realize just how warm he had been before.

"Is Luke's marriage some kind of problem for you?" Cash asked.

Dark blue eyes watched Mariah with a curiosity that was suddenly more predatory than sensual. She knew beyond a doubt that any threat to his sister's marriage would be taken head-on by the big man who was watching her the way a hawk watched a careless field mouse.

"No problem," Mariah said faintly, fighting the tears that came from nowhere to strangle her voice. She felt her uncertain self-control fragmenting and was too tired to care. "I should have guessed he would be married by now."

"Who are you?"

The question was as blunt as the rock hammer hanging from a loop on Cash's wide leather belt. The cold steel tool looked softer than his narrowed eyes. The almost overwhelming sense of being close to hard, barely restrained masculinity increased the more Mariah looked at Cash—wide, muscular shoulders, flat waist, lean hips, long legs whose power was hinted at with each supple shift of his weight. Cash was violently male, yet his hand on her arm had been gentle. Keeping that in mind, she tried to smile up at him as she explained why she was no threat to his sister's marriage.

"I'm Mariah MacKenzie. Luke's sister." Still trying to smile, Mariah held out her hand as she said, "Pleased to meet you, Mr. McQueen."

"Cash." The answer was automatic, as was his taking of Mariah's hand. "You're Luke's *sister?*"

Even as Cash asked the question, his senses registered the soft, cool skin of Mariah's hand, the silken smoothness of her wrist when his grip shifted, and the racing of her pulse beneath his fingertips. Hardly able to believe what he had heard, he looked again into Mariah's eyes. Only then did he realize that he had been so struck by her sexual appeal that he had overlooked her resemblance to Luke. He, too, had tawny topaz eyes and hair so brown it was almost black.

But Mariah's resemblance to her brother ended there. All five feet, eight inches of her was very definitely female.

Beneath the worn jeans and faded college T-shirt were the kinds of curves that made a man's hands feel both empty and hungry to be filled. Cash remembered the smooth resilience of her arm when he had steadied her, and then he remembered the warmth beneath the soft skin.

"What in hell brings you back to the Rocking M after all these years?"

There was no way for Mariah to explain to Cash her inchoate longings for a lost home, a lost family, a lost childhood. Each time she opened her mouth to try, no words came.

"I just wanted to—to see my brother," she said finally.

Cash glanced at his wrist. His new black metal watch told the time around the globe, was guaranteed to work up to a hundred and eighty feet underwater and in temperatures down to forty below zero. It was his third such watch in less than a year. So far, it was still telling time. But then, he hadn't been out prospecting yet. The repeated shock of rock hammer or pickax on granite had done in the other watches. That, and panning for gold in the Rocking M's icy mountain creeks.

"Luke won't be in from the north range until dinner, and probably not even then," Cash said. "Carla is in Cortez shopping with Logan. They aren't due back until late tomorrow, which means that unless the Blackthorns get in early from Boulder, there won't be anyone to cook dinner except me. That's why I don't expect Luke back. Neither one of us would walk across a room to eat the other's cooking."

Mariah tried to sort out the spate of names and information, but had little success. In the end she hung on to the only words that mattered: Luke wouldn't be back for several hours. After waiting and hoping and dreaming for so many years, the hours she had left to wait seemed like an eternity. She was tired, discouraged and so sad that it was all she could do not to put her head on Cash's strong shoulder and cry. Her feelings were irrational, but then so was her whole hopeful journey back to the landscape of her childhood and her dreams.

It will be all right. Everything will work out fine. All I have to do is hang on and wait just a little longer. Luke will be here and he'll remember me and I'll remember him and everything will be all right.

Despite the familiar litany of reassurance Mariah spoke in the silence of her mind, the tears that had been making her throat raspy began to burn behind her eyelids. Knowing it was foolish, unable to help herself, she looked out across the ranch yard to MacKenzie Ridge and fought not to cry.

"Until then, someone had better go take a look at your car," Cash continued. "How far back down the road did it quit?"

He had to repeat the question twice before Mariah's wide golden eyes focused on him.

"I don't know."

The huskiness of Mariah's voice told Cash that she was fighting tears. A nearly tangible sadness was reflected in her tawny eyes, a sadness that was underlined by the vulnerable line of her mouth.

Yet even as sympathy stirred strongly inside Cash, bitter experience told him that the chances were slim and none that Mariah was one-tenth as vulnerable as she looked sitting on the porch swing, her fingers interlaced too tightly in her lap. Helpless women always found some strong, willing, stupid man to take care of them.

Someone like Cash McQueen.

Mariah looked up at Cash, her eyes wide with unshed tears and an unconscious appeal for understanding.

"I guess I'll wait here until..." Mariah's voice faded at the sudden hardening of Cash's expression.

"Don't you think your time would be better spent trying to fix your car?" Cash asked. "Or were you planning on letting the nearest man take care of it for you?"

The brusque tone of Cash's voice made Mariah flinch. She searched his eyes but saw none of the warmth that had been there before she had told him who she was.

"I hadn't thought about it," she admitted. "I didn't think about anything but getting here."

Cash grunted. "Well, you're here."

His tone made it clear that he was less than delighted by her presence. Fighting tears and a feeling of being set adrift, Mariah told herself that it was silly to let a stranger's disapproval upset her. She looked out toward the barn, blinked rapidly, and finally focused on the building. Its silhouette triggered childhood memories, Luke playing hide-and-seek with her, catching her and lifting her laughing and squirming over his head.

"Yes, I'm here," Mariah said huskily.

"And your car isn't."

"No." She banished the last of the memories and faced the big man who was watching her without pleasure. "I'll need something to carry water."

"There's a plastic water can in the barn."

"Is there a car I could drive?"

Cash shook his head.

Mariah thought of the long walk she had just made and

was on the edge of suggesting that she wait for her brother's return before she tried to cope with her car. Cash's coolly appraising look put an end to that idea. She had received that look too many times from her stepfather, a man who took pleasure only in her failures.

"Good thing I wore my walking shoes," Mariah said with forced cheerfulness.

Cash muttered something beneath his breath, then added, "Stay here. I'll take care of it for you."

"Thank you, but that's not necessary. I can—"

"The hell you can," he interrupted abruptly. "You wouldn't get a hundred yards carrying two gallons of water. Even if you did, you wouldn't know what to do once you got there, would you?"

Before Mariah could think of a suitable retort, Cash stepped off the porch and began crossing the yard with long, powerful strides. He vanished behind the barn. A few minutes later he reappeared. He was driving a battered Jeep. As he passed the porch she realized that he didn't mean to stop for her.

"Wait!" Mariah called out, leaping up, sending the swing gyrating. "I'm going with you!"

"Why?" Cash asked, watching with disfavor as Mariah ran up to the Jeep.

"To drive the car back, of course."

"I'll tow it in."

It was too late. Mariah was scrambling into the lumpy passenger seat. Without a word Cash gunned the Jeep out of the yard and headed toward the dirt road that was the Rocking M's sole connection to the outer world.

The Jeep's canvas cover did little to shield the occupants

from the wind. Hair the color of bittersweet chocolate flew in a wild cloud around Mariah's shoulders and whipped across her face. She grabbed one handful, then another, wrestling the slippery strands to a standstill, gathering and twisting the shining mass into a knot at the nape of her neck. As the wind picked apart the knot, she tucked in escaping strands.

Cash watched the process from the corner of his eye, intrigued despite himself by the glossy, silky hair and the curve of Mariah's nape, a curve that was both vulnerable and sexy. When he realized the trend of his thoughts, he was irritated. Surely by now he should have figured out that the more vulnerable a girl appeared, the greater the weapon she had to use on men such as himself—men who couldn't cure themselves of the belief that they should protect women from the harshness of life.

Stupid men, in a word.

"Luke didn't say anything about expecting you."

Although Cash said nothing more, his tone made it plain that he thought the ranch—and Luke—would have been better off without Mariah.

"He wasn't expecting me."

"What?" Cash's head swung for an instant toward Mariah.

"He doesn't know I'm coming."

Whatever Cash said was mercifully obliterated by the sudden bump and rattle as the Jeep hurtled over the cattle guard set into the dirt road. Mariah made a startled sound and hung on to the cold metal frame. The noise of wheels racing over the cattle guard, plus the smell of nearby grass and the distant tang of evergreens, triggered a dizzying rush of memories in Mariah.

Eyes the color of my own. Clever hands that made a doll whole again. Tall and strong, lifting me, tossing me, catching me and laughing with me. Dark hair and funny faces that made me smile when I wanted to cry.

There were other memories, too, darker memories of arguments and sobbing and a silence so tense Mariah had been afraid it would explode, destroying everything familiar. And then it had exploded and her mother's screams had gone on and on, rising and falling with the howling December storm.

Shivering in the aftermath of a storm that had occurred fifteen years ago, Mariah looked out over the hauntingly familiar landscape. She had recognized MacKenzie Ridge before she had seen the ranch buildings at its base. The rugged silhouette was burned into her memory. She had watched her home in the rearview mirror of her grandparents' car, and when the ranch buildings had vanished into a fold of land, she had sobbed her loss.

It hadn't been the house she mourned, or even the father who had been left behind. She had wept for Luke, the brother who had loved her when their parents were too consumed by private demons to notice either of their children.

That's all in the past. I've come home. Everything will be all right now. I'm finally home.

The reassuring litany calmed Mariah until she looked at the hard profile of the man who sat within touching distance of her. And she wanted to touch him. She wanted to ask what she had done to make him dislike her. Was it simply that she was alive, breathing, somehow reminding him of an unhappy past? It had been that way with her stepfather, an instant masculine antagonism toward another man's child that nothing Mariah did could alter.

What would she do if Luke disliked her on sight, too?

CHAPTER TWO

ARMS ACHING, MARIAH HELD UP THE rumpled hood of her car while Cash rummaged in the engine compartment, muttering choice phrases she tried very hard not to overhear. A grimy, enigmatic array of parts was lined up on the canvas cloth that Cash had put on the ground nearby. Mariah looked anxiously from the greasy parts to the equally greasy hands of the big man who had taken one look at her sedan's ancient engine and suggested making a modern junk sculpture of it.

"When was the last time you changed the oil?"

The tone of voice was just short of a snarl. Mariah closed her eyes and tried to think.

"I can't remember. I wrote it in the little book in the glove compartment, but I needed paper for a grocery list so I—"

The rest of what Mariah said was lost beneath a rumble of masculine disgust. She caught her lower lip between her teeth and worried the soft flesh nervously.

"When was the last time you added water to the radiator?"

That was easy. "Today. Several times. Then I ran out."

Slowly Cash's head turned toward Mariah. In the shadow of the hood his eyes burned like dark, bleak sapphire flames. "What?"

Mariah swallowed and spoke quietly, calmly, as though gentleness and sweet reason was contagious.

"I always put water in the radiator every day, sometimes more often, depending on how far I'm going. Naturally I always carry water," she added, "but I ran out today. After that little town on the way in—"

"West Fork," Cash interrupted absently.

"That's the one," she said, smiling, encouraged by the fact that he hadn't taken her head off yet.

Cash didn't return the smile.

Mariah swallowed again and finished her explanation as quickly as possible. "After West Fork, there wasn't any place to get more water. I didn't realize how long it would take to get to the ranch house, so I didn't have enough water. Every time I stopped to let things cool off, more water leaked out of the radiator and I couldn't replace it, so I wouldn't get as far next time before it boiled and I had to stop. When I recognized MacKenzie Ridge I decided it would be faster to walk."

Shaking his head, muttering words that made Mariah wince, Cash went back to poking at the dirty engine. His hands hesitated as he was struck by a thought.

"How far did you drive this wreck?"

"Today?"

"No. From the beginning of your trip."

"I started in Seattle."

"Alone?"

"Of course," she said, surprised. Did he think she'd hidden a passenger in the trunk?

Cash said something sibilant and succinct. He backed out from beneath the hood, wiped his hands on a greasy rag and glared at the filthy engine; but he was seeing Mariah's lovely, uncertain smile, her clean-limbed, sexy body and her haunting aura of having been hurt once too often. He guessed that Mariah was a bit younger than his own sister, Carla, who was twenty-three. It made Cash furious to think of a girl who seemed as vulnerable as Mariah driving alone in a totally unreliable car from Seattle to the Rocking M's desolate corner of southwestern Colorado.

Cash took the weight of the hood from Mariah's hands and let the heavy metal fall into place with a resounding crash.

"What in hell were you thinking of when you set off across the country in this worthless piece of crud?"

Mariah opened her mouth. Nothing came out. She had driven the best vehicle she could afford. What was so remarkable about that?

"That's what I thought. You didn't think at all." Disgusted, Cash threw the greasy rag on top of the useless parts. "Well, baby, this wreck is D.O.R."

"What?"

"Dead on Road," Cash said succinctly. "I'll tow it to the ranch house, but the only way you'll get back on the road is with a new engine and you'd be a fool to spend that kind of money on this dog. From the wear pattern on the tires I'd guess the frame is bent but good. I know for damn sure the body is rusted through in so many places you could use it as a sieve. The radiator *is* a sieve. The battery is a pile of corrosion. The spark plugs are beyond belief. The carburetor—" His hand slashed the air expressively. "It's a miracle you got this far."

Mariah looked unhappily at the rumpled sedan. She started to ask if Cash were sure of his indictment, took one look at the hard line of his jaw and said nothing. Silently she watched while he attached her dead car to the Jeep. In spite of her unhappiness, she found herself appreciating the casual strength and coordination of his movements, a masculine grace and expertise that appealed to her in a way that went deeper than words.

Unfortunately, it was obvious to Mariah that the attraction wasn't mutual. After several attempts, she gave up trying to make small talk as she and Cash bumped down the one-lane dirt road leading toward the ranch house. Rather quickly the wind pulled apart the knot she had used to confine her hair. The silky wildness seethed around her face, but she didn't notice the teasing, tickling strands or the occasional, covert glances from Cash.

Mariah's long trip from Seattle in her unreliable car, her disappointment at not seeing Luke, her attraction to a man who found her aggravating rather than appealing—everything combined to drain Mariah's customary physical and mental resilience. She felt tired and bruised in a way she hadn't since her mother had died last year and she had been left to confront her stepfather without any pretense of bonds between them. Nor had her stepfather felt any need to pretend to such bonds. Immediately after the funeral, he had put a frayed cardboard carton in Mariah's hands and told her, *Your mother came to me with this. Take it and go.*

Mariah had taken the carton and gone, never understanding what she had done to earn her stepfather's coldness.

She had returned to her tiny apartment, opened the carton, and found her MacKenzie heritage, the very heritage that her mother had refused ever to discuss. Holding a heavy necklace of rough gold nuggets in one hand, turning the pages of a huge family Bible with the other, Mariah had wept until she had no more tears.

Then she had begun planning to get back to the only home she had ever known—the Rocking M.

The Jeep clattered over the cattle guard that kept range cows from wandering out of the Rocking M's huge home pasture. Shrouded by dark memories, Mariah didn't notice the rattling noise the tires made as they hurtled over pipe.

Nor did Cash. He was watching Mariah covertly, accurately reading the signs of her discouragement. No matter how many times he told himself that Mariah was just one more female looking for a free ride from a man, he couldn't help regretting being so blunt about the possibilities of fixing her car. The lost look in her eyes was a silent remonstration for his lack of gentleness. He deserved it, and he knew it.

Just as Cash was on the verge of reaching for Mariah and stroking her hair in comfort, he caught himself. In silent, searing terms he castigated himself for being a fool. A child learned to keep its hands out of fire by reaching out and getting burned in the alluring dance of flames. A man learned to know his own weaknesses by having them used against himself.

Cash had learned that his greatest weakness was his bone-deep belief that a man should protect and cherish those who weren't as strong as himself, especially women and children. The weakest woman could manipulate the strongest man simply by using this protective instinct against him. That was what Linda had done. Repeatedly. After too much pain, Cash had finally realized that the more vulnerable a woman appeared, the greater was her ability to deceive him.

If the pain had gone all the way to the bone, so had the lesson. It had been eight years since Cash had trusted any woman except Carla, his half sister, who was a decade younger than he was and infinitely more vulnerable. From the day of her birth, she had returned his interest and his care with a generous love that was uniquely her own. Carla gave more than she received, yet she would be the first one to deny it. For that, Cash loved and trusted Carla, exempting her from his general distrust of the female of the species.

Wrapped in their separate thoughts, sharing a silence that was neither comfortable nor uneasy, Cash and Mariah drove through the home pasture and up to the ranch buildings. When he parked near the house, she stirred and looked at him.

"Thank you," she said, smiling despite her own weariness. "It was kind of you to go out of your way for a stranger."

Cash looked at Mariah with unfathomable dark eyes, then shrugged. "Sure as hell someone had to clean up the mess you left. Might as well be me. I wasn't doing anything more important than looking at government maps."

Before Mariah could say anything, Cash was out of the Jeep. Silently she followed, digging her keys from her big canvas purse. She unlocked the trunk of her car and was reaching for the carton her stepfather had given her when she sensed Cash's presence at her back.

"Planning on moving in?" he asked.

Mariah followed Cash's glance to the car's tightly packed trunk. Frayed cardboard cartons took up most of the space. A worn duffel crammed as full as a sausage was wedged in next to the scarred suitcase she had bought at a secondhand shop. But it wasn't her cheap luggage that made her feel ashamed, it was Cash's cool assumption that she had come to the Rocking M as a freeloader.

Yet even as Mariah wanted fiercely to deny it, she had to admit there was an uncomfortable core of truth to what Cash implied. She did want to stay on at the Rocking M, but she didn't have enough money to pay for room and board and fix her car, too.

The screen door of the ranch house creaked open and thudded shut, distracting Cash from the sour satisfaction of watching a bright tide of guilt color Mariah's face.

"Talk about the halt leading the lame," said a masculine voice from the front porch. "Are you towing that rattletrap or is it pushing your useless Jeep?"

"That's slander," Cash said, turning toward the porch. He braced his hands on his hips, but there was amusement rather than anger in his expression.

"That's bald truth," the other man retorted. "But not as bald as those sedan's tires. Surprised that heap isn't sitting on its wheel rims. Where in hell did you—" The voice broke off abruptly. "Oh. Hello. I didn't see you behind Cash. I'll bet you belong to that, er, car."

Mariah turned around and looked up and felt as though she had stepped off into space.

She was looking into her own eyes.

"L-Luke?" she asked hoarsely. "Oh, Luke, after all these years is it really you?"

Luke's eyes widened. His pupils dilated with shock. He searched Mariah's face in aching silence, then his arms opened, reaching for her. An instant later she was caught up in a huge bear hug. Laughing, crying, holding on to her brother, Mariah said Luke's name again and again, hardly able to believe that he was as glad to see her as she was to see him. It had been so long since anyone had hugged her. She hadn't realized how long until this instant.

"Fifteen years," Mariah said. "It's been fifteen years. I thought you had forgotten me."

"Not a chance, Muffin," Luke said, holding Mariah tightly. "If I had a dime for every time I've wondered where you were and if you were happy, I'd be a rich man instead of a broke rancher."

Hearing the old nickname brought a fresh spate of tears to Mariah. Wiping her eyes, smiling, she tried to speak but was able only to cry. She clung more tightly to Luke's neck, holding on as she had when she was five and he was twelve and he had comforted her during their parents' terrifying arguments.

"Without you, I don't know what would have happened to me," she whispered.

Luke simply held Mariah tighter, then slowly lowered her back to the ground. Belatedly she realized how big her brother had become. He was every bit as large as Cash. In fact, she decided, looking from one man to the other, they were identical in size.

"We're both six foot three," Luke said, smiling, reading his sister's mind in the look on her face. "We weigh the same, too. Just under two hundred pounds."

Mariah blinked. "Well, I've grown up, too, but not that much. I'm a mere five-eight, one twenty-six."

Luke stepped back far enough to really look at the young woman who was both familiar and a stranger. He shook his head as he cataloged the frankly feminine lines of her body. "Couldn't you have grown up ugly? Or at least skinny? I'll be beating men back with a whip."

Mariah swiped at tears and smiled tremulously. "Thanks. I think you're beautiful, too."

Cash snorted. "Luke's about as beautiful as the south end of a northbound mule. Never could understand what Carla saw in him."

Instantly Mariah turned on Cash, ready to defend her big brother. Then she realized that Luke was laughing and Cash was watching him with a masculine affection that was like nothing she had ever encountered. It was as though the men were brothers in blood as well as in law.

"Ignore him, Muffin," Luke said, hugging Mariah again. "He's just getting even for my comments about his ratty, unreliable Jeep." He looked over Mariah's head at Cash. "Speaking of ratty and unreliable, what's wrong with her car?"

"Everything."

"Um. What's right with it?"

"Nothing. She started in Seattle. It's a damned miracle she got this far. Proves the old saying—God watches over fools and drunks."

"Seattle, huh?" Luke glanced at the open trunk, accurately assessed its contents and asked, "Did you leave anything you care about behind?"

Mariah shook her head, suddenly nervous.

"Good. Remember the old ranch house where we used to play hide-and-seek?"

She nodded.

"You can live there."

"But..." Mariah's voice died.

She looked from one large man to the other. Luke looked expectant. Cash wore an expression of barely veiled cynicism. She remembered his words: *Planning on moving in?* Unhappily she looked back at Luke.

"I can't just move in on you," she said.

"Why not?"

"What about your wife?"

"Carla will be delighted. Since Ten and Diana started living part-time in Boulder, there hasn't been a woman for Carla to talk to a lot of the time. She hasn't said anything, but I'm sure she gets a little lonely. The Rocking M is hard on women that way."

Though Luke said nothing more, Mariah sensed all that he didn't say, their mother's tears and long silences, their father's anger at the woman who couldn't adjust to ranch life, a woman who simply slipped through his fingers into a twilight world of her own making.

"But I can't—" Mariah's voice broke. "I can't pay my way. I only have enough money for—"

Luke talked over her stumbling words. "Don't worry. You'll earn your keep. Logan needs an aunt and Carla sure as hell will need help a few months down the road. Six and a half months, to be exact."

The cynical smile vanished from Cash's mouth as the implication of Luke's words sank in.

"Is Carla pregnant?" Cash demanded.

Luke just grinned.

Cash whooped with pleasure and gave Luke a bone-cracking hug.

"It better be a girl, this time," Cash warned. "The world needs more women like Carla."

"I hear you. But I'll be damned grateful for whatever the good Lord sends along. Besides," Luke added with a wolfish smile, "if at first we don't succeed…"

Cash burst out laughing.

Mariah looked from one grinning man to the other and felt a fragile bubble of pleasure rise and burst softly within her, showering her with a feeling of belonging she had known only in her dreams. Hardly able to believe her luck, she looked around the dusty, oddly luminous ranch yard and felt dreams and reality merge.

Then Mariah looked at the tall, powerful man whose eyes were the deepest blue she had ever seen, and she decided that reality was more compelling than any dream she had ever had.

CHAPTER THREE

"ARE YOU SURE YOU'RE A MACKENZIE?" Cash asked Mariah as he removed another slab of garlic pork from the platter. "No MacKenzie I know can cook."

"Carla can," Luke pointed out quickly.

"Yeah, but that's different. Carla was born a McQueen."

"And Mariah was born a MacKenzie," Nevada Blackthorn said matter-of-factly as he took two more slices of meat off the platter Mariah held out to him. "Even a hardrock miner like you should be able to figure that out. All you have to do is look at her eyes."

"Thanks," Mariah said.

She smiled tentatively at the dark, brooding man whose own eyes were a startlingly light green. Nevada had been introduced to her as the Rocking M's *segundo,* the second in command. When his brother Ten was gone, Nevada was the foreman, as well. He was also one of the most unnerving men Mariah had ever met. Not once had she seen a smile flash behind his neatly trimmed beard. Yet she had no feeling that he disliked her. His reserve was simply part of his nature, a basic solitude that made her feel sad.

Cash watched Mariah smile at Nevada. Irritation pricked at Cash even as he told himself that if Mariah wanted to stub her toe on a hard piece of business like Nevada, it wasn't Cash's concern.

Yet no sooner had Cash reached that eminently reasonable decision when he heard himself saying, "Don't waste your smiles on Nevada. He's got no more heart than a stone."

"And you've got no more brain," Nevada said matter-of-factly. Only the slight crinkling at the corners of his eyes betrayed his amusement. "Like Ten says—Granite Man."

"Your brother was referring to my interest in mining."

"My brother was referring to your thick skull."

Cash grinned. "Care to bet on that?"

"Not one chance in hell. After a year of watching you play cards, I know why people nicknamed you Cash." Nevada glanced sideways at Mariah. "Never play cards with a man named Cash."

"But I like to play cards," she said.

"You do?" Cash asked, looking at her sharply.

Mariah nodded.

"Poker?"

Dark hair swung as Mariah nodded again.

"I'll be damned."

Nevada lifted one black eyebrow. "Probably, but not many men would brag about it."

Luke snickered.

Cash ignored the other men, focusing only on Mariah. It was easy to do. There was an elegance to her face and a subtle lushness to the curves of her body that caught Cash anew each time he looked at her. Even when he reminded himself that Mariah's aura of vulnerability was false, he remained interested in the rest of her.

Very interested.

"Could I tempt you into a hand or two of poker after dinner?" he asked.

"No!" Luke and Nevada said simultaneously.

Mariah looked at the two men, realized they were kidding—sort of—and smiled again at Cash. "Sure. But first I promised to show the MacKenzie family Bible to Luke."

An unreasonable disappointment snaked through Cash.

"Maybe after that?" Mariah asked hesitantly, looking at Cash with an eagerness she couldn't hide, sensing his interest despite his flashes of hostility. Though she had never been any man's lover, she certainly knew when a man looked at her with masculine appreciation. Cash was looking at her that way right now.

When Mariah passed the steaming biscuits to Cash, the sudden awareness of him that made her eyes luminous brought each of his masculine senses to quivering alert. Deliberately he let his fingertips brush over Mariah's hands as he took the warm, fragrant food from her. The slight catch of her breath and the abrupt speeding of the pulse in her throat told Cash how vividly she was aware of him as a man.

Covertly, Cash glanced at Luke, wondering how he would react to his sister's obvious interest in his best friend. Luke was talking in a low voice with Nevada about the cougar tracks the *segundo* had seen that morning in Wildfire Canyon. Cash looked back to Mariah, measuring the sensual awareness that gave her eyes the radiance of candle flames and made the pulse at the base of her soft throat beat strongly.

Desire surged through Cash, shocking him with its speed and ferocity, hardening him in an aching torrent of blood. He fought to control his torrential, unreasonable hunger for Mariah by telling himself that she was no better looking than a lot of women, that he was thirty-three, too old to respond this fast, this totally, to his best friend's sister. And in any case Mariah was just one more woman hungry for a lifetime sinecure—look at how quickly she had moved in on the Rocking M. Her token protests had been just that. Token.

"You're a good cook," Nevada said, handing Mariah the salt before she had time to do more than glance in the direction of the shaker. "Hope Luke can talk you into staying. From what Ten has told me, the Rocking M never had a cook worth shooting until Carla came along. But by January, Carla won't feel much like cooking."

"How did you know?" Luke asked, startled. "Dr. Chacon just confirmed it today."

Nevada shrugged. "Small things. Her skin. Her scent. The way she holds her body."

Cash shook his head. "Your daddy must have been a sorcerer. You have the most acute perceptions of anyone I've ever met."

"Chalk it up to war, not sorcery," Nevada said, pouring himself a cup of coffee. "You spend years tracking men through the night and see what happens to your senses. The

Blackthorns come from a long line of warriors. The slow and the stupid didn't make the cut."

Nevada set the coffeepot aside and glanced back at Luke. "If you want, I'll check out that new cougar as soon as Ten gets back. I couldn't follow the tracks long enough to tell if it was male or female. Frankly, I'm hoping the cat is a young male, just coming out of the high country to mate and move on."

"I hope so, too. Wildfire Canyon can't support more than one or maybe two adult cats in a lean season. Long about February, some of the cattle in the upland pastures might get to looking too tasty to a big, hungry cat." Luke sipped coffee and swore softly. "I need to know more about cougars. The old ranchers say the cats are cow killers, the government says the cats only eat rabbits and deer...." Frowning, Luke ran a hand through his hair. "Check into the new tracks when Ten comes back, but I can't turn you loose for more than a day or two. Too damned short-handed."

"Need me?" Cash asked, trying and failing to keep the reluctance from his voice. He had been planning on getting in at least a week of prospecting in the Rocking M's high country. He no longer expected to find Mad Jack's lost mine, but he enjoyed the search too much to give it up.

"Maybe Luke needs you, but I don't," Nevada said. "When it comes to cows you make a hell of a good ranch mechanic."

Mariah looked at Cash and remembered his disgust with the state of her car's engine. "Are you a mechanic?"

Luke snickered. "Ask his Jeep. It runs only on alternate Thursdays."

"The miracle is that it runs at all," Nevada said. "Damned thing is even older than Cash is. Better looking, too."

"I don't know why I sit and listen to this slander," Cash complained without heat.

"Because it's that or do dishes. It's your turn, remember?" Luke asked.

"Yeah, but I was hoping you'd forget."

"That'll be the day." Luke pushed back from the table, gathered up his dishes and headed for the kitchen. "Nevada, you might want to stick around for the MacKenzie family show-and-tell. After all, some of them are your ancestors, too."

Nevada's head turned toward Luke with startling speed. "What?"

There was a clatter of dishes from the kitchen, then Luke came back to the big "mess hall" that adjoined the kitchen. He poured himself another cup of potent coffee before he looked down at Ten's younger brother with an odd smile.

"Didn't Ten tell you? The two of us finally figured it out last winter. We share a pair of great-great-grandparents—Case and Mariah MacKenzie."

"Be damned."

"No doubt," Cash said slyly, "but no man wants to brag about it, right?"

Nevada gave him a sideways glance that would have been threatening were it not for the telltale crinkling around Nevada's eyes. Luke just kept on talking, thoroughly accustomed to the masculine chaffing that always accompanied dinners on the Rocking M.

"Case was the MacKenzie who started the Rocking M,"

Luke explained as he looked back at Cash. "Actually, Mariah should have been one of your ancestors. Her grand-daddy was a gold prospector."

"He was? Really?" Mariah said eagerly, her voice lilting with excitement. "I never knew that Grandpa Lucas was a prospector."

Luke blinked. "He wasn't."

"But you just said he was."

Simultaneously Nevada spoke. "I don't remember my parents talking about any MacKenzie ancestors."

"No, I didn't," Luke said to Mariah. Then, to Nevada, "I'm not surprised. It wasn't the kind of relationship that families used to talk about."

When Nevada and Mariah began speaking at once, Cash stood up with a resigned expression and began carrying dirty dishes into the kitchen. No one noticed his comings and goings or his absence when he stayed in the kitchen. Once he glanced through the doorway, saw Luke drawing family trees on a legal tablet and went back to the dishes. The next time Cash looked out, Mariah was gone. He was irrationally pleased that Nevada had remained behind. The bearded cowhand was too good-looking by half.

Cash attacked the counters with unusual vigor, but before he had finished, he heard Mariah's voice again.

"Here it is, Nevada. Proof positive that we're kissing kin."

The dishrag hit the sink with a distinct smack. Wiping his hands on his jeans, Cash moved silently across the kitchen until he could see into the dining room. Mariah stood next to Luke. She was holding a frayed cardboard carton as though it contained the crown jewels of England.

"What's that?" Luke asked, eyeing the disreputable box his sister was carrying so triumphantly to the cleared table.

"This is the MacKenzie family Bible," she said in a voice rich with satisfaction and subdued excitement.

There was a time of stretching silence ended by the audible rush of Luke's breath as Mariah removed the age-worn, leather-bound volume from the box. The Bible's intricate gilt lettering rippled and gleamed in the light.

Nevada whistled softly. He reached for the Bible, then stopped, looking at Mariah.

"May I?" he asked.

"Of course," she said, holding the thick, heavy volume out to him with both hands. "It's your family, too."

While Cash watched silently from the doorway, Nevada shook his head, refusing to take the book. Instead, he moved his fingertips across the fragile leather binding, caressing it as though it were alive.

The sensuality and emotion implicit in that gesture made conflicting feelings race through Cash—irritation at the softness in Mariah's eyes as she watched the unsmiling man touch the book, curiosity about the old Bible itself, an aching sense of time and history stretching from past to present to future; but most of all Cash felt a bitter regret that he would never have a child who would share his past, his present or his future.

"How old is this?" Nevada asked, taking the heavy book at last and putting it on the table.

"It was printed in 1867," Mariah said, "but the first entry isn't until the 1870s. It records the marriage of Case MacKenzie and Mariah Elizabeth Turner. I've tried to make out the date, but the ink is too blurred."

As she spoke, Mariah turned to the glossy pages within the body of the Bible where births, deaths and marriages were recorded. Finger hovering just above the old paper, she searched the list of names quickly.

"There it is," she said triumphantly. "Matthew Case MacKenzie, our great-grandfather. He married a woman called Charity O'Hara."

Luke looked quickly down the page of names, then pointed to another one. "And there's your great-grand-daddy, Nevada. David Tyrell MacKenzie."

Nevada glanced at the birthdate, flipped to the page that recorded marriages and deaths, and found only a date of death entered. David Tyrell MacKenzie had died before he was twenty-six. Neither his marriage nor the births of any of his children had been recorded.

"No marriage listed," Nevada said neutrally. "No children, either."

"There wasn't a marriage," Luke said. "According to my grandfather, his uncle David was a rover and a loner. He spent most of his time living with or fighting various Indian tribes. No woman could hold him for long."

Nevada's mouth shifted into a wry line that was well short of a smile. "Yeah, that's always been a problem for us Blackthorns. Except for Ten. He's well and truly married." Nevada flipped the last glossy pages of the register, found no more entries and looked at Luke. "Nothing here. What makes you think we're related?"

"Mariah—no, not you, Muffin, the first Mariah. Anyway, she kept a journal. She mentioned a woman called Winter Moon in connection with her son David. Ten said your great-grandmother's name was Winter Moon."

Nevada nodded slowly.

"There was no formal marriage, but there was rumor of a child. A girl."

"Bends-Like-the-Willow," Nevada said. "My grandmother."

"Welcome to the family, cousin," Luke said, grinning and holding out his hand.

Nevada took it and said, "Well, you'll have no shortage of renegades in the MacKenzie roster now. The Blackthorns are famous for them. Bastards descended from a long line of bastards."

"Beats no descent at all," Luke said dryly.

Only Mariah noticed Cash standing in the doorway, his face expressionless as he confronted once again the fact that he would never know the sense of family continuity that other people took for granted. That, as much as his distrust of women, was the reason why he hadn't married again.

And why he never would.

CHAPTER FOUR

CASH TURNED BACK TO THE KITCHEN and finished cleaning it without taking time out for any more looks into the other room. When he was finished he poured himself a cup of coffee from the big pot that always simmered on the back of the stove and walked around the room slowly, sipping coffee. Finally he sat down alone at the kitchen table. The conversation from the dining room filtered through his thoughts, sounds without meaning.

His dark blue eyes looked at the kitchen walls where Carla had hung kitchen utensils that had been passed down through generations of MacKenzies and would be passed on to her own children. Cash's eyes narrowed against the pain of knowing that he would leave no children of his own when he died.

For the hundredth time he told himself how lucky he was to have a nephew whose life he was allowed to share. When he traced Logan's hairline and the shape of his jaw, Cash could see his own father and himself in his half-sister's child. If Logan's laughter and curiosity and stubbornness made Cash ache anew to have a child of his own, that was too bad. He would just have to get over it.

"...real gold?"

"It is. The nuggets supposedly came from Mad Jack's mine."

Nevada's question and Mariah's answer were an irresistible lure for Cash. He set aside his cooled cup of coffee and went into the room that opened off the kitchen.

Mariah was sitting between Luke and Nevada, who was looking up from the handful of faded newspaper clippings and letters he had collected from the Bible. Despite his question, Nevada spared only a moment's glance for the gold that rippled and flowed between Mariah's hands like water. The necklace of nuggets linked by a long, heavy gold chain didn't interest Nevada as much as the faded, smudged marks on the brittle paper he held.

"Cash?" Luke called out without looking up. "What the hell is taking you so—oh, there you are. Remember the old jewelry I thought was lost? Look at this. Mother must have taken the chain when she left Dad. Muffin brought it back."

Cash's large, powerful hand reached over Mariah's shoulder. Her breath came in swiftly when his forearm brushed lightly against the curve of her neck and shoulder. His flesh was hard, radiating vitality, and the thick hair on his arm burned with metallic gold highlights. When he turned his hand so that it was palm up, Mariah saw the strong, raised, taut veins centered in his wrist, silent testimony to the times when his heart had had to beat strongly to feed the demands he made on his muscular body.

The sudden desire to trace the dark velvet branching of Cash's life was so great that Mariah had to close her eyes before she gave in to it.

"May I?" Cash asked.

Too shaken by her own reaction to speak, Mariah opened her eyes and handed the loops of chain over to Cash. She told herself it was an accident that her fingertips slid over his wrist, but she knew she lied. She also knew she would never forget the hard strength of his tendons or the alluring suppleness of the veins beneath the clean, tanned skin.

Silently Mariah watched Cash handle the necklace, testing its weight with his palm and the hardness of random nuggets with his fingernail. Very faint marks appeared on the rough gold, legacy of his skillful probing.

"High-test stuff," Cash said simply. "Damn few impurities. I couldn't tell without a formal assay, but I'd guess this is about as pure as gold gets without man's help."

"Is it from Mad Jack's mine?" Mariah asked.

Cash shrugged, but his eyes were intent as he went from nugget to nugget on the old necklace, touching, probing, measuring the malleable metal against his own knowledge and memories. Then, saying nothing, he took Mariah's hand and heaped the necklace in it. Gold chain whispered and moved in a cool fall over both sides of her palm, but the weight of the nuggets that remained in her palm kept the necklace from falling to the table.

Cash pulled a key from his jeans pocket. Dangling from the ring was a hollow metal cylinder about half the size of his thumb. With a deftness that was surprising for such big hands, he unscrewed the cylinder.

"Hold out your other hand," he said to Mariah.

She did, hoping that no one else sensed the sudden race of her heart when Cash's hand came up beneath hers, steadying it and cupping her fingers at the same time. Holding her with one hand, he upended the cylinder over her palm. She made a startled sound when a fat gold nugget dropped into her hand. The lump was surprisingly heavy for its size.

Carefully Cash selected a strand of chain and draped it over her palm so that one of the necklace nuggets rested next to the nugget he had taken from the cylinder. There was no apparent difference in the color of the gold, or in the texture of the surface. Both lumps of gold were angular and rough rather than rounded and smooth. Both were of a very deep, richly golden hue.

"Again, without an assay it's impossible to be sure," Cash said, "but…" He shrugged.

Mariah looked up at Cash with eyes the color of gold. "They're from Mad Jack's mine, aren't they?"

"I don't know. I've never found the mine." Cash looked down into Mariah's eyes and thought again of golden heat, golden flames, desire like a knife deep in his loins. "But I'd bet my last cent that these nuggets came from the same place, wherever that is."

"You mentioned that Case kept a journal," Mariah said, her voice a husky rasp that made Cash's blood thicken.

"Yes," Luke answered, though his sister hadn't looked at him, having eyes only for the gold in her hands—and for Cash, the man who hunted for gold.

"Didn't he say where the mine was?" she asked.

"No. All we know for sure was that Case had saddlebags full of gold from Mad Jack's mine."

"Why?"

"He was going to give it to Mad Jack's son. Instead he gave it to Mariah, Mad Jack's granddaughter."

That caught Mariah's attention. "You mean it's really true?" she asked, turning quickly toward Luke. "You weren't just joking? We're really related to Mad Jack?"

"Sure. Where else do you think the nuggets in that necklace came from? It used to be a man's watch chain. Mariah had it made for Case as a wedding gift. The chain came down through the family, staying with whichever son held the Rocking M. Until Mother left." Luke shrugged. "I guess she thought she had earned it. Maybe she had. God knows she hated every minute she ever spent on the ranch."

Mariah looked at the gold heaped on her palm, shining links infused with a legacy of both love and hatred. Yet all she said was "That explains the modern clasp. I assumed the old one had fallen apart, but watch chains don't need clasps, do they?" Without hesitation she poured the long, heavy chain and bulky nuggets into a heap in front of Luke. "Here. It belongs to you."

He looked startled. "I didn't mean—"

"I know you didn't," she interrupted. "It's still yours. It belongs with the man who holds the Rocking M. You."

"I've been thinking about that. Half of what I inherited should be—"

"No." Mariah's interruption was swift and determined. "The ranch was meant to be the inheritance of whichever MacKenzie son could hold it. Mariah's letters made that quite clear."

"That might have been fair in the past, but it sure as hell isn't fair now."

"It wasn't fair that our parents couldn't get along or that

Mother had a nervous breakdown or that Dad drank too much or that I was taken away from the only person who really loved me. You." Mariah touched Luke's hand. "Lots of life isn't fair. So what?" Her smile was a bittersweet curve of acceptance. "You offered me a home when I had none. That's all I hoped for and more than I had any right to expect. Or accept."

"You'll by God accept it if I have to nail your feet to the floor," Luke said, squeezing Mariah's hand.

She laughed and tried to blink away the sudden tears in her eyes. "I accept. Thank you."

Luke picked up the gold chain and dumped it back in Mariah's hand. She tilted her palm, letting the heavy, cool gold slide back to the table.

"Mariah," he began roughly. "Damn it, it's yours."

"No. Make it back into a watch chain and wear it. Or give it to Logan. Or to your next child. Or to whichever child holds the Rocking M. But," Mariah added, speaking quickly, overriding the objections she saw in her brother's tawny eyes, "that doesn't mean I wouldn't like a gold necklace of my own. So, with your permission, I'll go looking for Mad Jack's mine. I've always believed I would find a lost gold mine someday."

Luke laughed, then realized that Mariah was serious. Smiling crookedly, he said, "Muffin, Cash has been looking for that mine for—how many years?"

"Nine."

Startled, Mariah looked up at Cash. "You have?"

He nodded slightly.

"And if a certified, multi-degreed geologist, a man who makes his living finding precious metals for other people—" began Luke.

"You do?" interrupted Mariah, still watching Cash with wide golden eyes.

He nodded again.

"—can't find Mad Jack's lost mine," Luke continued, talking over his sister, "then what chance do you have?"

Mariah started to speak, then sighed, wondering how she could explain what she barely understood herself.

"Remember how you used to put me to bed and tell me stories?" she asked after a few moments.

"Sure. You would watch me all wide-eyed and fascinated. Nobody ever paid that much attention to me but you. Made me feel ten feet tall."

She smiled and said simply, "You were. I would lie in bed and forget about Mother and Dad yelling downstairs and I'd listen to you talking about the calves or the new colts or some adventure you'd had. Sometimes you'd sneak in with cookies and a box full of old pictures and we would make up stories about the people. And sometimes you'd talk about Mad Jack and his mine and how we would go exploring and find it and buy everything the ranch didn't have so Mother would be happy on the Rocking M. We used to talk about that a lot."

In silent comfort Luke squeezed Mariah's hand. "I remember."

She leaned forward with an urgency she couldn't suppress. "I've always believed I can find that mine. I'm Mad Jack's own blood, after all. Please, Luke. Let me look. What harm can there be in that?" Despite the need driving her, Mariah smiled teasingly and added, "I'll give you half of whatever I find, cross my heart and hope to die."

Luke laughed, shaking his head, unable to take her seriously. "Muffin, this is a big damned ranch. It's a patchwork quilt of outright ownership, plus lease lands from three government agencies, plus water rights and mineral rights and other things only a land lawyer or a professional gold hunter like Cash would understand."

"I'll learn."

"Oh hell, honey, if you found anything in Rocking M's high country land but granite and cow flops, I'd give it to you without hesitation and you know it, but—"

"Sold!" Mariah crowed, interrupting before Luke could say anything she didn't want to hear. She looked at Nevada and Cash. "You heard him. You're my witnesses."

Nevada looked up, nodded, and returned his attention to one of the old pieces of paper he held.

Cash was much more attentive to Mariah. "I heard," he said, watching her closely. "But just what makes you so sure that mine is on the Rocking M?"

"Mariah said it was. It's in her letter to the son who inherited the ranch."

Luke looked up at Cash. "You were right. Damn. I was hoping that mine would never…" He shrugged and said no more.

Silently Cash took the single nugget from Mariah's hand. A few deft movements returned the gold to its cylinder.

"What do you mean, Cash was right?" she asked. "And why were you hoping he was wrong?"

There was a pause before Luke said anything. When he finally did speak, he answered only her first question.

"When Mother cleaned out the family heirlooms, she overlooked a fat poke of gold, all that was left from Case's saddlebags. I showed the poke to Cash. He took one look and knew the gold hadn't come from any of the known, old-time strikes around here."

"Of course," Mariah said. "The MacKenzie gold wasn't found in placer pockets."

Cash looked at Mariah with renewed interest. "How did you know?"

"I did my homework." She held up her hand, ticking off names with her fingers. "The strikes at Moss Creek, Hard Luck, Shin Splint, Brass Monkey, Deer Creek, and Lucky Lady were all placer gold. Some small nuggets, a lot of dust. Everything was smooth from being tumbled in water." Mariah gestured toward the necklace. "For convenience we call those lumps of gold 'nuggets,' but I doubt they spent any real time in the bottom of a stream. If they had, they would be round or at least rounded off. But they're rough and asymmetrical. The longer I thought about it, the more certain I was that the lumps came from 'jewelry rock.'"

"What's that?" Luke asked.

Cash answered before Mariah could. "It's an old miner's term for quartz that is so thickly veined with pure gold that the ore can be broken apart in your bare hands. It's the richest kind of gold strike. Veins of gold like that are the original source of all the big nuggets that end up in placer pockets when the mother lodes are finally eroded away and washed by rain down into streams."

"Is that what you think Mad Jack's mine is?" Luke persisted. "A big strike of jewelry rock?"

"I wasn't sure. Except for the chunk you gave me—" Cash flicked his thumbnail against the cylinder "—the poke was filled with flakes and big, angular grains, the kind of thing that would come from a crude crushing process of really high-grade ore." Thoughtfully Cash stirred the chain with a blunt fingertip. Reflected light shifted and gleamed in shades of metallic gold. "But if these nuggets all came from Mad Jack's mine, it was God's own jewelry box, as close to digging pure gold as you can get this side of Fort Knox."

Luke said something unhappy and succinct beneath his breath.

Mariah looked at her brother in disbelief. "What's wrong with that? I think it's fantastic!"

"Ever read about Sutter's Mill?" he asked laconically.

"Sure. That was the one that set off the California gold rush in 1849. It was one of the richest strikes in history."

"Yeah. Remember what happened to the mill?"

"Er, no."

"It was trampled to death in the rush. So was a lot of other land. I don't need that kind of grief. We have enough trouble keeping pothunters out of the Anasazi ruins on Wind Mesa and in September Canyon."

"What ruins?" Mariah asked.

"They're all over the place. Would you like to see them?" Luke asked hopefully, trying to sidetrack her from the prospect of gold.

"Thanks, but I'd rather look for Mad Jack's mine."

Cash laughed ruefully. When he spoke, his voice was rich with certainty. "Forget it, Luke. Once the gold bug bites you, you're hooked for life. Not one damn thing is as bright as the shine of undiscovered gold. It's a fever that burns out everything else."

Luke looked surprised but Mariah nodded vigorously,

making dark brown hair fly. She knew exactly what Cash meant.

Looking from Cash to Mariah, Nevada raised a single black eyebrow, shrugged, and returned his attention to the paper he was very gently unfolding on the table's surface.

"Smile," Mariah coaxed Luke. "You'd think we were talking about the Black Death."

"That can be cured by antibiotics," he shot back. "What do you think will happen if word gets out that there's a fabulous lost mine somewhere up beyond MacKenzie Ridge? A lot of our summer grazing is leased from the government, but the mineral rights *aren't* leased. There are rules and restrictions and bureaucratic papers to chase, but basically, when it comes to prospecting, it's come one, come all. Worst of all, mineral rights take precedence over other rights."

Mariah looked to Cash, who nodded.

"So we get a bunch of weekend warriors making campfires that are too big," Luke continued, "carrying guns they don't know how to use, drinking booze they can't hold, and generally being jackasses. I can live with that if I have to. What I can't live with is when they start tearing up the fences and creeks and watersheds. This is a cattle ranch, not a mining complex. I want to keep it that way."

"But…" Mariah's voice faded. She began worrying her lower lip between her teeth. "Does this mean I can't look for Mad Jack's mine?"

Luke swiped his fingers through his hair in a gesture of frustration. "No. But I want you to promise me two things. First, I don't want you telling anyone about Mad Jack's damned missing mine. That goes for Nevada, too. And I mean no one. Cash didn't even tell Carla."

"No problem," Nevada said. He looked at Cash with blunt approval. "You've been looking for nine years, huh? I like a man who can keep his mouth shut."

Cash's lips made a wry line and he said not one word.

"No problem for me, either," Mariah said, shrugging. "I don't have anyone to tell but you and you already know. What's the second thing?"

"I don't want you going out alone and looking for that damned mine," Luke said. "That's wild, rough country out there."

Mariah was on the verge of agreeing when she stopped. "Wait a minute. I can't tell anyone, right?"

Luke nodded.

"And you, Nevada and Cash are the only other ones who know. Right?"

"Carla knows," Luke said. "I told her myself."

"So five people know, including me."

"Right."

"Tell me, older brother—how much time do you have to spend looking for lost mines?"

"None," he said flatly.

"Nevada?"

He looked toward Luke, but it was Cash who spoke first.

"Nevada has cougar tracking duty. That takes care of his spare time for the summer."

The satisfaction in Cash's voice was subtle but unmistakable. Luke heard it. His smile was so small and swift that only Nevada saw it.

Mariah didn't notice. She was looking at Cash with hopeful eyes, waiting for him to volunteer. He didn't seem to notice her.

"No one prospects the high country in the winter," Luke said unhelpfully.

Mariah simply said, "Cash?"

"Sorry," he said. "That country is too rough for a tenderfoot like you."

"I've camped out before."

Cash grunted but was obviously unimpressed.

"I've hiked, too."

"Who carried your pack?"

"I did."

He grunted again. The sound wasn't encouraging.

Inspiration struck Mariah. "I'll do the cooking. I'll even do the dishes, too. Please?"

Cash looked at her luminous golden eyes and the graceful hand resting on his bare forearm in unconscious pleading. Desire shot through him at the thought of having her pleading with him for his skill as a lover rather than his expertise in hunting for gold.

"*No,*" Cash said, more roughly than he had intended.

Mariah flinched as though she had been slapped. Hastily she withdrew her hand from his arm.

For an instant Luke's eyes widened, then narrowed with a purely male assessment. Soon his mouth shifted into a smile that was both sympathetic and amused as he realized what Cash's problem was.

"If I were you, Granite Man," Nevada drawled calmly, "I'd change my mind."

Cash shot the other man a savage look. "You're not me."

"Does that mean you're volunteering to go gold hunting?" Mariah said to Nevada, hoping her voice didn't sound as hurt as she felt by Cash's harsh refusal.

"Sorry, Muffin," Luke said, cutting across anything Nevada might have wanted to say. "I'm too shorthanded as it is. I can't afford to turn loose of Nevada."

"Damn shame," Nevada said without heat. "Hate to see a good treasure map go to waste."

"What?" Luke and Cash said together.

Silently Nevada pushed a piece of paper toward Mariah. Cash bent over her shoulder, all but holding his breath so that he wouldn't take in her fragile, tantalizing scent.

"I'm a warrior, not a prospector," Nevada said, "but I've read more than one map drawn by a barely literate man. Offhand, I'd guess this one shows the route to Mad Jack's mine."

CHAPTER FIVE

WITH A HARSHLY SUPPRESSED SOUND of disgust and anger, Cash looked from the age-darkened, brittle paper to Mariah's innocent expression.

No wonder she was so eager to trade her nonexistent rights of inheritance in exchange for Luke's permission to prospect on the Rocking M—she has a damned map to follow to Mad Jack's mine!

Yet Mariah had looked so vulnerable when she had pleaded with Cash for his help.

Sweet little con artist. God. Why are men so stupid? And why am I so particularly stupid!

Mariah glanced from the paper to Nevada and smiled wryly. "I got all excited the first time I looked at it, too. Then I looked again. And again. I stared until I was cross-eyed, but I still couldn't make out two-thirds of the chicken scratches. Even if I assume Mad Jack drew this—and that's by no means a certainty—he didn't even mark north or south in any way I can decipher. As for labeling any of the landmarks, not a chance. I suspect the old boy was indeed illiterate. There's not a single letter of the alphabet on the whole map."

"He didn't need words. He read the land, not books." Nevada turned the map until the piece of paper stood on one chewed corner. "That's north," he said, indicating the upper corner.

"You're sure?" she asked, startled. "How can you tell?"

"He's right," Cash said an instant later. He stared at the map in growing excitement. "That's Mustang Point. Nothing else around has that shape. Which means...yes, there. Black Canyon. Then that must be Satan's Bath, which leads to the narrow rocky valley, then to Black Springs..." Cash's voice trailed off into mutterings.

Mariah watched, wide-eyed, as local place names she had never heard of were emphasized by stabs of Cash's long index finger. Then he began muttering words she had heard before, pungent words that told her he had run into a dead end. She started to ask what was wrong, but held her tongue. Luke and Nevada were standing now, leaning over the map in front of her, tracing lines that vanished into a blurred area that looked for all the world as though someone long ago had spilled coffee on the paper, blotting out the center of the map.

"Damn, that's enough to peeve a saint," Cash said, adding a few phrases that were distinctly unsaintly. "Some stupid dipstick smudged the only important part of the map. Now it's useless!"

"Not quite," Luke said. "Now you know the general area of the ranch to concentrate on."

Cash shot his friend a look of absolute disgust. "Hell, Luke, where do you think I've been looking for the past two years?"

"Oh. Devil's Peak area, huh?"

Cash grunted. "It's well named. It has more cracks and crannies, rills and creeks than any twelve mountains. It looks like it's been shattered by God's own rock hammer. I've used the line shack at Black Springs for my base. So far, I've managed to pan the lower third of a single small watershed."

"Find anything?"

"Trout," Cash said succinctly.

Mariah licked her lips. "Trout? Real, free-swimming, wild mountain trout?"

A smile Cash couldn't prevent stole across his lips. "Yeah. Sleek, succulent little devils, every one of them."

"Fresh butter, a dusting of cornmeal, a pinch of—"

"Stop it," groaned Cash. "You're making me hungry all over again."

"Does Black Springs have watercress?" she asked, smiling dreamily.

"No, but the creek does farther down the valley, where the water cools. Black Springs is hot."

"Hot? Wonderful! A long day of prospecting, a hot bath, a meal of fresh trout, camp biscuits, watercress salad...." Mariah made a sound of luxuriant anticipation.

Luke laughed softly. Cash swore, but there was no heat in it. He had often enjoyed nature's hard-rock hot tub. The meal Mariah mentioned, however, had existed only in his dreams. He was a lousy cook.

"Then you'll do it?" Mariah asked eagerly, sensing that

Cash was weakening. "You'll help me look for Mad Jack's mine?"

"Don't push, Muffin," Luke said. "Cash and I will talk it over later. Alone."

"I'll give you half of my half," she said coaxingly to Cash, ignoring her older brother.

"Mariah—" began Luke.

"Who's pushing?" she asked, assuming an expression of wide-eyed innocence. "*Moi?* Never. I'm a regular doormat."

Nevada looked at Cash. "You need this map?"

"No."

"Then if nobody minds, I'd like to pass it along to some people who are real good at making ruined documents give up their secrets."

Cash started to ask questions, then remembered where—and for whom—Nevada had worked before he came to the Rocking M.

"Fine with me," Cash said. "The map belongs to Luke and Mariah, though."

"Take it," said Luke.

"Sure. Who are you sending it to?" Mariah asked.

"Don't worry. They'll take good care of it," Nevada said, folding the map delicately along age-worn creases.

"But where are you sending it?"

Mariah was talking to emptiness. Nevada had simply walked away from the table. The back door opened and closed quietly.

"I didn't mean to make him mad."

"You didn't," Luke said, stretching. "Nevada isn't long on social niceties like smiling and saying excuse me. But he's a damned good man. One of the best. Just don't ever push him," Luke added, looking directly at Cash. "Even you. Nevada doesn't push worth a damn."

Cash smiled thinly. "My mother didn't hatch any stupid chicks. I saw Nevada fight once. If I go poking around in that lion's den, it will be with a shotgun."

"But where is Nevada taking the map?" Mariah asked in a plaintive voice.

"I don't know," Luke admitted. "I do know you'll get it back in as good shape as it was when Nevada took it. Better, probably."

"Then you must know where he's taking it."

"No, but I can make an educated guess."

"Please do," Mariah said in exasperation.

Luke smiled. "I'd guess that map will end up in an FBI lab on the east coast. Or some other government agency's lab. Nevada wasn't always a cowboy." Luke stretched and yawned again, then looked at Mariah. "Did you get everything moved into the old house?"

"Yes."

"All unpacked?"

"Well, not quite."

"Why don't you go finish? I'll be along in a few minutes to make sure you have everything you need."

"Why do I feel like I'm being told to leave?"

"Because you are."

Mariah started to object before she remembered that Luke wanted to talk with Cash in private about going prospecting with her.

"I'm not six years old anymore," she said reasonably. "You can talk in front of me."

It was as though she hadn't spoken.

"Don't forget to close the bathroom window," Luke said, "unless you want a battle-scarred old tomcat sleeping on your bed."

Mariah looked at Cash. "Why do you let him insult you like that?"

There was a two-second hesitation before Cash laughed out loud, but the sudden blaze in his eyes made Mariah's heart beat faster.

Shaking his head, Luke said, "Good night, Muffin."

"Don't forget to bring my cookies and milk," she retorted sweetly, "or I'll cry myself to sleep."

Luke grabbed Mariah, hugged her and ruffled her hair as though she were six years old again. Laughing, she stood on tiptoe and returned the favor, then found herself suddenly blinking back tears.

"Thank you, Luke," she said.

"For what?"

"Not throwing me out on my ear when I turned up without warning."

"Don't be silly. This is your home."

"No," she whispered, "it's yours. But I'm grateful to share it for a while."

Before Luke could say anything else, she kissed his cheek and walked quickly from the dining room. Cash stood and watched the outer door for a long, silent moment, admiring the perfection with which Mariah played the role of vulnerable child-woman. She was very good. Even better than Linda had been, and Linda had fooled him completely. Of course, Linda had had a real advantage. She had told him something he would have sold his soul to believe—that she was carrying his child.

What he hadn't known until too late was that Linda had been sleeping with another man. That was another thing women were good at—making each man feel like he was the only one.

"You don't have to worry about Nevada," Luke said calmly.

Startled, Cash turned toward his friend. "What do you mean?"

"Oh, he's a handsome son, but it's you Mariah keeps looking at." Deadpan, Luke added, "Which proves that there's no accounting for taste."

"Despite the beard, Nevada isn't a prospector," Cash pointed out coolly, "and the lady's heart is obviously set on gold."

"The lady was looking at you before she knew you were a prospector. And you were looking at her, period."

Cash's eyes narrowed into gleaming slits of blue. Before he could say anything, Luke was talking again.

"Yeah, yeah, I know, it puts a man between a rock and a hard place when he wants his best friend's little sister. Hell, I ought to know. I spent a lot of years wanting Carla."

"Not as many as she spent wanting you."

Luke smiled crookedly. "So I was a prize fool. If it weren't for her matchmaking older brother, I'd still be waking up alone in the middle of the night."

"Is that what you're doing now? Matchmaking? Is that why you want me to go prospecting with Mariah? You figure we'll find something more valuable and permanent than gold?"

Wincing at Cash's sardonic tone, Luke raked his fingers through his hair as he said, "The area around Devil's Peak is damned wild country."

Cash looked at the ceiling.

"I can't let her go alone," Luke continued.

Cash looked at his hands.

"I can't take her myself."

Cash looked at the floor.

"I need every cowhand I've got, and five more besides."

Cash looked at the table.

Luke swore. "Forget it. I'll get Nevada to—"

"*Hell,*" Cash interrupted fiercely, angered by the thought of throwing Mariah and Nevada together in the vast, lonely reaches of the Rocking M's high country. Cash pinned Luke with a black look. "All right, I'll do it. But I'm usually gone for weeks at a time. Have you thought about that?"

"Mariah said she was a camper. Besides, there's always the Black Springs line shack."

"Damn it, that's not what I mean and you know it! Your sister is one very sexy female."

Luke cocked his head to one side. "Interesting."

A snarl was Cash's only answer.

"No, I mean it," Luke continued. "Not that I think Mariah is a dog, but sexy wouldn't be the word I'd use to describe her. Striking, maybe, with those big golden eyes and lovely smile. Warm. Quick. But not sexy."

"I wouldn't describe Carla as sexy, either."

"Then you're blind."

"No. I'm her brother."

"Point taken," Luke said, grinning.

There was silence, then Cash spoke in a painfully reasonable tone of voice. "Look. It takes half a day just to get to the Black Springs line shack by horseback. From there, it's a hard scramble up boulder-choked creeks and steep canyons. There's no way we can duck in, poke around for a few hours, and duck out. We'll be spending a lot of nights alone."

"I trust you."

"Then you are a damned fool," Cash said, spacing each word carefully.

"You trusted me in the wilds of September Canyon with Carla," Luke pointed out.

"Yeah. Think about it. Carla ended up pregnant and alone."

Luke grimaced. "You're not as big a fool as I was."

"Damn it—"

"Mariah is twenty-two," Luke continued over Cash's words, "college educated, a consenting adult in every sense of the word. I trust you in exactly the same way you trusted me, and for the same reason. You may be hardheaded as hell and not trust women worth a damn, but you would never touch a girl unless she wanted you to. Mariah will never be safer in that way than when she is with you. Beyond that, whatever happens or doesn't happen between the two of you is none of my business."

For a minute there was no sound in the dining room. Cash stood motionless, his hands jammed in his back pockets, his mind racing as he assessed the situation and the man he loved more than most men loved their blood brothers. In the end, there was only one possible conclusion: Luke meant every word he had said.

Well, at least I won't have to worry about getting Mariah pregnant the way Luke did Carla.

But Cash's bitterly ironic thought remained unspoken. It wasn't the sort of thing a man talked about.

"I'll hold you to that," Cash said finally.

Luke nodded, then smiled widely and gave Cash an affectionate whack on his shoulder. "Thanks for getting me off the hook. I owe you one."

"Like hell. I spend more time here than I do in my apartment in Boulder."

"So move here. You can build at the other end of the big pasture, just across the stream from Ten and Diana. Plenty of space."

"One of these days you're going to say that and I'm going to take you up on it."

"Why do you think I keep saying it?" Luke stretched and yawned. "Damn, I wish Carla were home. I never sleep as well when she's gone."

"You're breaking my heart. Go to bed."

"Mariah's waiting for me."

"I'll tell her what we decided," Cash said. "With luck, she'll change her mind when she finds out Nevada won't be her trusty wilderness guide."

"Are you deaf as well as blind? I keep telling you, it's not Nevada she's looking at!"

Cash turned on his heel and left the room without saying another word, but he let the outside door close behind him hard enough to make a statement about his temper.

Outside, the cool summer darkness was awash with stars and alive with the murmur of air sliding down from the highlands to the long, flat valley that was the Rocking M's center. Lights burned in the bunkhouse and in the old ranch house. Cash moved with the swift, ground-covering strides of a man who has spent much of his adult life walking over wild lands in search of the precious metals that fed civilization's endless demands. Though he wore only a shirt and jeans, he didn't notice the crisp breeze. He knocked on the front door of the old ranch house with more force than courtesy.

"Come in, Luke. It's open."

"It's Cash. Is it still open?"

Mariah looked down at her oversize cotton nightshirt and bare feet. For an instant she wished she were wearing Spanish lace, Chinese silk and French perfume. Then she sighed. As angry as Cash sounded, she could be naked and it wouldn't make a speck of difference.

What is it about me that irritates him?

There was no answer to the question, other than the obvious one. He wasn't wild about the idea of being saddled with her out in the backcountry, just as he hadn't been wild about helping her with her car. He looked at her as a helpless, useless burden. That shouldn't surprise her. Her stepfather had felt precisely the same way.

Mariah opened the door and stifled an impulse to slam it shut before Cash could come in. He towered over her, looming out of the darkness like a mountain, and his eyes were black with anger.

"Come in, or would you rather bite my head off out in the yard?"

The sound Cash made could most politely be described as a growl. He stepped forward. Mariah retreated. A gust of wind sucked the door shut.

Cash looked at the nightshirt that should have concealed Mariah's curves but ended up teasing him by draping softly over her breasts and hips. Desire tightened his whole body, hammering through him with painful intensity. The thought of being alone with her night after night was enough to make him slam his fist into the wall from sheer frustration.

"What do you know about wild country?" Cash asked savagely.

"It's where gold is found."

He hissed a single word, then said, "This won't be a trendy pseudo-wilderness trek along a well-beaten path maintained by the National Park Service. Can you even ride a horse?"

"Yes."

"Can you ride rough country for half a day, then scramble over rocks for another half day?"

"If I have to."

"The line shack leaks and it rains damn near every night. The only privy is a short-handled shovel. At the end of a hard day you have to gather firewood, haul water, wash out your socks so you won't blister the next day, eat food you're too tired to cook properly, sleep on a wood floor that has more drafts than bare dirt would and—"

"You make it sound irresistible," Mariah interrupted. "I accept."

"Damn it, you aren't even listening!"

"You aren't telling me anything I don't already know."

"Then you better know this. We'll be alone out there, and I mean *alone*."

Mariah met Cash's dark glance without flinching and said, "I've been alone since I was dragged off the Rocking M fifteen years ago."

Cash jammed his hands into his back pockets. "That's not what I meant, lady. Up on Devil's Peak you could scream your pretty head off and no one would hear."

"You would."

"What if I'm the one making you scream? Have you thought about that?"

"Frankly, you're making me want to scream right now."

There was a charged silence.

Mariah smiled tentatively and put her hand out in silent appeal. "I know what you're trying to say, Cash, but let's be honest. I don't have the kind of looks that drive a man crazy with desire and we both know it. Just as we both know you don't want to take me across the road, much less spend a few weeks in the wild with me. But I'm going to Devil's Peak. I've been dreaming of looking for Mad Jack's mine as long as I can remember. Come hell or high water, that's what I'm going to do."

Cash looked down at the pale, graceful hand held out to him in artful supplication. He remembered how cool and silky Mariah's fingers had felt when they had rested on his bare forearm. He remembered how quickly her hand had warmed at his touch. He wondered if all of her would catch fire that fast.

The thought made him burn.

"I'll take care of packing the supplies and horses," Cash said coldly, "because sure as hell you won't know how. We leave in five hours. If you aren't ready, I'll leave without you."

"I'll be ready."

Cash turned and left the house before Mariah could see just how ready he was right now.

CHAPTER SIX

FIVE HOURS LATER MARIAH PULLED open the front door before Cash could knock. Silently he stared at her, noting the lace-up shoes, faded jeans, an emerald turtleneck T-shirt beneath a black V-necked sweater and a long-sleeved man's flannel shirt that ended at her hips. The arms of a windbreaker were tied casually around her neck. The outfit should have made her look as appealing as a mud post, but it was all he could do not to run his hands over her to find the curves he knew waited beneath the sensible trail clothes.

"Here," Cash said, holding out a pair of cowboy boots. "Luke said to wear these if they fit. They're Carla's."

While Mariah tried on the boots, Cash glanced around. She had packed a lot less gear than he had expected. A military surplus backpack was stuffed tightly and propped against the wall. Other military surplus items were tied to the backpack—canteen, mess kit and the like. Extra blankets had been rolled up and tied with thongs.

"Where's your sleeping bag?" he asked.

"I don't have one."

"What the hell are you planning to sleep on?"

"My side, usually. Sometimes my stomach."

Cash clenched his jaw. "What about hiking boots?"

"My shoes are tougher than they look." Mariah stood and stamped her feet experimentally. "They're long enough, but they pinch in the toes."

"That's how you know they're cowboy boots," Cash retorted.

Mariah glanced at Cash's big feet. He was wearing lace-up, rough-country hiking boots that came to just below his knees. The heels were thick enough to catch and hold the edge of a stirrup securely. She had priced a similar pair in Seattle and decided that she would have to find Mad Jack's mine before she could afford the boots.

She bent down, tied her shoes to the backpack, and picked it up. "Ready."

Cash's long, powerful arm reached out, snagged Mariah's impromptu bedroll, and stuffed it none too gently into her hands. "Don't forget this."

"You're too kind," she muttered.

"I know."

Empty-handed, Cash followed Mariah to the corral. Four horses waited patiently in the predawn darkness. Two of them were pack animals. The other two were saddled. Cash added Mariah's scant baggage to one of the existing packs and lashed everything securely in place. Moments later he stepped into the saddle of a big, rawboned mountain horse, picked up the lead rope of the pack animals and headed out into the darkness without so much as a backward look.

"It won't work," Mariah said clearly. "I don't need your help to carry my stuff. I don't need your help to get on a horse. I don't need your help for one damned thing except to make Luke feel better!"

If Cash heard, he didn't answer.

Mariah went to the remaining horse, untied it and mounted a good deal less gracefully than Cash had. It had been six years since she had last ridden, but the reflexes and confidence were still there. When she reined the small mare around and booted it matter-of-factly in the ribs, it quickly trotted after Cash's horse. The mare was short-legged and rough-gaited, but amiable enough for a child to ride.

An hour later Mariah would have traded the mare's good temperament for a mean-spirited horse with a trot that didn't rattle her teeth. The terrain went up and down. Steeply. If there was a trail, Mariah couldn't make it out in the darkness, which meant that she spent a lot of time slopping around in the saddle because there was no way for her to predict her horse's next movements. She would be lucky to stand up at the end of three more hours of such punishment, much less hike with a backpack up a steep mountain and look for gold until the sun went down.

Don't forget the bit about hauling water and washing your socks, Mariah advised herself dryly. *On second thought, do forget it. No socks could be that dirty.*

When dawn came, it was a blaze of incandescent beauty that Mariah was too uncomfortable to fully appreciate. Whichever way she turned in the saddle, her body complained.

Even so, she felt the tug of undiscovered horizons expanding away in all directions. It was exciting to be in a place where not so much as a glimpse of man was to be seen. For all that she could tell, she and Cash might have been the first people ever to travel the land. Wild country rolled away from her on all sides in pristine splendor, shades of green and white and gray, evergreens and granite.

Mixed in with the darker greens of conifers was the pale green of aspens at the higher elevations, a green that was subtly repeated by grassy slopes at the lower elevations and occasional meadows in between. Ahead, Devil's Peak loomed in black, shattered grandeur, looking like the eroded ruins of a volcano rather than the granite peak Mariah had expected.

I wonder why Cash is searching for gold on a volcano's flanks? All the strikes I've read about were in granite, not lava.

Mariah would have asked Cash to explain this reasoning to her, but she had promised herself that she wouldn't speak until he did. Not even to ask for a rest break. Instead, she just hooked one leg around the saddle horn and rode sidesaddle for a time. She prayed there would be enough strength left in her cramped muscles to keep her upright after she dismounted.

As the sun rose, its heat intensified until it burned through the high country's crystalline air. The last chill of night quickly surrendered to the golden fire. Mariah began shedding layers of clothing until only the long-sleeved, fitted ski shirt remained. She unzipped the turtleneck collar and shoved up the sleeves, letting the breeze tease as much of her skin as it could reach.

At the end of four hours, Mariah rather grimly reined the mare down a narrow rocky crease that opened into a tiny valley. Although Cash had been only a few minutes ahead of her, he had already unloaded the pack animals and was in the act of throwing his saddle over the corral railing. Even as Mariah resented it, she envied his muscular ease of movement. She pulled her horse to a halt and slowly, carefully, began to dismount.

Two seconds later she was sitting in the dirt. Her legs simply hadn't been able to support the rest of her. She gritted her teeth and was beginning the tedious job of getting to her feet when she felt herself picked up with dizzying speed. The world shifted crazily. When it settled again, she was being carried like a child against Cash's chest.

"I thought you said you could ride," Cash said harshly.

"I can." Mariah grimaced. "I just proved it, remember?"

"And now you won't be able to walk."

"*Quelle* shock. Wasn't that the whole idea? You didn't want me looking for gold with you and now I won't be able to. Not right away, at any rate. I'll be fine as soon as my legs start cooperating again and then you'll be out of luck."

Cash's mouth flattened into a hard line. "How long has it been since you were on a horse?"

"About a minute."

Against his will, Cash found himself wanting to smile. Any other woman would have been screaming at him or crying or doing both at once. Despite the grueling ride, Mariah's sense of humor was intact. Biting, but intact.

And she felt exciting in his arms, warm and supple, soft, fitting him without gaps or angles or discomfort. He shifted her subtly, savoring the feel of her, silently urging her to relax against his strength.

"Sorry, honey," he said. "If I had known how long it had been since—"

"Pull my other leg," Mariah interrupted. Then she smiled wearily. "On second thought, don't. It might fall off."

"How long has it been since you've ridden?" he asked again.

"Years. Six blessed, wonderful years."

Cash said something savage.

"Oh, it's not that bad," Mariah said.

"You sure?"

"Yeah. It's worse."

He laughed unwillingly and held her even closer. She braced herself against the temptation to put her head on the muscular resilience of his chest and relax her aching body. Her head sagged anyway. She sighed and gave herself to Cash's strength, figuring he had plenty to spare.

"A soak in the hot springs will help," he said.

Mariah groaned softly at the thought of hot water drawing out the stiffness of her muscles.

"My swimsuit is in my backpack," she said. "Better yet, just give me a bar of soap and throw me in as is. That way I won't have to haul water to wash my socks."

Laughing soundlessly, shaking his head, Cash held Mariah for a long moment in something very close to a hug. She might be an accomplished little actress in some ways, but she was good company in others. Linda hadn't been. When things didn't go according to her plan—and often even when they did—she pouted and wheedled like a child after candy. At first it had been gratifying to be the center of Linda's world. Gradually it had become tedious to be cast in a role of father to a manipulative little girl who would never grow up.

A long, almost contented sigh escaped Mariah's lips, stirring the hair that pushed up beneath Cash's open collar.

A visible ripple of response went through him as he felt her breath wash over his skin. He clenched his jaw and walked toward the corral fence.

"Time to stand on your own two feet," he said tightly.

With the unself-consciousness of a cat, Mariah rubbed her cheek against Cash's shirt and admitted, "I'd rather stand on yours."

"I figured that out the first time I saw you."

The sardonic tone of Cash's voice told Mariah that the truce was over. She didn't know what she had done to earn either the war or the truce. All she knew was that she had never enjoyed anything quite so much as being held by Cash, feeling the flex and resilience of his body, being so close to him that she could see sunlight melt and run through his hair like liquid gold.

When Cash's left arm released Mariah's legs, everything dipped and turned once more, but slowly this time. Instinctively she put her arms around his neck, seeking a stable center in a shifting world. Held securely more by the hard power of his right arm than by both her own arms, Mariah felt her hips slide down the length of Cash's body with a slow intimacy that shook her. Her glance flew to his face. His expression was as impassive as granite.

"Grab hold of the top rail," Cash instructed.

Mariah reached for the smooth, weathered wood with a hand that trembled. As she twisted in Cash's arms, the fitted T-shirt outlined her breasts in alluring detail, telling of the soft, feminine flesh beneath.

He wondered whether her nipples were pink or dusky rose or even darker, a vivid contrast to the pale satin of her skin. He thought of bending down and caressing her breasts with his tongue and teeth, drawing out the nipples until they felt like hot, hard velvet and she twisted beneath him, crying for release from the passionate prison of their lovemaking.

Don't be a fool, Cash told himself savagely. *No woman ever wants a man like that. Not really. Not so deep and hard and wild she forgets all the playacting, all the survival calculations, all the cunning.*

Yet, despite the cold lessons of past experience, when Cash looked down at Mariah curled softly in his arms, blood pulsed and gathered hotly, driven by the redoubled beating of his heart, blood surging with a relentless force that was tangible proof of his vulnerability to Mariah's sensual lures. Silently he cursed the fate that gave men hunger and women the instinctive cunning to use men's hunger against them.

"Put both hands on the rails," he said curtly.

When Mariah tried to respond to the clipped command, she found she couldn't move. Cash's arm was a steel band holding her against a body that also felt like steel. Discreetly she tried to put some distance between herself and the man whose eyes had the indigo violence of a stormy twilight. The quarter inch she gained by subtle squirming wasn't enough to allow her left hand to reach across her body to the corral fence. She tried for another quarter inch.

"What the hell do you think you're doing?" Cash snarled.

"I'm trying to follow your orders."

"When did I order you to rub against me like a cat in heat?"

Shock, disbelief and indignation showed on Mariah's face, followed by anger. She shoved hard against his chest. "Let go of me!"

She might as well have tried to push away the mountain itself. All her struggles accomplished were further small movements that had the effect of teaching her how powerful and hard Cash's body was—and how soft her own was by comparison. The lesson should have frightened her. Instead, it sent warmth stealing through her, gentle pulses of heat that came from the secret places of her body. The sensations were as exquisite as they were unexpected.

"C-Cash…?"

The catch in Mariah's voice sent a lightning stroke of desire arcing through Cash. For an instant his arm tightened even more, pinning Mariah to the hungry length of his body. Then he spun her around to face the corral, clamped her left hand over the top rail of the corral and let go of her. When her knees sagged, he caught her around the ribs with both hands, taking care to hold her well away from his body. Unfortunately there was nothing he could do about her breasts curving so close to his fingers, her soft flesh moving in searing caress each time she took a breath.

"Stand up, damn it," Cash said through clenched teeth, "or I swear I'll let you fall."

Mariah took in a shuddering breath, wondering if the jolting ride to Black Springs had scrambled her brains as well as her legs. The weakness melting her bones right now owed nothing to the hours on horseback and everything to the presence of the man whose heat reached out to her, surrounding her. She took another breath, then another, hanging on to the corral fence with what remained of her strength.

"I'm all right," Mariah said finally.

"Like hell. You're shaking."

"I'll survive."

With a muttered word, Cash let go of Mariah. His hands hovered close to her, ready to catch her if she fell. She didn't. She just sagged. Slowly she straightened.

"Now walk," he said.

"What?"

"You heard me. Walk."

A swift look over her shoulder told Mariah that Cash wasn't kidding. He expected her not only to stand on her rubbery legs but also to walk. Painfully she began inching crabwise along the corral fence, hanging on to the top rail with both hands. To her surprise, the exercise helped. Strength returned rapidly to her legs. Soon she was moving almost normally. She turned to give Cash a triumphant smile, only to discover that he was walking away. She started after him, decided it was a bit too soon to get beyond reach of the corral fence's support, and grabbed the sun-warmed wood again.

By the time Mariah felt confident enough to venture away from the fence, Cash had the horses taken care of and was carrying supplies into the line shack. The closer she walked to the slightly leaning building, the more she agreed that "shack" was the proper term. Tentatively she looked in the front—and only—door.

Cash hadn't been lying when he described the line shack's rudimentary comforts. Built for only occasional use by cowhands working a distant corner of the Rocking M's summer grazing range, the cabin consisted of four walls, a ceiling, a plank floor laid down over dirt, and two windows. The fireplace was rudely constructed of local rocks. The long tongue of soot that climbed the exterior stone above the hearth spoke eloquently of a chimney that didn't draw.

"I warned you," Cash said, brushing by Mariah.

"I didn't say a word."

"You didn't have to."

He dumped her backpack and makeshift bedroll on the floor near the fireplace. Puffs of dust arose.

"If you still want to go to Black Springs, put on your swimsuit," Cash said, turning away. "And wear shoes unless you want to ride there."

"Ride?" she asked weakly. "Uh, no thanks. How far is it?"

"I never measured it."

Mariah's small sigh was lost in the ghastly creaking the door made as it shut. She changed into her swimsuit as quickly as her protesting leg muscles allowed. The inexpensive tank suit was made of a thin, deep rose fabric that fit without clinging when it was dry. Wet, it was another matter. It would cling more closely than body heat. Since Mariah had been dry when she purchased the suit, she hadn't known about its split personality.

"Hey, tenderfoot. You ready yet?"

Groaning, Mariah finished tying her shoelaces and struggled to her feet. "I'm coming."

As she stood, she felt oddly undressed. If she had been barefoot in the bathing suit, she would have had no problem. But somehow wearing shoes made her feel...naked. She grabbed her windbreaker and put it on. The lightweight jacket was several sizes too big. Normally she wore it over a blouse and bulky sweater, so the extra room was appreciated. With only the thin tank suit to take up room, the windbreaker reached almost halfway down her thighs, giving her a comforting feeling of being adequately covered.

When Cash heard the front door creak, he turned around. His first impression was of long, elegant, naked legs. His second impression was the same. He felt a nearly overwhelming desire to unzip the jacket and see what was beneath. Anything, even the skimpiest string bikini, would have been less arousing than the tantalizing impression of nakedness lying just beneath the loose black windbreaker.

Mariah walked tentatively toward Cash, wondering at the harsh expression on his face.

"Which way to the hot tub?" she asked, her voice determinedly light.

Without a word Cash turned and walked around to the back of the cabin. Mariah followed as quickly as she could, picking her way along the clear stream that ran behind the cabin. Even if her legs hadn't been shaky, she would have had a hard time keeping up with Cash's long stride. When her path took her on a hopscotch crossing of the creek, she bent and tested the temperature of the water. It was icy.

"So much for my hot tub fantasy," she muttered.

The racing, glittering water came from a narrow gap in the mountainside that was no more than fifty yards from the cabin. Inside the gap the going became harder, a scramble along a cascade that hissed and foamed with the force of its downhill race. The rocks were dark, almost black, which only added to the feeling of chill. Just when Mariah was wondering if the effort would be worth it, she realized that the mist peeling off the water was warm.

A hundred feet later the land leveled off to reveal a series of graceful, stair-step pools that were rimmed by smooth travertine and embroidered by satin waterfalls no more than three feet high. As Mariah stared, a shiver of awe went over her. The pools could not have been more beautiful if they had been designed by an artist and built of golden marble.

The water in the lowest pool was a pale turquoise Mariah had seen only on postcards of tropical islands. The water in the next pool was a luminous aquamarine. The water in the last pool shaded from turquoise to aquamarine to a clear, very dark blue that was the exact shade of Cash's eyes. At the far end of the highest pool, the water was so deep it appeared black but for swirls of shimmering indigo where liquid welled up from the depths of the earth in silent, inexhaustible pulses that had begun long before man ever walked the western lands and would continue long after man left.

Slowly Mariah sank to her knees and extended her hand toward the jeweled beauty of the pool. Before she could touch the water, Cash snatched her hand back.

"I've cooked trout at this end of Black Springs. Sometimes the downstream end of the pool is cool enough to bear touching for a few moments. Most often it isn't. It depends."

"On what?"

Cash didn't answer her directly. "You get hot springs when groundwater sinks down until it reaches a body of magma and then flashes into superheated steam," he said, absently running his thumb over Mariah's palm as he looked at the slowly twisting depth of Black Springs. "The steam slams up through cracks in the country rock until the water bursts through to the surface of the land in a geyser or a hot spring. Most often the water never breaks the surface. It simply cools and sinks back down the cracks until it encounters magma, flashes to steam and surges upward again."

Mariah made a small sound, reflection of the sensations

that were radiating up from her captive hand. Cash looked away from the water and realized that his thumb was caressing Mariah's palm in the rhythm of the water pulsing deep within the springs. With a muttered word, he released her hand.

"I can tell you how a hot spring works, but I can't tell you why some days Black Springs is too hot and other days it's bearable. So be careful every day. Even on its best behavior, Black Springs is dangerously hot a foot beneath the surface."

"Is the water drinkable?" she asked.

"Once it cools off the trout love it. So do I. It has a flavor better than wine."

Mariah stared wistfully at the beautiful, intensely clear, searingly hot water. "It looks so wonderful."

"Come on," Cash said, taking pity on her. "I'll show you the best place to soak out the aches." He led her back to the middle pool. "The closer you are to the spring, the hotter the water. Start at the lower end and work your way up until you're comfortable." He started to turn away, then stopped. "You *do* swim, don't you?"

Mariah glanced at the pool. "Sure, but that water is hardly deep enough for me to get wet sitting down."

"The pool is so clear it fools your eyes. At the far end, the water is over my head." Cash turned away. "If you're not back in an hour, I'll come back and drag you out. I'm hungry."

"You don't have to wait for me," she said, setting shoes and socks aside.

"The hell I don't. You're the cook, remember?"

CHAPTER SEVEN

ON THE FOURTH DAY, MARIAH DIDN'T have to be awakened by the sound of the front door creaking as Cash walked out to check on the horses. She woke up as soon as sunrise brightened the undraped windows. Silently she struggled out of her tangle of blankets. Although she still ached in odd places and she wished that she had brought a few more blankets to cushion the rough wood floor, she no longer woke up feeling as though she had been beaten and left out in the rain.

Shivering in the shack's chill air, Mariah knelt between her blankets and Cash's still-occupied sleeping bag as she worked over the ashes of last night's fire. As always, she had slept fully clothed, for the high mountain nights were cold even in summer. Yet as soon as the sun shone over the broken ramparts of Devil's Peak, the temperature rose swiftly, sometimes reaching the eighties by noon. So while

Mariah slept wearing everything she had brought except her shoes, she shed layers throughout the morning, adding them again as the sun began its downward curve across the sky.

Enough coals remained in the hearth to make a handful of dry pine needles burst into flames after only a few instants. Mariah fed twigs into the fire, then bigger pieces, and finally stove-length wood. Despite the fireplace's sooty front, little smoke crept out into the room this morning. The chimney drew quite well so long as there wasn't a hard wind from the northeast.

When she was satisfied with the fire's progress, Mariah turned to the camp stove that she privately referred to as Beelzebub. It was the most perverse piece of machinery she had ever encountered. No matter how hard or how often she pumped up the pressure, the flame wobbled and sputtered and was barely hot enough to warm skin. When Cash pumped up the stove, however, it put out a flame that could cut through steel.

With a muttered prayer, Mariah reached for the camp stove. A tanned, rather hairy hand shot out of Cash's sleeping bag and wrapped around her wrist, preventing her from touching the stove.

"I'll take care of it."

"Thanks. The thing hates me."

There was muffled laughter as a flap of the partially zipped sleeping bag was shoved aside, revealing Cash's head and bare shoulders. Another big hand closed over Mariah's. He rubbed her hand lightly between his own warm palms. Long, strong, randomly scarred fingers moved almost caressingly over her skin. She shivered, but it had nothing to do with the temperature in the cabin.

"You really *are* cold," he said in a deep voice.

"You're not. You're like fire."

"No, I mean it," Cash said. He propped himself up on one elbow and pulled Mariah's hands toward himself. "Your fingers are like ice. No wonder you thrash around half the night. Why didn't you tell me you were cold?"

"Sorry." Mariah tugged discreetly at her hands. They remained captive to Cash's enticing warmth. "I didn't mean to keep you awake."

"To hell with that. Why didn't you tell me?"

"I was afraid you'd use it as an excuse to make me go back."

Cash hissed a single harsh word and sat up straight. The sleeping bag slithered down his torso. If he was wearing anything besides the bag, it didn't show. Although Mariah had seen Cash at Black Springs dressed in only cutoff jeans, somehow it just wasn't the same as seeing him rising half-naked from the warm folds of a sleeping bag. A curling, masculine pelt went in a ragged wedge from Cash's collarbones to a hand span above his navel. Below the navel a dark line no thicker than her finger descended into the undiscovered territory concealed by the sleeping bag.

"It's not worth getting upset about," Mariah said quickly, looking away. "Any extra calories I burn at night I replace at breakfast, and then some. Speaking of which, do you want pancakes again? Or do you want biscuits and bacon? Or do you just want to grab some trail mix and go prospecting? I'm going with you today. I'm not stiff anymore. I won't be a drag on you. I promise."

There was a long silence while Cash looked at Mariah and she looked at the fire that was struggling to burn cold wood. Deliberately he cupped her hands in his own, brought them to his mouth, and blew warm air over her chilled skin. Before she had recovered from the shock of feeling his lips brushing over her palms, he was rubbing her hands against his chest, holding her between his palms and the heat of his big body. It was like being toasted between two fires.

"Better?" he asked quietly after a minute.

Mariah nodded, afraid to trust her voice.

With a squeeze so gentle that she might have imagined it, Cash released her hands and began dressing. For a few moments Mariah couldn't move. When she went to measure ingredients for biscuits, her hands were warm, but trembling. She was glad Cash was too busy dressing to notice.

The front door creaked as he went outside. A few minutes later it creaked again when he returned. The smell of dew and evergreen resin came back inside with him.

"If that's biscuits and bacon, make a double batch," Cash said. "We'll eat them on the trail for lunch."

"Sure." Then the meaning of his words penetrated. Mariah turned toward him eagerly. "Does that mean I get to come along?"

"That's what you're here for, isn't it?" Cash asked curtly, but he was smiling.

She grinned and turned back to the fire, carefully positioning the reflector oven. She had discovered the oven in a corner of the shack along with other cooking supplies Cash rarely ever used. Her first few attempts to cook with the oven had been a disaster, but there had been little else for her to do except experiment with camp cooking while Cash was off exploring and she was recovering from the ride to Devil's Peak.

Mariah had been grateful to be able to keep the disasters a secret and pretend that the successes were commonplace.

It had been worth all the frustration and singed fingertips to see Cash's expression when he walked into the line shack after a day of prospecting and found fresh biscuits, fried ham, baked beans with molasses and a side dish of fresh watercress and tender young dandelion greens waiting for him.

While the coffee finished perking on the stove and the last batch of bacon sizzled fragrantly in the frying pan, Mariah sliced two apples and piled a mound of bacon on a tin plate. She surrounded the crisp bacon with biscuits and set the plate on the floor near the fireplace, where a squeeze bottle of honey was slowly warming. She poured two cups of coffee and settled cross-legged on the floor in front of the food. The position caused only a twinge or two in her thigh muscles.

"Come and get it," Mariah called out.

Cash looked up from the firewood he had been stacking in a corner of the shack. For a moment he was motionless, trying to decide which looked more tempting—the food or the lithe young woman who had proven to be such good company. Too good. It would have been much easier on him if she had been sulky or petulant or even indifferent— anything but humorous and quick and so aware of him as a man that her hands shook when he touched her.

The tactile memory of Mariah's cool, trembling fingers still burned against his chest. It had taken all of his self-control not to pull her soft hands down into the sleeping bag and let her discover just how hot he really was.

Damn you, Luke. Why didn't you tell me to leave your sister alone? Why did you give me a green flag when you know me well enough to know I don't have marriage in mind? And why can't I look at Mariah without getting hot?

There was no answer to Cash's furious thoughts. There was only fragrance and steamy heat as he pulled apart a biscuit, and then a rush of pleasure as he savored the flavor and tenderness of the food Mariah had prepared for him.

They ate in a silence that was punctuated by the small sounds of silverware clicking against metal plates, the muted whisper of the fire and the almost secretive rustle of clothes as one or the other of them reached for the honey. When Cash could eat no more, he took a sip of coffee, sighed, and looked at Mariah.

"Thanks," he said.

"For what?"

"Being a good cook."

She laughed, but her pleasure in the compliment was as clear as the golden glow of her eyes. "It's the least I could do. I know you didn't want me to come with you."

"And you're used to being not wanted, aren't you." There was no question in Cash's voice, simply the certainty that had come of watching her in the past days.

Mariah hesitated, then shrugged. "Harold—my mother's second husband—didn't like me. Nothing I did in fifteen years changed that. I spent most of those years at girls' boarding schools and summer camps." She smiled crookedly. "That's where I learned to ride, hike, make camp fires, put up a tent, cook, sew, give first aid, braid thin plastic thongs into thick useless cords, make unspeakably ugly things in clay, and identify poisonous snakes and spiders."

"A well-rounded education," Cash said, hiding a grin.

Mariah laughed. "You know, it really was. A lot of girls never get a chance at all to be outdoors. Some of the girls hated it, of course. Most just took it in stride. I loved it. The trees and rocks and critters didn't care that your real father never wrote to you, that your stepfather couldn't stand to be in the same room with you, or that your mother's grip on reality was as fragile as a summer frost."

Cash drained his coffee cup, then said simply, "Luke wrote to you."

"What?"

"Luke has written to you at least twice a year for as long as I've known him," Cash said as he poured himself more coffee. "Christmas and your birthday. He sent gifts, too. Nothing ever came back. Not a single word."

"I didn't know. I never saw them. But I wrote to him. Mother mailed…" Realization came, darkening Mariah's eyes. "She never mailed my letters. She never let me see Luke's."

The strained quality of Mariah's voice made Cash glance up sharply. Reflected firelight glittered in the tears running down her cheeks. He set aside his coffee and reached for her, brushing tears away with the back of his fingers.

"Hey, I didn't mean to hurt you," Cash said, stroking her cheek with a gentleness surprising in such a big man.

"I know," Mariah whispered. "It's just…I used to lie awake and cry on Christmas and my birthday because I was alone. But I wasn't alone, not really, and I didn't even know it." She closed her eyes and laced her fingers tightly together to keep from reaching for Cash, from crawling into his lap and asking to be held. "Poor Luke," she whispered. "He must have felt so lonely, too." She hesitated, then asked in a rush, "Your sister loves Luke, doesn't she? Truly loves him?"

"Carla has always loved Luke."

Mariah heard the absolute certainty in Cash's voice and let out a long sigh. "Thank God. Luke deserves to be loved. He's a good man."

Cash looked down at Mariah's face. Her eyes were closed. Long, dark eyelashes were tipped with diamond tears. All that kept him from bending down and sipping teardrops from her lashes was the certainty that anything he began wouldn't end short of his becoming her lover. Her sadness had made her too vulnerable right now—and it made him too vulnerable, as well. The urge to comfort her in the most elemental way of all was almost overwhelming. He wanted her far too much to trust his self-control.

"Yes," Cash said as he stood up in a controlled rush of power. "Luke is a good man." He jammed his hands into his back jeans pockets to keep from reaching for Mariah. "If we're going to get any prospecting done, we'd better get going. From the looks of the sky, we'll have a thunderstorm by afternoon."

"The dishes will take only a minute," Mariah said, blotting surreptitiously at her cheeks with her shirttail.

It was longer than a minute, but Cash made no comment when Mariah emerged from the cabin wearing her backpack. He put his hand underneath her pack, hefted it, and calmly peeled it from her shoulders.

"I can carry it," Mariah said quickly.

Cash didn't even bother to reply. He simply transferred the contents of her backpack to his own, put it on and asked, "Ever panned for gold?"

She shook her head.

"It's harder than it looks," he said.

"Isn't everything?"

Cash smiled crookedly. "Yeah, I guess it is." He looked at Mariah's soft shoes, frowned and looked away. "I'm going to try a new area of the watershed. It could get rough, so I want you to promise me something."

Warily Mariah looked up. "What?"

"When you need help—and you will—let me know. I don't want to pack you out of here with a broken ankle."

"I'll ask for help. But it would be nice," she added wistfully, "if you wouldn't bite my head off when I ask."

Cash grunted. "Since you've never panned for gold and we're in a hurry, I'll do the panning. If you really want to learn, I'll teach you later. Come on. Time's a-wasting."

The pace Cash set was hard but not punishing. Mariah didn't complain. She was certain the pace would have been even faster if Cash had been alone.

There was no trail to follow. From time to time Cash consulted a compass, made cryptic notes in a frayed notebook, and then set off over the rugged land once more, usually in a different direction. Mariah watched the landscape carefully, orienting herself from various landmarks each time Cash changed direction. After half an hour they reached a stream that was less than six feet wide. It rushed over and around pale granite boulders in a silver-white blur that shaded into brilliant turquoise where the water slowed and deepened.

Cash shrugged out of his backpack and untied a broad, flat pan, which looked rather like a shallow wok. Pan in one hand, short-handled shovel in the other, he sat on his heels by the stream. With a deft motion he scooped out a shovel full of gravel from the eddy of water behind a boulder. He dumped the shovel-load into the gold pan, shook it, and picked over the contents. Bigger pieces of quartz and granite were discarded without hesitation, despite the fact that some of them had a golden kind of glitter that made Mariah's heart beat faster and her breath catch audibly.

"Mica," Cash explained succinctly, dumping another handful of rocks back in the stream.

"Oh." Mariah sighed. Her reading on the subject of granite, gold, and prospecting had told her about mica. It was pretty, but it was as common as sand.

"All that glitters isn't gold, remember?" he asked, giving her an amused, sideways glance.

She grimaced.

Cash laughed and scooped up enough water to begin washing the material remaining in the bottom of the gold pan. A deft motion of his wrists sent the water swirling around in a neat circle. When he tilted the pan slightly away from himself, the circular movement of the water lifted the lighter particles away from the bottom of the pan. Water and particles climbed the shallow incline to the rim and drained back into the stream. After a minute or two, Cash looked at the remaining stuff, rubbed it between his fingers, stared again, and flipped it all back into the stream. He rinsed the pan, attached it and the shovel to his backpack again, and set off upstream.

"Nothing, huh?" Mariah said, scrambling to keep up.

"Grit, sand, pea gravel, pebbles. Granite. Some basalt. A bit of chert. Small piece of clear quartz."

"No gold?"

"Not even pyrite. That's fool's gold."

"I know. Pyrite is pretty, though."

Cash grunted. "Leave it to a woman to think pretty is enough."

"Oh, right. That's why men have such a marked preference for ugly women."

Cash hid a smile. For a time there was silence punctuated by scrambling sounds when the going became especially slippery at the stream's edge. Twice Mariah needed help. The first time she needed only a steadying hand as she scrambled forward. The second time Cash found it easier simply to lift her over the obstacle. The feel of his hands on her, and the ease with which he moved her from place to place, left Mariah more than a little breathless. Yet despite the odd fluttering in the pit of her stomach, her brain continued to work.

"Cash?"

The sound he made was encouraging rather than curt, so Mariah continued.

"What are we doing?"

"Walking upstream."

"Why are we walking upstream?"

"It's called prospecting, honey. Long hours, backbreaking work and no pay. Just like I told you back at the ranch house. Remember?"

Mariah sighed and tried another approach.

"We're looking for Mad Jack's mine, right?" she asked.

"Right."

"Mad Jack's gold was rough, which meant it didn't come out of a placer pocket in a stream, right?"

"Right."

"Because placer gold is smooth."

"Right."

The amusement in Cash's tone was almost tangible. It was also gentle rather than disdainful. Knowing that she was being teased, yet beguiled by the method, Mariah persisted.

"Then why are you panning for Mad Jack's nonplacer mine?"

Cash's soft laughter barely rose above the sound of the churning stream. He turned around, made a lightning grab and had Mariah securely tucked against his chest before she knew what was happening. With a startled sound she hung on to him as he crossed the stream in a few strides, his boots impervious to the cold water.

"Wondered when you'd catch on," Cash said.

He set Mariah back on her feet, releasing her with a slow reluctance that was like a caress. His smile was the same. A caress.

"But the truth is," he continued in a deep voice, resolutely looking away from her, "I *am* panning for that mine. Think about it. Gold is heavy. Wherever a gold-bearing formation breaks the surface, gradually the matrix surrounding the gold weathers away. Gold doesn't weather. That, and its malleability, is what makes it so valuable to man."

Mariah made an encouraging sound.

"Anyway, the matrix crumbles away and frees the gold, which is heavy for its size. Gravity takes hold, pulling the gold downhill until it reaches a stream and sinks to the bottom. Floods scoop out the gold and beat it around and drop it off farther downstream. Slowly the gold migrates downhill, getting more and more round until the nugget settles down to bedrock in a deep placer pocket."

"Mad Jack's gold is rough," Mariah pointed out.

"Yeah. I'm betting that canny old bastard panned a

nameless stream and found bits of gold that were so rough they had to have come from a place nearby. So he panned that watershed, tracking the color to its source—the mother lode."

Cash looked back at Mariah to see if she understood. What he saw were wisps of dark, shiny hair feathered across her face, silky strands lifted by a cool wind. Before he could stop himself, he smoothed the hair away from her lips and wide golden eyes. Her pupils dilated as her breath came in fast and hard.

"You see," he said, his voice husky, "streams are a prospector's best friend. They collect and concentrate gold. Without them a lot of the West's most famous gold strikes would never have been made."

"Really?"

The breathless quality of Mariah's voice was a caress that shivered delicately over Cash.

"They're still looking for the mother lode that put Sutter's Mill on the map," he murmured, catching a lock of her hair and running it between his fingers.

The soft sound Mariah made could have been a response to his words or to the fragile brush of Cash's fingertips at her hairline. With a stifled curse at his inability to keep his hands off her, Cash opened his fingers, releasing Mariah from silken captivity.

"Anyway," he said, turning his attention back to the rugged countryside, "I'm betting Mad Jack was panning a granite-bottomed stream, because only a fool looks for gold in lava formations, and that old boy was nobody's fool."

"You're not a fool, either," Mariah said huskily, grabbing desperately for a safe topic, because it was that or grab Cash's hand and beg him to go on touching her. "So why were you prospecting the Devil's Peak area before you saw Mad Jack's map? Until we got to this stream, I didn't see anything that looked like granite or quartzite or any of the 'ites' that are usually found with gold. Just all kinds of lava. Granted, I'm no expert on gold hunting, but…"

"This area wasn't my first choice," Cash said dryly. "Almost two years ago I was having a soak in Black Springs when I realized that Devil's Peak is basically a volcano rammed through and poured out over country rock that's largely granite. Where the lava has eroded enough, the granite shows through. And where there's granite, there could be gold." He smiled, gave Mariah a sideways glance, and admitted, "I was glad to see that ratty old map, though. I've been panning up here for two years and haven't gotten anything more to show for it than a tired back."

"No gold at all?"

"A bit of color here and there. Hobbyist flakes, the kind you put in a magnifying vial and show to patient friends. Nothing to raise the blood pressure."

"Darn, I was hoping that—trout!" Mariah said excitedly, pointing toward the stream.

"What?"

"I just saw a trout! Look!"

Smiling down at Mariah, barely resisting the urge to fold her against his body in a long hug, Cash didn't even glance at the stream that had captured her interest.

"Fish are silver," he said in a deep voice. "We're after gold. We'll catch dinner on the way back."

"How can you be so sure? The fish could be hiding under rocks by then."

"They won't be."

Mariah made an unconvinced sound.

"I bet we'll catch our fill of trout for dinner tonight," Cash said.

"What do you bet?"

"Loser cleans the fish."

"What if there are no fish to clean?"

"There will be."

"You're on," she retorted quickly, forgetting Nevada's advice about never gambling with a man called Cash. "If we don't get fish, you do dishes tonight."

"Yeah?"

"Yeah."

"You're on, lady." Cash laughed softly and tugged at a silky lock of Mariah's hair once more. "Candy from a baby."

"Tell me that while you're doing dishes."

Cash just laughed.

"It's not a bet until we shake on it," she said, holding out her hand.

"That's not how it works between a man and a woman."

He took her hand and brought it to his mouth. She felt the mild rasp of his growing beard, the brush of his lips over her palm, and a single hot touch from the tip of his tongue. She thought Cash whispered *candy* when he straightened, but she was too shaken to be sure.

"Now it's a bet," he said.

CHAPTER EIGHT

"HOW'S IT GOING?" CASH ASKED.

Mariah looked up from the last fish that remained to be cleaned. "Better for me than for the trout."

He laughed and watched as she prepared the fish for the frying pan with inexpert but nonetheless effective swipes of his filleting knife.

Cash had expected Mariah to balk at paying off the bet, or at the very least to sulk over it. Instead, she had attacked the fish with the same lack of complaint she had shown for sleeping on the shack's cold, drafty floor. Only her unconscious sigh of relief as she rinsed the last fish—and her hands—in the icy stream told Cash how little she had liked the chore.

"I'll do the dishes," he said as she finished.

"Not a chance. It's the only way I'll get the smell of fish off my hands."

Cash grabbed one of Mariah's hands, held it under his nose and inhaled dramatically. "Smells fine to me."

"You must be hungry."

"How did you guess?"

"You're alive," she said, laughing up at him.

Smiling widely, Cash grabbed the tin plate of fish in one hand. The other still held Mariah's water-chilled fingers. He pulled her to her feet with ease.

"Lady, you have the coldest hands of any woman I've ever known."

"Try me after I've done the dishes," she retorted.

He smiled down at her. "Okay."

Mariah's stomach gave a tiny little flip that became a definite flutter when Cash pulled her fingers up his body and tucked them against the warm curve of his neck. Whether it was his body heat or the increased beating of her own heart, Mariah's fingers warmed up very quickly. She slanted brief, sideways glances at Cash as they walked toward the line shack, but he apparently felt that warming her cold hands on his body was in the same category as helping her over rough spots in the trail—no big deal. Certainly it wasn't something for him to go all breathless over.

But Mariah was. Breathless. Each time Cash touched her she felt strange, almost shaky, yet the sensations shimmering through her body were very sweet. Even as she wondered if Cash felt the same, she discarded the idea. He was so matter-of-fact about any physical contact that it made her response to it look foolish.

"Listen," Cash said, stopping suddenly.

Mariah froze. From the direction of Devil's Peak came a

low, fluid, rushing sound, as though there were a river racing by just out of sight. Yet she knew there wasn't.

"What is it?" she whispered.

"Wind. See? It's bending the evergreens on the slope like an invisible hand stroking fur. The rain is about a quarter mile behind."

Mariah followed the direction of his pointing finger and saw that Cash was right. Heralded by a fierce, transparent cataract of wind, a storm was sweeping rapidly toward them across the slope of Devil's Peak.

"Unless you want the coldest shower you ever took," Cash said, "stretch those long legs."

A crack of thunder underlined Cash's words. He grabbed the plate of fish from Mariah and pushed her in the direction of the cabin.

"Run for it!"

"What about you?"

"Move, lady!"

Mariah bolted for the cabin, still feeling the imprint of Cash's hand on her bottom, where he had emphasized his command with a definite smack. She barely beat the speeding storm back to the line shack's uncertain shelter.

Cash, who had the plate of slippery fish to balance, couldn't move as quickly as Mariah. The difference in reaching shelter was only a minute or two, but it was enough. He got soaked. Swearing at the icy rain, Cash bolted through the line shack's open door and kicked it shut behind him. Water ran off his big body and puddled around his feet.

"Put all the stuff that has to stay dry over there," Cash said loudly, trying to be heard over the hammering of rain on the roof.

Mariah grabbed bedding, clothes and dry food and started stacking them haphazardly in the corner Cash had indicated. He set aside the fish and disappeared outside again. Moments later he returned, his arms piled high with firewood. The wood dripped as much as he did, adding to the puddles that were appearing magically on the floor in every area of the cabin but one—the corner where Mariah was frantically storing things. Cash dumped the firewood near the hearth and went back outside again. Almost instantly he reappeared, arms loaded with wood once more. With swift, efficient motions he began stacking the wood according to size.

"Don't forget the kindling," he said without looking up.

Quickly Mariah rescued a burlap sack of dry pine needles and kindling from the long tongue of water that was creeping across the floor. Before the puddle could reach the dry corner, gaps in the wooden planks of the floor drained the water away.

"At least it leaks on the bottom, too," Mariah said.

"Damn good thing. Otherwise we'd drown."

Thunder cracked and rolled down from the peak in an avalanche of sound.

"What about the horses?" Mariah asked.

"They'll get wet just like they would at the home corral."

Cash stood up and shook his head, spraying cold drops everywhere.

"We had a dog that used to do that," Mariah said. "We kept him outside when it rained. In Seattle, that was most of the time."

She started to say something else, then forgot what it was. Cash was peeling off his flannel shirt and arranging it on a series of nails over the hearth. The naked reality of his strength fascinated her. Every twist of his body, every motion, every breath, shifted the masculine pattern of bone and muscle, sinew and tendon, making new arrangements of light and shadow, strength and grace.

"Is something wrong?" Cash said, both amused and aroused by the admiration in Mariah's golden eyes.

"Er...you're steaming."

"What?"

"You're steaming."

Cash held out his arms and laughed as he saw that Mariah was right. Heat curled visibly up from his body in the line shack's chilly air.

"I'll get you a shirt before you freeze," Mariah said, turning back to the haphazard mound she had piled in the corner. She rummaged about until she came up with a midnight-blue shirt that was the color of Cash's eyes in the stormy light. "I knew it was here."

"Thanks. Can you find some jeans, too?"

The voice came from so close to Mariah that she was startled. She glanced around and saw bare feet not eight inches away. Bare calves, too. And knees. And thighs. And— hastily she looked back at the pile of dry goods, hoping Cash couldn't see the sudden color burning on her cheeks or the clumsiness of her hands.

But Cash saw both the heat in Mariah's cheeks and the trembling of her fingers as she handed him dry jeans without looking around.

"Sorry," he said, taking the jeans from her and stepping into them. "In these days of co-ed dorms, I didn't think the sight of a man in underwear would embarrass you."

"There's rather a lot of you," Mariah said in an elaborately casual voice, then put her face in her hands. "I didn't mean it the way it sounded. It's just that you're bigger than most men and…and…"

"Taller, too," Cash said blandly.

Mariah made a muffled sound behind her hands, and then another.

"You're laughing at me," he said.

"No, I'm strangling on my feet."

"Try putting them in your mouth only one at a time. It always works for me."

Mariah gave up and laughed out loud. Smiling, Cash listened to her laughter glittering through the drumroll of rain on the roof. He was still smiling when he went down on one knee in front of the fire and stirred it into life.

"What do you say to an early dinner and a game of cards?" Cash asked.

"Sure. What kind of game?"

"Poker. Is there any other kind?"

"Zillions. Canasta and gin and Fish and Old Maid and—"

"Kid games," Cash interrupted, scoffing. He looked over his shoulder and saw Mariah watching him. "We're too old for that."

The gleaming intensity of Cash's eyes made Mariah feel weak.

"I just remembered something," she said faintly.

"What?"

"Never play cards with a man called Cash."

"It doesn't apply. My name is Alexander."

"I'm reassured."

"Thought you would be."

"I'm also broke."

"That's okay. We'll play for things we have lots of."

"Like what?"

"Pine needles, smiles, puddles, kisses, raindrops, that sort of thing." Without waiting for an answer, Cash turned back to the fire. "How hot do you need it for trout? Or do you want to cook them over the camp stove?"

Blinking, Mariah tried to gather her scattered thoughts. Cash couldn't have mentioned kisses, could he? She must have been letting her own longing guide her hearing down false trails.

"Trout," she said tentatively.

"Yeah. You remember. Those slippery little devils you cleaned." He smiled. "The look on your face... Never bet anything you mind losing, honey."

Abruptly Mariah was certain she had heard his list of betting items very clearly, and kisses had definitely been one of them.

And he had nearly gotten away with it.

"Cash McQueen, you could teach slippery to a fish."

He laughed out loud, enjoying Mariah's quick tongue. Then he thought of some other ways he would like to enjoy that tongue. The fit of his jeans changed abruptly. So did his laughter. He stood in a barely controlled rush of power and turned his back on Mariah.

"You'll need light to cook," he muttered.

He crossed the shack in a few long strides, ignoring the puddles, and yanked a pressurized gas lantern from its wall hook. He pumped up the lantern with short, savage strokes, ripped a wooden match into life on his jeans and lit the lantern. Light pulsed wildly, erratically, until he adjusted the gas feed. The lantern settled into a hard, bright light whose pulses were so subtle they were almost undetectable. He brought the lantern across the room and hung it on one of the many nails that cowhands had driven into the line shack's walls over the years.

"Thank you," Mariah said uncertainly, wondering if Cash had somehow been insulted by being called slippery. But his laughter had been genuine. Then he had stopped laughing and that, too, had been genuine.

With a muffled sigh Mariah concentrated on preparing dinner. While she worked, Cash prowled the six-foot-by-nine-foot shack, putting pans and cups and other containers under the worst leaks. Rain hammered down with the single-minded ferocity of a high-country storm. Although it was hours from sunset, the light level dropped dramatically. Except for occasional violent flashes of lightning, the hearth and lantern became isolated islands of illumination in the gloom.

Both Cash and Mariah ate quickly, for the metal camp plates drained heat from the food. Cash stripped the sweet flesh from the fish bones with a deftness that spoke of long practice. Cornbread steamed and breathed fragrance into the chilly air. When there was nothing left but crumbs and memories, Mariah reached for the dishes.

"I'll do them," Cash said. "You've had a hard day."

"No worse than yours."

Cash didn't argue, he simply shaved soap into a pot with his lethally sharp pocketknife, added water that had been warming in the bucket by the hearth and began washing dishes. Mariah rinsed and stacked the dishes to one side to drain, watching him from the corner of her eyes. He had rolled up his sleeves to deal with the dishes. Each movement he made revealed the muscular power of his forearms and the blunt strength in his hands.

When the dishes were over and Cash sat cross-legged opposite Mariah on the only dry patch of floor in the cabin, lantern light poured over him, highlighting the planes of his face, the sensual lines of his mouth, and the sheer power of his body. As Cash quickly dealt the cards, Mariah watched him with a fascination she slowly stopped trying to hide.

The cards she picked up time after time received very little of her attention. As a result, the pile of dried pine needles in front of her vanished as though in an invisible fire. She didn't mind. She was too busy enjoying sitting with Cash in a cabin surrounded on the outside by storm and filled on the inside by the hushed silence of pent breath.

"Are puddles worth more than pine needles?" Mariah asked, looking at the three needles left to her.

"Only if you're thirsty."

"Are you?"

"I've got all the water I can stand right now."

Mariah smiled. "Yeah, I know what you mean. Well, that lets out raindrops, too. I guess I have to fold. I'm busted."

Cash nudged a palm-size pile of needles from his pile over to her side of the "table."

"What's that for?" she asked.

"Your smile."

"Really? All these needles? If that's what a smile is worth, how much for a kiss?"

Abruptly Cash looked up from his cards. His glance moved almost tangibly over Mariah's face, lingering with frank intensity on the curving line of her lips. Then he looked back at his cards, his expression bleak.

"More than either of us has," he said flatly.

Several hands were played in silence but for the hissing of the lantern and the slowly diminishing rush of rain. Cash kept winning, which meant that he kept dealing cards. As he did, the lantern picked out various small scars on his hands.

"How did you get these?" Mariah asked, touching the back of Cash's right hand with her fingertips.

He froze for an instant, then let out his breath so softly she didn't hear. Her fingers were cool, but they burned on his skin, making him burn, as well.

"You pan gold for more than a few minutes in these streams and your hands get numb," Cash said. His voice was unusually deep, almost hoarse, reflecting the quickening of his body. "I've cut myself and never even known it. Same for using the rock hammer during cold weather. Easiest thing in the world to zing yourself. What my own clumsiness doesn't cause, flying chips of rock take care of."

"Clumsy?" Mariah laughed. "If you're clumsy, I'm a trout."

"Then you're in trouble, honey. I'm still hungry."

"I'm a very, very *young* trout."

Cash smiled grimly. "Yeah. I keep reminding myself of that. You're what…twenty-two?"

Startled by the unexpected question, Mariah nodded.

"I teach grad students who are older than you," Cash said, his tone disgusted.

"So?"

"So quit looking at me with those big golden eyes and wondering what it would be like to kiss me."

Mariah's first impulse was to deny any such thoughts. Her

second was the same. Her third was embarrassment that she was so transparent.

"You see," Cash said flatly, pinning Mariah with a look, "I'm wondering the same thing about you. But I'm not a college kid. If I start kissing you, I'm going to want more than a little taste of all that honey. I'm going to want everything you have to give a man, and I'm going to want it until I'm too damn tired to lick my lips. I get hard just watching you breathe, so teasing me into kissing you would be a really dumb idea, unless you're ready to quit playing and start screwing around." He watched Mariah's face, muttered something harsh under his breath, and threw a big handful of pine needles into the pot. "Call and raise you."

"I d-don't have that many needles."

"Then you lose, don't you?" he asked. And he waited.

How much is a kiss worth?

Mariah didn't speak the words aloud. She didn't have to. She knew without asking that a kiss would be worth every needle in the whole forest. In electric silence she looked at Cash's mouth with a hunger she had never felt before. The days of beard stubble enhanced rather than detracted from the smooth masculine invitation of his lips. And he was watching her with eyes that burned. He had meant his warning. If she teased him into kissing her, she had better be prepared for a lot more than a kiss.

The thought both shocked and fascinated Mariah. She had never wanted a man before. She wanted Cash now. She wanted to be kissed by him, to feel his arms around her, to feel his strength beneath her hands. But she had never been a man's lover before. She wasn't sure she was ready tonight, and Cash had made it very clear that there would be no way for her to test the water without getting in over her head.

"I guess I lose," Mariah whispered. "But it isn't fair."

"What isn't?"

"Not even one kiss, when you must have kissed a hundred other women."

"Don't bet on it. I'm very particular about who gets close to me." Abruptly Cash closed his eyes against the yearning, tentative flames of desire in Mariah's golden glance. "The game is over, Mariah. Go to bed. Now."

Without a word Mariah abandoned her cards, rushed to her feet and began arranging her blankets for the night. After only a few moments she was ready for bed. She kicked out of her shoes, crawled into the cold nest she had made and began shivering. The first few minutes in bed at night, and the first few out of it in the morning, were the coldest parts of the day.

Cash stood up and moved around the cabin, listening to the rain. When he had checked all the pans he turned off the lantern and knelt to bank the fire. Although Mariah tried not to watch him, it was impossible. Firelight turned his hair to molten gold and caressed his face the way she wanted to. Closing her eyes, shivering, she gripped the blankets even more tightly, taking what warmth she could from them.

"Here."

Mariah's eyes snapped open. Cash was looming above her. His hands moved as he unfurled a piece of cloth and pulled it over her. One side of the cloth was a metallic silver. The other was black.

"What is it?"

"Something developed by NASA," Cash said. He knelt next to Mariah and began tucking the odd blanket around her with hard, efficient movements. "It works as good on earth as it does in space. Reflects heat back so efficiently I damn near cook myself if I use it. I just bring it along for emergencies. If I'd known earlier how cold you were, I'd have given it to you."

Mariah couldn't have answered if her life depended on it. Even with blankets in the way, the feel of Cash's hands moving down her sides as he tucked in the odd cloth was wonderful.

Suddenly Cash shifted. His hands flattened on the floor on either side of Mariah's head. He watched her mouth with an intensity that left her weak. Slowly his head lowered until he was so close she could taste his breath, feel his heat, sense the hard beating of his heart.

"Cash...?" she whispered.

His mouth settled over hers, stealing her breath, sinking into her so slowly she couldn't tell when the kiss began. At the first touch of his tongue, she made a tiny sound in her throat. A shudder ripped through Cash, yet his gradual claiming of Mariah's mouth didn't hasten. Gently, inevitably, he turned his head, opening soft feminine lips that were still parted over the sighing of his name. The velvet heat of Mariah's mouth made him dizzy. The tiny sounds she made at the back of her throat set fire to him. He rocked his head back and forth until her mouth was completely his, and then he drank deeply of her, holding the intimate kiss until her breathing was as broken and rapid as his own. Only then did he lift his head.

"You're right," Cash said hoarsely. "It isn't fair."

There was a rapid movement, then the sound of Cash climbing fully clothed into his sleeping bag.

It was a long time before either of them got to sleep.

CHAPTER NINE

MARIAH SAT ON A SUN-WARMED boulder and watched Cash pan for gold in one of the nameless small creeks along the Devil's Peak watershed. Sunlight fell over the land in a silent golden outpouring that belied the chilly summer night to come. Stretching into the warmth, smiling, Mariah relished the clean air and the sun's heat and the feeling of happiness that had grown within her until she found herself wanting to laugh and throw her arms out in sheer pleasure.

The first days at the line shack had been hard, but after that it had been heaven. By the sixth day Mariah no longer awoke stiff every morning from a night on the hard floor and Cash no longer looked for excuses not to take her prospecting. By the eleventh day Mariah no longer questioned the depth of her attraction to Cash. She simply accepted it as she accepted lightning zigzagging through darkness or sunlight infusing the mountains with summer's heat.

Or the way she had accepted that single, incredible kiss.

Since then, Cash had been very careful to avoid touching Mariah but his restraint only made him more compelling to her senses. She had known men who wouldn't have hesitated to push her sexually if they had sensed such a deep response on her part. The fact that Cash didn't press for more was a sign to Mariah that he, too, cherished the glittering emotion that was weaving between the two of them, growing stronger with each shared laugh, each shared silence, drawing them closer and closer each day, each hour, each minute. Their closeness was becoming as tangible as the water swirling in Cash's gold pan, a transparent, fluid beauty stripping away the ordinary to reveal the gleaming gold beneath.

Shivering with a delicious combination of pleasure and anticipation each time she looked at Cash, Mariah told herself to be as patient as he was. When Cash was as certain of the strength of their emotion as she was, he would come to her again, ask for her again.

And this time she would say yes.

"Find anything?" Mariah asked, knowing the answer, wanting to hear Cash's voice anyway.

She loved the sound of it, loved seeing the flash of Cash's smile, loved the masculine pelt that had grown over his cheeks after eleven days without a razor, loved seeing the flex and play of muscles in his arms, loved...*him.*

"Nope. If the mine is up this draw, nothing washed down into the creek. I'll try a few hundred yards farther up, just to be sure."

Before Cash could flip the gritty contents of the pan back into the small creek, Mariah bent over his shoulder, bracing herself against his strength while she stirred through the gold pan with her fingertip. After a time she lifted her hand and examined her wet fingertip. No black flakes stuck to the small ridges on the pad of her finger. No gold ones stuck, either.

Mariah didn't care. She had already found what she sought—a chance to touch the man who had become the center of her world.

"Oh, well," she said. "There's always the next pan."

Cash smiled and watched while Mariah absently dried her fingertip on her jeans. A familiar heat pulsed through him as he looked at her. The desire he had felt the first time he saw her had done nothing but get deeper, hotter, harder. Despite the persistent ache of arousal, Cash had never enjoyed prospecting quite so much as he had in the past week. Mariah was enjoying it, too. He could see it in her smile, hear it in her easy laughter.

And she wanted him. He could see that, too, the desire in her eyes, a golden warmth that approved of everything he did, everything he said, every breath he took. He knew his eyes followed her in the same way, approving of every feminine curve, every golden glance, every breath, everything. He wanted her with a near-violent hunger he had never experienced before. All that kept him from taking what she so clearly wanted to give him was the bitter experience of the past, when he had so needed to believe a woman's lies that he had allowed her to make a fool of him. Yet no matter how closely Cash looked for cracks in Mariah's facade of warmth and vulnerability, so far he had found none.

It should have comforted him. It did not. Cash was very

much afraid that his inability to see past Mariah's surface to the inevitable female calculation beneath was more a measure of how much he wanted her than it was a testimony to Mariah's innate truthfulness.

But God, how he wanted her.

Cash came to his feet in a swift, coordinated movement that startled Mariah.

"Is something wrong?"

"No gold here," Cash said curtly. He secured the gold pan to his backpack with quick motions. "We might as well head back. It's too late to try the other side of the rise today."

Mariah looked at the downward arc of the sun. "Does that mean there will be time for Black Springs before dinner?"

The eagerness in Mariah's voice made Cash smile ruefully. He had been very careful not to go to the hot springs with Mariah if he could avoid it. He had enough trouble getting to sleep at night just remembering what she looked like bare-legged and wearing a windbreaker. He didn't need visions of her in a wet bathing suit to keep him awake.

"Sure," he said casually. "You can soak while I catch dinner downstream."

Disappointed at the prospect of going to the springs alone, Mariah asked, "Aren't you stiff after a day of crouching over ice water?"

Cash shrugged. "I'm used to it."

Using a shortcut Cash had discovered, they took only an hour to get back to the line shack. While he picketed the horses in fresh grass, Mariah changed into her tank suit and windbreaker. When she appeared at the door of the cabin,

Cash glanced up for only an instant before he lowered his head and went back to driving in picket stakes.

With a disappointment she couldn't conceal, Mariah started up the Black Springs path. After a hundred yards she turned around and headed back toward the cabin. Cash had just finished picketing the last horse when he spotted Mariah walking toward him.

"What's wrong?"

"Nothing. I just decided it would be more fun to learn how to handle a gold pan than it would be to soak in an oversize hot tub."

Cash's indigo glance traveled from the dark wisps of hair caressing Mariah's face to the long, elegant legs that were naked of anything but sunlight.

"Better get some more clothes on. The stream is a hell of a lot colder than Black Springs."

"I wasn't planning on swimming."

"You'll get wet anyway. Amateurs always do."

"But it's hot. Look at you. You're in shirtsleeves and you're sweating."

He didn't bother to argue that the sun wasn't warm. If he had been alone, he would have been working stripped to the waist. But he wasn't alone. He was with a woman he wanted, a woman who wanted him, a woman he was trying very hard to be smart enough not to take.

"If you plan on learning how to pan for gold," Cash said flatly, "you better get dressed for it."

Mariah threw up her hands and went back to the line shack before Cash changed his mind about teaching her how to pan for gold at all. She tore off the windbreaker and yanked on jeans over her shoes. Without looking, she grabbed a shirt off the pile of clothes that covered her blankets. She was halfway out the door before she realized that the shirt belonged to Cash.

"Tough," she muttered, yanking the soft navy flannel into place over her tank suit and fastening the snaps impatiently. "He wanted me to be dressed. I'm dressed. He didn't say whose clothes I had to wear."

There was no point in fastening the shirt's cuffs, which hung down well past her fingertips, just as the shoulders overhung hers by four inches on either side. The shirttails draped to her knees. Yet when Cash wore the shirt, it fit him without wrinkles or gaps.

"Lord, but that man is big," Mariah muttered. "It's a good thing he doesn't bite."

Impatiently she shoved the cuffs up well past her elbows, tied a hasty knot in the tails, grabbed the gold pan and shovel and ran back to where Cash was still working on the horses.

"I'm ready," Mariah said breathlessly.

Cash looked up, blinked, tried not to smile and failed completely. He released the horse's hoof he had been cleaning and stood up.

"Next time, don't wear such a tight shirt," he said, deadpan.

"Next time," Mariah retorted, "don't leave your tiny little shirt on my blankets when I'm in a hurry."

Snickering, Cash shook his head. "Let me get my fishing rod. We'll start in the riffles way up behind the shack. The creek cuts through a nice grassy place just above the willow thicket. Grass will be a lot easier on your knees than gravel."

"Don't you need gravel to pan gold?"

"Only if you expect to find gold. You don't. You're just learning how to pan, remember?"

"Boy, wouldn't you be surprised if I found nuggets in that stream."

"Nope."

Mariah blinked. "You wouldn't be surprised?"

"Hell no, honey. I'd be dead of shock."

Her smile flashed an instant before her laughter glittered in the mountain silence, brighter than any gold Cash had ever found. Unable to resist touching her, he ruffled her hair with a brotherly gesture that was belied by the sudden heat and tension of his body. The reaction came every time he touched her, no matter how casually, which was why he tried not to touch her at all.

Unfortunately for Cash's peace of mind, there was no satisfactory way to teach Mariah how to pan for gold without touching her or at least getting so close to her that not touching was almost as arousing as touching would have been. The soft pad of grass beneath their feet, the liquid murmur of the brook and the muted rustle of nearby willows being stroked by the breeze did nothing to make the moment less sensually charged.

Mariah's own response to Cash's closeness didn't help ease the progress of the lessons at all. When he put his hands next to hers on the cold metal in order to demonstrate the proper panning technique, she forgot everything but the fact that Cash was close to her. Her motions became shaky rather than smooth, which defeated the whole point of the lessons.

"It's a good thing the pan is empty," Cash muttered finally, watching Mariah try to imitate the easy swirling motion of proper panning. "The way you're going at it, any water in that pan would be sprayed from hell to breakfast."

"It looks so easy when you do it," Mariah said unhappily. "Why can't I get the rhythm of it?"

Cursing himself silently, knowing he shouldn't do what he was about to do, Cash said, "Here, try it this way."

Before common sense could prevent him, he stepped behind Mariah, reached around her and put his hands over hers on the pan. He felt the shiver that went through her, bit back a searing word and got on with the lesson.

"You can pan with either a clockwise or counterclockwise motion," Cash said through clenched teeth. "Which do you prefer?"

Mariah closed her eyes and tried to stifle the delicious shivering that came each time Cash brushed against her. Standing as close as they were, the sweet friction occurred each time either of them breathed.

"Damn it, Mariah, wake up and concentrate! Which way do you want to pan?"

"C-count."

"What?"

"Counter." She dragged in a ragged breath. "Counterclockwise."

With more strength than finesse, Cash moved his hands in counterclockwise motions, dragging Mariah's hands along. The circles he made weren't as smooth as usual, but they were a great improvement on what she had managed alone. The problem was that, standing as they were, Cash couldn't help but breathe in Mariah's fragile, elementally female fragrance. Nor could he prevent feeling her warmth all the way down to his knees.

And if he kept standing so close to her, there would be a lot less innocent kind of touching that he couldn't—or wouldn't want to—prevent.

Yet brushing against Mariah was so sweet that Cash couldn't force himself to stop immediately. He continued to stand very close to her for several excruciating minutes, teaching her how to pan gold and testing the limits of his self-control at the same time.

"That's it," Cash said abruptly, letting go of Mariah's hands and stepping back. "You're doing much better. I'm going fishing."

"But—how much water do I put in the pan?" Mariah asked Cash's rapidly retreating back.

"As much as you can handle without spilling," he answered, not bothering to turn around.

"And how much gravel?"

There was no answer. Cash had stepped into the willow thicket and vanished.

"Cash?"

Nothing came back to Mariah but the sound of the wind.

She looked at the empty gold pan and sighed. "Well, pan, it's just you and me. May the best man win."

At first Mariah tried to imitate Cash and crouch on her heels over the stream while she panned. The unaccustomed position soon made her legs protest. She tried kneeling. As Cash had predicted, kneeling was more comfortable, but only because of the thick mat of streamside grass. Kneeling on gravel wouldn't have worked.

Alternating between crouching and kneeling, Mariah concentrated on making the water in the pan turn in proper circles. As she became better at it, she used more water.

While she worked, sunlight danced across the brook, striking silver sparks from the water and pouring heat over the land.

Patiently Mariah practiced the technique Cash had taught her, increasing the amount of water in the pan by small amounts each time. The more water she used, the greater the chance that she would miscalculate and drench herself with a too-energetic swirl of the pan. So far she had managed to make her mistakes in such a way as to send the water back into the stream, but she doubted that her luck would hold indefinitely.

Just when Mariah was congratulating herself on learning how to pan without accidents, she made an incautious movement that sent a tidal wave of ice water pouring down her front. With a stifled shriek she leaped to her feet, automatically brushing sheets of water from Cash's shirt and her jeans. The motions didn't do much good as far as keeping the clothes dry, but Mariah wasn't particularly worried. Once the first shock passed, the water felt rather refreshing. Except in her right shoe, which squished.

Mariah kicked off her shoes and socks, relishing the feel of sun-warmed grass on bare feet. Sitting on her heels again, she dipped up more water in the pan. Just as she was starting to swirl the water, she sensed that she wasn't alone any longer. She spun around, spilling water down her front again. She brushed futilely at the drops, shivered at the second onslaught of ice water, and smiled up at Cash in wry defeat.

He was standing no more than an arm's length away, watching her with heavy-lidded eyes and a physical tension that was tangible.

"Cash? What's wrong?"

"I was just going to ask you the same thing."

"Why?"

"You screamed."

"Oh." Mariah gestured vaguely to her front, where water had darkened the flannel shirt to black. "I goofed."

"I can see that."

Cash could see a lot more, as well. His soaked shirt clung lovingly to Mariah's body, doing nothing to conceal the shape of her breasts and much to emphasize them. The frigid water had drawn her nipples into hard pebbles that grew more prominent with each renewed pulse of breeze.

Watching Cash, Mariah shivered again.

"You should go back to the line shack and change out of those wet clothes," he said in a strained voice. "You're cold."

"Not really. The shirt is clammy, but I can take care of that without going all the way back to the cabin."

While Mariah spoke, her hands picked apart the loose knot in the bottom of Cash's shirt. She had undone the bottom two snaps before his fingers closed over hers with barely restrained power.

"What the hell do you think you're doing?" he demanded.

"Giving my bathing suit a chance to live up to its no-drip, quick-dry advertising."

Cash looked down into Mariah's topaz eyes, felt the smooth promise of her flesh against his knuckles and could think of nothing but how easy it would be to strip the clothes from her and find out whether the feminine curves that had been haunting him were as beautiful as he had dreamed.

"Bathing suit?" he asked roughly. "You're wearing a bathing suit under your clothes?"

Mariah nodded because she couldn't speak for the sudden tension consuming her, a tension that was more than equalled in Cash's hard body.

The sound of a snap giving way seemed very loud in the hushed silence, as did Mariah's tiny, throttled gasp. Cash's hands flexed again and another snap gave way.

Mariah made no move to stop him from removing the shirt. She hadn't the strength. It was all she could do to stand beneath the sultry brilliance of his eyes while snap after snap gave way and he watched her body emerge from the dripping folds of his shirt. Where the thin fabric of the tank suit was pressed wetly against her body, everything was revealed.

Cash's breath came out in a sound that was almost a groan. "God, woman, are you sure that suit is legal?"

Mariah looked down. The high, taut curves of her breasts were tipped by flesh drawn tightly against the shock of cold water. Every change from smooth skin to textured nipple was faithfully reflected by the thin, supple fabric. She made a shocked sound and tried to cover her breasts.

It was impossible, for Cash's hands suddenly were holding Mariah's in a vise that was no less immovable for its gentleness. He looked at her breasts with half-closed eyes, too unsure of his own control to touch her. Nor could he give up the pleasure-pain of seeing her. Not just yet. She was much too alluring to turn away from.

There was neither warning nor true surprise when Cash's hands released Mariah's so that he could sweep the wet shirt from her faintly trembling body. Warm, hard palms settled on her collarbones. Long masculine fingers caressed the line of her jaw, the curve of her neck, the hollow of her throat, and the gentle feminine strength of her arms all the way to her wrists.

Too late Mariah realized that the straps of her tank suit had followed Cash's hands down her arms, leaving not even the flimsy fabric between her breasts and the blazing intensity of his eyes.

"You're perfect," Cash said hoarsely, closing his eyes like a man in pain. "So damn perfect."

For long, taut moments there was only the sound of Cash's rough breathing.

"Cash," Mariah said.

His eyes opened. They were hungry, fierce, almost wild. His voice was the same way, strained to breaking. "Just one word, honey. That's all you get. Make damn sure it's the word you want to live with."

Mariah drew in a long, shaking breath and looked at the man she loved.

"Yes," she whispered.

CHAPTER TEN

CASH SAID NOTHING, SIMPLY BENT AND took the pink velvet tip of one breast into his mouth. The caress sent streamers of fire through Mariah's body. Her breath came out in a broken sound of pleasure that was repeated when she felt the hot, silky rasp of his tongue over her skin. Cash's warm hands enveloped her waist, kneading the flesh sensuously while his mouth tugged at her breast.

Even as Mariah savored the delicious fire licking through her body, Cash's hands shifted. Instants later her jeans were undone and long, strong fingers were pushing inside the wet denim, sliding over the frail fabric of her bathing suit, seeking the heat hidden between her thighs, finding it, stroking it in the same urgent rhythms of his mouth shaping her breast.

The twin assaults made Mariah's knees weaken, forcing her to cling to Cash's upper arms for balance. The heat and hardness of the flexed muscles beneath her hands surprised her. They were a tangible reminder of Cash's far greater physical power, a power that was made shockingly clear when he lifted her with one arm and with the other impatiently stripped away her wet jeans, leaving only the fragile tank suit between her body and his hands.

"Cash?" Mariah said, unable to control the trembling of her voice as the beginnings of sweet arousal turned to uncertainty.

His only answer was the sudden spinning of the world when he carried her down to the sun-warmed grass. Hungrily he took her mouth and in the same motion pinned her legs beneath the weight of his right thigh, holding her stretched beneath him while his hands plucked at her nipples and his tongue thrust repeatedly into her mouth.

Mariah couldn't speak, could barely breathe, and had no idea of how to respond to Cash's overwhelming urgency. After a few minutes she simply lay motionless beneath his powerful body, fighting not to cry. That, too, proved to be beyond her abilities. When Cash tore his mouth from hers and began kissing and love-biting a path to her ear, the taste of tears was plain on her cheek.

"What the hell...?" he asked.

Baffled, he levered himself up until he could look down into Mariah's eyes. They were huge against the paleness of her skin, shocking in their darkness. Whatever she might have said a few minutes ago, it was brutally clear right now that she didn't want him.

"What kind of game are you playing?" Cash demanded savagely. "If you didn't want sex, why the hell did you say yes?"

Mariah's lips trembled when she tried to form words, but

no words came. She no more knew what to say than she had known what to do. Tears came more and more quickly as her self-control disintegrated.

Cash swore. "You're nothing but a little tease whose bluff got called!"

With a searing word of disgust, Cash rolled aside, turning completely away from Mariah, not trusting himself even to look at her. If it weren't for his overwhelming arousal, he would have gotten to his feet and walked off. Bitterly he waited for the firestorm to pass, hating the realization that he had been so completely taken in by a woman. Again.

"I'm not a tease," Mariah said after a moment of struggling to control her tears. "I d-didn't say no."

"You didn't have to," Cash snarled. "Your body said it loud and clear."

There was a long moment of silence, followed by Mariah's broken sigh and a shaky question.

"How was I supposed to respond?"

Cash began to swear viciously; then he stopped as though he had stepped on solid ground only to find nothing beneath his feet but air. He turned toward Mariah and stared at her, unable to believe that he had heard her correctly.

"What did you say?" he asked.

"How was I supposed to respond?" she repeated shakily. "I couldn't even move. What did you want me to do?"

Cash's eyes widened and then closed tightly. An indescribable expression passed over his face, only to be replaced by no expression at all.

"Have you ever had a lover?" Cash asked neutrally.

"No," Mariah whispered. "I never really wanted one until you." She turned her face away from Cash, not able to cope with any more of his anger and contempt. Her eyes closed as her mouth curved downward. "Now I wish I'd had a hundred men. Then I would have known how to give you what you want."

Cash said something appalling beneath his breath, but the words were aimed at himself rather than at Mariah. Grimly he looked from her slender, half-naked form to the scattered clothes he had all but torn off her body. He remembered his own uncontrolled hunger, his hands on her breasts and between her legs in a wildness that only an experienced, very hungry woman would have been able to cope with. Mariah was neither.

"My fault, honey, not yours," Cash said wearily. He took off his shirt, wrapped it around Mariah like a sheet and gently took her into his arms. "I wanted you so much I lost my head. That's a sorry excuse, but it's all I have. I'm sure as hell old enough to know better."

Mariah looked up at him with uncertain golden eyes.

"Don't be afraid," he said, kissing her forehead. One hand moved down her back in slow, comforting strokes. "It's all right, honey. It won't happen again."

The easy, undemanding hug Cash gave Mariah was like a balm. With a long sigh, she rested her head against his chest. When she moved slightly, she realized that his pelt of curling hair had an intriguing texture. She rubbed her cheek against it experimentally. Liking the feeling, she snuggled even closer.

"I wasn't afraid," Mariah whispered after a moment.

Cash made a questioning sound, telling Mariah that he hadn't heard her soft words.

"I wasn't afraid of you," Mariah said, tilting back her

head until she could see Cash's eyes. "It was just…things were happening so fast and I wanted to do what you wanted but I didn't know how."

The soothing rhythm of Cash's hand hesitated, then continued as he absorbed Mariah's words.

"Virginity doesn't guarantee sexual inexperience," he said after a time. "You're both, aren't you? Virgin and inexperienced."

"There's no such thing as a sexually experienced virgin," Mariah muttered against his chest.

He laughed softly. "Don't bet on it, honey. My ex-wife was a virgin, but she had my pants undone and her hands all over me the first time we made out."

Mariah made an indecipherable noise that sounded suspiciously like "Virgin my fanny."

"Say again?" Cash said, smiling and tilting Mariah's face up to his.

She shook her head, refusing to meet his eyes. He laughed softly and bent over her mouth. His lips brushed hers once, twice, then again and again in tender motions that soon had her mouth turning after his, seeking him in a kiss less teasing than he was giving her. He seemed to give in, only to turn partially aside at the last instant and trace her upper lip with his tongue. The sensuous caress drew a small gasp from her.

Very carefully Cash lifted his head, took a slow breath and tucked Mariah's cheek against his chest once more. She gave a rather shaky sigh and burrowed against him. Hesitantly her hands began stroking him in the same slow rhythms that he was stroking her. His chest was hot beneath the silky mat of hair, and his muscles moved sleekly. Closing her eyes, she memorized his strength with her hands, enjoying the changes in texture from silky hair to smooth skin, savoring his heat and the muscular resilience of his torso.

When Mariah's hand slid down to Cash's waist, hovered, then settled on the fastening of his jeans, his breath came in with an odd, ripping sound.

"Would you like having my hands all over you?" Mariah asked tentatively.

A shudder of anticipation and need rippled over Cash, roughening his voice. "Hell yes, I'd like it. But," he added, capturing both her hands in one of his, preventing her from moving, "not unless you'd like it, too."

"There's only one way to find out...."

With a sound rather like a groan, Cash dragged Mariah's hands up to his mouth. "Let's wait," he suggested, biting her fingers gently. "There are other things you might like better at first."

"Like what?"

"Like kissing me."

Cash bent over Mariah's lips, touched the center of her upper lip with the tip of his tongue, then retreated. He returned again, touched, retreated, returned, touched and retreated once more. The slow, sensual teasing soon had Mariah moving restlessly in his arms, trying to capture his lips, failing, trying again and again until with a sound of frustration she took his head between her hands.

The cool, course silk of Cash's growing beard was an intense contrast to the heat and satin smoothness of his lips. The difference in textures so intrigued her that she savored them repeatedly with soft, darting touches of her tongue. When his lips opened, her tongue touched only air...and then the tip of his tongue found hers, touched, retreated, touched, withdrew. The hot caresses lured her deeper and yet deeper into his mouth, seducing her languidly, completely, until finally she was locked with him in an embrace as urgent as the one that had dismayed her a few minutes earlier.

But this time Mariah wasn't dismayed. This time she couldn't taste Cash deeply enough, nor could she be tasted deeply enough by him in turn. She clung to him, surrendering to and demanding his embrace at the same time, wholly lost in the shimmering sensuality of the moment. When he would have ended the kiss, she made a protesting sound and closed her teeth lightly on his tongue. With a hoarse rush of breath, Cash accepted the seductive demand and made one of his own in return, nipping at her lips, her tongue, sliding into the hot darkness behind her teeth until he had total possession of her mouth once more.

Gently Cash urged Mariah over onto her back. When she was lying against the soft grass once more, he settled onto her body in slow motion, easing apart her legs, letting her feel some of his weight while he explored the sweet mouth he had claimed with rhythmic strokes of his tongue.

Mariah made a soft sound at the back of her throat and arched against Cash's hard body. She couldn't imagine what had been wrong with her before, why his weight had frightened and then paralyzed her. The feel of his weight was delicious, maddening, incredibly arousing. Her only dilemma was how to get closer to him, how to ease the sweet aching of her body by pressing against his, soft against hard, fitting so perfectly.

When Cash's hips moved against Mariah, fire splintered in the pit of her stomach. She gasped and arched against him in an instinctive effort to feel the fire again. The sound he made was half throttled need, half triumph at having ignited the passion he had been so certain lay within her. Reluctantly, teasingly, he moved aside, lifting his body and his mouth from hers, releasing her from a sensual prison she had no desire to leave. Smiling, he looked down into her dazed topaz eyes. He was breathing too fast, too hard, but he didn't care. Mariah was breathing as quickly as he was.

"I think we can say with certainty that you like kissing me," Cash murmured.

Mariah's only answer was to capture his face between her hands once more, dragging his mouth back to hers. But he evaded her with an easy strength that told her he had been only playing at being captive before. He took her hands in his, interlacing them and rubbing against the sensitive skin between her fingers at the same time. When he could lace himself no more tightly to her, he flexed his hands, gently stretching her fingers apart. Her eyes widened as fire raced through her in response to the unexpected sensuality of the caress.

Smiling darkly, Cash flexed his hands once more as he bent down to Mariah.

"Want to taste me again?" he asked against her mouth.

Mariah's lips opened on a warm outrush of breath. The tip of her tongue traced his smile. He lifted his head just enough to see the sensual invitation of her parted lips revealing the glistening pink heat that waited for him. He wondered if she would open the rest of her body to him so willingly, and if he would slide into it with such sultry ease. With a throttled groan Cash took what Mariah offered and gave her his own mouth in return.

Slowly he pulled Mariah's hands above her head until she

was stretched out beneath him. Each slow thrust of his tongue, each flexing of his hands, each hoarse sound he made was another streamer of fire uncurling deep inside Mariah's body. She twisted slowly, hungrily, trying to ease the aching in her breasts and at the apex of her thighs. When Cash lifted his head and ended the kiss, she felt empty, unfinished. She whimpered her protest and tried to reach for him, but her arms were still captive, stretched above her head in sensual abandon.

Mariah's eyes opened. Cash was watching her body's sinuous, restless movement with eyes that smoldered. Breathless, she followed his glance. The shirt he had used to cover her had long since fallen aside, leaving her bare to the waist once more. Her nipples were tight and very pink. One breast showed faint red marks, legacy of his first, wild hunger.

The memory of Cash's mouth went through Mariah in a rush of fire, tightening her body until her back arched in elemental reflex. When she saw the reaction that went through Cash, shaking his strength, she arched again, watching him, enjoying the heat of his glance and the sun pouring over her naked breasts.

"If you keep that up, I'm going to think you've forgiven me for this," he said in a deep voice, touching the vague mark on her breast caressingly. "Have you forgiven me, honey?"

"Yes."

The sound was more a sigh than a word. Mariah twisted slowly, trying to bring Cash's hand into more satisfying contact with her breast, but she could not. Cash still held her arms stretched above her head, her wrists held in his left hand, her body softly pinned beneath his right hand.

"If I promise to be very gentle, will you let me kiss you again?"

This time Mariah's answer was a sound of anticipation and need that made Cash ache. Slowly he bent down to her. His tongue laved the passionate mark on her breast, then kissed it so gently she shivered.

"I'm sorry," Cash whispered, kissing the mark once more. "I didn't mean to hurt you."

"You didn't, you just surprised me," Mariah said moving restlessly, wanting more than the gentle torment of his lips. "I know you won't hurt me. And I—I liked it. Cash? *Please.*"

Cash wanted to tell Mariah what her trust and sensual pleas did to him, but he couldn't speak for the passion constricting his throat. With exquisite care he caught the tip of first one breast then the other between his teeth. The arching of her body this time was purely reflex, as was the low sound of pleasure torn from her throat when he drew her nipple into his mouth and tugged it into a taut, aching peak. When he released her she made a sound of protest that became a moan of pleasure when he captured her other breast and began drawing it into a sensitive peak, pulling small cries of passion from her.

Mariah didn't know when Cash released her hands. She only knew that the heat of his skin felt good beneath her palms, and the flexed power of his muscles beneath her probing fingers was like a drug. She couldn't get enough of it, or of him.

A lean, strong hand stroked from Mariah's breasts to her thighs and back again while Cash's mouth plucked at her hardened nipple in a sensual teasing that made her breath break into soft cries. Long fingers slid beneath the flimsy tank suit and kneaded her belly, savoring the taut muscles and resilient heat. Gradually, imperceptibly, inevitably, his hand eased down until he could feel the silken thicket concealing her most vulnerable flesh. When he could endure teasing himself no longer, he slid farther down, finding and touching a different, hotter softness.

Mariah's eyes opened and her breath came in with a startled gasp that was Cash's name.

"Easy, honey. That doesn't hurt you, does it?"

"No. It just—" Mariah's breath broke at another gliding caress. "It's so—" Another gasp came, followed by a trembling that shook her.

Mariah looked up at Cash with wide, questioning eyes, only to find that he was watching the slow twisting of her half-clothed body as he caressed her intimately. The stark sensuality of the moment made heat bloom beneath her skin, embarrassment and desire mingling. When his hand slid from between her legs, she made a broken sound of protest. An instant later she felt the fragile fabric of her tank suit being drawn down her legs until she was utterly naked. She saw the heavy-lidded blaze of Cash's eyes memorizing the secrets he had revealed, and she was caught between another rush of embarrassment and passion. He was looking at her as though he had never seen a nude woman before.

"You're beautiful," Cash breathed, shaken and violently aroused by Mariah's smooth, sultry body.

One of his big hands skimmed from her mouth to her knees, touching her reverently, marveling at the sensual contrast between her deeply flushed nipples and the pale cream of her breasts. The soft mound of nearly black curls fascinated him. He returned again and again to skim their promise, lightly seeking the honeyed softness he knew lay within.

Shivering with a combination of uncertainty and arousal, Mariah watched Cash cherish her body with slow sweeps of his hand. The dark intensity of his eyes compelled her, the tender caresses of his fingertips reassured her, the hot intimacy of seeing his hand touching the secret places of her body made her blush.

"Cash?" she asked shakily.

"If it embarrasses you," Cash said without looking up, "close your eyes. But don't ask me to. I've never touched a woman half so beautiful. If you weren't a virgin, I'd be doing things to you right now that would make you blush all the way to the soles of your feet."

"I already am," she said shakily.

A dark, lazy kind of smile was Cash's only answer. "But you like this, don't you?"

His knuckles skimmed the dark curls again, turning Mariah's answer into a broken sigh of pleasure.

"Good," he whispered, bending down to kiss her lips slowly, then rising once more, wanting to watch her. "I like it, too. There's something else I know I'll like doing. I think you'll like it even better."

Cash's fingertips caressed Mariah's thighs, sliding up and down between her knees, making her shiver. Watching her, he smiled and caressed her soft inner thighs again and again, gently easing them apart. When she resisted, he bent and took her mouth in a kiss that was sweet and gentle and deep. The rhythmic penetration and withdrawal of his tongue teased her, as did the sensual forays of his mouth over her breasts.

Soon Mariah's eyelids flickered shut as thrill after thrill of pleasure went through her. She forgot that she was naked and he was watching her, forgot that she was uncertain and he was tremendously strong, forgot her instinctive protection of the vulnerable flesh between her legs. With a moan she arched her back, demanding that he do something to ease the tightness coiling within her body.

The next time Mariah lifted, pleading for Cash, sensual heat bloomed from within the softness no man had ever touched. And then Cash's caress was inside her, testing the depth of her response, his touch sliding into her sleek heat until he could go no farther. Mariah made a low sound that could have been pain or pleasure. Before Cash could ask which, he felt the answer in the passionate melting of her body around his deep caress. The instant, fierce blaze of his own response almost undid him.

With a hoarse groan of male need, Cash sought Mariah's mouth, found it, took it in hungry rhythms of penetration and retreat. She took his mouth in return while her hands moved hungrily over his head, his chest, his back, half-wild with the need he had called from her depths. When he finally tore his mouth away from hers in an agonizing attempt to bring himself under control, Mariah's nails scored heedlessly on his arms in silent protest.

Cash didn't complain. He was asking for all of her response each time he probed caressingly within her softness and simultaneously rubbed the sleek bud that passion had drawn from her tender flesh. Mariah's quickening cries and searing meltings were a fire licking over him, arousing him violently, yet he made no move to take her. Instead, his hands pleasured and enjoyed her with an unbridled sensuality that was as new to him as it was to her, each of his caresses a mute demand and plea that was answered with liquid fire.

Finally Cash could bear no more of the sensuous torment. It was as difficult as tearing off his own skin to withdraw from Mariah's softness, but he did. The lacings of his boots felt harsh, alien, after the silky perfection of her aroused body. He yanked off his boots and socks with violent impatience, wanting only to be inside her. Shuddering with the force of his suppressed need, he fought for control of the passion that had possessed him as completely as it had possessed her.

"Is it—is it supposed to be—like this?" Mariah asked, breathing too hard, too fast, watching Cash with wild golden eyes.

"I don't know," Cash said, reaching for his belt buckle, looking at her with eyes that were black with desire. "But I'm going to find out."

Mariah's eyes widened even more as Cash stripped out of his clothes and turned toward her. Admiration became uncertainty when she looked from the muscular strength of his torso to the blunt, hard length of his arousal. She looked quickly back up to his eyes.

"If it were as bad as you're thinking now," Cash said huskily, drawing her body close to his, "the human race would have died out a long time ago."

Mariah's smile was too brief, too shaky, but she didn't withdraw from him. When Cash rubbed one of her hands slowly across his chest, she let out a long breath and closed her eyes, enjoying his newly familiar textures. Her fingertips grazed one of his smooth, flat nipples, transforming it into a nail head of desire. The realization that their bodies shared similarities beneath their obvious differences both comforted and intrigued her. She sought out his other nipple with her mouth. A slow touch of her tongue transformed his masculine flesh into a tiny, tight bud.

"You *do* like that," Mariah whispered, pleased by her discovery.

A sound that was both laughter and groan was Cash's only answer. Then her hand smoothed down his torso and breath jammed in his throat, making speech impossible. The tearing instants of hesitation when she touched the dense wedge of hair below Cash's waist shredded his control. Long fingers clamped around her wrist, dragging her hand to his aching flesh, holding her palm hard against him while his hips moved in an agony of pleasure. She made an odd sound, moved by his need. Abruptly he released her, afraid that he had shocked her.

Mariah didn't lift her hand. Her fingers curled around Cash, sliding over him in sweet, repeated explorations that pushed him partway over the brink. When she touched the sultry residue of his desire, she made a soft sound of discovery and wonder. She could not have aroused him more if she had bent down and tasted him.

Cash groaned hoarsely and clenched his teeth against the release that was coiled violently within his body, raging to be free. With fingers that trembled, he pulled Mariah's hand up to his mouth and bit the base of her palm, drawing a passionate sound from her. His hand caressed down the length of her body, sending visible shivers of response through her. When he reached the apex of her thighs, he had only to touch her and she gave way before him, trusting him.

He settled his weight slowly between her thighs, easing

them apart even more, making room for his big body. She was sleek, hot, promising him a seamless joining. He pushed into her, testing the promise, savoring the feverish satin of her flesh as it yielded to him.

"Cash."

He forced himself to stop. His voice was harsh with the pain of restraint. "Does it hurt?"

"No. It—" Mariah's breath fragmented as fire streaked through her. "I—"

Even as her nails scored Cash's skin, he felt the passionate constriction and then release of her body. The hot rain of her pleasure eased his way, but not enough. Deliberately he slid his hand between their joined bodies, seeking and finding the velvet focus of her passion. Simultaneously his mouth moved against her neck, biting her with hot restraint. Fire and surprise streaked through Mariah, and then fire alone, fire ripping through her, filling her as Cash did, completely, a possession that transformed her.

Mariah's eyes opened golden with knowledge and desire.

"You feel like heaven and hell combined," Cash said, his voice rough with passion. "Everything a man could want."

Mariah tried to speak but could think of no words to describe the pleasure-pain of having so much yet not quite enough...heaven and hell combined. She closed her eyes and moved her hips in a sinuous, languid motion, caressing Cash as deeply as he was caressing her. Exquisite pleasure pierced her, urging her to measure him again and then again, but it wasn't enough, it was never enough, she was burning. She twisted wildly beneath the hands that would have held her still.

"Mariah," Cash said hoarsely. "Baby, stop. You don't know what you're doing to me. I—"

His voice broke as her nails dug into the clenched muscles of his hips. Sweet violence swept through him, stripping away his control. He drove into her seething softness, rocking her with the force of his need, giving all that she had demanded and then more and yet more, becoming a driving force that was as fast and deep within her as the hammering of her own heart.

At a distance Mariah heard her own voice crying Cash's name, then the world burst and she could neither see nor hear, she was being drawn tight upon a golden rack of pleasure, shuddering, wild, caught just short of some unimaginable consummation, unborn ecstasy raking at her nerves.

For an agonizing moment Cash held himself away from Mariah, watching her, sensing her violent need as clearly as he sensed his own.

"Mariah. Look at me. *Look at me.*"

Her eyelids quivered open. She looked at Cash and saw herself reflected in his eyes, a face drawn by searing pleasure that was also pain.

"*Help me,*" she whispered.

With a hoarse cry that was her name, Cash drove deeply into Mariah once more, sealing their bodies together with the profound pulses of his release. Her body shivered in primal response, ecstasy shimmering through her, burning, bursting in pulses of pleasure so great she thought she would die of them. She clung to Cash, absorbing him into herself, crying as golden fire consumed her once more.

Cash drank Mariah's cries while ecstasy unraveled her, giving her completely to him and unraveling him completely in turn. Passion coiled impossibly, violently, within him once more. The elemental force was too overwhelming to fight. He held her hard and fast to himself, pouring himself into her again and again until there was no beginning, no end, simply Mariah surrounding him with the golden fury of mutual release.

CHAPTER ELEVEN

MARIAH FLOATED ON THE HOT CURRENTS at the upstream end of the middle pool, keeping herself in place with languid motions of her hands. The sky overhead was a deep, crystalline blue that reminded her of Cash's eyes when he looked at her, wanting her. A delicious feeling shimmered through her at the memories of Cash's body moving over hers, his shoulders blocking out the sky, his powerful arms corded with restraint, his mouth hungry and sensual as it opened to claim her.

If only they had been able to leave the cellular phone behind, they would have remained undisturbed within Black Springs's sensual silence. But their peace was disturbed by the phone's imperious summons. It woke them from their warm tangle of blankets on the shack's wooden floor. Mariah appreciated the emergency safeguard the phone represented, but she resented its intrusion just the same.

Cash had picked up the phone, grunted a few times and

hung up. Mariah had fallen asleep again, not awakening until Cash had threatened to throw her in the stream. He had taken one look at the slight hesitation in her movements as she crawled out of his sleeping bag and had sent her to Black Springs to soak. When she had tried to tell him that she wasn't really sore from the long, sweet joining of their bodies, he hadn't listened.

But she wasn't sore. Not really. She was just deliciously aware of every bit of herself, a frankly female awareness that was enhanced by the slight tenderness he deplored.

"Have I ever told you how lovely you are?"

Mariah's eyes opened and she smiled.

Cash was standing at the edge of the pool, watching her with dark blue eyes and a hunger that was more unruly for having been satisfied so completely. He knew beyond doubt what he was missing. He had sent her to the hot springs because he was afraid he wouldn't be able to keep his hands off her if she stayed in the cabin. Now he was certain he wouldn't be able to keep his hands to himself. The thin, wet fabric of her suit clung to every lush line of her body, reminding him of how good it had felt to take complete possession of her softness.

The cutoff jeans Cash wore in Black Springs didn't conceal much of his big body. Certainly not the desire that had claimed him as he stood watching Mariah.

"I'm not sure lovely is the right word for you," Mariah said, smiling. "Potent, certainly."

The shiver of desire that went over his skin as she looked at Cash did nothing to cool his body.

"Kiss me?" Mariah asked softly, holding a wet, gently steaming hand toward him.

"You're hard on my good intentions," he said in a deep voice, wading into the pool.

"Should that worry me?"

"Ask me this afternoon, when you're two hours into a half-day ride back to the ranch house."

"We have to go back so soon again?" Mariah asked, unable to hide her dismay. "Why?"

"I just got a ten-day contract in Boulder. Then I'll be back and we can go gold hunting again."

"Ten days..."

The soft wail wasn't finished. It didn't need to be. Mariah's tone said clearly how much she would miss Cash.

"Be grateful," Cash said thickly. "It will give you time to heal. I'm too damn big for you."

"I don't need time. I need...you."

The sound Cash made could have been laughter or hunger or both inextricably mixed. The water where Mariah was floating came to the middle of his thighs, not nearly high enough to conceal what her honest sensuality did to him. His former wife had used sex, not enjoyed it. At least not with him. Maybe Linda had liked sex with the father of her child.

I should be grateful that I can't get Mariah pregnant. Holding back would be impossible with her.

"Cash? Is something wrong?"

"Just thinking about the past."

"What about it?"

Without answering, Cash pulled Mariah into his arms and gave her a kiss that was hotter than the steaming, gently seething pool.

DISCREETLY MARIAH SHIFTED POSITION in the saddle. After she had recovered from the initial trip to the line shack, Cash had insisted that she ride every day no matter where she was. Thanks to that, and frequent rest breaks, she wasn't particularly sore at the moment. She was very tired of her horse's choppy gait, however. Next time she would insist on a different horse.

"Are you doing okay?" Cash asked, reining in until he came alongside Mariah.

"Better than I expected. My horse missed her calling. She would have made a world-class cement mixer."

"You should have said something sooner. We'll trade."

Mariah looked at Cash and then at the small mare she rode. "Bad match. You're too big."

"Honey, I've seen Luke ride that little spotted pony all day long."

"Really? Is he a closet masochist?"

Cash smiled and shook his head. "He saves her for the roughest country the ranch has to offer. She's unflappable and surefooted as a goat. That's why Luke gave her to you. But the rough country is behind us, so there's no reason why we can't switch horses."

Before Mariah could object any more, Cash pulled his big horse to a stop and dismounted. Moments later she found herself lifted out of the saddle and into his embrace.

"You don't have to do this," she said, putting her arms around Cash's neck. "I was finally getting the hang of that spotted devil's gait."

"Call it enlightened self-interest. Luke will peel me like a ripe banana if I bring you back in bad shape. I'm supposed to be taking care of you, remember?"

"You're doing a wonderful job. I've never felt better in my life."

Mariah's smile and the feel of her fingers combing through his hair sent desire coursing through Cash. The kiss he gave her was hard and deep and hungry. His big hands smoothed over her back and hips until she was molded to him like sunlight. Then he tore his mouth away from her alluring heat and lifted her onto his horse. He stood for a moment next to the horse, looking up into Mariah's golden eyes, his hand absently stroking the resilience of her thigh while her fingertips traced the lines of his face beneath the growth of stubble.

"What are you thinking?" Mariah asked softly.

Cash hesitated, then shrugged. "Even though we'll sleep separately on the ranch, a blind man could see we're lovers."

It was Mariah's turn to hesitate. "Is that bad?"

"Only if Luke decides he didn't mean what he said about you and me."

"What did he say?"

"That you wanted me," Cash said bluntly. "That you were past the age of consent. That whatever the two of us did was our business."

Mariah flushed, embarrassed that her attraction to Cash had been so obvious from the start.

"I hope Luke meant it," Cash continued. "He and Carla are the only home I'll ever have. But what's done is done. We might as well have the pleasure of it because sure as hell we'll have the pain."

The bleak acceptance in Cash's voice stunned Mariah. Questions crowded her mind, questions she had just enough self-control not to ask. Cash had never said anything to her about their future together beyond how long he would be gone before he came back to the Rocking M and the two of them could go gold hunting again.

I haven't said anything about the future, either, Mariah reminded herself. *I haven't even told him that I love him. I keep hoping he'll tell me first. But maybe he feels the same way about speaking first. Maybe he's waiting for me to say something. Maybe...*

Cash turned, mounted the smaller horse, picked up the pack animals' lead ropes and started down the trail once more. Mariah followed, her thoughts in a turmoil, questions ricocheting in her mind.

By the time the ranch house was in sight, Mariah had decided not to press Cash for answers. It was too soon. The feelings were too new.

And she was too vulnerable.

It will be all right, Mariah told herself silently. *Cash just needs more time. Men aren't as comfortable with their emotions as women are, and Cash has already lost once at love. But he cares for me. I know he does.*

It will be all right.

As they rode up to the corral, the back door of the ranch house opened and Nevada came out to meet them. At least Mariah thought the man was Nevada until she noticed the absence of any beard.

"It's about time you got back!" Cash called out. "If I don't sée Carolina more often, she won't recognize me at all."

The man took the bridle of Mariah's horse and smiled up at her. "With those eyes, you've got to be Luke's little sister, Mariah. Welcome home."

Mariah grinned at the smiling stranger who was every bit

as handsome as his unsmiling younger brother. "Thanks. Now I know what Nevada looks like underneath that beard. You must be Tennessee."

"You sure about that?" Ten asked.

"Dead sure. With those shoulders and that catlike way of walking, you've got to be Nevada's older brother."

Ten laughed. "It's a shame Nevada's not the marrying kind. You'd make a fine sister-in-law."

Cash gave Ten a hard glance. Ten had no way of knowing that Mariah's gentle interest in Nevada was a raw spot with Cash. No matter how many times he told himself that Mariah had no sexual interest in Nevada, Cash kept remembering his bitter experience with Linda. It had never occurred to him that she was sleeping with another man. After all, she had come to him a virgin.

Like Mariah.

"Put your ruff down," Ten drawled to Cash, amused by his response to the idea of Nevada and Mariah together. "Nevada was the one who told me the lady was already taken."

"See that he remembers it."

Ten shook his head. "Still the Granite Man. Hard muscles and a skull to match. You sure you didn't just buy your Ph.D. from some mail-order diploma mill?"

Laughing, Cash dismounted. When Ten offered his hand to help Mariah dismount, Cash reached past the Rocking M's foreman and lifted her out of the saddle. When Cash put her down, his arm stayed around her.

"Not that I don't trust you, ramrod," Cash said dryly to Ten. "It's just that you're handsome as sin and twice as hard."

The left corner of Ten's mouth turned up. "That's Nevada you're thinking of. I'm hard as sin and twice as handsome."

Cash snickered and shook his head. "Lord, what are we going to do if Utah comes home to roost?"

Mariah blinked. "Utah?"

"Another Blackthorn," Cash explained.

"There are a lot of them," Ten added.

"Don't tell me," Mariah said quickly. "Let me guess. Fifty, right? Who got stuck being called New Hampshire?"

The two men laughed simultaneously.

"My parents weren't that ambitious," Ten said. "There are only eight of us to speak of."

"To speak of?" Mariah asked.

"The Blackthorns don't run to marriage, but kids have a way of coming along just the same." Ten smiled slightly, thinking of his own daughter.

"Is Carolina awake?" Cash asked.

"I hope not. She'll be hungry when she wakes up and Diana isn't due back from our Spring Valley house for another hour. She and Carla are measuring for drapes or rugs or some darn thing." Ten shook his head and started gathering up reins and lead ropes. "Life sure was easier when all I had to worry about was a blanket for my bedroll."

"Crocodile tears," Cash snorted. "You wouldn't go back to your old life and you know it. Hell, if a man even looks at Diana more than once, you start honing your belt knife."

"Glad you noticed," Ten said dryly.

"Not that you need to," Cash continued, struck by something he had never put into words. "Diana is a rarity among females—a one-man woman."

"And I'm the lucky man," Ten said with tangible satisfaction as he led the horses off. "You two go on up to the big house and watch Carolina sleep. I'll take care of the horses for you."

When Cash started for the house, Mariah slipped from his grasp. "I've got to clean up before Carla gets back. I don't want to get off on the wrong foot with Luke's wife."

"Carla won't care what you look like. She's too damn happy that Logan finally shook off that infection and both of them can stay on the ranch again instead of in my apartment in Boulder. Besides, I happen to know Carla's dying to meet you."

"You go ahead," Mariah urged. "I'll catch up as soon as I've showered."

He tipped up Mariah's chin, kissed her with a lingering heat that made her toes curl, and reluctantly released her.

"Don't be long," Cash said huskily.

She almost changed her mind about going at all, but the thought of standing around in camp clothes while meeting Carla stiffened Mariah's determination. As her brother's wife and the sister of the man she loved, Carla was too important to risk alienating. Bitter experience with Mariah's stepfamily had taught her how very important first impressions could be.

Putting the unhappy past out of her mind, Mariah hurried toward the old ranch house. She had her blouse half-unbuttoned when she opened the front door, only to encounter Nevada just inside the living room. He was carrying a huge carton.

"Don't stop on my account," he said, appreciation gleaming in his eyes.

Hastily Mariah fumbled with a button, trying to bring her décolletage under some control.

"Relax," he said matter-of-factly. "I'm just a pack animal."

"Funny," she muttered, feeling heat stain her cheeks. "To me you look like a man called Nevada Blackthorn."

"Optical illusion. Hold the door open and I'll prove it by disappearing."

"What are you hauling?" she asked, reaching for the door, opening it only a few inches.

"Broken crockery."

"What?"

"Ten and Diana are finally moving the Anasazi artifacts out of your way. I'm taking the stuff to their new house in Spring Valley."

"That's not necessary," Mariah said. "I don't want to be a bother. I certainly don't need every room in the old house. Please. Put everything back. Don't go to any trouble because of me."

The fear beneath Mariah's rapid words was clear. Even if Nevada hadn't heard the fear, he would have sensed it in the sudden tension of her body, felt it in the urgency of the hand wrapped around his wrist.

"You'll have to take that up with Ten and Diana," Nevada said calmly. "They were looking forward to having all this stuff moved into their new house where they could work on it whenever they wanted." He saw that Mariah didn't understand yet. "Diana is an archaeologist. She supervises the September Canyon dig. Ten is a partner in the Rocking M. He owns the land the dig is on."

Slowly Mariah's fingers relaxed their grip on Nevada's wrist, but she didn't release him yet.

"You're sure they don't mind moving their workroom?" she asked.

"They've been looking forward to it. Would have done it sooner, but Carolina came along a few weeks early and upset all their plans."

Mariah smiled uncertainly. "If you're sure…"

"I'm sure."

"Just what are you sure of?" Cash's voice asked coldly, pushing the door open. Bleak blue eyes took in Mariah's partially unbuttoned blouse and her hand wrapped around Nevada's wrist.

"I was just telling her that Diana and Ten don't mind clearing out their stuff," Nevada said in a voice as emotionless as the ice-green eyes measuring Cash's anger. "Your woman was afraid she'd be kicked off the ranch if she upset anyone."

"My woman?"

"She lit up like a Christmas tree when she heard your voice. That's as much a man's woman as it gets," Nevada said. "Now if you'll get out of my way, I'll get out of yours."

There was a long silence before Cash stepped aside. Nevada brushed past him and out the front door. Only then did Mariah realize she was holding her breath. She closed her eyes and let out air in a long sigh.

When she opened her eyes again, Cash was gone.

CHAPTER TWELVE

MARIAH SHOWERED, DRIED HER HAIR, dusted on makeup and put on her favorite casual clothes—a tourmaline green blouse and matching slacks. She checked her appearance in the mirror. Everything was tucked in, no rips, no missing buttons, no spots. Satisfied, she turned away without appreciating the contrast of very dark brown hair, topaz eyes and green clothes. She had never seen herself as particularly attractive, much less striking. Yet she was just that—tall, elegantly proportioned, with high cheekbones and large, unusually colored eyes.

Mentally crossing her fingers that everything would go well with Carla, Mariah grabbed a light jacket and headed for the big house. No one answered her gentle tapping on the front door. She opened it and stuck her head in.

"Cash?" she called softly, not wanting to wake Carolina if she were still sleeping.

"In here," came the soft answer.

Mariah opened the door and walked into the living room. What she saw made her throat constrict and tears burn behind her eyelids. A clean-shaven Cash was sitting in an oversize rocking chair with a tiny baby tucked into the crook of his arm. One big hand held a bottle that looked too small in his grasp to be anything but a toy. The baby was ignoring the bottle, which held only water. Both tiny hands had locked onto one of Cash's fingers. Wide, blue-gray eyes studied the man's face with the intensity only young babies achieved.

"Isn't she something?" Cash asked softly, his voice as proud as though he were the baby's father rather than a friend of the family. "She's got a grip like a tiger."

Mariah crept closer and looked at the smooth, tiny fingers clinging to Cash's callused, much more powerful finger.

"Yes," Mariah whispered, "she's something. And so are you."

Cash looked away from the baby and saw the tears magnifying Mariah's beautiful eyes.

"It's all right," she said softly, blinking away the tears. "It's just...I thought men cared only for their own children. But you care for this baby."

"Hell, yes. It's great to hold a little girl again."

"Again?" Mariah asked, shocked. "Do you have children?"

Cash's expression changed. He looked from Mariah to the baby in his arms. "No. No children." His voice was flat, remote. "I was thinking of when Carla was born. It was Dad's second marriage, so I was ten years old when Carla came along. I took care of her a lot. Carla's mother was pretty as a rosebud, and not much more use. She married

Dad so she wouldn't have to support herself." Cash shrugged and said ironically, "So what else is new? Women have lived off men since they got us kicked out of Eden."

Although Mariah flinched at Cash's brutal summation of marriage and women, she made no comment. She suspected that her mother's second marriage had been little better than Cash's description.

Cash looked back to the baby, who was slowly succumbing to sleep in his arms. He smiled, changing the lines of his face from forbidding to beguiling. Mariah's heart turned over as she realized all over again just how handsome Cash was.

"Carla was like this baby," Cash said softly. "Lively as a flea one minute and dead asleep the next. Carla used to watch me with her big blue-green eyes and I'd feel like king of the world. I could coax away her tears when no one else could. Her smile…God, her smile was so sweet."

"Carla was lucky to have a brother like you. She was even luckier to keep you," Mariah whispered. "Long after my grandparents took me from the Rocking M, I used to cry myself to sleep. It was Luke I was crying for, not my father."

"Luke always hoped that you were happy," Cash said, looking up at Mariah.

"It's in the past." Mariah shrugged with a casualness that went no deeper than her skin. "Anyway, I was no great bargain as a child. The man my mother married was older, wealthy, and recently widowed. I met him on Christmas Day. I had been praying very hard that the special present my mother had been hinting at would be a return trip to the Rocking M. When I was introduced to my new 'father' and his kids, I started crying for Luke. Not the best first impression I could have made," Mariah added unhappily. "A disaster, in fact. Harold and his older kids resented being saddled with a 'snot-nosed, whining seven-year-old.' Boarding schools were the answer."

Cash muttered something savage under his breath.

"Don't knock them until you've tried them," Mariah said with a wry smile. "At least I was with my own kind. And I had it better than some of the other outcasts. I got to see Mother most Christmases. And I got a good education."

The bundle in Cash's arm shifted, mewing softly, calling his attention back from Mariah. He offered little Carolina the bottle again. Her face wrinkled in disgust as she tasted the tepid water.

"Don't blame you a bit," Cash said, smiling slightly. "Compared to what you're used to, this is really thin beer."

Gently he increased the rhythm of his rocking, trying to distract the baby from her disappointment. It didn't work. Within moments Carolina's face was red and her small mouth was giving vent to surprisingly loud cries. Patiently Cash teased her lips with his fingertip. After a few more yodels, the baby began sucking industriously on the tip of his finger.

"Sneaky," Mariah said admiringly. "How long does it last?"

"Until she figures out that she's working her little rear end off for nothing."

Car doors slammed out in the front yard. Women's voices called out, to be answered from the vicinity of the barn.

"Hang in there, tiger," Cash said. "Milk is on the way."

Mariah smoothed her clothes hastily, tucked a strand of hair behind her ear and asked, "Do I look all right?"

Cash looked up. "It doesn't matter. Carla isn't so shallow that she's going to care what you look like."

Mariah heard the edge in Cash's voice and knew he was still angry about finding her with Nevada. But before she could say anything, the front door opened and a petite, very well built woman hurried in.

"Sorry I'm late. I—oh, hello. What gorgeous eyes. You must be Luke's sister. I'm Diana Blackthorn. Excuse me. Carolina is about to do her imitation of a cat with its tail in a wringer. Thanks, Cash. You have a magic touch with her. Even Ten would have had a hard time keeping the lid on her this long."

Diana whisked the small bundle from Cash's arms and vanished up the staircase, speaking to Carolina in soothing tones at every step.

Mariah blinked, not sure that she had really seen the honey-haired woman at all. "That was an archaeologist?"

"Um," Cash said tactfully.

"Ten's wife?"

"Um."

"Whew. No wonder he smiles a lot."

"Ask Diana and she'll tell you that she'd trade it all for four more inches of height."

"She can have four of mine if I can have four of hers," Mariah said instantly.

Cash came out of the rocking chair in a fluid motion and pulled Mariah close. His hands slid from her hips to her waist and on up her body, stopping at the top of her rib cage. Watching her, he eased his hands underneath her breasts, taking their warm weight into his palms, teasing her responsive nipples with his thumbs, smiling lazily.

"You're too damn sexy just the way you are," Cash said, his voice gritty, intimate, as hot as the pulse suddenly speeding in Mariah's throat. "I've never seen anything as beautiful as you were this morning in that pool wearing nothing but steam. *You watched me take you.* The sweet sounds you made then almost pushed me over the edge. Just thinking about it now makes me want to—"

"Hi, Nevada. Is that another box of shards? Good. Put them in Diana's car. Here, Logan, chew on this instead of Nosy's tail. Even if the cat doesn't mind it, I do."

The voice from the front porch froze Cash. He closed his eyes, swore softly, and released Mariah. He turned toward the front door, blocking Mariah's flushed face with his body.

"Where's my favorite nephew?" Cash called out.

"Your only nephew," Carla said, smiling as she walked into the living room. "He's a one hundred percent terror again. How's my favorite brother?"

"Your only brother, right?" Cash bent down and scooped up Logan in one arm. "Lord, boy. What have you been eating—lead? You must have gained ten pounds."

As a toddler, Logan wasn't exactly a fountain of conversation. Action was more his line. Laughing, he grabbed Cash's nose and tried to pull it off.

"That's not the way to do it," Cash said, grabbing Logan's nose gently. Very carefully Cash pulled and made a sucking, popping noise. Moments later he triumphantly held up his hand. The end of his thumb was pushed up between his index and second finger to imitate Logan's snub nose. "See? Got it! Want me to put it back on?"

With an expression of affection and amusement, Carla watched her brother and her son. Then she realized that someone was standing behind Cash. She looked around his broad shoulders and saw a woman about her own age and height hastily tucking in her blouse.

"Hello?"

Mariah bit her lip and gave up trying to straighten her clothes. "Hi, I'm—"

"Mariah!" Carla said, smiling with delight. She stepped around Cash and gave Mariah a hug. "I'm so glad you came home at last. When the lawyer told Luke his mother was dead, there was no mention of you at all. We had no way to contact you. Luke wanted so much to share Logan with you. And most of all he wanted to know that you were happy."

Mariah looked into Carla's transparent, blue-green eyes and saw only welcome. With a stifled sound, Mariah hugged Carla in return, feeling a relief so great it made her dizzy.

"Thank you," Mariah said huskily. "I was so afraid you would resent having me around."

"Don't be ridiculous. Why would anyone resent you?" Carla stared into Mariah's huge, golden-brown eyes. "You mean it. You really were worried, weren't you?"

Mariah tried to smile, but it turned upside down. "Families don't like outsiders coming to live with them."

Cash spoke without looking up from screwing Logan's nose back into place. "As you might guess from that statement, Mariah's mother didn't pick a winner for her second husband. In fact, he sounds like a real, um, prince. Kept her in boarding schools all year round."

"Why didn't he just send you back to the Rocking M?" Carla asked Mariah.

"Mother refused. She said the Rocking M was malevolent. It hated women. She could feel it devouring her. Just

talking about it upset her so much I stopped asking."
Mariah looked past Carla to the window that framed
MacKenzie Ridge's rugged lines. "I never felt that way about
the ranch. I love this land. But as long as Mother was alive,
I couldn't come back. She simply couldn't have coped with
it."

"You're back now," Carla said quietly, "and you're
staying as long as you want."

Mariah tried to speak, couldn't, and hugged her sister-in-
law instead.

Cash watched the two women and told himself that no
matter why Mariah had originally come to the Rocking M,
she was genuinely grateful to be accepted into Luke's family.
And, Cash admitted, he couldn't really blame Mariah for
wanting a place she could call home. He felt the same way.
The Rocking M, more than his apartment in Boulder, was
his home. Only on the Rocking M were there people who
gave a damn whether he came back from his field trips or
died on some godforsaken granite slope.

Almost broodingly Cash watched Mariah and his sister
fix dinner. With no fuss at all they went about the business
of cooking a huge meal and getting to know one another.
As he looked at them moving around the kitchen, Cash
realized that the two women were similar in many ways.
They were within a year of each other in age, within an inch
in height, graceful, supremely at home with the myriad tools
used to prepare food, willing to do more than half of any
job they shared; and their laughter was so beautiful it made
him ache.

*Linda never wanted to share anything or do any work. I
thought it was just because she was young, but I can see that*

wasn't it. She was the same age then as Mariah is now. Linda was just spoiled. Mariah may have come here looking for room and board—and a crack at Mad Jack's mine—but at least she's not afraid to work for it.

Best of all, Mariah doesn't whine.

No. Not best of all. What was best about Mariah, Cash conceded, was her incandescent sensuality. After Linda, he had never found it difficult to control himself where women were concerned. Mariah was different. He wanted her more, not less, each time. It was just as well that he was going to Boulder. He needed distance from Mariah's fire, distance and the coolness of mind to remember that a woman didn't have to be spoiled in order to manipulate a man. She simply had to be clever enough to allow him to deceive himself.

Cash was still reminding himself of how it had been with Linda when he let himself into the old house in the hour before dawn. He knew he should be on the road, driving away, putting miles between himself and Mariah. Yet he couldn't bring himself to leave without saying goodbye to her.

The front door of the old house closed softly behind Cash. An instant later he heard a whispering, rushing sound and felt Mariah's soft warmth wrapping around him, holding him with a woman's surprising strength. His arms came around her in a hard hug that lifted her feet off the floor.

Her tears were hot against his neck.

"Mariah?"

She shuddered and held on to Cash until she could trust her voice. "I couldn't sleep. I heard you loading the Jeep. I thought you weren't even going to say goodbye to me. Please don't be angry with me over Nevada. I like him but it's nothing to what I feel about you. I—"

But Cash's mouth was over hers, sealing off her words. The taste of him swept through her, making her tremble. His arms shifted subtly, both molding and supporting her body, stroking her over his hard length, telling her without a word how perfectly they fit together, hard against soft, key against lock, male and female, hunger and fulfillment.

It took an immense amount of willpower for Cash to end the kiss short of taking Mariah down to the floor and burying himself in her, ending the torment that raked him with claws of fire.

"Don't leave me," Mariah whispered when Cash lowered her feet back to the floor. "Not yet. Hold me for just a little longer. Please? I—oh, Cash, it's so cold without you."

She felt the tremor that went through Cash, heard his faint groan, and then the world tilted as he picked her up once more. Moments later he put her on the bed, grabbed the covers and pulled them up beneath her chin. She struggled against the confining sheet and comforter, trying to get her arms free, but it was impossible.

"Warm enough?" he asked. "I don't want you getting sick." His voice was too deep, too thick, telling of the heavy running of his blood. "You didn't get much sleep last night, I couldn't keep my hands off you in the pool, it was a long ride back and then you cooked a meal for twelve."

"Carla did most of the work and—"

"Bull. I was watching, honey."

"—and I loved your hands on me in the pool," Mariah said quickly, talking over Cash's voice. "I love your mouth. I love your body. I love—"

His mouth came down over hers again, ending the husky flow of words that were like tiny tongues of fire licking over him.

"I shouldn't have taken you this morning," Cash said when he managed to tear himself away from Mariah's sweet, responsive mouth. "Damn it, honey, you're not used to having a man yet, and you make me so hard and hungry."

"The pool must have magic healing properties," Mariah whispered, looking up at Cash with wide golden eyes. In the vague golden illumination cast by the night-light, Cash was little more than a dense man-shadow, a deep voice and powerful hands holding her imprisoned within the soft cocoon of bed covers. "And when I couldn't sleep tonight I took a long soak in the tub. I'm not sore, not even from the ride back. If you don't believe it, touch me. You'll see that I'm telling the truth. I know you want me, Cash. I felt it when you hugged me. Touch me. Then you'll know I want you, too."

"Mariah," he whispered.

Cash kissed her again and again, tiny, fierce kisses that told of his restraint and need. When she made soft sounds of response and encouragement, he deepened the kiss. As their tongues caressed, hunger ripped through him, loosening his hold on the bedclothes for a few moments.

It was all Mariah needed. She kicked aside the soft, enfolding covers even as she reached for Cash. He groaned when he saw her elegant, naked legs and the cotton nightshirt that barely came below her hips. Then she took his hand in hers and began smoothing it down her body.

He could have pulled away and they both knew it. He was far stronger than she was, more experienced, more able to control the hot currents of hunger that coursed through his body. But Mariah's abandoned sensuality disarmed him completely. When her breasts tightened and peaked visibly beneath cloth, he remembered how it felt to hold her in his mouth, shaping and caressing her while cries of pleasure shivered from her lips.

Even before Mariah guided Cash's hand to the sultry well of her desire, he suspected he was lost. When he touched the liquid heat that waited for him, he knew he was. He tried not to trace the soft, alluring folds and failed. He skimmed them again, probing delicately, wishing that his profession hadn't left his fingertips so scarred and callused. She deserved to be caressed by something as silky and unmarked as her own body.

"Baby?" Cash whispered. "Are you sure?"

The answer he received was a broken sound of pleasure and a sensual melting that took his doubts and his breath away. When he started to lift his hand, Mariah's fingers tightened over his wrist, trying to hold him.

"Cash," Mariah said urgently, "don't leave yet. Please stay with me for a little more. I—"

"Hush, honey," Cash said, kissing away Mariah's words. "I'm not going far." He laughed shakily. "I couldn't walk out of here right now if I had to. Don't you know what you do to me?"

"No," she whispered. "I only know what you do to me. I've never felt anything close to it. I didn't even know it was possible to feel so much. It's like I've been living at night all my life and then the sun finally came up."

The words were more arousing than any caress Cash had ever received. His hands shook with the force of the hunger pouring through him.

Mariah watched while Cash stripped away his clothes with careless, powerful motions that were very different from the tender caresses he had given to her just moments before. The nebulous glow of the tiny night-light turned Cash's skin to gold and the hair on his body to a dark, shimmering bronze. Each movement he made was echoed by the black velvet glide of shadows over his muscular body.

Cash watched Mariah as he kicked aside the last of his clothes and stood naked before her. Mariah's eyes were heavy lidded, the color of gold, shining, and they worshiped all of him, even the full, hard evidence of his desire. Still looking at him, she reached for the bottom button on her nightshirt with fingers that trembled.

Cash rested one knee on the mattress, making it give way beneath his weight. One long finger traced from the instep of Mariah's foot, up the calf, behind the knee, then slowly up the inside of her thighs. When her leg flexed in response, he smiled slowly.

"That's it, little one. Show me you want me," Cash whispered. "Make room for me between those beautiful legs."

Mariah's long legs shifted and separated. He followed each movement with dark, consuming eyes and light caresses. Slowly he knelt between her legs, watching her, seeing the same sensual tension in her that had taken his body and drawn it tight on wires of fire.

For a moment Cash didn't move, couldn't move, frozen by the beauty of Mariah's body and the trust implicit in her vulnerable position. Slowly, irresistibly, his hands pushed aside her unbuttoned nightshirt, smoothing it down over her shoulders and arms, stopping at her wrists, for he had become distracted by the rose-tipped, creamy invitation of her breasts.

Mariah made a murmurous sound of pleasure that became a soft cry as his mouth found one nipple and pulled it into a tight, shimmering focus of pleasure. When she arched up in sensual reflex, the nightshirt slid down beneath her back to her hips, stopping there, holding her hands captive. She didn't notice, for Cash's hands were smoothing up her legs, making her tremble in anticipation of the pleasure to come. When he touched her very lightly, she shivered and cried out.

"It occurred to me," Cash said, his voice deep and slow, "that something as soft as you shouldn't have to put up with hands as callused as mine."

Mariah would have told Cash how much she loved his hands, but couldn't. The feel of his tongue probing silkily into her navel took her breath away. Glittering sensations streaked through her body at the unexpected caress.

"You should be touched by something as hot and soft as you are," Cash said. He sampled the taut skin of Mariah's belly with his tongue, smiling to feel the response tightening her. His tongue flicked teasingly as he slid down her body. "Since it's too late for you to go out and find some soft gentleman to be your lover, we'll just have to do the best we can with what we've got, won't we?"

Mariah didn't understand what Cash was talking about. As far as she was concerned he was perfect as a lover. She was trying to tell him just that when she felt the first sultry touch of his tongue. The intimacy of the kiss shocked her. She tried to move, only to find her legs held in her lover's gentle, immovable hands and her wrists captive to the tangled folds of her nightdress.

"Cash—you shouldn't—I—"

"Hush," he murmured. "I've always wondered what a woman tastes like. I just never cared enough to find out. But I do now. I want you, honey. And that's what you are. Honey."

Cash's voice was like his mouth, hungry, hot, consuming. The words Mariah had been trying to speak splintered into a pleasure as elemental as the man who was loving her in hushed, wild silence. For long moments she fought to speak, to think, to breathe, but in the end could only give herself to Cash, twisting slowly, drawn upon a rack of exquisite fire.

By the time Cash finally lifted his head, Mariah was shaking and crying his name, balanced on the jagged breakpoint of release. He sensed that the lightest touch would send her over the edge. Knowing he should release her from her sensual prison, Cash still held back, loving the sound of her voice crying for him, loving the flushed, petal-softness of her need, loving the raggedness of her breathing matching his own.

At last he bent down to her once more, seeking the satin knot of sensation he had called from her, touching it with the tip of his tongue.

With a husky cry that was his name, Mariah was overcome by an ecstasy that convulsed her with savage delicacy. Cash held her and smiled despite the shudders of unfulfilled need that were tearing him apart. Caressing her softly, he waited for her first, wild ecstasy to pass. Then he gently flexed her legs, drawing them up her body until she was completely open to him. With equal care he fitted his body to hers, pressing very, very slowly into her.

When he looked up, he saw Mariah watching him become a part of her. He felt the shivering, shimmering ripples of pleasure that were consuming her all over again, ecstasy renewed and redoubled by his slow filling of her body. The knowledge that she welcomed the deep physical interlocking as much as he did raced through Cash, sinking all the way into him, calling to him at a profound level, luring him so deeply into Mariah that he couldn't tell where she ended and he began, for there was no difference, no separation, no boundary, nothing but their shared body shuddering in endless, golden pulses of release.

And in the pauses between ecstasy came Mariah's voice singing a husky litany of her love for Cash.

CHAPTER THIRTEEN

KISS ME GOODBYE, HONEY. THE SOONER I go, the sooner I'll be back.

Mariah had heard those same words of parting from Cash many times in the five months since she had come to the Rocking M, including the one time she had declared her love. Cash's goodbyes were woven through her days, through her dreams, a pattern of separations and returns that had no end in sight. Even though Cash was no longer teaching at the university, his consulting work rarely allowed him to spend more than two weeks at a time at the Rocking M. More often, he was free for only a handful of incandescent days, followed by several weeks of loneliness after he left. Each time Mariah hoped that he would invite her to Boulder, but he hadn't.

Nor had Cash told Mariah that he loved her.

He must love me. Surely no man could make love to a

woman the way Cash does to me without loving her at least a little. Carla and Luke assume Cash loves me. So does everyone else on the Rocking M. He just can't say the words. And is that so important, after all? His actions are those of a man in love, and that's what matters.

Isn't it?

Mariah had no doubt about her own feelings. She had never expected to love anyone the way she loved Cash—no defenses, nothing held back, an endless vulnerability that would have terrified her if Cash hadn't been so clearly happy to see her each time he came back to the ranch.

He was gone for only four days this time and he called every night and we talked for hours about nothing and everything and we laughed and neither one of us wanted to hang up. He loves me. He just doesn't say it in so many words.

It will be all right. If he hadn't wanted children he would have used something or seen that I did. But he never even mentioned it.

The emotional fragility that had plagued Mariah for too many weeks sent tears clawing at the back of her eyes. It had been more than four months since her last period. Soon she wouldn't be able to hide the life growing within her by leaving her pants unbuttoned and wearing her shirts out. Cash had noticed the new richness in the curves of her body but hadn't guessed the reason. Instead, he had teased her about the joys of regular home cooking.

He loves children and kids love him. He'll be a wonderful father.

It will be all right.

Fighting for self-control, unconsciously pressing one hand

against her body just below her waist, Mariah stood on the small porch of the old house and stared out through the pines at the road that wound through the pasture. She thought she had seen a streamer of dust there a moment ago, the kind of boiling rooster tail of grit that was raised by Cash's Jeep when he raced over the dirt road to be with her again.

"Are you going to tell him this time?"

Mariah started and turned away from the road. Nevada Blackthorn stood a few feet away, watching her with his uncanny green eyes.

"Tell who what?" she asked, off balance.

"Tell Cash that he's going to be a daddy sometime next spring." Nevada swore under his breath at the frightened look Mariah gave him. "Damn it, woman, you're at least four months along. You should be going to a doctor. You should be taking special vitamins. If you don't have sense enough to realize it, I do. Have you ever seen a baby that was too weak to cry? Babies don't have any control over their lives," he continued ruthlessly. "They're just born into a world that's more often cruel than not, and they make the best of it for as long as they can until they either die or grow up. Too often, they die."

Mariah simply stared at Nevada, too shocked to speak. The bleakness of his words was more than matched by his eyes, eyes that were looking at her, noting each telltale difference pregnancy had made.

"You must have decided to have the baby," Nevada said, "or you would have done something about it months ago. A woman who has guts enough to go through with a pregnancy should have guts enough to tell her man about it."

"I've tried." Mariah made a helpless gesture. "I just can't find the right time or the right words."

Because Cash has never said he loves me. But she couldn't say that aloud. She could barely stand to think it.

"The two of you go off looking for gold at least twice a month, but there's never enough time or words for you to say 'I'm pregnant'?" Nevada hissed a word beneath his breath. "If you don't have the guts to tell Cash this time, I'll take you into Cortez after he leaves. Dr. Chacon is a good man. He'll tell you what the baby needs and I'll make damn sure you get it."

Mariah looked at Nevada and knew he meant every word. He was as honest as he was hard. If he said he would help her, he would. Period.

"You're a good man," she said softly, touching his bearded jaw with her fingertips. "Thank you."

"You can thank me by telling Cash." Despite the curtness of Nevada's voice, he took Mariah's hand and squeezed it encouragingly. "You've got about twenty seconds to find the right words."

"What?"

"He's here."

Mariah spun to face the road. When she saw that Cash's battered Jeep had already turned into the dusty yard of the old house, her face lit up. She ran to the Jeep and threw herself into Cash's arms as he got out.

Cash lifted her, held her close, and looked at Nevada over Mariah's shoulder. Nevada returned the cool stare for a long moment before he turned and walked toward the bunkhouse without a backward glance.

"What did Nevada want?" Cash asked.

Mariah stiffened. Cash's voice was every bit as hard as Nevada's had been.

"He just—he was wondering when you would get here," she said hurriedly.

It was a lie and both of them knew it.

Cash's mouth flattened at the surprise and the pain tearing through him. Somehow he hadn't expected Mariah to lie. Not to him. Not about another man.

A freezing fear congealed in Cash as he realized how dangerously far he had fallen under Mariah's spell.

"Nevada wanted something else, too," Mariah said quickly, hating having told the lie. "I can't tell you what. Not yet. Before you leave, I'll tell you. I promise. But for now just hold me, Cash. Please hold me. I've missed you so!"

Cash closed his eyes and held her, feeling her supple warmth, a warmth that melted the ice of her half lie, leaving behind a cold shadow of memory, a forerunner of the betrayal he both feared and expected.

"Did you miss me?" Mariah asked. "Just a little?"

The uncertainty in her voice caught at Cash's emotions. "I always miss you. You know that."

"I just—just wanted to hear it."

Cash pulled away from Mariah until he could look down into her troubled golden eyes. The unhappiness he saw there made his heart ache despite his effort to hold himself aloof. "What is it, Mariah? What's wrong?"

She shook her head, took a deep breath and smiled up at the man she loved. "When you hold me, nothing is wrong. Come to the big house with me. Let me lust after you while I make dinner."

His expression changed to a lazy kind of sensuality that

sent frissons of anticipation over Mariah's nerves. Smiling, Cash dipped his head until he could take her mouth in a kiss that left both of them short of breath.

"I'd rather you lusted after me in the old house where we can do something about it," Cash said, biting Mariah's lips with exquisite care, wanting her even more than he feared wanting her.

"So would I. But then I'd never get around to cooking dinner and the cowhands would rebel."

Laughing despite the familiar hunger tightening his body, Cash slowly released Mariah, then put his arm around her waist and began walking toward the big house. The time of reckoning and payment would come soon enough. Anticipating it would only diminish the pleasure of being within reach of Mariah's incandescent sensuality.

"I don't want to be responsible for a Rocking M rebellion," he said.

"Neither do I," Mariah answered, putting her arm around Cash's lean waist. "I tried to do as much of dinner as possible ahead of time, but Logan and Carolina decided they didn't want a nap."

Cash looked down at Mariah questioningly. "Where are Diana and Carla?"

"I'm watching the kids during the morning so Diana and Carla can work on the artifacts that keep coming in from September Canyon."

"And you're cooking six nights a week for the whole crew."

"I love to cook."

"And Diana is making an archaeologist out of you three nights a week."

"She's a very good teacher."

"And you're taking correspondence courses in commercial applications of geology. And technical writing."

Mariah nodded. "I have my first job, too," she said proudly. "The Four Corners Regional Museum wants to do a splashy four-color book about the history of the area. They commissioned specialists for each section of the book, then discovered that having knowledge isn't the same thing as being able to communicate knowledge through writing."

Ruefully Cash smiled. Despite the fact that his profession required writing reports of his fieldwork, he knew his shortcomings in that department. In fact, he had begun writing all his reports on the Rocking M. Not only did it give him more time with Mariah, he had discovered that she had a knack for finding common words to describe esoteric scientific data. He had been the one to suggest that Mariah pursue technical writing, since she obviously had a flair for it.

"So," Mariah continued, "I'm translating the geology and archaeology sections into plain English. If they like my work, I have a chance to do the whole book for them."

Cash stopped, caught Mariah's face between his hands, kissed her soundly and smiled down at her. "Congratulations, honey. When did you find out?"

"This morning. I wanted to call, but you were already on the road. I thought you would never get here. It's such a long drive. And in the winter…"

Mariah's voice trailed off. They both knew that driving to the Rocking M from Boulder was tedious under good conditions, arduous during some seasons and impossible when storms turned segments of the ranch's dirt roads into goo that even Cash's Jeep couldn't negotiate.

The difficulty of getting to the Rocking M wasn't a subject Cash wanted to pursue. If Mariah hadn't been Luke's sister, Cash would have asked her to stay with him in Boulder months ago. But that was impossible. It was one thing to go gold hunting with Mariah or to steal a few hours alone with her in the old house before both of them went to sleep in separate beds under separate roofs. It was quite another thing to set up housekeeping outside of marriage with his best friend's little sister.

The obvious solution was marriage, but that, too, was impossible. Even if Cash brought himself to trust Mariah completely—especially if he did—he wouldn't ask her to share a childless future with him. Even so, he found himself coming back to the idea of marriage again and again.

Maybe Mariah wouldn't mind. Maybe she would learn to be like me, accepting what can't be changed and enjoying Logan and Carolina whenever possible. Maybe...

And maybe not. How can I ask her to give up so much? No matter how much she thinks she loves me, she wants children of her own. I can see it every time she looks at Logan and then looks at me with a hunger that has nothing to do with sex. She wants my baby. I know it as surely as I know I can't give it to her.

But God, I can't give her up, either. I'm a fool. I know it. But I can't stop wanting her.

There wasn't any answer to the problem that circled relentlessly in Cash's mind, arguments and hopes repeated endlessly with no solution in sight. No matter how many times Cash thought about Mariah and himself and the future, he had no answer that he wanted to live with. So he did what he had always done since he had realized what being effectively sterile meant. He put the future out of his mind and concentrated on the present.

"Come on," Cash said, kissing Mariah's forehead. "I'll peel potatoes while you tell me all about your new job."

If he noticed the uncertainty in her smile, he didn't mention it, any more than she mentioned the fact that he was gripping her hand as though he expected her to run away.

MOTIONLESS, AWARE ONLY OF his own thoughts, Cash let himself into the old ranch house in the velvet darkness that comes just before dawn. Mariah didn't expect him. They had decided to spend the day at the ranch and not leave for Black Springs until the following dawn.

But Cash hadn't been able to stay away. He had awakened hours before, fought with himself, and finally lost. He had just enough self-control not to go into Mariah's bedroom and wake her up by slowly merging their bodies. Fighting the need that never left him even when he had just taken her, Cash went into the house and sat in what had once been Diana's workroom and gradually had evolved into an office for him and a library for Mariah's increasing collection of books.

He didn't even bother to turn on the light. He just pulled out one of the straightback chairs, faced it away from the table, and tried to reason with his unruly body and mind. His body ignored him. His mind supplied him with images of a night at the line shack when Mariah had teased him because his body steamed in the frosty autumn air. He had teased her, too, but in other ways, drawing from her the sweet cries of desire and completion that he loved to hear. The thought of hearing those cries again was a banked fire in Cash's big body, and the fire was no less hot for being temporarily controlled.

The sound of the bedroom door opening and Mariah's light footsteps crossing the living room sent a wave of desire through Cash that was so powerful he couldn't move. A light in the living room came on, throwing a golden rectangle of illumination onto the workroom floor. None of the light reached as far as Cash's feet.

"Cash?"

"Sorry, honey. I didn't mean to wake you up."

Mariah was silhouetted in the doorway. The shadow of her long flannel nightshirt rippled like black water.

"I'm here."

"What are you doing sitting in the dark?"

"Watching the moonlight. Thinking."

The huskiness of Cash's deep voice made Mariah's heartbeat quicken. She walked through the darkened room and stood in front of Cash.

"What are you thinking about?" she asked softly.

"You."

Big hands came up and wrapped around Mariah's wrists. She whispered his name even as he tugged her down into his lap. He kissed her deeply, shifting her until she sat astride his legs and he could rock her hips slowly against his body. The heavy waves of his need broke over her, sweeping away everything but the taste and feel and heat of the man she loved. When his hands found and teased her breasts, she made rippling sounds of hunger and pleasure.

When Mariah unfastened her nightshirt to ease his way, Cash followed the wash of moonlight over her skin with his tongue until she moaned. Soon her nightshirt was undone and he was naked to the waist and his jeans were open and her hands were moving over him, loving the proof of his passion, making him tighten with desire.

"If you don't stop, we'll never make it to bed," Cash said, his voice hoarse.

"But you feel so good. Better each time. You're like Black Springs, heat welling up endlessly."

Cash's laugh was short and almost harsh. "Only since I've known you."

Without warning he lifted Mariah off his lap.

"Cash?"

"Honey, if I don't move now, I won't be able to stand up at all. I want you too much."

Despite Cash's words, he made no move to get up. When Mariah's hands pushed at his jeans, tugging them down until she had the freedom of his body, he didn't object. He couldn't. He could hardly breathe for the violence of the need hammering through him. When she touched him, the breath he did have trickled out in a groan that sounded as though it had been torn from his soul.

Mariah's eyes widened and her breath caught in a rush of sensual awareness that was as elemental as the power of the man sitting before her. Her fingertips traced Cash gently again. Closing his eyes, he gave himself to her warm hands. When the caressing stopped a few moments later, he couldn't prevent a hoarse sound of protest. He heard a rustling sound, sensed Mariah's nightshirt sliding to the floor, and shuddered heavily. When he opened his eyes she was standing naked in front of him.

"Can people make love in a chair?" Mariah asked softly.

Before the words were out of her mouth, Cash's hand was

caressing her inner thighs, separating them, seeking the sultry heat of her. She shivered and melted at the caress. When his touch slid into her, probing her softness, her knees gave way. Swaying, she grabbed his shoulders for balance.

"Cash?" she whispered. "Can we?"

"Sit on my lap and find out," he said, luring her closer and then closer still, easing her down until she was a balm around his hard, aching flesh and her name was a broken sigh on his lips. "Each time—better."

For Mariah, the deep rasp of Cash's voice was like being licked by loving fire. She leaned forward to wrap her arms around his neck. The movement caused sweet lightning to flicker out from the pit of her stomach. She moved again, seeking to recapture the stunningly pleasurable sensation. Again lightning curled through her body.

"That's right," Cash said huskily, encouraging Mariah's sensual movements. "Oh, yes. Like that, honey. Just…like… that."

Shivering, moving slowly, deeply, repeatedly, giving and taking as much as she could, Mariah fed their mutual fire with gliding movements of her body. When the languid dance of love was no longer enough for either of them, Cash's hands fastened onto her hips, quickening her movements. Her smile became a gasp of pleasure when he flexed hard against her, enjoying her as deeply as she did him.

He watched her, wanting all of her, breathing dark, hot words over her until control was stripped away and he poured himself into her welcoming softness. Mariah held herself utterly still, drinking Cash's release, loving him, feeling her own pleasure beginning to unravel her in golden pulses that radiated through her body, burning gently through to her soul.

And then there was a savage flaring of ecstasy that swept everything away except her voice calling huskily to Cash, telling him of her love and of their baby growing within her womb....

For an instant Cash couldn't believe what he was hearing. "What?"

"I'm pregnant, love," she whispered, leaning forward to kiss him again.

Suddenly Cash believed it, believed he was hearing the depth of his own betrayal from lips still flushed with his kisses. He had thought he was prepared for it, thought that a woman's treachery had nothing new to teach him.

He had been wrong. He sat rigid, transfixed by an agony greater than any he had ever known...and in its wake came a rage that was every bit as deep as the passion and the pain.

"You're pregnant," Cash repeated flatly, a statement rather than a question.

He could control his voice, but not the sudden, violent rage snaking through his body, a tension that was instantly transmitted to the woman who was so intimately joined with him.

"Yes," Mariah said, trying to smile, failing, feeling the power of Cash's fingers digging into her hips. "Didn't you want this? You never tried to prevent it and you like children and I thought..."

Her voice died into a whisper. She swallowed, but no ease came to her suddenly dry throat. In the moonlight Cash looked like a man carved from stone.

"No, I never tried to prevent it," Cash said. "I never spend time trying to make lead into gold, either."

He heard his own words as though at a vast distance, an echo from a time when he could speak and touch and feel, a time when betrayal hadn't spread like black ice through his soul, freezing everything.

"I don't understand," Mariah whispered.

"I'll just bet you don't."

With bruising strength Cash lifted Mariah from his lap, kicked out of his entangling clothes and stood motionless, looking through her as though she weren't there. She had the dizzying feeling of being trapped in a nightmare, unable to move, unable to speak, unable even to cry. She had imagined many possible reactions to her pregnancy, even anger, but nothing like this, an absolute withdrawal from her.

"Cash?" Mariah whispered.

He didn't answer. In electric silence he studied the deceptively vulnerable appearance of the woman who stood with her face turned up to him, moonlight heightening both the elegance and the fragility of her bone structure.

She's about as fragile as a rattlesnake and a hell of a lot more dangerous. She's one very shrewd little huntress. No one will believe that I'm not the father of her baby. I could go to the nearest lab and get back the same result I got years ago, when Linda told me she was pregnant—a chance I was the father, but not much of one.

But Cash had wanted to believe in that slim chance. He had wanted it so desperately that he had blinded himself to any other possibility.

Luke would feel the same way this time. Rather than believe that his beloved Muffin was a liar, a cheat and a schemer, Luke would believe that Mariah was carrying Cash's baby. If Cash refused to marry Mariah, it would drive a wedge between himself and Luke. Perhaps even

Carla. Then there would be nothing left for Cash, nowhere on earth he could call home. He had no choice but to accept the lie and marry the liar.

It was as nice a trap as any woman had ever constructed for a foolish man.

Except for one thing, one detail that could not be finessed no matter how accomplished a huntress Mariah was. There was one way to prove she was lying. It would take time, though. Time for the baby to be born, time for its blood to be tested, time for the results to be compared with Cash's own blood. Then, finally, it would be time for truth.

"When is it due."

Cash didn't recognize his own voice. There was no emotion in it, no resonance, no real question, nothing but a flat requirement that Mariah give him information.

"I d-don't know."

"What does the doctor say."

"I haven't been to one." Mariah interlaced her fingers and clenched her hands in order to keep from reaching for Cash, touching him, trying to convince herself that she actually knew the icy stranger standing naked in the darkness while he interrogated her. "That's—that's what Nevada wanted. He said he'd take me into see Dr. Chacon if I didn't tell you this time."

So that's who fathered her bastard. I should have known. God, how can one man be such a fool?

Suddenly Cash didn't trust his self-control one instant longer. Too many echoes of the past. He had known the trap. He had taken the bait anyway.

So be it.

Mariah watched as Cash dressed. Though he said nothing

more, his expression and his abrupt handling of his clothes said very clearly that he was furious. Uncertainly Mariah tried to dress, but her trembling fingers forced her to be satisfied with simply pulling her nightshirt on and leaving it unfastened. When she looked up from fumbling with the nightshirt, Cash was standing at the front door watching her as though she were a stranger.

"Congratulations, honey. You just got a name for your baby and a free ride for the length of your pregnancy."

"What?"

"We're getting married. That's what you wanted, isn't it?"

"Yes, but—"

"We'll talk about it later," Cash said, speaking over Mariah's hesitant words. "Right now, I'm not in the mood to listen to any more of your *words*."

The door opened and closed and Mariah was alone.

CHAPTER FOURTEEN

*I*T WILL BE ALL RIGHT. *H*E JUST NEEDS *some time to get used to the idea. He must care for me. He wouldn't have asked me to marry him if he didn't care for me, would he? Lots of men get women pregnant and don't marry them.*

It will be all right.

The silent litany had been repeated so often in Mariah's mind during the long hours after dawn that the meaning of the words no longer really registered with her. She kept seeing Cash's face when he had told her that she would have a free ride and a name for the baby.

When we're married I'll be able to show Cash how much I love him. He must care for me. He doesn't have to marry me, but he chose to. It will be all right.

The more Mariah repeated the words, the less comfort they gave. Yet the endless, circling words of hope were all she had to hold against a despair so deep that it terrified her, leaving sweat cold on her skin, and a bleak, elemental cry of loss vibrating beneath her litany of hope.

Cash would marry her, but he did not want the child she was carrying. He would marry her, but he didn't believe in her love. He would marry her, but he thought she wanted only his name and the money to pay for her pregnancy. He would marry her, but he believed he had been caught in the oldest trap of all.

And how can I prove he's wrong? I have no money of my own. No home. No job. No profession. I'm working toward those things, but I don't have them yet. I have nothing to point to and say, "See, I don't need your apartment, your food, your money. I just need you, the man I love. The only man I've ever loved."

But she could not prove it.

"Mariah? You awake?"

For a wild instant she thought the male voice belonged to Cash, but even as she spun toward the front door with hope blazing on her face, she realized that it was Nevada, not Cash. She went to the front door, opened it, and looked into the pale green eyes that missed not one of the signs of grief on her face.

"Are you feeling all right?" Nevada asked.

Mariah clenched her teeth against the tears that threatened to dissolve her control. Telling Nevada what had happened would only make things worse, not better. Cash had always resented the odd, tacit understanding between Nevada and Mariah.

Nor could she tell Luke, her own brother, because telling him would in effect force him to choose between his sister and Cash, the man who was closer to him than any brother could be. No good could come of such a choice. Not for her. Not for Cash. And most of all, not for Luke, the brother who had opened his arms and his home to her after a fifteen-year separation.

"I'm...just a little tired." Mariah forced a smile. She noticed the flat, carefully wrapped package in Nevada's hand and changed the subject gratefully. "What's that?"

"It's yours. It came in yesterday, but I didn't have time to get it to you."

Automatically Mariah took the parcel. She looked at it curiously. There was no stamp on the outside, no address, no return address, nothing to indicate who the package was for, who had sent it or where it had come from.

"It's yours, all right," Nevada said, accurately reading Mariah's hesitation.

"What's underneath all that tape?"

"Mad Jack's map."

"Oh. I suppose they found where the mine was."

Nevada's eyes narrowed. There was no real curiosity in Mariah's voice, simply a kind of throttled desperation that was reflected in her haunted golden eyes.

"I didn't ask and they didn't tell me," Nevada said after a moment. "They just sent it back all wrapped up. I'm giving it to you the same way I got it."

Mariah looked at the parcel for a long moment before she set it aside on a nearby table. "Thank you."

"Aren't you going to open it?"

"I'll wait for...Cash."

"Last time I saw him, he was in the kitchen with Carla." Nevada looked closely at Mariah, sensing the wildness seething just beneath her surface. "You told Cash about the baby."

Mariah shivered with pent emotion. "Yes. I told him."

Without another word Mariah stepped off the porch and headed for the big house. She couldn't wait for a moment longer. Maybe by now Cash had realized that she hadn't meant to trap him. Maybe by now he understood that she loved him.

It will be all right.

Mariah was running by the time she reached the big house. She raced through the back door and into the kitchen, but no one was around. Heart hammering, she rushed into the living room. Cash was there, standing next to Carla. His hand was over her womb and there was a look of wonder on his face.

"It's moving," he said, smiling suddenly. "I can feel it moving!"

The awe in Cash's voice made Mariah's heart turn over with relief. Surely a man who was so touched by his sister's pregnancy could accept his own woman's pregnancy.

"Moving? I should say so." Carla laughed. "It's doing back flips."

A healthy holler from the second-floor nursery distracted Carla. "Logan just ran out of patience." She hurried out of the room. "Hi, Mariah. The coffee is hot."

"Thank you," Mariah said absently.

She walked up to Cash, her face suffused with hope and need. She took his hand and pressed it against her own womb.

"I think I've felt our baby moving already. But you have to be very still or you won't—"

Mariah's words ended in a swift intake of breath as Cash jerked his hand away, feeling as though he had held it in fire. The thought of what it might be like to actually feel his own child moving in the womb was a pain so great it was all he could do not to cry out.

"I can't feel a damned thing," Cash said roughly. "I guess my imagination isn't as good as yours."

He spun away, clenching his hands to conceal their fine trembling. When he spoke, his voice was so controlled as to be unrecognizable.

"I'll leave tomorrow to make the arrangements. After we're married, you'll stay here."

Mariah heard the absolute lack of emotion in Cash's voice and felt ice condense along her spine.

"What about you?" she asked.

"I'll be gone most of the time."

Tears came to Mariah's eyes. She could no more stop them than she could stop the spreading chill in her soul.

"Why?" she asked. "You never used to work so much."

"I never had a wife and baby to take care of, did I."

The neutrality of Cash's voice was like a very thin whip flaying Mariah's nerves. She swallowed but it did nothing to relieve the aching dryness of her mouth or the burning in her eyes.

"If you don't want me to be your wife," Mariah said in a shaking voice, "why did you ask me to marry you?"

Cash said something savage beneath his breath, but Mariah didn't give up. Anything, even anger, was better than the frigid lack of emotion he had been using as a weapon against her.

"Other men get women pregnant and don't marry them," she said. "Why are you marrying me?"

"I could hardly walk out on my best friend's sister, could I? And you have Carla wrapped around your little finger, too. They would think I was a real heel for knocking you up and then not marrying you."

"That's why…?" Mariah shuddered and felt the redoubling of the chill despair that had been growing in the center of her soul.

"Carla and Luke are the only family I have or ever will have," Cash continued with savage restraint.

"That's not true," Mariah said raggedly. "You have me! You have our baby!"

She went to Cash in a rush, wrapping her arms around him, holding him with all her strength. It was like holding granite. He was unyielding, rigid, motionless but for the sudden clenching of his hands when Mariah's soft body pressed against his.

"We'll be a family," she said. Her lips pressed repeatedly against his cheek, his neck, his jaw, desperate kisses that said more than words could about yearning and loneliness, love and need. "Give us a chance, Cash. You enjoyed being with me before, why not again?"

While Mariah spoke, her hands stroked Cash's back, his shoulders, his hair, the buttons of his shirt; and then her mouth was sultry against his skin. When she felt the involuntary tremor ripping through his strong body, she made a small sound in the back of her throat and rubbed her cheek against his chest.

"You enjoyed my kisses, my hands, my body, my love," Mariah said, moving slowly against Cash, shivering with the pleasure of holding him. "It can be that way again."

Cash moved with frightening power, pushing Mariah away at arm's length, holding her there. Black fury shook him as he listened to his greatest dream, his deepest hungers, his terrifying vulnerability used as weapons by the woman he had trusted too much.

"I'll support you," he said through his clenched teeth. "I'll give your bastard a name. But I'll be damned if I'll take another man's leavings to bed."

Shock turned Mariah's face as pale as salt.

"What are you saying?" she whispered hoarsely. "This baby is yours. You must know that. I came to you a virgin. You're the only man I've ever loved!"

Cash's mouth flattened into a line as narrow as the cold blaze of his eyes.

"A world-class performance, right down to the tears trembling in your long black eyelashes. There's just one thing wrong with your touching scenario of wounded innocence. I'm sterile."

Mariah shook her head numbly, unable to believe what she was hearing. Cash kept talking, battering her with the icy truth, freezing her alive.

"When I was sixteen," Cash said, "Carla came down with mumps. So did I. She recovered. So did I...after a fashion. That's why I never worried about contraceptives with you. I couldn't get you pregnant."

"But you did get me pregnant!"

"You're half right." Cash's smile made Mariah flinch. "Settle for half, baby. It's more than I got."

"Listen to me," Mariah said urgently. "I don't care what you had or when you had it or what the doctors told you afterward. They were wrong. Cash, you have to believe me. I love you. I have never slept with another man. *This baby is yours.*"

For an instant Cash's fingers dug harshly into Mariah's

shoulders. Then he released her and stepped back, not trusting himself to touch her any longer.

"You're something else." He jammed his hands into the back pockets of his jeans. "Really. Something. For the first time in my life I'm grateful to Linda. If she hadn't already inoculated me against your particular kind of liar, I'd be on my knees begging your forgiveness right now. But she did inoculate me. She stuck it in and then she broke it off right at the bone."

"I—"

Cash kept right on talking over Mariah's voice.

"Virginity is no proof of fidelity," he said flatly. "Linda was a virgin, too. She told me she loved me, too. Then she told me she was pregnant. Sound familiar?" He measured Mariah's dismay with cold eyes. "Yeah, I thought it would. The difference was, I believed her. I was so damned hungry to believe that I'd gotten lucky, hit that slim, lucky chance and had gotten her pregnant. We hadn't been married five months when she came and told me she was leaving. Seems her on-again, off-again boyfriend was on again, and this time he was willing to pay her rent."

Mariah laced her fingers together in a futile attempt to stop their trembling.

"You loved her," Mariah whispered.

"I loved the idea of having gotten her pregnant. I was so convinced she was carrying my baby that I told her she couldn't have a divorce until after the baby was born. Then she could leave, but not with the baby. It would stay with me. Well, she had the baby. Then she had a blood test run on it. Turns out I hadn't been lucky. The baby wasn't mine. End of story."

Cash made a short, thick sound that was too harsh to be a laugh. "Want to know the really funny part? I never believed Linda loved me, but I was beginning to believe that you did. You got to me in a way Linda never did." He looked at Mariah suddenly, really looked at her, letting her see past the icy surface to the savage masculine rage beneath. "Don't touch me again. You won't like what happens."

Mariah closed her eyes and swayed, unable to bear what she saw in Cash's face. His remoteness was as terrifying as her own pain.

Suddenly she could take no more. She turned and ran from the house. The chilly air outside settled the nausea churning in her stomach. Walking swiftly, shivering, she headed for the old ranch house. The pines surrounding the old house were shivering, too, caressed by a fitful wind.

When the front door closed behind Mariah, she made a stifled sound and swayed, hugging herself against a cold that no amount of hope could banish. Slowly she sank to her knees, wishing she could cry, but even that release was beyond her.

It will be all right. It has to be. Somehow I'll make him believe me.

Slim chance, isn't that what you said? But it came true, Cash. It came true and now you won't believe in it. In my love. In me. And there's nothing I can do. Nothing!

Mariah swayed and caught her balance against the table that stood near the front door. A small, flat package slid off. Automatically she caught it before it hit the floor.

Slim chance.

Almost afraid to believe that hope was possible, Mariah stripped off paper and tape until Mad Jack's map fell into her hands. With it was a cover letter and a copy of the map. There was no blank area on the copy, no ancient stain, no blur, nothing but a web of dotted lines telling her that she and Cash had been looking at the wrong part of Devil's Peak.

Will you believe I love you if I give you Mad Jack's mine?
Will that prove to you that I'm not after a free ride like your
stepmother and your wife? Will you believe me if...

With hands that trembled Mariah refolded the copy and put it in her jeans. Silently, quickly, she went to the workroom cupboard and changed into her trail clothes. When she was ready to leave, she pulled out a sheet of notepaper and wrote swiftly.

I have nothing of value to give you, no way to make you believe. Except one. Mad Jack's mine. It's yours now. I give it to you. All of it.

I'll find the mine and I'll fill your hands with gold and then you'll have to believe I love you. When you believe that, you'll know the baby is yours.

Slim chance.
But it was the only chance Mariah had.

CHAPTER FIFTEEN

THE MEMORY OF MARIAH'S LOST, frightened expression rode Cash unmercifully as he worked over his Jeep. No matter how many times he told himself she was an accomplished little liar, her stricken face contradicted him, forcing him to think rather than to react from pain and rage.

And reason told Cash that no matter how good an actress Mariah was, she didn't have the ability to make her skin turn pale. She didn't have the ability to make the black center of her eyes dilate until all the gold was gone. She didn't have the ability...but those things had happened just the same, her skin pale and her eyes dark and watching him as though she expected him to destroy her world as thoroughly as she had destroyed his.

With a savage curse Cash slammed shut the Jeep's hood and went to the old house. The instant he went through the front door, he knew the house was empty. He could feel it.

"Mariah?"

No one answered his call. With growing unease, Cash walked through the living room. Shreds of wrapping paper and tape littered the floor. On the table near the door was a typed note and what looked like Mad Jack's faded old map. Cash read the note quickly, then once more.

There was no mistake. A copy of the map had been in the package, a clean copy that supposedly showed the way to Mad Jack's mine. Automatically Cash glanced out the window, assessing the weather. Slate-bottomed clouds were billowing over the high country.

Mariah wouldn't risk it just for money. She would count on Luke to support her even if I refused.

Yet even as the thought came, Cash discarded it. Mariah had been very careful to take nothing from Luke that she didn't earn by helping Carla with Logan and the demands of being a ranch wife. That was one of the things Cash had admired about Mariah, one of the things that had gotten through his defenses.

As he turned away from the small table, he saw another piece of paper that had fallen to the floor. He picked it up, read it, and felt as though he were being wrenched apart.

It can't be true. It...can't...be.

Cash ran to the workroom and wrenched open the cupboard that held Mariah's camping clothes. It was empty.

That little fool has gone after Mad Jack's mine.

Cash looked at his watch. Three hours since Mariah had tried to seduce him and his treacherous body had responded as though love rather than lies bound him to her. Three hours since he had told her that he was sterile. Three hours since she had looked at him in shock and had tried to convince him that the baby was his. Three hours since she had looked at his face and fled.

Three hours, a treasure map, and a high-country storm coming down.

Cursing under his breath, Cash began yanking drawers open, pulling out cold-weather gear he hadn't used since the past winter. After he changed clothes, he started cramming extra clothing into a backpack. Then he remembered the Rocking M's cellular telephones. When Mariah and Cash weren't hunting gold, one of those phones was kept in the old house's tiny kitchen.

The phone was missing from its place on the kitchen counter. Cash ran out to his Jeep, opened the glove compartment and pulled out his own battery-operated unit. He punched in numbers, praying that Mad Jack's map kept Mariah out of canyons that were too steep and narrow for the signal to get in or out. Cellular phones worked better than shortwave radio, but the coverage wasn't complete. Twentieth-century technology had its limitations. The Rocking M's rugged terrain discovered every one of them.

The ringing stopped. No voice answered.

"Mariah? It's Cash."

Voiceless sound whispered in response, a rushing sense of space filled with something that was both more and less than silence.

"Mariah, turn around and come back."

There was a long, long pause before her answer came.

"No. It's my proof. When I find it you'll know I love you and then maybe, just maybe, you'll…"

Cash strained to hear the words, but no more came.

"Mariah. Listen to me. I don't want the damned mine.

Turn around and head back to the ranch before it starts snowing."

"It already did. Then it rained a little and now it's just sort of slushy. Except for the wind, it's not too cold."

But Mariah was shivering. He could hear it in the pauses between words, just as he could hear the shifting tone of her voice when she shivered.

"Mariah, you're cold. Turn around and come back."

"No. The mine is here. It has to be. I'll find it and then I'll have p-proof that slim chances are different from none. Life's a lottery and you're one of the l-luckiest men alive. I'm going to find your mine, Cash. Then you'll have to b-believe me. Then everything will be all right. Everything will be..."

The phone went dead.

Quickly Cash punched up the number again, ignoring the first chill tendrils of fear curling through his gut.

It can't be.

Mariah didn't answer the phone. After ten rings Cash jammed the phone into his jacket pocket, zipped the pocket shut and ran to the corral.

Slim chance.

Ice crystallized in the pit of Cash's stomach, displacing the savagery that had driven him since the instant Mariah had told him she was pregnant.

In three hours it would be freezing up in the high country. Mariah didn't have any decent winter gear. She didn't even have enough experience in cold country to know how insidious hypothermia could be, how it drained the mind's ability to reason as surely as it drained the body's coordination, cold eating away at flesh until finally the person was defenseless.

Three hours. Too much time for the cold to work on Mariah's vulnerable body. Doubly vulnerable. Pregnant.

Slim chance.

Oh God, what if I was wrong?

Trying not to think at all, Cash caught and bridled two horses. He saddled only one. Leading one horse, riding the other, Cash headed out of the ranch yard at a dead run. Mariah's trail was clear in the damp earth and slanting autumn light. Holding his mount at a hard gallop, Cash followed the trail she had left, forcing himself to think of nothing but the task in front of him. After half an hour he stopped, switched his saddle to the spare horse and took off again at a fast gallop, leading his original mount.

Although the dark, wind-raked clouds rained only fitfully, the ground was glistening with cold moisture. In the long afternoon shadows, puddles wore a rime of ice granules left by the passage of a recent hailstorm. The horses' breaths came out in great soft plumes, only to be torn away by the rising wind.

Except for the wind, it's not too cold.

Mariah's words haunted Cash. He tried not to think of how cold it was, how quickly wind stripped heat from even his big body. Even worse than the cold was the fitful rain. He would have preferred snow. In an emergency, dry snow could be used as insulation against the wind, but the only defense from rain was shelter. Otherwise wind simply sucked out all body heat through the damp clothes, leaving behind a chill that drained a person's strength so subtly yet so completely that most people didn't realize how close they were to death until it was too late; they thought they stopped shivering because their bodies had miraculously become warm again.

MARIAH LOOKED AT THE MAP ONCE more, then at the dark lava slope to her right. There was a pile of rocks that looked rather like a lizard, but there was no lightning-killed tree nearby. Shrugging, she reminded herself that more than a century had passed since Mad Jack drew the map. In that amount of time, a dead tree could have fallen and been absorbed back into the land. Carefully Mariah reined her mount around until the lizard was at her back. The rest of the landmarks fit well enough.

Shivering against the chill wind, she urged her horse downhill, checking every so often in order to keep the pile of rocks at her back. The horse was eager to get off the exposed slope. It half trotted, half slid down the steep side of a ravine. The relief from the wind was immediate.

With a long sigh, Mariah gave the horse its head and tucked her hands into the huge pockets of her jacket. Once in the ravine, the only way to go was downhill, which was exactly the way Mad Jack had gone. Her fingers were so cold that she barely felt the hard weight of the cellular phone she had jammed into one of the oversize pockets and forgotten.

I'll count to one hundred. If I don't see any granite by then, I'll get out of the ravine and head for Black Springs. It can't be more than twenty minutes from here, just around the shoulder of the ridge. It will be warm there.

Mariah had counted to eighty-three when she saw a spur ravine open off to the right. The opening was too small and too choked with stones for the horse to negotiate. Almost afraid to breathe, much less to believe, she dismounted and hung on to the stirrup until circulation and balance returned to her cold-numbed body. Scrambling, falling, getting up again, she explored the rocky ravine.

When Mariah first saw the granite, she thought it was a patch of snow along the left side of the ravine. Only as she got closer did she realize that it was rock, not ice, that gleamed palely in the fading light. The pile of rubble she crawled over to reach the granite had been made by man. The shattered, rust-encrusted remains of a shovel proved it.

Breathing quickly, shivering, Mariah knelt next to the small hole in the mountainside that had been dug by a man long dead. Inside, a vein of quartz gleamed. It was taller than she was, thicker, and running through it like sunlight through water was pure gold.

Slowly Mariah reached out. She couldn't feel the gold with her chilled fingers, but she knew it was there. With both hands she grabbed a piece of rocky debris and used it as a hammer. Despite her clumsiness, chunks of quartz fell away. Pure gold gleamed and winked as she gathered the shattered matrix in both hands. She shoved as much as she could in her oversize jacket pockets, then stood up. The weight of the rocks staggered her.

Very slowly Mariah worked her way back down the side ravine to the point where she had left her horse. It was waiting patiently, tail turned toward the wind that searched through the main ravine. Mariah tried to mount, fell, and pulled herself to her feet again. No matter how she concentrated, she couldn't get her foot through the stirrup before she lost her balance.

And her pocket was jeering at her again. It had jeered at her before, but she had ignored it.

Mariah realized that it was the cellular phone that was jeering. With numb fingers she groped through the pieces of rock and gold until she kept a grip on the phone long enough to pull it from her pocket and answer. The rings stopped, replaced by the hushed, expectant sound of an open line.

"Mariah? Mariah, it's Cash."

The phone slid through Mariah's fingers. She made a wild grab and caught the unit more by luck than skill.

"Mariah, talk to me. Where are you? Are you warm enough?"

"Clumsy. Sorry." Mariah's voice sounded odd to her own ear. Thick. Slow.

"Where are you?"

"Devil's Peak. But isn't hell warm? I'm warm, too. I think. I was cold after the rain. Now I'm tired."

The words were subtly slurred, as though she had been drinking.

"Are you on the north side of Devil's Peak?" Cash asked, his voice as hard and urgent as the wind.

Mariah frowned down at the phone as she struggled with the concept of direction. Slowly a memory of the map formed in her mind.

"And…west," she said finally.

"Northwest? Are you on the northwest side?"

Mariah made a sound that could have meant anything and leaned against her patient horse. The animal's warmth slowly seeped into her cold skin.

"Are you above timberline?" Cash asked.

"No."

"Are there trees around you?"

"Rocks, too. Gray. Looked like snow. Wasn't."

"Look up the mountains. Can you see me?"

Mariah shook her head. All she could see was the ravine.

"Can't." She thought about trying to mount the horse again. "Tired. I need to rest."

"Mariah. Look up the mountain. You might be able to see me."

Grumbling, Mariah tried to climb out of the ravine. Her hands and feet kept surprising her. She persisted. After a while she could at least feel her feet again, and her hands. They hurt. She still couldn't claw her way out of the crumbling ravine, however.

"I can't," she said finally.

"You can't see me?"

"I can't climb out of the ravine." Mariah's voice was clearer. Moving around had revived her. "It's too steep here. And I'm cold."

"Start a fire."

She looked around. There wasn't enough debris in the bottom of the ravine for a fire. "No wood."

She shivered suddenly, violently, and for the first time became afraid.

"Talk to me, Mariah."

"Do you get lonely, too?" Then, before Cash could say anything, she added, "I wish...I wish you could have loved me just a little bit. But it will be all right. I found the mine and now it's yours and now you have to believe me...don't you?" Her voice faded, then came again. "It's so cold. You were so warm. I loved curling up against you. Better each time...love."

Cash tried to speak but couldn't for the pain choking him. He gripped the phone so hard that his fingers turned white. The next words he heard were so softly spoken that he had a hard time following them. And then he wished he hadn't been able to understand the ragged phrases pouring from Mariah.

"It will be all right … everything will be fine … it will be …"

But Mariah was crying. She no longer believed her own words.

A horse's lonesome whinny drifted up faintly from below. Cash's horse answered. He reined his mount toward the crease in the land where Mariah's tracks vanished. Balancing his weight in the stirrups, he sent his horse down the mountainside at a reckless pace. Minutes later the ravine closed around Cash, shutting out all but a slice of the cloudy sky.

"Mariah!" Cash called. *"Mariah!"*

There was no answer but that of her horse whinnying its delight into the increasing gloom.

Instants after Cash saw Mariah's horse, he saw the dark splotch of her jacket against the pale swath of granite. He dismounted in a rush and scrambled to Mariah. At the sound of his approach, she pushed herself upright and held out her hands. Quartz crystals and gold gleamed richly in the dying light.

"See? I've p-proved it. Now will you b-believe me?" she whispered.

"All you've proved is that you're a fool," Cash said, picking Mariah up in a rush, ignoring the gold that fell from her hands. "It will be dark in ten minutes—I'm damned lucky I found you at all!"

Mariah tried to say something but couldn't force herself to speak past the defeat that numbed her more deeply than any cold.

Her gift of the gold mine had meant nothing to Cash. He still didn't believe in her. She had risked it all and had nothing to show for it but the contempt of the man she loved.

He was right. She was a fool.

CHAPTER SIXTEEN

BROODINGLY CASH WATCHED MARIAH. In the silence and firelight of the old line shack she looked comfortable despite the stillness of her body. Wearing dry clothes and his down sleeping bag, sitting propped up against the wall, coffee steaming from the cup held between her hands, Mariah was no longer cold. No shivers shook her body. Nor was she clumsy anymore. The pockets bulging with gold-shot rock had been as much to blame for her lack of coordination as the cold.

She's fine, Cash told himself. *Any fool could see that. Even this fool. So why do I feel like I should call her on the cellular phone right now?*

That's easy, fool. She's never been farther away from you than right now. Your stupidity nearly killed her. You expect her to thank you for that?

Flames burnished Mariah, turning her eyes to incandescent gold, heightening the color that warmth had returned to her skin.

"More soup?" Cash asked, his voice neutral.

"No, thank you."

Her voice, like her words, was polite. Mariah had been very polite since they had come to the line shack. She had protested only once—when he stripped her out of her damp clothes and dressed her in the extra pair of thermal underclothes he had brought in the backpack. When he had ignored her protest, she had fallen silent. She had stayed that way, except when he asked a direct question. Then she replied with excruciating politeness.

Not once had she met his eyes. It was as though she literally could not bear the sight of him. He didn't really blame her. He would break a mirror right now rather than look at himself in it.

"Warm enough?" Cash asked, his voice too rough.

It must have been the tenth time he had asked that question in as many minutes, but Mariah showed no impatience.

"Yes, thank you."

Cash hesitated, then asked bluntly, "Any cramps?"

That question was new. He heard the soft, ripping sound her breath made as it rushed out.

"No."

"Are you sure?"

"Yes. I'm fine. Everything is..." The unwitting echo of Mariah's past assurances to herself went into her like a knife. Without finishing the sentence, Mariah took a sip of coffee, swallowed and regained her voice. "Just fine, thank you."

But her eyelids flinched and the hands holding the coffee tightened suddenly, sending a ripple of hot liquid over the side. A few drops fell to the sleeping bag.

"I'm sorry," she said immediately, blotting at the drops with the sleeve of her discarded shirt. "I hope it won't stain."

"Pour the whole cup on it. I don't give a damn about the sleeping bag."

"That's very kind of you."

"*Kind?* Good God, Mariah. This is me, Cash McQueen, the fool you wanted to marry, not some stranger who just wandered in off the mountain!"

"No," she said in a low voice, blotting at the spilled coffee.

"What?"

There was no answer.

Fear condensed into certainty inside Cash. With a harsh curse he put aside his own coffee cup and sat on his heels next to Mariah.

"Look at me."

She kept dabbing at the bag, refusing to look at him.

Cash's big hand fitted itself to her chin. Gently, inexorably, he tilted her face until she was forced to meet his eyes. Then his breath came out in a low sound, as though he had been struck. Beneath the brilliant dance of reflected flames, Mariah's eyes were old, emotionless, bleak.

He looked into Mariah's golden eyes, searching for her, feeling her slipping away, nothing but emptiness in all the places she had once filled. The cold tendrils of fear that had been growing in Cash blossomed in a silent black rush, and each heartbeat told him the same cruel truth: she no longer loved the man whose lack of trust had nearly killed her. She couldn't even stand the sight of him.

Cash had thought he could feel no greater pain than he had when Mariah told him she was pregnant. He had been wrong.

"Are you sure you feel all right?" he asked, forcing the words past the pain constricting his body. "You're not acting like the same girl who went tearing up a stormy mountain looking for gold."

"I'm not," she whispered.

"What?"

"I'm not the same. I've finally learned something my step-father spent fifteen years trying to teach me."

Cash waited.

Mariah said nothing more.

"What did you learn?" he asked when he could no longer bear the silence.

"You can't make someone love you. No matter what you do, no matter how hard you try…you can't. I thought my stepfather would love me if I got good grades and made no demands and did everything he wanted me to do." Mariah closed her eyes, shutting out the indigo bleakness of Cash's glance. "It didn't work. After a while I didn't care very much.

"But I didn't learn very much, either. I thought you would love me if only I could prove that I loved you, but all I proved was what a fool I was. You see, I had it all wrong from the start. I thought if you believed me, you would love me. Now I know that if you loved me, *then* you would believe me. So we both had a long, cold ride for nothing."

"Not for nothing," Cash said, stroking Mariah's cheek, wanting to hold her but afraid she would refuse him. "You're safe. That's something, honey. Hell, that's everything."

"Don't. I don't need pity. I'm warm, dry and healthy, thanks to you. I did thank you, didn't I?"

"Too many times. I didn't come up here for your thanks."

"I know, but you deserve thanks just the same. If my stepfather had had a chance to get rid of me, he wouldn't have walked across the street to avoid it, much less climbed a mountain in a hailstorm."

Cash's breath hissed in with shock as he realized what Mariah was implying.

"I appreciate your decency," she continued, opening her eyes at last. "You don't need to worry about losing your home with Luke and Carla because of my foolishness. Before I leave, I'll be sure they understand that none of this was your fault."

Too quickly for Cash to prevent it, Mariah pulled free of his hand, set her coffee cup aside and unzipped the sleeping bag. His hand shot out, spread flat over her abdomen and pinned her gently in place.

"What are you saying?" Cash asked, his voice dangerously soft.

Mariah tried to prevent the tremor of awareness that went through her at his touch. She failed. Somehow she had always failed when it came to love.

"I'm leaving the Rocking M. You don't have to marry me just to ensure your welcome with Luke and Carla," Mariah said, her voice careful. "You'll always have a home with them."

"So will you." Cash's eyes searched hers, looking for the emotions that he had always found in her before, praying that he hadn't raced up the mountain only to lose her after all. "You'll have a home. Always. I'll make sure of it."

Mariah closed her eyes again and fought against the emotions that were just beneath her frozen surface.

"That's very generous of you," Mariah said, her voice husky with restraint. "But it's not necessary." She tried to get up, but Cash's big hand still held her captive. "May I get up now?" she asked politely.

"Not yet."

Cash's big hand moved subtly, almost caressingly. He couldn't free Mariah. Not yet. If he let her go he would never see her again. He clenched his jaw against the pain of an understanding that had come too late. He tried to speak, found it impossible, and fought in silence to control his emotions. When he could speak again, his voice was a harsh rasp.

"Look at me, Mariah."

She shook her head, refusing him.

"Do you hate me so much?" he asked in a low, constrained voice.

Shocked, Mariah opened her eyes.

"You have every right," Cash continued. "I damn near killed you. But if you think I'm going to let you go, you're as big a fool as I was. You loved me once. You can learn to love me again." He shifted his weight onto his knees as he bent down to her. "Forgive me, Mariah," he whispered against her lips. "Love me again. I need you so much it terrifies me."

Mariah would have spoken then, but he had taken her breath. Trembling, she opened her lips beneath his, inviting his kiss. She sensed the tremor that ripped through him, felt the sudden iron power of his arms, tasted the heat and hunger of his mouth. The world shifted until she was lying down and he was with her, surrounding her with a vital warmth that was so glorious she wept silently with the sheer beauty of it.

Suddenly Cash's arms tightened and he went very still.

"Cash? What's wrong?"

"Didn't you feel it?" he asked, his voice strained.

"What?"

"Our baby." Cash closed his eyes but could not entirely conceal the glitter of his tears. "My God," he breathed. *"I felt our baby move."*

"Are you certain?"

His eyes opened. He smiled down at Mariah, sensing the question she hadn't asked. He kissed her gently once, twice, then again and again, whispering between each kiss.

"I'm very certain."

"Cash?" she whispered, her eyes blazing with hope.

"I love you, Mariah," he said, kissing her hand, holding it against his heart. "I love you so damned much."

Laughing, crying, holding on to Cash, Mariah absorbed his whispered words and his warmth, his trust and his love, and gave her own in return. He held her, loving her with his hands and his voice and his body, until finally they lay at peace in each other's arms, so close that they breathed the same scents, shared the same warmth…and felt the butterfly wings of new life fluttering softly in Mariah's womb.

Cash's big hand rested lightly over Mariah's womb.

"Go to sleep, little baby. Mom and Dad are right here. Everything is all right."

WARRIOR

CHAPTER ONE

SHE'S THE WRONG WOMAN IN THE WRONG place at the wrong time, Nevada Blackthorn thought, *and she's headed right for me.*

Nevada watched her approach in disbelief. Most people took one look at his light green eyes and unsmiling mouth and decided to strike up a conversation with someone else. Anyone else. This woman was different. She had taken one look at him and hadn't looked anywhere else.

With a grace that was totally unconscious, Eden Summers worked her way through the bar's crowded room, heading instinctively toward the dark, broad-shouldered man who sat alone. Very much alone. No one in the packed room came within arm's length of the man with the unflinching gaze and black, closely cut beard.

Even if she hadn't been told to "ask the guy with the beard" about supplies, Eden would have been drawn to this man. His isolation attracted rather than worried her. She was accustomed to working with solitary, wild animals.

"Hi, I'm Eden Summers," she said, smiling when she finally reached the bar. The lack of an answering smile didn't deter her. She would have felt better if she could have seen the color of his eyes, but they were shadowed by the brim of the black Stetson that he wore. "The man at the gas station said the store was closed, but that you might open it so I could buy supplies."

Eden's voice was like her smile, warm without being flirtatious. The tone was husky, as though she hadn't talked to anyone in hours. Nevada wondered if she would sound that way first thing in the morning, and if her taste would be half as sweet as her smile.

Even as he tried to push the sensual speculations aside, Nevada felt the rush of his body changing to meet the uncalculated femininity of Eden herself. It had been a long, long time since he had responded to a woman like that—quick and hot and hard, suddenly filled with a need as elemental as breathing itself.

"The man you're looking for is Bill," Nevada said, his voice roughened by the fierce racing of his blood. "He's the bartender."

"Oh. Sorry. Wrong beard." Eden's large hazel eyes went from Nevada's sleek, well-trimmed pelt to the bartender's rowdy chin fur. "That's Bill?"

Nevada nodded.

"Thanks," she said, smiling as she turned away.

Nevada nodded again and said nothing more. Nor did he smile. His bleak green glance went from Eden's lithe, alluring body to the faces of the men in West Fork's only bar. Every male in the packed, seething room had taken Eden's measure the instant she had come in the door. There was more than casual curiosity in their looks. Whether Eden knew it or not, the two other women present in the bar could most politely be described as working girls. Saturday in West Fork was their busiest time. They had been in and out of the bar and the adjoining motel with the regularity of clocks striking off the quarter hour.

When Eden turned away from Nevada, the men in the bar realized that she wasn't his date. Nor was there any other man hovering in the background, waiting for her. She was alone.

Instantly the men became more aggressive in their interest. In a town with one gas station, one general store, one café, one motel and one bar—all of which were collectively known as the OK Corral—strangers weren't that common. An unknown, attractive young woman with a graceful walk and a generous smile was unheard of.

And she had no man escorting her, no man to discourage the blunt sexual interest of the males in the bar.

Normally the lack of an escort wouldn't have been a problem for a woman, even in the wildest areas of the Four Corners Country of southwestern Colorado. But today wasn't normal. Today was West Fork's Eighth Annual Rattlesnake Roping Contest, an event that drew every bored, restless young man for a hundred miles around. As the snakes were still sleeping off winter—a fact that the men had counted on—approximately forty healthy males had spent the dreary March Saturday drinking beer, swapping lies and coarse jokes, ragging newcomers, passing comments about the availability and desirability of local females, playing practical jokes, and generally being a pain in the butt to everyone in the bar who wasn't at least four beers under the weather.

Nevada had been watching his second beer go flat and trying to decide which would be less tedious—helping the town's lone mechanic to patch a leaky gas tank on the Rocking M's pickup truck or watching the brawl that would inevitably break out in a bar jammed with bored young cowboys. On the whole, Nevada had been leaning toward patching leaky gas tanks when he had looked up and seen a flash of pale blond hair and the kind of easy-moving walk that was guaranteed to bring him to attention.

It had done the same for the other denizens of the OK Corral, who immediately assumed that the pretty stranger had come to West Fork for the kind of action that its bar was famous—or infamous—for delivering on a Saturday night.

Nevada knew that the other men's assumption was wrong. It wasn't just that Eden wore jeans, outdoor shoes and a hip-length down jacket. It was something both more subtle and more final than her lack of party clothes that told Nevada this woman was different. The openness and generosity in Eden's smile when she greeted him had announced that she wasn't in the market for sex. Women who were for sale were neither spontaneous nor uncalculating in their approach to life or men.

Unfortunately, Saturday in the bar at the OK Corral was the day and the place where pros and semipros came to display their shopworn wares. Eden's gentle manner and open smile didn't belong in the OK Corral's sexual marketplace, but she was there just the same.

Wrong place, wrong time, wrong woman.

And the longer she stayed there, the more insistent the men would become about attracting her attention.

With increasing irritation Nevada listened to the men nearby speculate on the subject of Eden's sexual expertise and price. He watched from the corner of his eye as the bartender came around the bar and stood close to Eden under the pretext that he couldn't hear her over the crude background comments. Standing that close wasn't necessary. Nevada, who was four feet away, could hear Eden all too well. She had a voice like summer, rich with warmth and life. The sensual promise in her voice made blood beat visibly at the base of Nevada's throat.

"The man at the filling station said you were closed, but that you might open the store so I could buy supplies," Eden said, speaking quickly, ignoring the catcalls and crass propositions coming from behind her. "There's no other store between here and the government cabin. I've driven all day, and there's supposed to be a storm in the high country tomorrow so I'll have to leave before dawn or take a chance on getting snowed out. As it is, I'll need a room for the night."

"No problem," Bill said, leaning back long enough to pull a room key from a board beneath the bar. He handed the key to Eden. "What else do you need?"

Before Eden could answer, a voice called out, "Yeah, that's it, Bill. Find out what she needs and I'll give it to her!"

Nevada didn't have to turn and look to know that the voice belonged to a young cowhand called Jones. Tall, well built and almost as handsome as he thought he was, Jones had earned his reputation as a lady-killer, drinker and fighter. Nevada's brother Tennessee had fired Jones from the Rocking M ranch. Since then, Jones had spent more time raising hell than working cattle. The cowboys drinking with Jones were the same as he was, too old to be boys and too undisciplined to be men.

Eden pocketed the key and acted as though she and the bartender were alone in the room.

"I need basics, mostly. Salt, sugar, flour, coffee—"

Jones inserted a stream of words that would have made a seasoned streetwalker wince. Nevada was the only man sober enough, and perceptive enough, to notice Eden's almost invisible flinching at the ugly language. But that was her only reaction.

"Hey, babe, look at me when I talk to you!" Jones yelled. "Pieces like you give me a pain. You sell it all over town and then act like you're a nun when a man tells you what he wants and how he wants it!"

Nevada's hand tightened on his beer bottle, a reflex as involuntary as his own arousal in Eden's presence. Slowly he relaxed his fingers.

Eden unzipped her jacket and pulled a small tablet from an inside pocket, praying that no one would notice the fine tremor of her fingers. She had dealt with too many wild animals not to have a sixth sense for danger. She was in danger now. What was a coarse verbal assault could change at any moment into something worse. The men around her had drunk enough to be uninhibited but not unable—and she was a stranger who had walked into their territory with nothing more to protect her than whatever basic goodness might exist beneath the veneer of civilization.

If the situation were different, Eden wouldn't have worried about being alone with even the cowboy who was running his mouth at her expense right now. But he had made his brags in front of the pack. Now he had to dominate her or lose face. It was an old, old story among animals.

And man was definitely an animal.

While Eden flipped through the tablet to find her supply list, Jones started wondering aloud what she would look like without her clothes, stripping her verbally, adding fuel to the savage fires that always burned just beneath the restraints of civilization.

Nevada turned and looked at Jones and the four men who were urging him on. The rest of the men in the room didn't notice Nevada's abruptly predatory intensity. They were watching Eden with the single-minded purpose of a pack of jackals closing in on their prey.

A glance at Eden told Nevada that she sensed the building ugliness. Beneath her calm expression was an animal wariness that increased with every deep voice that joined the chorus egging Jones on. Nevada had heard similar mutterings from men before, and with each guttural word civilization had been eroded a bit more until finally the savagery beneath broke free, destroying everything in its path that wasn't stronger and more vicious than itself.

With a feeling of acute relief, Eden found her supply list, tore it out, and handed it to the bartender. Not by so much as a fast sideways glance did she acknowledge that there was any other man in the room.

"This is all I need," she said.

Reluctantly Bill looked away from the opening in Eden's jacket to the piece of paper. He took it, scanned it quickly, and shrugged.

"Yeah, I got everything." His smile was just short of a leer as he looked back at Eden. "The store's in the next room.

I'll unlock it for you. When you're done, holler and I'll open up the cash register."

"Thank you," Eden said, zipping her jacket again despite the stuffy heat of the bar. "I appreciate your kindness."

Bill had the grace to look uncomfortable.

With half-closed eyes, Nevada watched Eden follow the bartender through the inner door that joined the store and the bar. As though sensing that Nevada was watching, the bartender came back quickly and resumed selling drinks. The door joining the two rooms remained open. From where he sat at the bar, Nevada was in a position to watch both Eden and Jones without appearing to notice either one.

Through some eccentricity of the heating system, the empty store was even hotter than the crowded bar. Eden hesitated, then peeled off her stifling down jacket and worked quickly, finding supplies and stacking them on the checkout counter. When she was finished, she walked to the doorway. Backlit by the bright lights of the store, her distinctly feminine silhouette was a siren call far older than civilization.

A silence came over the bar.

"I'm ready, Bill."

Jones's hand shot out and fastened on the bartender's arm. "I'll take care of the little lady."

Jones grabbed his half-empty beer bottle and headed for the store. Four of his friends quickly followed. Although many of the men in the crowded bar looked around uneasily, no one stepped forward to stop Jones. Alone, the cowboy was bad enough. At the head of a pack, he was more trouble than anyone wanted to take on.

Except Nevada.

With a deceptively lazy motion Nevada came off the bar stool and stood between Jones and the path to Eden.

"Get out of my way," Jones said.

Nevada said nothing.

With a quick, practiced motion, Jones flicked his beer bottle against the side of the bar. The lower third of the bottle disintegrated, leaving behind the smooth neck and three wicked blades of glass.

Nevada neither moved nor spoke. He simply watched Jones and his four friends with the pale, unblinking green eyes of a cougar.

In the electric silence, Eden's harsh intake of breath was as clear as a scream. From her position in the doorway she could see that the dark, aloof stranger she had spoken to earlier was even more isolated now than he had been when she first walked into the barroom. She looked at Bill, who was backing away from the bar as quickly as he could, making clear that he wanted no part of whatever fight developed. The rest of the patrons obviously felt the same way. They were backing up as quickly as possible, leaving a wide clearing around the other men.

Alone, Nevada waited, feeling the world change as it always did when he was fighting, time stretching, dragging, nailed to the ground, leaving him free to move and other men mired in slow motion. It was a primitive physiological gift, a trick of the adrenal glands, a quirk that had been passed down through centuries of Blackthorn warriors; adrenaline coursing through his body with each rapid heartbeat, speeding him up, a warrior's reflex that had saved Blackthorn lives when other, slower men had died.

Eden saw the subtle shifting of his body, the electric tension of a cougar set to spring.

"No!" Eden called, her voice tight with fear for him. "Damn it—no! There are five of them and you're not even armed!"

Having reached the same conclusion, Jones rushed forward, closing the distance between himself and Nevada.

Nevada moved.

His hands flashed out, grabbing Jones, then he pivoted, throwing him against the bar so hard that bottles danced and skidded. As Nevada finished the pivot, he smoothly converted his momentum into a different kind of force, lashing out with hands and feet in an intricate sequence. Two of Jones's buddies went to their knees and then onto their faces. One staggered backward and fell. The remaining cowboy grabbed one of his dazed friends, yanked him to his feet and headed for the exit.

Even though Eden was accustomed to seeing big cats take their prey, the speed, coordination and precision of Nevada's attack shocked her. He was so quick that individual motions blurred. Only the results were clearly visible. Three men down, two men running away.

Nevada's pale glance flicked over the remaining inhabitants of the bar, dismissed them as a source of danger, and came back to focus on Jones. With a silent, gliding stride, Nevada started forward to teach the cowboy the kind of lesson a man would be lucky to survive. But at the moment Nevada didn't really care about Jones's future. Better men had died and the world had kept on turning.

Just as Nevada reached for Jones, two slender, determined hands locked around one of Nevada's wrists. He could easily have shaken off the hands, but the combination of softness and strength was quintessentially feminine, disarming him. Eden smelled of sunshine and her breath was a rush of warmth flowing over him.

"Don't," Eden said softly, holding on to Nevada's hard arm, seeing his eyes for the first time. A cougar's eyes, pale green, bottomless, hell unleashed and waiting to spring. She brought his unresisting hand to her face. Her lips brushed his palm. "Please. He's not worth what it would cost you."

Eden felt the tiny shudder that ripped through Nevada's strength, sensed the gradual uncoiling of steel muscles, and breathed her thanks into his hard palm. Slowly her fingers slid from his arm until she no longer touched him.

Restrained by nothing more tangible than his acceptance of Eden's plea, Nevada reached once more for Jones. He lifted the heavy cowboy to his feet in a single motion. Stunned, Jones sagged between Nevada's hands.

"That's your free one," Nevada said calmly. "Understand?"

Jones tried to speak, couldn't, and nodded. Nevada opened his hands, releasing the cowboy. Jones staggered, caught himself on a bystander, then pushed free and reeled toward the front door. He didn't even pause to look at the two groaning men who had followed him into the fight.

"Take them with you," Nevada said.

His voice was still soft, but it carried clearly through the stunned silence of the room. Struggling, limping, able to use only one arm, Jones got the two other men upright and out the door.

Nevada turned to the bartender. "Total her bill."

"Sure thing, Nevada," the man said hastily. "Right away."

His hurried footsteps were the only sound in the bar. Nevada turned and looked at each man in the room as the tense silence stretched. Smoothly he stepped behind Eden, putting his hands on her shoulders.

"Gentlemen," Nevada said softly, his tone transforming the word into an insult, "I want you to meet Eden Summers. In the future you will treat her the same as you would Carla, Diana, Mariah or any other Rocking M woman."

Nevada said no more. He didn't have to.

"Go get your supplies," Nevada said, squeezing Eden's shoulders reassuringly before he released her.

While Eden paid her bill, Nevada shrugged into his shearling jacket, leaned casually against the bar and waited for the groceries to be bagged.

Slowly the other men in the bar turned away and began talking in subdued voices. Most of the conversations centered around the fight. Or rather, around Nevada. Tennessee Blackthorn's lethal fighting skills were well-known. Nevada's had often been speculated upon, but no one had been curious enough to rattle his cage and find out for sure.

Until tonight. West Fork had just discovered that the aloof, silent cowhand called Nevada was every bit as skilled at fighting as he was at tracking cougars—and he was known as the best cat-tracker in five states.

When Eden was ready, Nevada helped her carry the supplies. Outside a raw March wind combed the streets, sending shivers of motion over puddles that had just begun to freeze in the early evening chill. Where there was no snow, the landscape had taken on a vague hint of green, promise of the hot summer to come. For now, it was promise only. The earth itself was still locked within winter's cold.

In the distance an isolated group of mountains rose against the darkening sky. Clouds gathered and slowly seethed around the peaks. Other clouds stretched in a wind-smoothed front across the icy arch of the sky. Eden glanced overhead, saw the weather front that was supposed to bring snow, and debated whether or not to take on the rough road between West Fork and the government cabin that would be her home until June.

"You'll be safe enough at the motel," Nevada said, following Eden's glance at the weather front. "No one will bother you now."

The subtle rasp in Nevada's deep voice intrigued Eden. But then, everything about him intrigued her, and had from the first instant she had seen him.

"Thank you," she said quietly. "If I had known what West Fork was like, I would have bought my supplies in Cortez."

Nevada shrugged. "Most of the time West Fork is real quiet. You just came on the one Saturday a year when the local half-wits get together and howl. Two hours earlier and no one would have been drunk enough to run off at the mouth. Two hours later and they would have been too drunk to care who came through the door."

"I doubt that you ever get that drunk," Eden said matter-of-factly. She braced a sack of supplies on her hip as she unlocked the truck's door. "You're too disciplined."

Nevada gave Eden a sharp look, but before he could ask her how she had known that about him, he saw a huge, dark shadow moving inside the cab of the weather-beaten truck.

"Good God—is that a wolf?" Nevada demanded.

Eden smiled. "You're mostly right. The rest is husky." The

truck's door grated as it opened. "Hello, Baby. You ready to stretch your legs a bit?"

A black tail waved and sounds of greeting that were a cross between a growl and a muffled yip came from the wolf's thickly furred throat. The instant Nevada moved toward the truck, the sounds became a definite growl and the tail ceased waving.

"It's all right, Baby. Nevada is a friend."

The growls ended. Yellow eyes looked at Nevada for a comprehensive instant. Then, accepting the stranger, Baby leaped to the ground.

"Baby?" Nevada asked dryly. "He's got to go at least a hundred and twenty pounds."

"One hundred and thirty-three. But he started small. I found him in a hunter's trap when he was half-grown. The leg healed almost as good as new, but not quite. In the wild, the difference would have slowly killed him."

"So you kept him."

Eden made a murmurous sound of agreement as she leaned into the passenger side of the truck to deposit supplies.

"Do you make a habit of collecting and taming wild animals?"

"No." Eden stacked two sacks where a passenger's feet would have gone. "I'm a wildlife biologist, not a zookeeper. If I find wild animals that are hurt, I heal them and turn them loose again. If I kept them, there's nothing I could give them that would compensate for the loss of their freedom."

Silently Nevada handed over the sacks he was carrying. As he did, Eden noticed that he had cut his left hand in the fight. She dumped the sacks in the truck and took Nevada's hand between her own.

"You're hurt!"

Nevada looked down into Eden's eyes. In the fading light of day her eyes were almost green, almost gold, almost amber, almost blue gray, a shimmer of colors watching him, as though every season, every time, lived behind her eyes. Her hands on his skin had the healing warmth of summer, the softness of spring sunshine. He wanted nothing more than to bend down and take her mouth, her body, sinking into her until he couldn't remember what it was like to be cold.

But that would only make the inevitable return of ice all the more painful.

"I'm fine," he said, removing his hand.

Eden took Nevada's hand again. The renewed touch of her skin sent hunger searching through every bit of his big body, making his muscles clench with need.

"Nevada," she said, remembering what the bartender had called him. "That's your name, isn't it?"

Nevada nodded curtly, trying to ignore the exquisite heat of Eden's breath as she examined his hand again.

"You're bleeding, Nevada. Come with me to the motel room. I'll clean the cut and—"

"No."

His rough refusal surprised her. She looked up into eyes as cold and bleak as a winter moon.

"It's the least I can do to thank you for being a gentleman," Eden said softly.

"Take me to your motel room?" Nevada asked, his tone sardonic.

"You know that isn't what I meant."

"Yes. But I mean it." Nevada freed his left hand, hesitated, then let out his breath with a whispered curse. His fingertip skimmed the curve of Eden's lower lip with aching slowness. "Stay away from me, Eden. I'm a warrior, not a knight in shining armor, and I want you more than all the men in that bar put together."

Abruptly Nevada turned and walked away, leaving Eden standing motionless in the icy twilight, watching him with a mixture of shock and deeply sensual speculation in her eyes.

CHAPTER TWO

THE BIG APPALOOSA THREW UP ITS head and snorted.

"Take it easy, you knothead," Nevada said soothingly. Then, without turning around, he added, "'Morning, Ten. Hear anything from Mariah and Cash?"

Tennessee Blackthorn was accustomed to his brother's uncanny ability to tell when he was being approached from behind, and by whom. Even so, Ten had hoped that after almost two years on the Rocking M, Nevada would lose some of the habits of a guerrilla warrior. But he hadn't. He had the same fighting edge to his reflexes and senses that he had had in the mountains of Afghanistan, where he had taught warriors with flintlocks how to defeat soldiers with tanks. Nevada had the same intense discipline and concerted lack of emotion that he had learned in Afghanistan. Even the Rocking M's cowhands had given up betting on when—or under what circumstances—Nevada Blackthorn would truly smile.

"Cash called late yesterday," Ten said. "Mariah's doctor said she was fine. Apparently she missed the flu that was going around here."

"Good."

"Speaking of being sick, are you sure you should be on your feet? That was a fair fever you were running yesterday."

"I'm glad Mariah isn't sick," Nevada said, settling the saddle gently over the skittish Appaloosa. "She and Cash should have fine, strapping children. I'm looking forward to hearing another healthy baby around here hollering for mama to bring his next meal. Carla's new baby is really something." Nevada cinched up the saddle girth with a swift, smooth motion, moving so quickly that the horse had no time to object. "Like your Carolina. That's one fine set of lungs the little lady has. She and Logan make a real pair."

Ten smiled dryly and accepted that Nevada wasn't going to talk about flu, rest, and a cold ride into the mountains. "Glad you like having babies around. Mariah will give us two more little screamers sometime in May or June."

Nevada looked over his shoulder. "Twins?"

"Yeah. Cash was so excited he could hardly talk. He and Mariah had been hoping, but they hadn't said anything until they were sure everything was fine."

"Tell her to be extra careful. Twins tend to be born small, and small babies have a harder time."

"Tell her yourself. She'll be here tomorrow."

"I won't." Nevada gestured with his head toward MacKenzie Ridge. "I'm going to spend a few days tracking cats. Supposed to be fresh snow by afternoon up toward

Wildfire Canyon. It may be the last tracking snow of the winter."

And maybe, just maybe, when I'm chasing cats rather than fighting fever dreams, I'll be able to see something other than extraordinary hazel eyes and a warm mouth that trembles at the lightest touch of a man's finger.

The back door of the ranch house slammed as someone left the dining room. The Appaloosa shied wildly. Nevada cursed in the silence of his mind and brought his attention back to the horse.

"I can see why Luke gelded that one," Ten muttered. "Target has more brains in his spotted butt than between his ears."

Nevada shrugged. "As long as you pay attention, he's the best winter horse on the Rocking M." With the unconscious ease of a man performing a familiar task, Nevada gathered the roping rein, stepped into the stirrup and mounted in a single easy motion. "Especially in fresh snow. Target's big enough not to get bogged down in the drifts."

"Wouldn't life be simpler if you just shot the cougars with a tranquilizer dart, put a radio collar on them and tracked them from the air?"

"Simpler? Maybe. A hell of a lot more expensive for sure. And a hell of a lot less fun for the cats—and me."

Ten laughed softly. "That's what Luke said. I didn't argue." Ten started to turn away, then remembered something else. "You know that old cabin just beyond Wildfire Canyon?"

"The one at the end of that abandoned logging road?"

Ten nodded. "A guy from the government called yesterday to tell us that some cougar specialist will be using the cabin as a base camp for the next month or two, depending on the cats. So if you find signs of someone moving around in the high country, don't worry. Luke and I agreed to give free access to Rocking M land as long as we got a copy of whatever report is filed about the cougars."

At the word *cabin,* Nevada went very still. A conversation that was three days old echoed in his mind.

There's no other store between here and the government cabin.

"Did anyone mention the name of the cat expert?" Nevada asked.

"I don't think so. Why?"

For a moment Nevada said nothing, remembering Eden's gentle voice and surprisingly strong hands, and the utter lack of fear in her eyes when she had seen the elemental violence in his.

Do you make a habit of collecting and taming wild animals?

No. I'm a wildlife biologist, not a zookeeper.

Eden's voice, her scent, the tactile memory of her alluring warmth…they had haunted Nevada's waking hours. They might have haunted his sleep as well, but he would never know. It was a pact he had made with himself years ago. He never remembered dreams.

"There was a young woman in West Fork last Saturday," Nevada said evenly. "She said something about being a wildlife expert."

"Last Saturday?" Ten said, his gray eyes narrowing.

Though Nevada had said nothing, word of the fight had gone through the Four Corners area of Colorado like forked lightning.

Nevada nodded.

"A woman, huh?"

Nevada nodded again.

"Pretty?" Ten asked, his handsome face expressionless.

"Why? You getting tired of Diana?"

The idea was so ridiculous that Ten laughed aloud. Then his smile vanished and he looked every bit as hard as his younger brother.

"The next time you go one on five," Ten said, "I'd take it as a personal favor if you'd let me guard your back. Luke made the same offer. So did Cash."

The left corner of Nevada's mouth turned up very slightly, as close as he ever came to a smile. "Cash, too, huh? Does that mean he's finally forgiven me for noticing that Mariah was pregnant before he did?"

"When a man is unsure of a woman, he's apt to be a bit blind," Ten said in a bland voice.

"He's apt to be a horse's butt."

"Your turn will come."

"Yours sure did," Nevada retorted, remembering the tense months before Ten had finally admitted that he was irrevocably bound to Diana. "I'll tell you, Tennessee, if I never tangle with you again, it will be too soon."

"Yeah, well, the hands are taking bets on that one too, especially since word got out that Utah's coming back as soon as he gets out of the hospital. Guess he's finally gotten his fill of jungle fighting."

"At least they don't need to worry about Utah getting in a brawl over a woman. Not since Sybil." Nevada leaned forward in the saddle. A flick of his hand freed the packhorse's lead rope from the corral railing. "The real shame about Sybil is that she wasn't a man," Nevada continued, reining Target toward the mountains. "If she were a man, I'd have killed her."

Before Ten could speak, Nevada kicked the big Appaloosa. "Shake a leg, Target. We've got a long ride ahead."

Even with the eager, powerful Appaloosa beneath him, it was afternoon before Nevada rode into Wildfire Canyon's wide mouth. In all but the worst winter storms, the canyon's alignment with the prevailing winds kept the flat floor swept relatively free of snow. Patches of evergreens clothed the sloping sides of the canyon, tall trees whose ages were almost all the same. The fire that had given the canyon its name had swept through eighty years before, burning the living forest to ash, leaving behind a ghost forest of heat-hardened skeletons. A few of those skeletons still stood upright amid the new forest, their weather-smoothed shapes silver and black in the full sun or moonlight.

The on-again, off-again warmth of March had melted the snow in places, revealing dark ground. Snowdrifts remained in narrow gullies and ravines, and beneath the most dense forest cover. Yet even in the higher altitudes, winter was slowly losing its white grip on the land. Water sparkled and glittered everywhere, testimony to melting snow. Drops gathered into tiny rivulets, joined in thin streams, merged into small, rushing creeks. Today the drops would freeze again, but only for a short time. Soon they would be free to run down to the distant sea once more.

Soon, but not yet. The storm that had threatened three days before hadn't materialized. It was coming now, though. As Target followed the zigzagging trail that led out of the northern end of Wildfire Canyon, Nevada could smell the storm on the wind, feel it in the icy fingers ruffling his beard and making his eyes sting. Even the rocks around him weren't impervious. They had known the grip of countless winters, water silently freezing, expanding, splitting stones apart. Evidence of the silent, inexorable power of ice lay everywhere in the high reaches of the canyon, where slopes too steep to grow trees were covered with angular stones that had been chiseled from boulders and bedrock by countless picks of ice.

At the top of the steep trail, Nevada reined in and let Target rest for a few minutes. Between gusts of wind, the silence was complete. The tiniest sound came clearly through the air—a pebble rolling from beneath steel-shod hooves, a raven calling across the canyon. Target's ears flicked and twitched nervously as he tried to hear every sound. When a pebble dislodged by water clattered down the slope, the horse's nostrils flared, the skin on his shoulder flinched and he shied.

"Take it easy, boy," Nevada said in a soothing voice as he gathered in the roping rein more tightly.

Even as Nevada's left hand managed the reins, his right hand checked that the rifle was still in its saddle holster. The gesture was so automatic that he was unaware of it, legacy of commando training and years spent in places where to be unarmed was to die. The rifle's cold, smooth stock came easily into his hand, then settled back into the sheath.

Target snorted and bunched his haunches, wanting to be free of the pressure of the bit. Nevada glanced at the packhorse. Daisy was ignoring Target's nervousness.

"Settle down, knothead," Nevada said calmly. "If there was anything around but wind and shadows, Daisy would know it. She has a nose like a hound."

Target chewed resentfully on the bit as the wind gusted suddenly, raking the landscape with fingernails of ice.

Nevada tugged his hat down more firmly and guided the horse out onto the exposed slope. For the first hundred yards, a faint, ragged line across the wind-scoured scree was the only sign of a trail. The line had been left by generations of deer, cougars, and occasional Indians. In modern times, deer and cougars still used the game trail, as did Rocking M cowhands who were working both Wildfire Canyon and the leased grazing lands beyond.

Target was in the center of the scree when the black flash of a raven skimming over the land spooked him. Between one heartbeat and the next, Target tried to leap over his own shadow.

There was no time for Nevada to think, to plan, to escape. Reflex took over. Even as Target lost his footing on the loose stone, Nevada was kicking free of the stirrups, grabbing the rifle, and throwing himself toward the uphill side of the trail. Inches away from his rider's body, Target's powerful hooves flailed as the horse lost its balance and began rolling down the slope in a clattering shower of loose stone. Nevada fell too, turning and rolling rapidly, surrounded by loose rocks, no way to stop himself, nothing solid to hang on to.

At the bottom of the slope, a massive boulder stopped Nevada's body. Before the last stone in the small landslide had stopped rolling, Target staggered to his feet, shook himself thoroughly, and looked around. When nothing happened, the horse walked calmly to the edge of the recent slide and looked for something edible. A few minutes later the packhorse joined Target, having found a less dangerous way to the bottom of the slope.

Before long the gray sky lowered and dissolved into the

pale dance of countless snowflakes. The horses turned their tails to the wind and drifted before the storm.

Nevada lay unmoving, rifle in hand.

BABY'S ULULATING HOWL BROUGHT EDEN to her feet in a rush of adrenaline. The wolf had been running free all day, for Eden hadn't yet needed Baby's keen nose. She would put him to work after the storm had passed, leaving a fragile shawl of white over the land. Then she would roam widely, noting and recording the cat tracks that would show clearly in the fresh snow. Once the snow melted away, Baby's nose would make certain that Eden could follow the cats even across solid rock.

A steaming cup of coffee in her hand, Eden went to the cabin door, opened it and listened. The slow glide of snowflakes to the ground and muffled sounds limited visibility to a hundred feet.

Baby howled again, calling out in the eerie harmonics of his wolf father.

Eden listened closely and muttered, "Not his hunting song. Not his lonely song. Not his great-to-be-alive song."

The haunting cry rose again, closer now, piercing the snow's silence.

"I hear you, Baby. You're coming back to me."

A black shape materialized at the edge of the snowfall. With the ghostly silence of smoke, Baby came across the meadow clearing to the cabin. There was a brief hesitation in his gait, a slight asymmetry in his stride, which was the legacy of the steel trap that had maimed him years before.

Instead of greeting Eden and going about his business, Baby caught her hand delicately in his mouth and looked at her with intent yellow eyes. Curiosity leaped in Eden. Baby rarely insisted on having her attention. When he did, it was to warn her that they weren't alone any longer—men were somewhere near.

"Company is coming, hmm?" After what had happened in West Fork, Eden was glad for the presence of the huge, dark wolf. "Well, don't worry. I just made a big pot of coffee. Come on in, Baby. We'll greet whoever it is together."

Eden tried to withdraw her hand. Politely, gently, Baby's jaws tightened.

Curiosity gave way to a fresh rush of adrenaline in Eden. A picture condensed in her mind—eyes of pale icy green, a thick black pelt of hair and beard, a face that was too hard to be called handsome and too fiercely good-looking to be called anything else.

Stay away from me, Eden…. I want you more than all the men in that bar put together.

It was not the first time Eden had thought of the dark stranger who had come to her aid. His image condensed between her eyes and the hearth fire, the wild sky, the rugged land. He haunted her with questions that couldn't be answered.

Who are you, Nevada? Where are you? Is it your scent on the snow-wind that is calling to my wolf?

As soon as the hopeful thought came, Eden pushed it aside. Nevada hadn't looked back after he had walked away from her. He hadn't left any message for her the following morning. He hadn't even told her his last name.

Eden looked into Baby's eyes and wished futilely that she could truly communicate with him. Baby had been this insistent only once before, in Alaska, when it was a silvertip grizzly sniffing around downwind rather than a lonely trapper smelling smoke and hoping for a cup of fresh coffee.

"Are you sure it's important, Baby? Mortimer J. Martin, Ph.D., personally assured me there were no bears left in this part of the Lower Forty-eight. That's why I left my rifle with Dad."

Baby made a soft, somehow urgent sound deep in his throat and tugged on Eden's hand. Then he released her, trotted away about twenty feet and looked over his shoulder.

"You're sure? Compared to the Yukon there isn't enough snow to mention, but I'm really not dying for a hike in the white stuff. There's not enough snowpack for cross-country skis or snowshoes, which means—"

Baby whined softly, pleading in the only way he could. Then he threw back his head and howled. The hair on the back of Eden's neck stirred in primal response. Not even for the grizzly had Baby been so insistent.

"Baby, *stay.*"

Knowing without looking that the wolf would obey, Eden spun around and ran back into the cabin. She grabbed a canteen, filled it with hot coffee, banked the hearth fire, yanked on two layers of snow gear, shrugged into the backpack she always kept ready to go and ran out the front door in less than three minutes. She glanced at her watch, wondering how long she would be gone. If necessary she could live out of her backpack for several days. She would just as soon have the comforts of the cabin, however.

"Okay, Baby. Let's go."

The wolf didn't waste any time. He set off at a purposeful trot across the meadow through the evergreens. Eden walked swiftly behind, pacing herself so that she would neither tire quickly nor become sweaty. Sweat was one of the greatest hazards of snow country, for when a person stopped moving, sweat froze, creating a layer of ice against the skin that sapped warmth dangerously.

Baby was careful never to get out of Eden's sight. Nor did he run with his nose to the ground as though following a trail. Gradually Eden realized that Baby was retracing his own steps—in places where snow had gathered, his tracks went in both directions.

Eden had been following Baby for ten minutes when she saw the first hoofprints in a patch of snow. Two horses, one with a rein or a rope dragging. They were headed roughly southeast and she was headed roughly north. Baby ignored the horse sign even though Eden could see it was very fresh. The softly falling snow hadn't yet blurred the crisp edges of the tracks. She stopped, stared off through the snow and thought she saw a vague shape that could have been a horse standing in the shelter of a big evergreen.

"Baby!"

The wolf stopped, gave a short, sharp bark and resumed trotting.

After only an instant of hesitation, Eden kept on following Baby. She would trust the half-wild, half-tame animal's uncanny instincts. If Baby wasn't interested in the horse it was because he had more important game in mind.

Without turning aside even once, Baby retraced his own tracks. The forest ended at the foot of a scree slope. Automatically Eden checked the barren slope first. Even beneath the veil of falling snow, the story of what had happened was clear: at least one horse had come skidding and rolling down through the scree, starting a small rockslide in the process.

Hoofprints led away from the disturbed ground. There was no sign of any horse nearby.

Baby never hesitated. He darted over the loose debris left by the slide and sat near a massive boulder ten yards from Eden. There the slide had parted like water, leaving behind larger rocks before closing around the downhill side of the car-size boulder.

"Baby? What—"

Eden's breath broke, then came in harshly as she realized that something lay half-buried in the loose stone that had piled against the huge boulder.

A man.

His body blended with the rubble from the recent slide. Fresh snowfall was rapidly blurring all distinctions between stone and flesh. The man was motionless, yet hauntingly familiar. His bearded face was turned up to the chill softness of falling snow.

"Nevada!"

No motion answered Eden's cry.

CHAPTER THREE

EDEN SCRAMBLED THROUGH THE LOOSE debris and threw herself down at Nevada's side. Even as she ripped off her gloves and felt for his pulse, she saw the brassy glitter of spent shell casings scattered on top of the rocky rubble. A rifle was still gripped in Nevada's big right hand. The skin of his left wrist was cool but not chilled. He must have been conscious at some time since his fall, for he had fired the rifle repeatedly.

"Nevada," Eden said, pitching her voice to be both reassuring and distinct. Still talking, she moved back from him so that she could shrug out of her backpack and down jacket. "Nevada, can you hear me?"

A shudder rippled through his powerful body. His eyes opened, a cougar's eyes, trapped, dangerous. The fingers holding the rifle tightened. Eden didn't notice, for she was spreading her bright red jacket over his chest.

"Do you hurt anywhere?" she asked.

When Nevada's eyes focused on her, they changed. Life and light came back into them. He shook his head as though to clear it.

"If you can do that, you didn't break your neck."

Relief was bright in Eden's voice. Growing up on a homestead in Alaska had taught her the basics of first aid—splinting breaks, stitching up gashes, and the dangers of hypothermia, but spine injuries were beyond her skills.

And the thought of Nevada hurt bothered Eden deeply.

She pulled off the knitted ski hat she had worn underneath her jacket hood. A moment later she was leaning over Nevada, stretching the hat to cover Nevada's short black hair, tucking stray strands in, her face only inches from his, her breath bathing his cheeks above his beard, her soft hair touching him when she turned her head.

"There. That will help you to stay warm."

"Eden? What the hell are you doing out here?"

"Ask Baby. He dragged me out of a nice warm cabin and insisted I go for a walk in the snow."

Gently Eden lowered Nevada's head back to the ground, cushioned the rocks beneath with one of her jacket's quilted sleeves, and looked closely at Nevada's pale green eyes. Both pupils were the same size and he was studying her with an intensity that was almost tangible. Whatever else had happened in his fall, his faculties were intact.

"Thank God," Eden said too softly for Nevada to hear.

But he did, just as he felt the rushing warmth of the sigh she gave, as though the weight of the mountainside had just slipped from her shoulders.

"Baby must have found you earlier, sensed something

was wrong and came back to get me," Eden continued, tucking her bright jacket around Nevada's broad chest.

Nevada blinked, scattering snowflakes that had tangled in his thick black eyelashes. "Be damned. Thought I saw a wolf a while back, but there aren't any wolves around here, so I chalked it up to taking a header down the mountain."

"You did that, all right. Where do you hurt?"

"Nowhere."

Eden looked skeptical. "Then why are you lying here?"

"My left foot is wedged against the big boulder. When I couldn't dig myself out, I began firing my rifle three rounds at a time."

Eden nodded. Three spaced shots were a universal come-running signal. "Baby must have heard the shots or caught your scent on the wind." She turned back to the knapsack, pulled out the canteen, and took off the top. The coffee was still hot. She put the canteen in Nevada's hands. "This will help to warm you. Drink as much as you can while I look at your foot."

Nevada inhaled deeply. "Damn. That smells like real coffee."

"Guaranteed strong enough to grow hair on the bottom of your feet," Eden agreed as she began pulling on her gloves.

The corner of Nevada's mouth shifted unnoticeably beneath his beard as he lifted the canteen and drank deeply. The hot, rich liquid spread through his body like a benediction, warming everything it touched. Reluctantly he stopped drinking.

"You want some?" he asked.

"I'm plenty warm," Eden said. "Drink as much as you can hold."

"That will be all of it."

"Good."

While Nevada finished the coffee, Eden began pushing loose rock away from his hips and legs, clearing a way to the trapped ankle. As she worked, she tried not to notice the clean, powerful lines of his body. It was impossible. He was a large, healthy male animal, and he called to her senses in ways that disconcerted her.

Nevada licked the last drop of coffee from his mustache and watched Eden working over his legs. Her motions were sure, efficient and productive. Obviously she wasn't going to come apart in an emergency.

He liked that as much as he liked the breasts swaying beneath her ski jersey and pullover sweater and the decidedly female curves of her hips. But admiring Eden's body was having a pronounced effect on his own, so he concentrated on her face instead, memorizing the smooth skin of her cheeks, the changing colors of her hazel eyes, the tempting sweetness of her mouth.

Eden looked up, sensing Nevada's intense regard. He shifted his glance to the slope.

"You see any horses on the way here?" he asked.

"Just tracks. A big horse and a smaller one. Both are wearing winter shoes. Both are drifting south and east in front of the wind." Stones clattered and rattled, pushed by Eden's hands as she resumed digging. "I might have seen one of them under a big evergreen about five minutes up the trail, but I couldn't be sure. The smaller horse is dragging a rope or a rein. Neither of the horses is limping, although the bigger one rolled down the same slope you did. If there was any blood, it wasn't much. So relax. Your horses are better off than you are."

"Big horse. Small horse. Winter shoes. Rope." Nevada looked at Eden's clean profile and asked neutrally, "Where did you learn how to track?"

"Alaska."

"Horses?" he asked skeptically.

"Cats," Eden said, struggling to shove aside a rock that was smaller than a pony, but not much. "I studied lynx in the north woods. I came to Colorado to study cougars. After cats, tracking horses is a piece of cake."

Nevada's eyes changed, intensity returning. Eden was going to be living in the remote area around Wildfire Canyon, tracking the cougars that had returned to the Rocking M.

And so was he.

"Damn," Eden said under her breath. She braced her shoulder and tried again to shift the smaller of the two boulders that had trapped Nevada's foot. "Did you try pulling your foot out of your boot?"

"Yes. Rest before you start sweating."

She hesitated, then nodded. He was right. She sat back on her heels and breathed deeply, trying not to let her worry show. Nevada's left foot was securely wedged between a rock that was too big for her to shift and the massive boulder that had broken the back of the landslide. Loose rubble slithered and stirred and eased downhill every time she tried to dig him out.

"How's your head?" As Eden asked the question, her eyes were searching the slope for something to use as a lever against the smaller of the two boulders that were holding Nevada captive.

"I'll live."

"Dizzy? Double vision? Nausea?"

"No. I have a hard skull."

She smiled without looking at him, still searching for a lever. "I won't touch that line. How bad is your foot?"

"Cold is a good anesthetic."

"Too good. You were unconscious when I got here."

"I would have awakened in ten minutes and fired three more rounds."

Nevada's certainty made Eden look back at him.

"Hypothermia—" she began.

"It's not a problem yet," he interrupted flatly. "I've been a lot colder under a lot worse conditions and functioned just fine."

Eden tugged off one glove, grabbed Nevada's wrist and started counting. His pulse was strong. Cold hadn't slowed his body processes yet. And the quart of hot coffee would help hold the chill of the ground at bay.

"All right." Unconsciously Eden caressed Nevada's left wrist and his palm with her fingertips, reassured by his tangible heat and the resilience of his flesh. Like Baby, Nevada fairly radiated an elemental vitality. "Where did you learn to sleep and wake yourself whenever you wanted?"

"Afghanistan." His voice was clipped, foreclosing any other questions.

"They have some big mountains there, and a lot of mines," Eden said absently. She looked past him to the forest, focusing on a piece of deadfall that might work as a lever. "Are you a geologist?"

"No."

Despite the warning in Nevada's voice, Eden was beginning to ask another question when she felt wetness on her fingertips. She looked down and saw a trickle of blood across Nevada's hand. Ignoring his brief protest, she eased off his leather glove. A jagged, partially healed cut went across the back of his hand. The scab had been broken in one place. Fresh blood oozed slowly toward his tanned wrist.

Eden breathed Nevada's name and stroked the uninjured flesh on either side of the cut. Memories of anger and fear and the razor edges of a freshly broken beer bottle lanced through her.

"You should have let me take care of you," she said quietly.

"I don't need a woman to take care of me. I never have. I never will."

This time the warning in Nevada's voice got through.

"Really?" Eden asked casually. "Then I hope you're comfortable, cowboy. It may be a long time before a *man* comes along this particular piece of mountainside."

There was a tight silence before the left corner of Nevada's mouth shifted very slightly.

"You must be the exception that proves the rule," he said.

"Gosh, I'm so glad you explained that to me. I was beginning to wonder if you hadn't hit your head too hard on one of those rocks."

Suddenly Eden frowned and shifted her grip on Nevada's wrist. "Are you sure you feel all right? Your pulse is pretty fast right now."

"My resting pulse is in the low sixties."

"But—"

"I'm not resting."

"You have a point. But your pulse has increased in the past minute or two."

"If a man were leaning over me and stroking my wrist like a lover, my pulse wouldn't have budged."

It took a few moments for the meaning of Nevada's words to get past Eden's concern for him. A rising tide of color marked the exact instant of her understanding that she was cradling his hand between her own. Even worse, she was running her fingertips caressingly from the pulse point on his wrist to the base of his fingers and back again.

"Sorry," Eden said, dropping Nevada's hand. She pulled on her glove again and she spoke quickly. "I'm a tactile kind of person. When I'm nervous or worried or thinking hard, I tend to stroke things. You were within reach."

It was partly true. The rest of the truth was that there was something about Nevada Blackthorn that made Eden want to stroke him, to learn his textures and pleasures, to make him smile, to warm him, to...heal him.

And then set him free?

There was no answer except Eden's silent, inner cry of pain at the thought of Nevada turning away from her again. The depth of her reaction was irrational, and she knew it. She also knew it was as deep as a night sky, and as real. Knowing that, she stopped fighting her response to Nevada. Working in the wild as much as she did had taught her to accept things that did not make sense within the narrow cultural limits of modern rationality.

"Tactile, huh?" Nevada drawled. "Must make life interesting for the men around you."

"The only men in my life have fur and fangs and go on all fours."

Stones rattled as Eden went back to work clearing debris around Nevada's trapped ankle. It seemed that for every two handfuls she pushed aside, a handful more slithered down to fill the depression.

"Can you reach my backpack?" Eden asked after a few minutes.

Instead of answering, Nevada twisted his body, reached, and snagged the backpack. Any lingering questions Eden might have had as to Nevada's hidden injuries vanished. Except for the trapped foot, Nevada moved with supreme ease.

"What do you need?" he asked.

"Not me. You. This is trickier than I thought it would be. There's a survival blanket in the backpack. Turn the black side out."

Nevada didn't argue. Though neither of them had mentioned it, both knew it would take time to free his ankle—if it could be done at all. Even with the help of hot coffee, his big body couldn't hold heat indefinitely. Lying on the cold ground was slowly sapping his living warmth.

He opened the backpack and sorted through its contents with growing approval. Eden's fingers might be as hot and gentle as sunlight, and her breath might be as sweetly heady as wine, but she was no foolish little flower when it came to living in the wild. She had everything she might reasonably expect to need in an emergency, except a weapon.

Speculatively Nevada looked over at Baby, who was watching him with yellow eyes that missed nothing.

Maybe she doesn't need a gun after all. I'll bet Baby would go to war for her. Hell, so did I a few days ago.

I wonder if Jones has figured out yet just how lucky he was.

A snap of Nevada's wrist unrolled the survival blanket. He sat upright. The bright red of Eden's snow jacket slid away from his body as he put the empty canteen in the backpack. Wind blew across his chest, penetrating even his own shearling jacket's thick protection, making him shiver in a reflexive effort to warm himself.

Instantly Eden was at Nevada's side. She put the backpack aside and helped him to wrap the thin, incredibly warm material of the survival blanket around his body. She tried not to notice the intimacy of Nevada's breath on her face when she leaned over him, urging him to lie back. She tried not to breathe in fast and hard, taking his breath into her body, shivering at the realization that even in such a small way he was a part of her now.

"Lie down," Eden said, her voice low. "There's less of you for the wind to work on that way." Methodically she folded up her jacket and made a pillow for Nevada's head. "Here. I don't need this while I'm digging."

Nevada's senses were far too acute for him to have missed the telltale catching of Eden's breath, the new huskiness of her voice, the concern that went beyond that of one human being for another who needed help. She was intensely aware of him as a man.

Grimly Nevada tried to still his body's violent response to the knowledge that Eden was as drawn to him as he was to her. He succeeded in quelling the rush of his blood, but only up to a point. When Eden went to pull the survival blanket more snugly around his hips, she was confronted by the one thing Nevada couldn't control—the hard evidence of his response to her. The mixture of emotions on her face when she saw the fit of his jeans would have made anyone but Nevada smile.

"Reassured about my health?" he asked in a dry tone.

"Try astonished," Eden said faintly.

"Why? I'm a man, in case you hadn't noticed."

"In case *you* hadn't noticed, you're a man who is in a hell of a jam at the moment."

"So?"

"So I wouldn't think you'd be feeling very, er, lively," Eden muttered. She ducked her head, knowing her cheeks were red from much more than a cold wind.

"I accepted a long time ago that nobody gets out of life alive," Nevada said matter-of-factly. "Once you accept that you stop worrying about the details of when and where and how. Dead now or dead fifty years from now, dead is dead. And alive is alive, all the way, full max. I'm alive and you turn me on deep and quick and hard. I don't like that one damn bit, but there's nothing I can do about it."

Eden looked at him, a question in her eyes that she wouldn't ask. Nevada knew what that question was. He knew what the answer was, too.

"I don't like being turned on by you because you still believe in fairy tales like love. I know better. That's why I told you to stay away from me. But it didn't work out that way, did it?"

Slowly Eden searched Nevada's silver-green eyes, wondering what had made him the way he was and what might heal him so that he could live completely again.

"No, it didn't work out that way," Eden said, her voice both gentle and determined. "Life is always unexpected, Nevada. That's why laughter is vital and very real. And life always seeks life. That's why love is vital and very real. Not fairy tale. Reality."

"Sex is real," he said flatly. "Love is a game. I'm too old

to play games and you're too young to do anything else, so finish digging me out of this hole and say goodbye."

Eden looked at Nevada's icy eyes and knew that arguing with him would be futile. Yet she couldn't help reaching out to him, wanting to stroke the smooth skin of his cheek and the sleek pelt of his beard, to soothe and reassure him that he wasn't alone within the bleak world of his choosing.

With shocking speed Nevada's hand locked around Eden's wrist, preventing her from touching him.

"I'm trapped, but I'm a long way from helpless," he said coldly. "Dig or get the hell out of here and leave me alone."

Eden had no doubt that Nevada meant it: he would sooner lie trapped in a snowstorm than submit to a kind of touching that had nothing to do with sex.

The pain that came with Eden's understanding froze the breath in her throat, making her ache for whatever wounding had caused so deep a scar to form within Nevada, sealing off all emotion except an icy kind of rage.

Sudden tears burned behind Eden's eyes. She looked away quickly, knowing Nevada would have even less use for her tears than he had for her comforting touch. Saying nothing, she came to her feet and walked away from him. The falling snow was much thicker now, limiting visibility to less than ten feet. Baby whined softly in confusion, then trotted after Eden, leaving Nevada alone beneath the lowering sky.

When Eden returned five minutes later dragging a sturdy branch taller than she was, Nevada was just raising the rifle to his shoulder.

"Save the three bullets," Eden said. "There's no one else around to care. You're stuck with me."

Nevada lowered his rifle, grabbed the jacket he had been

using as a pillow and fired it in Eden's direction. "Put this on. It's cold."

Eden didn't bother to argue that she didn't need the jacket as long as she kept moving. Nor did she try to put the jacket back beneath Nevada's head as she wanted to do. She simply stepped over the bright mound of cloth and knelt near Nevada's trapped foot, examining it closely.

Nothing had changed. Just above the ankle bone, Nevada's boot was caught between heavy stones. After a struggle that left her breathing rapidly, she managed to wedge one end of the thick branch beneath the smaller of the two boulders.

Smaller, Eden thought with a fear that she concealed from Nevada. *Lord. That stone has to weigh more than Nevada and me put together. I hope the branch I found is strong enough. I hope I'm strong enough. By the time I could go for help and get back, it would be too late.*

"Do you still have feeling in your foot?" she asked tightly.

"Some."

"Too bad. This is going to hurt. Do try not to cry, cowboy. It would hurt my feelings."

Despite Nevada's determination to keep Eden at a distance, her deadpan instructions made the corner of his mouth move slightly. He shook his head and said, "I'll do my best."

"That's all I can ask, isn't it?" she said beneath her breath, thinking he couldn't hear. "Of you, of me, of anything."

Nevada did hear, but there was nothing he could say or do. Eden was right and he knew it. He just didn't like it.

Eden bent her legs, braced her shoulder beneath the branch and then began to straighten, pouring every bit of her feminine strength and determination into moving the stone, straining against a weight she was never meant to lift.

Putting his free foot against the smaller boulder, Nevada shoved hard. It had done no good before. It did no good now. He had no leverage, nothing but brute strength and no way to apply it effectively. He could wrench his trapped leg but he couldn't free himself.

Helplessly, his much greater strength useless, Nevada watched Eden strain against the stone again and again, spending herself recklessly in an attempt to free him. He cursed steadily, silently, wishing that he could do something, anything, to lighten her burden. She was too slender, too fragile, too gentle—like life itself, a flame burning against a vast icy darkness; she would break her heart and have nothing to show for it but the memory of pain and failure.

"Eden," Nevada said roughly, unable to bear watching her an instant longer. "Eden, stop!"

If she heard, she ignored him. A ragged sound was dragged from her throat as she strained to straighten her body, and in doing so force the boulder aside just a little, her muscles straining, just a few fractions of an inch—her body screaming—just enough for Nevada's foot to slide free of the rocky vise—her vision blurring and her breath burning in her chest until she sobbed.

The boulder grated as it shifted minutely.

It was all Nevada had been waiting for and more than he had thought possible. He shoved hard with his free leg against the boulder and at the same time yanked his trapped leg backward, ignoring the pain that shot through his ankle. After a few agonizing seconds his foot wrenched free of the boot and the rocky vise.

"I'm out!"

Instantly Eden let go of the branch and sank to her knees,

breathing in great gulps, trying to get enough oxygen to keep the world from receding down an endless black tunnel. When she finally succeeded, she realized that Nevada was kneeling next to her, his arms around her, supporting her. With a broken sigh she leaned against his strength.

"Sorry about the boot," Eden said when she had enough breath to spare for words.

"Never fit right anyway. Too big. Damn good thing, too."

Nevada leaned to the side, snagged Eden's jacket with one hand and began stuffing her into it. When he was finished, he caught her face between his big hands.

"Do you hurt anywhere?" he asked.

She shook her head.

"Don't ever do anything that stupid again. You can tear yourself up inside and never know until it's too late," Nevada said savagely. Then, before she could say anything, he asked, "Can you walk to the cabin?"

Eden nodded.

"Get going," he said. "You're sweaty. Don't stop to rest until you're in dry clothes."

"But—"

"*Move.*"

"What about you?" Eden persisted.

"I can take care of myself."

As he spoke, Nevada automatically wiped snow off the rifle, checked the load and the firing mechanism. Satisfied that everything was in working order, he used the butt of the rifle to lever himself to his feet. Circulation was returning to his left foot, but slowly. With the renewed flowing of blood came excruciating pain. Nevada ignored it. Using the rifle as a makeshift crutch, he took a step forward.

And fell full-length in the snow.

Even as Nevada rolled onto his side to lever himself upright again, Eden spoke quickly to Baby. The wolf hit Nevada squarely in the chest, knocked him back into the snow and put one very large paw on his chest. Nevada realized instantly that he wasn't going to get up again without fighting Baby. The prospect wasn't inviting.

Eden bent over Nevada, survival blanket in hand. "Wrap up. I'll be back with the horses as soon as possible."

Before she could straighten again, Nevada's hand flashed out and snared her wrist in an immovable grip. His eyes were as cold and bleak as his voice.

"Baby or no Baby, you damn well better be in dry clothes when I see you again, lady."

CHAPTER FOUR

WHEN EDEN RETURNED LEADING THE Appaloosa and the packhorse, she found Baby sitting next to Nevada. The animal's black paw was on the man's forearm. Yellow wolf's eyes stared into equally untamed silver-green ones. Neither one looked up when she walked in.

Eden had the distinct feeling that both males were enjoying measuring each other.

A single word called Baby off guard duty. He removed his big paw, stretched and waved his tail at Nevada in a silent offering of truce. Gravely Nevada took off his glove and held out his hand. Baby sniffed, ducked his head and offered it to be scratched.

"You're all bluff, aren't you, Baby?" Nevada asked.

A huge, gleaming wolf's grin was Baby's answer.

"Impressive. Who's your dentist?"

Eden smiled despite herself. She was still smiling when

Nevada's head turned and his pale green glance raked over her, taking in every detail of her appearance. Suddenly she was very grateful the horses had continued to drift in the direction of her cabin. Otherwise she wouldn't have taken the time to change into dry clothes before coming back to Nevada. Then she would have had to explain to him why it had been more important to get back to him quickly than it had been to find dry clothes for herself. She doubted that he would have found her arguments convincing.

Nevada folded the survival blanket, stuffed it in his jacket pocket and levered himself into a standing position.

"How's your foot?" Eden asked finally.

"It's there."

"I can see that," she muttered, leading the Appaloosa closer. "Does it hurt? Do you have any feeling in it? Is it frostbitten?"

"Are you cold?" he asked, ignoring her questions.

"Damn it, Nevada, I'm not the one who's hurt!"

"Neither am I. Guess that means we're both fine. Take it easy, you knothead."

At first Eden thought Nevada was referring to her. Then she realized he was talking to the spotted horse, which had shied when Nevada came awkwardly to his feet. That was the end of Nevada's awkwardness, however. He grabbed the saddle horn and vaulted into the saddle with catlike ease.

"Hand me my rifle."

For a moment Eden was too stunned to say anything. Nevada was going to ride off into the storm without so much as a thank-you. She could handle the lack of gratitude. What made her furious was the knowledge that he wasn't nearly as "fine" as he said he was. His face was too pale and she was afraid the stain of red over his cheekbones owed more to fever than windburn. But apparently Nevada was angry about being guarded by Baby, or too proud to admit he needed anything more from her, or both.

Eden handed the rifle up to Nevada, shrugged into her backpack and walked off up the trail toward the cabin without a word, too furious to trust herself to speak. Her short temper shocked her. Normally she was the last one to lose control—but normally she wouldn't have spent the last hour digging a man out of a hole before he froze to death. And not just any man. A man she had taken one look at and gone to with the absolute certainty of water running downhill to the waiting sea.

A man who thought love was a fairy tale.

A spotted flank materialized from the snowstorm in front of Eden. The Appaloosa was standing across the trail, blocking her way. At an unseen signal from Nevada, the horse turned toward her and then stood motionless once more. Nevada kicked his stockinged foot out of the left stirrup and leaned toward Eden, holding out his left arm.

"Climb on."

"I've never ridden," she said tightly.

"I've never had a wolf sicced on me. Learn something new every day."

"I didn't sic—"

"The hell you didn't. Grab hold of me."

Eden was never sure what happened next. All she knew was that the world swung suddenly, crazily. When things settled into place again she was behind the saddle, hanging on to Nevada with both hands, for he had become the stable center of an otherwise highly mobile world.

"Well you've got the first part right," Nevada said dryly.

"What?"

"You're hanging on."

She started to speak, only to make a high, startled sound when the horse moved. Target snorted and sidestepped lightly.

"Go easy on the screaming," Nevada said. "Target is skittish. That's how we got into trouble in the first place."

"You screamed?" she retorted.

Nevada turned around enough to look at Eden. His narrowed eyes gleamed like gems between his thick black eyelashes, but she would have sworn his look was one of amusement rather than anger. She decided that she liked that particular gleam in his eyes much better than the icy distance that was his normal response to the world.

Then Nevada's glance shifted to her mouth and Eden remembered the instant when his fingertip had caressed her lips. Her heart hesitated before it beat with increased speed.

"Does that quick little tongue of yours ever get you in trouble?" he asked finally.

The intriguing rasp was back in Nevada's voice, making Eden shiver.

"Only with you," she admitted. "Normally I'm rather quiet. But I love the sound of your voice, especially when it gets all slow and deep. Like now."

His eyes narrowed even more, all amusement gone, replaced by something as elemental as a wolf's howl. The searching intensity of Nevada's glance made Eden shiver. He turned away abruptly.

"Can Baby lead us to the cabin?" Nevada asked harshly.

"Yes."

"Then tell him to do it."

"Lead us home, Baby. *Home.*"

Baby turned and began trotting along the base of the scree slope. Nevada turned Target to follow the wolf's tracks. The instant the horse began moving, Eden made a stifled sound and clung very tightly to Nevada. He looked down, saw her arms wrapped around him, saw hands that were slender even inside gloves, knew that the hard rise of his flesh was only inches from those feminine hands, and tried not to swear aloud at the ungovernable rushing of his blood.

For several minutes there was a silence that was at least as uncomfortable as Nevada was.

"Nevada?"

He grunted.

"I wasn't making fun of your voice."

"I know."

"Then why are you angry?"

Nevada hesitated, then shrugged. "Some kinds of honesty are dangerous, Eden."

"I don't understand."

"Drop your hand down a few inches and you'll understand just fine."

Nevada's voice was remote, clipped. When Eden realized what he meant, she was glad he couldn't see her blazing cheeks. Beneath her embarrassment she was shocked. When Nevada had told her he lived every instant as though it were his last, he had meant it, and the proof was right at hand.

"Makes a girl wonder what it would take to cool you off," Eden muttered against his back, certain he wouldn't be able to hear.

He did, of course.

"Hell of a question," Nevada retorted. "Sure you want to hear the answer?"

Eden opened her mouth for an incautious reply, only to think better of it at the last instant. Before she closed her mouth, she felt the unanticipated, fragile chill of snowflakes dissolving on her tongue. Her eyes closed and she held her breath, waiting for the exquisite sensation to be repeated. As she waited, the world swayed gently beneath her and her arms clung to the living column of strength that was Nevada.

Suddenly Eden had a dizzying sense of the wonder of being alive and riding through a white storm holding on to a man whose last name she didn't even know, while snowflakes melted on her lips like secret kisses. She laughed softly and tipped her face back to the sky, giving herself to the miracle of being alive.

The sound of Eden laughing made Nevada turn toward her involuntarily, drawn by the life burning so vividly in her. He looked at her with a hunger that would have shocked her if she had seen it, but her eyes were closed beneath the tiny, biting caresses of snowflakes. When her eyes opened once more, he had already turned away.

"Nevada?"

He made a rough, questioning sound.

"What's your last name?"

"Blackthorn."

"Blackthorn," Eden murmured, savoring the name as though it were a snowflake freshly fallen onto her tongue. "What do you do when you're not rescuing maidens or falling down mountains, Nevada Blackthorn?"

"I'm *segundo* on the Rocking M when Tennessee is there. When he isn't, I'm ramrod."

"*Segundo?* Tennessee? Ramrod? Are we speaking the same language?"

The corner of Nevada's mouth lifted slightly. "A ramrod is a ranch foreman. A *segundo* is the ramrod's right-hand man. Tennessee is my brother."

"Is the Rocking M your family ranch?"

"After a fashion. We're the bastard line. The legitimate folks are the MacKenzies. Tennessee bought into the ranch when Luke MacKenzie's father was trying to drink himself to death. I own a chunk of the Devil's Peak area. Cash and Mariah gave it to me for a wedding gift."

For a few moments Eden was too stunned to breathe. "You're married?" she asked faintly.

"It was Cash and Mariah's wedding, not mine."

"They gave you a present on their wedding day," Eden said carefully.

Nevada nodded.

"Why?"

"It's a long story."

"I'm very patient."

"Could have fooled me."

"I doubt that much fools you," she said matter-of-factly.

Nevada thought of the instant he had seen Eden coming toward him in a smoky bar and his whole body had reached out to her with a primitive need that had shocked him. But he would have been a fool to talk about that, and Nevada Blackthorn was no fool.

"Mariah is Luke's sister," Nevada said. "She had a map to a gold mine that had come down through the family. The map wasn't much use because it was all blurred. I passed the map along to some people who are real good at making documents give up their secrets. When the map came back, I gave it to her. She found the mine, Cash found her, and they got married. They gave me a chunk of the mine as a wedding present."

The hint of a drawl in Nevada's voice told Eden that she was being teased. She didn't mind. She liked the thought that she could arouse that much playfulness in Nevada.

"Why do I feel you left something out?" she asked.

"Such as?"

"Such as how a *segundo* knows the kind of people who can make crummy old documents sit up and sing."

"I wasn't always a *segundo*."

Eden hesitated. The drawl was definitely gone from Nevada's voice. Even as she told herself she had no right to pry, she heard herself asking a question.

"What were you before you were a *segundo*?"

"What the Blackthorn men have been for hundreds of years—a warrior."

Vivid images from the fight in West Fork flashed before Eden's eyes, followed by other images. Nevada lying half-buried in a rock slide with a rifle in his hand. Nevada checking the rifle's firing mechanism with a few swift motions before he even tried to stand up. Nevada's bleak eyes and unsmiling mouth.

Warrior.

It explained a lot. Too much.

The vivid joy in life that Eden had experienced moments before drained away, leaving sadness in its place. Her arms tightened protectively around Nevada's powerful body as though she could somehow keep whatever might hurt him at bay. When she realized what she was doing, she didn't know whether to laugh or to weep at her own idiocy. Nevada needed protecting about as much as a bolt of lightning did.

But unlike lightning, Nevada could bleed and cry. And he had. She knew it as surely as she knew that she was alive.

Breathing Nevada's name, Eden moved her face slowly against the cool suede texture of his shearling jacket, wiping away the tears that fell when she thought of what Nevada must have endured in the years before he went to work for the Rocking M. The knowledge of his pain reached her as nothing had since the death of her little sister during Alaska's long, frigid night.

Nevada felt the surprising strength of Eden's arms holding him, heard his name breathed like a prayer into the swirling storm, sensed the aching depth of Eden's emotions. Without stopping to ask why, Nevada brought one of her gloved hands to his cheek and rubbed slowly. With a ragged sigh she relaxed against him.

For several minutes there was no sound but the tiny whispering of snowflakes over the land, the creak of cold leather, and the muffled hoofbeats of the two horses as Nevada held them to Baby's clear trail. When Nevada saw the outline of the cabin rising from the swirling veils of snow, he removed Eden's arms from around him.

"Time to let go, Eden. You're home."

Reluctantly Eden released Nevada. He swung his right leg over the front of the saddle, grabbed the saddle horn in his right hand and slid to the ground. Braced by his grip on the saddle horn, Nevada tentatively put weight on his left foot. There was pain, but he had expected it. What mattered was that the foot and ankle took his weight without giving way.

Nevada reached up, lifted Eden off the horse and lowered her to the icy ground.

"Legs still working?" he asked, holding on to her just in case.

Eden felt the hard length of Nevada pressed against her body and wondered if she would be able to breathe, much less stand. She nodded her head.

"Good. Go in and get a fire going while I take care of the horses."

"Your foot—"

"Go in and get warm," Nevada interrupted. "You'd just be in my way."

Eden would have argued, but Nevada had already turned around and begun loosening the cinch on Target's saddle. As she watched, he removed the heavy saddle easily and set it aside. There was a hesitation when he walked that reminded her of Baby—injured, but hardly disabled.

Besides, Nevada was right. She didn't know what to do with the horses.

Without a word Eden removed her backpack and jacket, shook snow from them and went into the cabin. Baby followed her in and went immediately to the coldest, draftiest spot in the cabin's single room. His thick fur had been grown for a Yukon winter. Until he shed some of his undercoat, a fire was redundant.

It took only a moment for Eden to stir the banked coals to life. That was one of the first things her parents had taught her about living in cold country—no matter how long or how short the absence was supposed to be, always leave the hearth in a state of instant readiness for the next fire. No more than a single match should be needed to bring light and warmth into a cabin.

Eden exchanged her snow boots for fleece-lined moccasins before she went to the ice chest to look for a quick meal. After sorting through the snow she had used to chill the contents of the ice chest, she found a package of chicken. Fresh vegetables were in a cardboard carton. She selected a handful, took the knife from her belt sheath and went to work.

By the time Nevada came in the front door carrying a pair of hiking boots in his hands, the cabin was warm from the fire and fragrant with the smell of chicken and dried herbs simmering together on a tall trivet over the fire. Eden looked up as Nevada took off her knit ski cap and rubbed his fingers through his short, black hair. He shrugged out of his thick shearling jacket, hung it on a nail next to hers, and walked unevenly toward the fire. Moments later he had removed his single cowboy boot and his socks and was toasting his bare feet by the flames. Bruises shadowed his left foot, which was also reddened from cold.

Eden set aside the vegetables she had been chopping and knelt next to Nevada's legs. She took his left foot between her hands and went over it with her fingertips, searching for swellings, cold spots that could be frostbite, or any other injury.

Silently Nevada's breath came in and stayed that way. Her fingers felt like gentle flames caressing his cold skin. Not by so much as a sideways look did she reveal that she knew what her touch was doing to him. The thought that Eden might be as innocent as she was alluring disturbed Nevada more deeply than her warm fingers.

"I told you I'm fine," he said. His voice was rough, irritable, for his body was reacting to Eden's touch once again.

"Your idea of fine and mine are different." Eden pressed her fingertips around a swelling. "Hurt?"

"No."

She examined his toes critically. Other than being cold, they showed no damage. She let go of his foot. Before he could prevent it, she had pressed her hand against his forehead. His temperature brought a frown to her face. She put her other hand against her own forehead for comparison.

"You're running a fever," she said.

Nevada grunted. He had been running a fever for the past hour or more. Tennessee had been right. He should have stayed out of the mountains. But he hadn't been able to. Since the fight in West Fork, Nevada had been too restless to stick around the Rocking M's tame winter pastures.

"Are you planning on riding out into the storm as soon as your feet warm up?" Eden asked evenly, removing her hand from Nevada's forehead. "Or are you going to be sensible and wait out the storm here?"

A pale green glance fixed on Eden with searching intensity. The warning Nevada had spoken to her once before hung in the air between them: *Stay away from me, Eden. I want you more than all the men in that bar put together.*

"Aren't you nervous about being alone with me in a cabin at the end of the world?" Nevada asked softly.

"No."

"You damned well should be."

"Why?"

Nevada said something rude under his breath.

"I know you want me," Eden said simply. "I also know you won't rape me. And not because of Baby. The way you fight, you probably could take care of a pack of wolves. But if I said no, you wouldn't so much as touch me. Even if I said yes..." She shrugged.

"You have more faith in me than I do."

Eden's smile was as beautiful as it was sad. "Yes, I know."
She stood up and went back to chopping vegetables.

Broodingly Nevada looked around the cabin. Once it had
been a base camp for hunters who were less interested in fine
decorator touches than in solid shelter from storms. In the far
corner of the room, next to Baby, there was a small potbel-
lied stove. A section of chimney pipe was missing. Obviously
Eden had decided it would be easier to stay warm near the
big fieldstone hearth than to fix the stove's broken chimney.

Narrowed green eyes inventoried the contents of the room
in a sweeping glance that missed nothing. Bedroll and
mattress laid out, clothes either hung on nails or put neatly
into the rough-hewn dresser, kitchen implements stacked on
overturned cartons, camp chairs, a small can of oil set near
the kitchen pump, a bucket of water to prime the pump, a
kerosene lantern as well as a battery model; it was apparent
that Eden was at home in the Spartan shelter.

Eden walked across the room, pushed a thick, faded
curtain aside, and looked out. Snow was coming down thick
and hard. Saying nothing, she let herself out of the cabin's
only door and closed it behind her. Instantly Baby came to
his feet and went to stand by the door. A minute later the
door opened again. Eden came in, dragging Nevada's packsacks behind. She kicked the door shut.

Without the awkwardness of wearing only one cowboy
boot to hamper him, Nevada moved with startling speed
and only the slightest limp. He took her hands from the
canvas packsacks.

"Put your bed near the hearth," Eden said. "The cabin
gets cold by dawn."

"Next time let me get my own gear. These sacks are too heavy for you."

Eden gave him a look out of hazel eyes that were almost molten gold with reflected flames. "You've been hurt and you're running a fever," she said with careful patience. "That makes us about even in the strength department."

"Bull," Nevada said succinctly.

With no visible effort he lifted both sacks, walked across the room and dumped the sacks to one side of the hearth. Eden stared. She knew how heavy those bags were. She'd had a hard time simply dragging them into the cabin.

"Okay, I was wrong," she said, throwing up her hands. "You can jump tall buildings in a single bound and catch bullets in your bare hands."

"Bare teeth," Nevada said without looking up.

"What?"

"You catch bullets with your teeth."

"You may," she retorted, "but I'm not that stupid."

"The hell you aren't." Nevada lifted his head and pinned her with a cougar's pale green glance. "You're alone in the middle of a snowstorm with a man who gets hard every time you lick your lips. And you *trust* me. That, lady, is damned stupid."

CHAPTER FIVE

Sensing that something was wrong, Eden awoke with a start. In the silent spaces between gusts of wind, she heard a man speaking in broken phrases, fragmented names, snatches of language that had no rational meaning. But they made sense emotionally. Someone was hurt, trapped, dying....

And it was happening over and over again.

Nevada.

Quickly Eden sat up and looked across the hearth to the place where Nevada had set up his bedroll and mattress. The room was so dark that she could see only an outline, a darker black that indicated Nevada was still there. The cold in the room was the penetrating chill of a winter that would not release the land into spring's life-giving embrace.

Without leaving her sleeping bag, Eden stirred the fire into life and added fuel. Flames surged up, bringing light and heat into the room. A swift glance told Eden that Nevada was only half-covered, restless, caught in the grip of fever or nightmare or both.

Eden unzipped her sleeping bag and slid out. Her double-layer, silk-and-wool ski underwear turned aside the worst of the chill, but the floor was icy on her bare feet. Silently she knelt next to Nevada, watching the contours of his face emerge from the darkness as flames licked over the wood.

A combination of stark shadows, black beard, shifting orange flames and physical tension drew Nevada's features into lines as harsh as they were compelling to Eden's senses. His torso was lean, muscular, highlighted by fire and midnight swirls of hair. He wore no shirt, nothing to keep the cold at bay.

Eden knelt at Nevada's side. As she had earlier in the day, she put her hand on his forehead to gauge his temperature.

The world exploded.

Within the space of two seconds Eden was jerked over Nevada's body, thrown on her back and stretched helplessly beneath his far greater weight while a hot steel band closed around her throat. In the wavering light Nevada's eyes were those of a trapped cougar, luminous with fire, bottomless with shadow, inhuman.

"*Nevada...*" Eden whispered, all she could say, for the room was spinning away.

Instantly the pressure vanished. Eden felt the harsh shudder that went through Nevada's body before he rolled aside, releasing her from his weight. She shivered with the cold of the cabin floor biting into her flesh, and with another, deeper cold, the winter chill that lay at the center of Nevada's soul.

"Next time you want to wake me up, just call my name. Whatever you do, don't touch me. Ever."

Nevada's voice was as remote as his eyes had been.

"That's the problem, isn't it?" Eden asked after a moment, her voice husky.

"What?"

"Touching. You haven't had enough of it. Not the caring kind, the warm kind, the gentle kind."

"Warmth is rare and temporary. Cruelty and pain aren't. A survivor hones his reflexes accordingly. I'm a survivor, Eden. Don't ever forget it. If you catch me off guard I could hurt you badly and never even mean to."

Eden closed her eyes and shivered against the icy cold. Suddenly she felt herself lifted again. She made a startled sound and stiffened.

"It's all right," Nevada said calmly. "I'm wide-awake now. Turn your face toward the fire."

The difference in temperature between the floor and Nevada's bed was disorienting. Eden let out a broken sigh of relief at the warmth and turned her face toward the dancing flames. When she felt Nevada's hand at her throat once more, she gave him a startled look. Nevada didn't notice. He was carefully peeling down the mock-turtleneck collar of her top. Gently his hand slid up beneath her chin, urging her to turn more fully toward the fire.

As Eden turned, a necklace of fine gold chain spilled from the scarlet fabric into Nevada's hand, drawn by the fragile weight of the ring she wore as a pendant. The shimmer of metal caught his eye. He looked more closely and saw that the ring was made of fine strands of smoothly braided gold. When he realized that the ring was too small to be worn by anyone but a very young child, he tipped his palm and let the gold slide away.

Firelight revealed no marks on the creamy surface of Eden's throat. With devastating gentleness Nevada's fingertips traced the taut tendons and satin skin. The startled intake of her breath followed by the visible, rapid surge of her pulse made Nevada's body tighten in a wild, sweeping rush that was becoming familiar to him around Eden.

Even as Nevada told himself he should be grateful that Eden's response to him came from fear rather than desire, he knew he wasn't grateful. He wanted nothing so much as to soothe with his tongue the tender flesh he had savaged, and then go on to find even warmer, more tender flesh and know its sweetness, as well.

But even if he were fool enough to start something he wasn't going to finish, Eden wouldn't be fool enough to want him. She finally understood what he was: a warrior, not a knight in shining armor.

Eden trembled again.

"Don't worry. I won't hurt you now," Nevada said.

The subdued rasp in his voice was like a hidden caress, making Eden ache to know more of his touch.

"I know," she whispered.

"Do you? You're trembling."

"I'm not used to…this."

"Take my word for it," Nevada said sardonically, "nearly being strangled isn't the sort of thing you get used to." His fingertips probed lightly at her soft skin. "Tender?"

Eden shook her head.

"Does it hurt when you talk?" he asked.

"No."

"Are you sure?"

She nodded.

"I don't believe you."

"But it's true," Eden said. "You didn't hurt me."

The throaty intimacy of her voice made Nevada burn. Very carefully he lifted his hand from Eden's warmth. He sat up in a tangle of sleeping bag and blankets, bringing her upright with him. The easy way he handled her weight served to underline his strength and her vulnerability—a vulnerability she stubbornly refused to acknowledge.

As Nevada released Eden, she reached up and put her palm on his forehead. He jerked back.

"You were lucky, Eden. Very lucky. Don't push it."

"You should take your own advice."

Nevada gave her a narrow look. "Meaning?"

"You're running a fever, but you plan on getting up at dawn and riding out of here."

Nevada shrugged. "I'll see what it looks like in the morning."

"White," Eden said succinctly.

"What?"

"It will look white. All of it. Even if it stops snowing, you won't be able to tell. The wind will strip off the new snow and blow it everywhere. White on white, sky and ground, everything and everywhere. If you don't believe me, listen to the wind. You would be a fool to go anywhere tomorrow, and survivors aren't fools."

Nevada turned and looked at Eden with unfathomable eyes. "Get back in your own bed. Fever or no fever, there's nothing you can do for me."

After a long, tight moment, Eden went back to her sleeping bag, crawled in and shivered until she was warm once more.

"Nevada?"

He grunted unencouragingly.

"What were you dreaming about?"

"Was I dreaming?"

"Yes. That's what woke me up."

Silence.

"Do you dream like that often?" she persisted.

"I don't know."

"How can you not know?"

"Survivors don't remember their dreams. That's how we stay sane."

Nevada rolled over and was asleep within moments.

Eden lay awake for a long time, thinking about survivors and listening to the wind rearrange layers of snow over the frozen land.

"BABY, GIVE THEM TO ME," Eden coaxed.

Baby moved just beyond her reaching fingers. Yellow eyes gleamed with unmistakable mischief. From either side of Baby's long muzzle dangled Nevada's socks. Plainly the wolf had no intention of giving up his prize.

Eden made a sudden grab. Baby danced backward and then half crouched, his muzzle on his front paws, his hindquarters in the air, his tail waving with delight at having suckered his mistress into playing with him.

Nevada looked up from stacking firewood next to the hearth, where the heat could dry out wood newly brought in from the snow.

"Good thing I have extra socks," he said. "Look's like that pair is a goner."

"Baby knows better, at least with my socks," Eden

said, exasperated. "Guess he figured yours were fair game. Baby, *drop.*"

Yellow eyes met hazel ones for a long moment. With a startlingly human look of disappointment, Baby opened his mouth. Socks dropped to the floor, no worse for the time spent in a wolf's jaws. Eden picked up the socks, tossed them in Nevada's direction, and rubbed both hands through Baby's thick neck fur, praising him for giving up his prize. Baby burrowed into her touch in return, stropping himself against her like a huge cat, plainly enjoying the physical contact.

Nevada watched through hooded eyes, oddly moved by the sight of the big, frankly savage-looking beast being petted by a woman who weighed less than the animal did and was considerably less well equipped to defend herself. As she buried her face in the wolf's fur, it didn't seem to occur to Eden that those long jaws and steel muscles could tear her apart.

You're a fool, Eden Summers. A sweet fool, but a fool just the same. You trust too much.

Baby made a sound that was a cross between a chesty growl and a throaty yap as he half crouched again, waving his tail, vibrating with a desire for energetic play after being penned up by the storm. Eden laughed and shoved against the wolf with both hands, sending him skidding across the smooth wooden floor. With a powerful scrambling of legs, Baby stopped his backward motion and romped toward Eden, who was braced on hands and knees, waiting for Baby's charge. Instead of running into Eden head-on, the wolf turned at the last instant, buffeting her with his shoulder.

If Eden hadn't been prepared, she would have been bowled over, but this was an old game for the two of them. She gave as good as she got, throwing her weight behind her shoulder as Baby raced by, sending him scrambling for purchase on the slick wood floor. Eden barely had a chance to recover her own balance before Baby was back for more. She survived a few more glancing passes before the wolf's greater strength and coordination sent her rolling.

Instantly Baby pivoted, scrambled for traction and started after his laughing mistress. Eden had just enough time to brace herself again before more than a hundred and thirty pounds of muscle and fur bounded into her. She shoved hard against Baby, knowing she was going to go spinning again but determined to give the wolf a good tussle.

Before Baby's shoulder could connect with Eden, she was lifted and set down behind Nevada. The wolf hit the man instead. Two strong hands shoved hard against steel muscles and thick fur. Baby went spinning and sliding across the cabin floor. He recovered, gave Nevada a look of glittering delight, and came full tilt across the cabin floor toward the man.

This time Nevada waited on all fours as Eden had. Muscular shoulder met muscular shoulder, Baby rebounded and went sliding and scrambling across the floor. When the wolf regained his balance, he gave Nevada a laughing, long-tongued grin and charged once more, holding back nothing of his strength as he had earlier in the game with Eden.

"You're in for it now, Nevada," Eden crowed breathlessly. "Baby hasn't had a decent wrestling match since Mark broke his arm, so Baby's loaded for bear—and with that sleek beard, you're looking like bear to him."

Just as Nevada turned to ask who Mark was, Baby sprang. Nevada went down in a tangle of arms, furry legs and waving black tail. Laughing hard at Nevada's comeuppance, trying to catch her breath at the same time, Eden sank onto her bed and applauded while wolf and warrior romped.

And a romp it was. Nevada and Baby caromed off ice chest and walls, supply sacks and packsaddle, firewood and empty water bucket. The room became a shambles of its former neat condition. Yet no matter how fast or exciting the wrestling became, both wolf and warrior kept individual weapons carefully sheathed. Fangs never sank into flesh, nor did steel fingers gouge. Claws might rake the floor, but nothing else. Unarmed combat tactics remained unused.

Finally Nevada wrestled Baby to the floor and pinned him there, both of them breathing hard. The wolf relaxed, baring his throat and belly to the warrior, accepting the end of the game. Nevada shook Baby gently by the scruff, spoke to him calmly, and released him. Baby sprang up, shook himself thoroughly, and stood panting and grinning up at Nevada. The left side of Nevada's mouth kicked up slightly in return. He sat on his heels and took the wolf's big head in his hands, rubbing the base of the erect ears and smoothing the thick fur.

"You're one hell of a fighter, old man," Nevada said quietly.

Baby's head turned. Big jaws gently closed over Nevada's right hand, then released him.

"That's meant to reassure you," Eden explained in a soft voice. "It's a wolf's kiss. Wolves aren't quite the same as dogs. They require different things from their friends, whether four-footed or two."

"What should I do to reassure Baby in return?"

"You already have."

"How?"

"You accepted his surrender, let him go with his dignity intact, and then praised him with your touch and your voice." Eden paused thoughtfully. "You read Baby very well, Nevada. Have you ever worked with undomesticated animals?"

"All my life."

"Really? What kind?"

"Men."

Eden started to laugh before she realized that there was more truth than humor in what Nevada said. Then she laughed anyway, a bittersweet and very human laughter, accepting what could not be changed in the nature of man and beast.

"Maybe if men had their signals of dominance and submission as well worked out as wolves," Eden said, "there would be fewer wars."

"I suspect we had our signals straight once. Then we got civilized and it all went to hell."

Nevada stood and stretched. His glance fell on the upside-down water bucket, the packsaddle standing on end, and other signs of the romp. The corners of his eyes crinkled slightly.

"Looks like I have my work cut out for me before we go cat hunting," Nevada said.

Eden's breath caught. She smiled brilliantly and said in a husky voice, "Thank you."

He gave her a sideways glance. "For not leaving you to clean up the mess?"

"No," she said, dismissing the room with a wave of her hand. "For staying here one more day. I know you think I'm silly for worrying about you, but I'm not. Spring, especially in a cold country, is the hardest season on animals. No matter how strong you are, the huge temperature swings stress your body. I've seen flu turn into pneumonia…"

Eden's voice dipped, almost broke and then steadied. "Anyway, if you had ridden off today I would have worried. Now I'll know where you are and if your fever is really gone."

"And if I've managed to stay on top of Target this time?" Nevada said dryly.

Eden's laugh was as soft as the creamy skin of her throat. She started to speak but could think of nothing to say except the truth.

"I'm glad you're staying, Nevada. Not just for my peace of mind, either. Even with fresh snow, no wind, and Baby's nose, finding cougars out there won't be easy. I suspect you're a good tracker."

"I get by."

The buried drawl in Nevada's voice told Eden that he was amused by something. She smiled slightly. "I'll just bet you do. You don't miss much, do you?"

"No."

Eden didn't need to be told any more. Nevada had lived on the razor edge of awareness for so long that he had forgotten there was any other way to live.

"I'll put your skills to work every chance I get," Eden said. "There's so little time."

"I heard you'd be here until June. At least, I heard the government cat expert would be here. That's you, isn't it?"

"After a fashion, but probably there will be more than

one cat expert coming and going. My grant money is private, administered through the university at Boulder, but I'm working in conjunction with a federal study of cougars. The whole study will cover a decade. My part will last only as long as the tracking snows do, unless I find a female that's denned up with cubs. Then I might be able to stretch things into May or June."

Nevada bent over, righted the packsaddle with an easy motion and asked, "What is your part?"

"A feasibility study."

"Of what?"

"Whether it's possible to monitor cougars without drugging them, putting on bulky radio collars, and then turning the cats loose to lead a supposedly normal life."

"Yeah, I always wondered how many animals the scientists lost that way," Nevada said dryly. "Drugs are tricky things, especially with cats. As for the radio collars..."

He shrugged, bent over a bedroll and began putting it back together with the smooth, efficient motions of a man who has done a task so often he no longer has to think about it. Eden worked alongside Nevada, watching him from the corners of her eyes, fascinated by his unconscious grace and his casual acceptance of his own physical strength.

"What about the radio collars?" Eden asked, realizing belatedly that Nevada had stopped talking and was watching her watch him.

"I'm no specialist," Nevada said, looking away from Eden, straightening a blanket with a casual snap of his wrist, "but I've noticed one thing about wild animals. If there's anything different about an animal, the others shun him. Or they attack him. Makes me wonder if anyone has thought about that when they wrap a few pounds of brightly packaged radio collar around a wild animal and turn it loose. Then the specialists come back every few days or weeks in a helicopter or a small plane and buzz the hell out of the local wildlife trying to track down the radio collar's signal."

"Somebody around here must have thought about it," Eden said. She knelt and began stacking firewood that had been scattered when Nevada had rolled into it. "Dr. Martin said my particular part of the grant money came from one of the local ranchers." Suddenly she turned and looked at Nevada. "Was it you?"

He hesitated fractionally in the act of righting the water bucket, then shrugged and said, "I'm a cowhand, not a rancher. Luke and Ten own the land."

Eden waited, certain that she was right. Only someone who respected and understood wildlife would have given money for a study that didn't disrupt the animals' normal lives. It was obvious that Nevada felt an unusual affinity for wild animals. She had never seen Baby take to a person with such ease.

"Both Luke and Ten admire the cougars, but they have their hands full raising kids and cattle," Nevada continued, "and at the same time they're protecting and excavating some of the Anasazi sites at September Canyon. On a ranch there's never enough money to do everything that should be done."

"So you paid for part of the grant."

Again, Nevada shrugged. "The cougars are staging a comeback around here. Now, I believe the cats live on wild food rather than on Rocking M beef, but I couldn't prove it even though I spent a lot of time chasing cats when I should have been chasing cattle. So I took some of the money from the gold mine Mariah found and told the university to find an expert who could study our cougars without drugging or harassing them."

"I won't drug the cats," Eden said. "But having Baby on their trail might constitute harassment."

Nevada's mouth shifted subtly beneath his beard. He reached down and ruffled the wolf's sleek fur. Baby leaned into the touch, enjoying it.

"Dogs have been chasing cats at least as long as men have been chasing women," Nevada said, giving Eden a brief, sidelong look. "I think the cats might even get a kick out of a good race. Cougars will run like hell, but once they're up in a tree, they relax. Hell, I've seen more than one cougar curl up for a nap in some tall timber while a pack of hounds went crazy barking down below." Frowning thoughtfully, Nevada turned away from scratching Baby's ears. "That reminds me—does Baby ever bark?"

"Rarely."

Nevada's mouth flattened. "Then you've got the wrong hunting dog no matter how good Baby's nose is. A cougar will run from a barking dog, even if it's no bigger than a Scottish terrier. But a dog that doesn't bark will be attacked, no matter how big it is."

"Don't worry. Cats are the exception to Baby's code of silence. When he's on a hot cat trail, Baby makes more noise than a pack of foxhounds."

"Good." Nevada looked around the room, which was neat once more. "That leaves just one other thing to settle before we go hunting. Who's Mark?"

Eden looked up, surprised by the sudden edge in Nevada's voice. "What?"

"Baby's wrestling partner," Nevada said flatly. "The man who broke his arm."

"Oh. That Mark. He's my brother."

Nevada grunted. "How many Marks do you know?"

"Just two."

Nevada waited, watching Eden with pale green eyes as she stacked the last piece of firewood, stood up and dusted her hands on her pants.

"The second Mark was my fiancé for a time," she continued. "Then he discovered that being lifelong friends wasn't the same thing as really wanting a woman. He took one look at Karen and knew something important had been missing from our relationship. They were married a month later."

Nevada had had a lot of practice reading people. He saw no indications of distress in Eden as she talked about her broken engagement. Her voice was even, supple, almost amused. Not at all the way it had been when she had discussed flu turning into pneumonia.

"You sound like you didn't mind losing Mark to another girl," Nevada said, walking slowly across the room toward Eden.

"I didn't lose him. We're still friends."

Skepticism showed in the arch of Nevada's black eyebrows. Eden watched with widening eyes as he came closer and then closer still, not stopping until he was so close that she could feel the heat from his big body.

"It's true," she said, puzzled by Nevada's intensity. "Mark and I are still friends."

"Then you were never lovers."

Eden made a soft, startled sound deep in her throat. "How did you know?"

"Easy. Once a man had you, he'd want you again with every breath he took." Nevada shrugged, but the silver-green intensity of his eyes didn't diminish. "Which means Mark never had you, because he let you go."

CHAPTER SIX

THE ELEMENTAL HARMONICS OF A WOLF'S howl shivered over the land before dissipating on the wind. Nevada froze, listening with every fiber of his body. The sound came again, rising and falling, a song sung to the primal memories that existed in every human soul. The eerie ululation faded into the wind. Silence reigned once more.

"A wolf's howl has to be one of the most beautiful sounds on earth," Nevada said in a hushed voice.

Eden didn't disagree. She had heard only one thing more compelling—Nevada's deep voice when he looked at her and told her that any man who had her would never let her go. Even now she could hardly believe Nevada had said it, meant it, and then turned away, picked up his rifle and calmly asked her if she was ready to go hunting.

The memories made Eden's fingers tremble as she cupped her hands around her mouth and answered Baby with a call that was more musical than a shout and less structured than a yodel. When she finished, Nevada looked at her expectantly.

"Baby's just checking in," Eden explained. "Now we know where he is and he knows where we are. No cats, though."

Nevada nodded. "He won't hit cougar sign on this side of the stream unless a new cat has moved in since I was here last. Once Baby gets to the other side of the stream, though, it shouldn't be long before he hits a trail. A young female staked out her territory there two years ago."

"How young? Did she have cubs?"

"The first year she didn't mate. But this year there was some real caterwauling around here for the two weeks she and her mate traveled together." The left corner of Nevada's mouth lifted a bit and he added blandly, "Seems like the young females always scream the loudest."

"There's a reason they scream," Eden said before she could think better of it.

"Really? What?"

All right, how am I going to get out of this one? Eden asked herself wryly, caught between embarrassment and amusement.

"Er, take my word for it," she said, knowing her cheeks were bright with something more than cold.

"Give me some words and I'll see how I take them."

"Better yet," Eden said quickly, thinking of a graceful exit from the topic, "I'll give you a textbook on cat anatomy."

"Did you bring it with you?"

She sighed. "No."

"Then we're back to words."

Eden suspected she was being teased. Nevada's eyes had

a definite crinkle at the corners. She took a deep breath, reminded herself that she and Nevada were both adults, and began speaking as though she were in a graduate seminar.

"Male cats are built to begin, but not to end, copulation. Therefore, disengagement must be rather uncomfortable for the females."

Nevada gave Eden a sideways glance. "I'm missing something."

"Barbs," she said succinctly.

The sleek black of Nevada's beard shifted a bit as his mouth quirked, but he said only, "Can't be all that bad—"

"Spoken like a true male," she muttered.

"—because the older females keep coming back for more," Nevada finished, ignoring Eden's interruption.

She saw the gleam in his eyes and knew that Nevada was teasing her. She struggled not to laugh. It was impossible. The wicked light in Nevada's eyes reminded her of Baby's when he had danced up to her with a mouthful of forbidden socks and lured her into play.

Nevada listened to the rippling warmth of Eden's laughter and silently decided that it was even more beautiful than a wolf's wild song. He fought the impulse to put an arm around Eden and hug her to his side, and then to bend down and taste lips whose tempting curves haunted him at every moment.

I should have left yesterday, storm or no storm. If I stay much longer I'm going to reach out and take what I need more than I need air.

Having her would be like sinking into fire, all hot and clean and wild, no boundaries, no restraints, nothing but the two of us and the fire burning higher and higher....

A wolf's howl leaped and twisted in the wild silence, calling to them, demanding their attention.

"He's found cat sign!" Eden said. She looked eagerly around the landscape, trying to decide on the quickest route to Baby. "It could be bobcat, I suppose."

"I'm betting it isn't," Nevada said promptly, heading toward the creek. "There's a big old fir on top of that rise. The lady cougar likes to lie up beneath the lowest limbs and watch the land."

"Hurry," Eden said, following. "Once Baby starts running, we may not see him again until he's ready to come into the cabin and chew the ice out from between his toes."

Nevada moved swiftly down the slope toward the creek that gleamed blackly between low banks of snow. Despite the snow that had fallen yesterday, neither Nevada nor Eden needed the snowshoes they had tied to their backpacks. Only in the steepest ravines or in the most dense forest was snowpack more than six inches deep. Yesterday's storm had filled in minor hollows and ripples, leaving behind a pristine surface that took and held tracks as though it had been designed for just that purpose.

Baby howled again. Then came a series of short, excited barks.

"He's seen the cat!" Eden said.

"Will he call off?"

"Doubt it. Not after being shut up in a car and then in the cabin."

Nevada leaped the stream with a lithe power that made Eden think enviously of a cougar. She judged the distance to the other side and skidded to a stop. If she jumped, she'd be asking for an icy dunking on landing and a twisted ankle in the bargain.

"Go on," she urged. "I'll catch up as soon as I find a safe way across. Try to get a look at the cat so we can identify it if we see it again. Once they're forty feet up a tree, cats are darned hard to see, much less identify, even with binoculars."

Nevada hesitated for only an instant before he took off up the rise toward a big fir tree.

Eden trotted—and occasionally slid and slithered—along the side of the creek, muttering about boulders concealed by snow and other traps for the unwary. Finally she came to a place where sun or wind or both had cleaned the rocks of snow. She jumped from boulder to boulder across the stream and headed up the rise. Soon she was following Nevada's tracks.

Lord, that man runs like a big cat. No slipping, no struggling for balance, nothing but clean, long-legged strides.

Baby's barks were faint now, continuous, and very excited.

Sounds like the cat is up a tree. That was fast work. Hope Nevada got a look before it was too late.

When Eden got to the top of the rise, she saw the place where the cougar had been stretched out on the ground beneath a low limb, watching the world in relaxed silence until a loudmouthed black wolf had appeared. Then all hell had cut loose. The cougar—for the size of the tracks left no doubt that a cougar had made them rather than a bobcat—had exploded out of cover, sending a shower of snow from lower branches. The cat had hit its full running stride instantly, racing over the sparsely wooded slope, heading uphill as cats always did when pursued.

Baby's barking ended abruptly, telling Eden that Nevada

had already caught up. Cocking her head, Eden listened, heard nothing to indicate that the chase was anything but over, and returned her attention to a particularly fine set of tracks the cougar had left. Baby wasn't going anywhere now. Neither was the cat. The tracks, however, were at the mercy of the rising wind and the sun. She had to photograph the tracks before they lost their fine, crisp edges.

Automatically Eden took off her backpack, opened it and went to work. She pulled out camera and ruler, lined up the ruler close to the tracks, adjusted the camera's macrozoom lens and triggered the shutter. In the forest silence, the *snick, snick, snick* of the shutter and the faint rubbing of her clothes against the snow when she knelt were the only sounds. When she was through measuring and photographing the prints, she took out a notebook and began to record information.

Eden was halfway through a sentence when she had the distinct feeling of being watched. She spun around. Nevada was standing less than an arm's length away.

"Lord, Nevada, you're a quiet man!"

"Sorry. I didn't mean to startle you."

Eden pushed a deep breath out of her lungs to slow her hammering heart, took a better grip on her pencil and resumed recording her observations.

"Did you get a look at the cougar?" she asked.

"It's the young female. She wintered well. Coat is thick and smooth, no sign of hesitation in her stride. I can't be positive, but I think she's nursing cubs. Her teats were swollen."

With a startled sound Eden jammed her notebook and pencil into her jacket pocket. "I'd better go call off Baby. I don't want a new mother getting panicked."

Nevada lifted Eden's backpack and started back up the trail. "Don't worry about the cougar. Last time I saw her, she was stretching out on a limb to watch Baby jawing at her from below."

"Will I be able to see her?" Eden asked, excited.

"Some."

"How much?"

"The black tip of her long, thick tail."

"Figures," Eden muttered. "Seems like all I ever see of my cats are silent ghosts sliding away at the corner of my eyes."

When Nevada and Eden arrived at the fir where Baby was leaping and yapping, not even the tip of a tail was to be seen. Eden called off Baby and went to work examining the tree through binoculars. Finally she spotted the cougar partway up the big evergreen.

The cat was indeed stretched out along a hefty limb, watching the activity below through half-closed eyes. So well did the cougar screen herself with greenery that Eden wouldn't have seen the animal at all if she hadn't yawned. The motion revealed an astonishing length of pink tongue, as well as teeth of intimidating size and sharpness. The yawn ended, the jaws began closing, and the pink tongue vanished.

An instant later, so did the cougar. Occasional tufts of snow rained down, revealing that the cat was still moving somewhere within the drooping, multiple arms of the tree. No matter how hard Eden looked through the binoculars, she couldn't see so much as a patch of the cat's thick, tawny fur.

Baby whined coaxingly, tired of having to be silent.

"Nope," Eden said to Baby as she lowered the binoculars. "Fun's over." She turned to Nevada. "Are you sure she was nursing?"

"It's more of a hunch. She's healthy, but tires fast, even for a cat. She took to a tree real quick, even though Baby wasn't close to her." Nevada shrugged and squinted up into the tree with pale green eyes. "I'm no expert, though."

"I'll take your instincts over the expertise of anyone I've ever worked with. You're a very noticing kind of man." Eden reached for her pack, which Nevada was still holding in one big hand. "Let's try backtracking from that big fir. If you're right about her having cubs, she'll have a den, too. Maybe we can find it."

"It would make our work a lot easier," Nevada agreed.

Eden heard the word *our* and felt a shiver of pleasure travel through her body. But if Nevada realized what he had implied, nothing was revealed on his face.

"The cougars over on the other side of MacKenzie Ridge," he continued, "have much bigger territories. Up here, the countryside supports more deer, so the cats get by with a lot less land. Even so, they can cover twenty, thirty miles a day looking for prey or for a mate or just keeping their boundary markers fresh."

"Speaking of food, my lunch is in my backpack." Eden tugged discreetly at one of the straps Nevada held.

"Hungry?"

Eden looked up. Nevada's light green eyes were very clear, the lashes surrounding them were ragged slices of midnight, and he was watching her with an intensity that made her breath shorten.

"Yes, I'm...hungry."

Her voice was too husky, but Eden was helpless to change it. Something in Nevada's eyes was making her blood shimmer wildly through her body, leaving chaos in its wake.

She would have moved, but felt unable to so much as take a step. Motionless she waited for him to say something.

"Nevada?" she whispered finally, looking up at him, wondering what was wrong, why she felt as though she were on the edge of a cliff and had only to spread her wings and fly...or fall endlessly, spinning away into infinity like a snowflake on the wind.

Nevada saw the yearning and uncertainty in Eden's wide hazel eyes, hissed a searing word between his teeth and let go of her backpack. The straps slid through her fingers. She grabbed awkwardly with both hands, but it was Nevada's extraordinary quickness that kept the pack from being dumped into the snow. Instead of giving the backpack to Eden, he slung it over one shoulder and turned back the way they had come.

For a moment Eden was too unsettled to follow. She watched Nevada stride through the widely spaced trees. He moved with a strength and silence that should have frightened her, but did not. His male grace and power tugged at her senses, just as the realization that she had never seen Nevada in any but dark clothes tugged at her emotions.

He wants me. He's never made any secret of it. So why won't he even kiss me?

The thought of being kissed by Nevada made Eden's blood shimmer wildly once more. Her breath came in hard, ragged, and she wanted nothing so much at that instant as the feel of Nevada's lips on her own.

Lord, if Mark had had this effect on me, we'd be married by now, with kids in the bargain.

The thought of having Nevada's children went through Eden like lightning, shaking her—another human being with a smile like hers and black hair like his, another person with curiosity and discipline and maybe, just maybe, a boy with his father's smooth coordination, his strength, his restraint.

Eden's breath rushed out, leaving her almost dizzy. She blinked and took several slow breaths as she looked around in the manner of a person who has awakened in a strange land. The snow-brushed trees were unchanged, the white glitter of sunswept snow was the same, and the tracks still showed as blue-white marks in the snow. Nothing in the world around her had changed.

Yet everything had changed. For the first time in Eden's life, her own inner world, the untouched, unviolated privacy of her dreams, had been transformed by the presence of a man.

I'm falling in love with Nevada.

No. Scratch that. It's past tense, over and done with, and I was the last one to know.

Baby whined and nudged Eden's hand. Absently she stroked his big head. He ducked, caught her gloved hand in his mouth and tugged. Immediately he had her full attention.

"You're right, Baby. It's time we left the mama cougar in peace. Or is it lunch you're after, hmm? Does your sharp nose know that all the food left with Nevada? Or do you sense that he's making off with my heart as well as my backpack?"

Yellow eyes watched Eden alertly.

"Yes, I know," she said in a low voice. "It's stupid of me to let someone walk off with something that vital. But my lack of sense is nothing new. A smart girl would have followed everyone's advice and let you die after finding you in that trap, rather than take a chance on getting savaged while trying to teach a wild young mostly-wolf to trust people again."

Baby cocked his head to the side, listening to Eden with every fiber of his mostly-wolf being. Then he made a soft sound deep in his throat and turned his head to look out across the land.

"Okay, boy, I get the message," Eden said. She swept her arm in the direction in which Nevada had gone. "Go catch up with lunch."

It was like releasing a catapult. Within three seconds Baby had reached his full stride and was running with his belly low to the ground and his tail streaming out like a dark banner. Eden followed more slowly, needing time to get a better grip on her unsettled and unsettling thoughts.

Nevada won't be an easy man to love. He's a winter man, shut down deep inside, waiting for a spring that hasn't come.

On the heels of Eden's thought came another, a realization as unflinching as winter itself.

Don't kid yourself. You're going into this with your eyes wide open or you're not going at all. Nevada isn't waiting for spring. He probably doesn't even believe spring exists. That's quite a difference.

It's a difference that could break my heart.

Yet even knowing that, Eden could no more walk away from Nevada now than she had been able to walk away years ago from a wild young wolf made savage by pain.

CHAPTER SEVEN

WITH UNNERVING QUICKNESS NEVADA pushed back from the long table where everyone on the Rocking M ate dinner.

"Good God, Nevada," Ten muttered as his brother turned away to leave. "You're as jumpy as a long-tailed cat in a roomful of rocking chairs. If you're so worried about that female that you can't sit through a whole meal, go check on her."

The ranch hands sitting around the Rocking M's table became silent. Nevada had indeed been edgy for the five days since he had ridden back down out of Wildfire Canyon missing one boot. Privately the hands had speculated that Target had dumped his rider down the scree slope out of self-preservation, but not one of the men had offered that theory within Nevada's hearing. After learning about the modern-day fight at the OK Corral, the cowhands had been very careful to give Nevada all the room he might need, and then extra space for good measure.

Nevada turned around with feline quickness. Narrowed, ice-green eyes focused on Ten.

"What female?" Nevada asked softly.

"The mama cougar, who else?" Ten said blandly as he poured gravy over his second serving of chicken. "We all know how worried you get over mothers." He winked at Mariah, who was at the moment very rounded out by her twins. "You always know women are pregnant before they do, and then you nag them like a maiden aunt to get them to take proper care of themselves. It's a wonder the human race ever got gestated without your help."

Nevada grunted.

Ten's wife, Diana, smiled at her plate. Carla, Mariah and Diana were all touched by Nevada's concern for them and their babies. It was so unexpected coming from a man as hard as Nevada was.

"Go ahead and check on that female again," Ten continued, carefully not looking at his brother, for Nevada wouldn't have missed the amused warmth in Ten's gray eyes. "We've got eleven hands now and two more coming tomorrow. Won't even miss you. Right, Luke?" Ten added as Luke walked in and sat down.

"Miss who?"

"My point exactly," Ten said.

Nevada looked sharply at his brother, saw only the top of a black head bent over a plateful of excellent food, and muttered something too low for Carla, Mariah or Diana to overhear.

A muffled cry came from the next room. Diana and Carla looked at each other as both pushed back from the table.

"Sit down, Diana," Nevada said. "I'll see what's bothering Carolina. Whatever it is isn't serious. You can tell by her cry."

Both Diana and Carla settled back into their chairs. Neither woman questioned Nevada's words, for they had quickly discovered that he had an uncanny ability to judge not only the identity of a child by its cry but also the urgency of the problem.

"Thanks," Diana said to Nevada's retreating back. Then, softly, she said to Ten, "Your brother is wasted as an uncle. He should have babies of his own to love."

Beneath the table Ten squeezed Diana's hand and said in a low voice, "Nevada's been through too many wars, honey. He doesn't trust life enough to risk loving a woman. And without love, there won't be any babies. The Blackthorns may be the bastard branch of the MacKenzie family, but we don't make babies with women we don't love." His thumb stroked over Diana's palm as he added wryly, "It just took me a while to figure that out in our case."

Diana smiled at Ten and laced her fingers through his.

Nevada's acute hearing had picked up every syllable of the conversation between Diana and her husband. Nevada didn't disagree with Ten's assessment of the Blackthorn clan. The day Nevada had discovered Diana could be pregnant and was definitely alone—because Ten was uncertain of his own ability to love—Nevada had taken his brother out to a lonely stretch of pasture and given him the fight Ten had been begging for since the day Diana had left the Rocking M.

It had been a learning experience for both men. One of

the things they had learned was that the love of a brother for a brother was a lot deeper than either had suspected.

"Well, little lady," Nevada said, bending down over Carolina's playpen and lifting her into his arms. "You're as fat and sassy as a summer storm. You want to cloud up and rain all over me?"

Carolina had no such intention now that one of her favorite human beings was within reach. She made a cooing, crowing sound of triumph and grabbed Nevada's beard. He endured the rough caress for a time before gently disengaging her small, surprisingly strong fingers.

"Easy does it," he murmured, rubbing his beard against Carolina's small hands and cheeks. "You'll have me bald before you're a year old."

She laughed with delight and grabbed for the intriguing chin fur again. Nevada blew on Carolina's head teasingly, stirring her silky black hair, the legacy of her Blackthorn father. Her eyes were Diana's—a dark, astonishingly clear blue. Carolina's smile was unique, a smile like sunrise, a contagion of warmth. Holding Carolina, turning his shoulders slowly from side to side, Nevada spoke softly.

"Just lonely, huh?" Nevada murmured, his deep voice gentle, almost a purr. "Well, don't you worry, little darling. Logan's almost over the flu. In a few days he'll be back to stealing your toys. For now, though, he's out of commission. Guess you'll have to settle for me tonight. But your 'uncle' Cash should be back from Boulder by the weekend. He's an even bigger sucker for little girls than I am."

Carolina cooed. Thick black eyelashes swept down over brilliant blue eyes. She curled up against Nevada's chest, yawned, rubbed her ear with a small fist, and relaxed completely. Thirty seconds later she was asleep.

Nevada stood for a long time, cradling the little girl's head with his hand, rocking her very gently, remembering too many babies who had been born into a war-torn land, babies too weak even to cry out, babies he had found too late....

"You're going to spoil her," Ten said from the doorway, but his smile was as affectionate as his voice.

"My pleasure," Nevada said, looking down at his sleeping niece. "She's such a healthy, pretty little thing. Your hair and Diana's eyes."

"And your smile," Ten said softly. "But Luke and I are the only ones who know about that. We're the only ones who remember you from the time before you gave up smiling."

Nevada shrugged slightly. "That's what happens when you wrestle with the devil and lose."

"Is it? I wrestled. I lost. And I learned to smile again anyway."

"Then you're a fool, Tennessee. Any man who lets emotions affect him is a fool."

"Any man who doesn't is dead in all the ways that matter, and you damn well know it. That's why you're standing there holding Carolina."

"She's hardly more than a baby. She needs to be held, needs to know she's not alone, needs..." Nevada shrugged again. "She needs holding, that's all."

"So do adults. Sometimes we need it most of all."

"At over six feet, you're a little big for cuddling," Nevada said dryly.

"Don't tell that to the Rocking M women," Ten retorted. "Luke, Cash and I would hate like hell to give up our ration of cuddling!"

Carolina stirred, complained sleepily and burrowed closer to Nevada.

Ten looked at his watch. "Bedtime. Hand her over to Daddy."

Nevada shifted Carolina into her father's arms. She opened her eyes, approved her new transportation, and promptly went back to sleep. Ten kissed the silky black hair and headed for the stairway.

"Ten?"

"Yeah?" Ten asked softly without looking back.

"If you're sure you don't need me around here, I think I'll head for Wildfire Canyon early tomorrow."

"Happy hunting."

Only Carolina could have seen Ten's wide, knowing smile, and she was asleep.

"Would you miss one of the ranch trucks?" Nevada continued. "We—I lost the cat's tracks on a windy slope way back up a canyon. Even a dog couldn't track her there. It's too steep for a horse, so I might as well drive up that old logging road and work back down from there."

"Take the black truck. Take extra supplies. Take anything you need to get the job done right, including time. For once we're not shorthanded. In other words, don't hurry back."

Sensing the buried amusement in Ten's voice, Nevada watched closely as his brother disappeared up the stairway, carrying the utterly relaxed child.

Abruptly Nevada turned away and went to the bunkhouse.

He packed what he would need, set his mental alarm clock for five hours of sleep and crawled into his cold bunk, trying not to remember what it had been like to hold Eden for just a few moments in his arms in an isolated cabin when she had been disturbed by his dark, unremembered dreams.

Nevada slept quickly, deeply, and he did not remember his dreams. Five hours later he awakened, dressed, and went to the black pickup truck. When he opened the door, a mélange of fragrances greeted him—Carla's chocolate chip cookies and Mariah's fudge brownies, a sack of freshly baked biscuits and a kettle of hearty beef stew that would feed him for several days.

The corner of Nevada's mouth turned up as Ten's words came back to him: *Don't tell that to the Rocking M women. Luke, Cash and I would hate like hell to give up our ration of cuddling!*

Something told Nevada that the women enjoyed it, too.

BY THE TIME NEVADA HAD NEGOTIATED the final washout on the abandoned logging road, he was beginning to wonder how Eden had managed the trip in the first place. If it hadn't been for the signs of her vehicle tracks, he would have sworn that no one had been over the road since the logging operation had been shut down a decade ago. In an emergency, it would be impossible to get to the cabin quickly—or to get away from it.

The anxiety that had been gnawing at Nevada ever since he had left Eden increased as the truck bumped and labored over the rutted, slushy track. He told himself there was no reason for him to be concerned about Eden's welfare. There had been no new storms, no word of strangers in the high country, nothing to set his mind to worrying. Even if there had been, Baby was a formidable bodyguard and Eden had been very much at home in the wild. Rationally, Nevada knew he didn't need to worry about her.

But he wasn't feeling very rational at the moment.

Eden haunted him like an echo down a lonely canyon, touching hidden places that even the sun couldn't reach. Nevada knew he wouldn't have any peace of mind until he assured himself that Eden was all right.

Impatient with himself for his own foolishness, Nevada braked to a stop in front of the isolated cabin. Beyond the cabin, the open, sparse forest began. Even before he turned off the engine, the anxiety that had been driving him intensified. There was smoke rising from the chimney but no one was coming out to greet him. Light green eyes noted every detail of the cabin. Though the weather had been clear, the only tracks Nevada could see in the melting snow went from the cabin around to the outhouse in back, with a single set of tracks detouring to the woodpile.

Eden hadn't left the cabin for anything but absolute necessities.

I knew it. Damn it, I never should have left her alone. Accidents happen. Hell, one happened to me!

Nevada left the truck and reached the cabin door in three long strides. He opened the door and automatically shut it behind him. Baby whined and rumbled a greeting.

"Hi," Eden said, then coughed before continuing in a raspy voice. "Baby told me company was coming, but he didn't say who."

Dressed in the long, scarlet ski underwear she used as pajamas, Eden was kneeling in front of the hearth, raking up the coals of last night's fire. Her hair was tangled and her normally luminous skin was the color of chalk except for the fever flags flying across her high cheekbones. With less than her usual ease, Eden pushed herself slowly to her feet.

"Sit down," she said, gesturing toward a camp chair. "It will be a few minutes until the coffee is ready."

"You're sick," Nevada said flatly, starting toward her.

"It's just—"

Eden's explanation ended in a startled sound as Nevada lifted her off her feet and returned her to her mattress and bedding without so much as a word of warning. Gently, implacably, he stuffed her under the covers. Against the dullness of her skin, her eyes appeared unnaturally brilliant.

"Nevada, what—"

Again Eden's words ended in a startled sound. Nevada's hands were beneath her ears, moving below her chin line and down her neck, probing gently, checking for swollen glands.

"Tender?" he asked curtly.

Wordlessly Eden shook her head. Nevada's eyes were so close, so intent, so beautiful in their concern. Her breath came in raggedly and she shivered at the feel of his hands touching her. Two long, elegantly masculine fingers settled over the pulse in her throat and pressed gently.

"Strong but much too fast," Nevada said.

Eden remembered taking Nevada's pulse and feeling it accelerate at her touch. She smiled crookedly and began to give his words back to him.

"If you were a woman—" she began.

"I'm not," he cut in.

"Yes. Definitely. There's a direct correlation between your masculinity and my pulse rate."

For a moment Eden would have sworn that Nevada was surprised. If he was, he recovered instantly.

"Feeling sassy, are we?" he asked in a dry voice.

"I can't speak for you, but in my case any sassiness is temporary."

"I'm glad you realize it. If your temperature isn't about a hundred and two, I'll eat that bedroll."

Eden let out a shaky breath. "Please don't. Even with Baby as a bunkmate I'd get awfully cold."

At the sound of his name, Baby came over, stuck his outrageously cold nose against Eden's neck and whimpered softly. She lifted her hands and rubbed the wolf's big head. Nevada felt a chill condense along his spine when he saw the trembling of her fingers. The pressure of her hands barely dented the wolf's thick fur.

"Damn it, Eden, you're as weak as a baby."

Eyes closed, she shook her head and smiled in Nevada's general direction. "It's just flu. I've survived much worse."

"Not when you were living alone in a cold cabin at the butt end of nowhere," Nevada said harshly.

"Wrong," she said, sighing, no longer fighting her exhaustion. "The last time I was sick I was living in a Yukon cabin that could teach cold to a glacier."

"What?"

"Mom and Dad were Alaskan homesteaders who believed in doing things the hard way."

"They left you alone when you were sick?" Nevada asked in disbelief.

"Dad was working the trap line and Mom was helping

Mrs. Thompson with her new baby. Besides, it was just a cold and Mark was there, too. Then Mark's ski-doo went through the river ice in front of the cabin…."

Eden's voice faded into a yawn. When she spoke again Nevada had to lean down to hear her slow words.

"By the time I helped him home…got his arm splinted… We were pretty sorry puppies for a day or two." She yawned again. "But we made it just fine."

"Splinted his arm?" Nevada asked.

Eden mumbled something that Nevada couldn't understand. Then she shivered and rolled onto her side, wrapping covers around herself.

With a few quick movements Nevada peeled off his heavy shearling coat and put it over her. Then he went to work on the fire. A few minutes later burnished orange flames leaped above the wood, sending heat into the room. With the competence of a man who has spent a lot of time cooking over open fires, Nevada went to work putting together a rich soup.

When Nevada turned back to Eden, she had drifted into a feverish sleep. Frowning, Nevada sat on his heels next to her, watching her intently. Though Eden's skin and lips were dry, she showed no sign of real dehydration. And while her color was chalky, it had none of the ash-gray or yellow tones of serious illness.

When Nevada put his palm on Eden's forehead, she made a murmurous sound and turned toward him as though seeking more of his touch.

Baby whined and nudged his mistress.

"She'll be all right," Nevada said, gently pushing the wolf's long, narrow muzzle away from Eden's cheek. "Let her sleep while I bring in the rest of the supplies. She won't be hungry when I wake her up, but she'll eat."

Eden slept on while Nevada came and went, emptying the truck and filling the cabin with the fragrance of food. She stirred several times when the sharp sounds of an ax striking wood came through the cabin's log walls, but she didn't awaken until Nevada pulled her half-upright across his lap, propped her against his chest and held a steaming mug of soup under her nose.

"Wake up, Sleeping Beauty."

"Not…beautiful," she mumbled.

Nevada disagreed, but he did it silently. "It's just as well, honey. I'm no genteel prince with a magic kiss for you."

Eden grumbled sleepily about being disturbed, yet even as she complained she turned and snuggled against Nevada, trusting him as completely as Carolina had. Without intending to, Nevada found himself setting the soup aside and holding Eden close while one big hand smoothed over her hair and forehead and cheek. He told himself that he was simply seeing if her temperature had dropped, but he didn't believe it. Nevada had never been very good at lying to himself.

"If you're not Sleeping Beauty," he said in a deep voice, "you must be Little Red Riding Hood. Wake up, Red."

Long, sable eyelashes stirred. Eyes that were green and gold and blue and gray, the color of every season, looked up at Nevada.

"You don't look like my grandmother."

"That's because I'm the wolf."

"Goody," Eden sighed, smiling and rubbing her cheek against Nevada's bearded jaw. "I've always had a weakness for furry beasts."

"The weakness is in your head," he retorted, his voice both hard and deep. He forced himself to turn away from the vulnerable spot just behind Eden's ear. "Furry beasts always have sharp teeth to use on tempting little morsels like you."

"Sounds exciting," she said, yawning. Then she made a sound of contentment and let her weight rest fully against Nevada. "Know something? You're much more comfortable than my mattress."

Eden smiled dreamily and curled more deeply into Nevada's lap. As she moved against him, the sleeping bag, extra blankets and coat slid off her shoulders, revealing the firm, curving lines of her breasts against the deep red of her ski underwear. When the chilly air seeped through red cloth, her nipples tightened.

Nevada's heartbeat hesitated for an instant before it resumed at a harder, quicker rate.

"Damn it, Eden, *sit up*."

"Sheesh…what a grouch."

Eden's attempts to sit up involved bracing herself against Nevada. Fever and sleepiness made her clumsy. Her hands slipped and fumbled down the length of his torso before coming to rest on his hard thighs. Even harder male flesh rose insistently only a fraction of an inch away from her right hand.

Nevada closed his eyes and told himself he was glad that Eden's hand hadn't come to rest a fraction of an inch to the left. He didn't believe that lie, either.

Slim fingers braced themselves on the clenched power of Nevada's thighs, but he sensed that Eden's balance was still uncertain, that her hands were sliding…

Abruptly Eden felt herself being lifted off Nevada's lap. Strong hands wrapped the shearling coat firmly around her and buttoned it, imprisoning her arms against her body.

"Warm enough?" Nevada asked through his teeth.

She nodded.

"Good." He grabbed the mug of warm soup. "Open your mouth."

She opened her mouth.

"Drink."

She drank, swallowed, licked her lips and said, "Nevada, what's wrong?"

"Drink."

Silently Eden drank from the mug that Nevada was holding against her mouth. When she finished the soup, she tried to lick the creamy mustache from her upper lip, couldn't reach all of it, and tried again.

Nevada closed his eyes and said something harsh beneath his breath.

"So I'm a little messy," Eden muttered. "What do you expect? I'm not used to being fed. If you'll let me out of this straitjacket I'll feed myself."

Nevada came to his feet in a tightly coordinated rush, stalked to the fire, ladled out another mug of soup and went back to Eden. His jacket was so big on her that she had managed to get her arms through the sleeves even though she was buttoned inside.

And now she was watching him with eyes whose color shifted at each leap of flame. She hadn't a third of his strength, she wasn't two-thirds of his weight, yet she was utterly calm. She trusted him with an unshakable certainty that was as arousing as it was infuriating.

"You just don't get it, do you?" Nevada asked tightly.

"Get what?"

"You're so damned vulnerable," he said, "and too damned sexy. I mean it, Eden. *Don't trust me.*"

She started to speak, looked at his bleak eyes, and shivered. But it wasn't fear that made her tremble, nor was it cold. It was the realization that Nevada was watching her the way a wild animal watches a winter campfire, both lured by and deeply wary of the dancing warmth, easing closer and closer only to snarl and spring back and circle once more, watching what it wants but is too wild and wary to take, watching her with eyes as cold as winter itself.

"I can no more help trusting you than you can help wanting me," Eden said finally. "I'm not nearly as fragile as you seem to think. And…and you must know that I want to touch you, too, Nevada. I'm not very good at hiding how I feel."

Eden watched the centers of Nevada's eyes expand, saw the sudden rush of blood in the pulse beating rapidly at his temple, and cleared her throat.

"May I have some more soup, please?" she asked in a trembling voice. "It's…it's very good."

With great care Nevada placed the mug in Eden's out-stretched hand, stood up and walked out of the cabin.

CHAPTER EIGHT

THE FIRST RED-GOLD TINT OF DAWN HAD barely seeped through the cabin window when Baby scratched at the door, looked toward Eden's sleeping bag, then pawed the door again.

"Lord, Baby," Eden muttered, sitting up, yawning. "Don't you ever sleep?"

Baby whined.

"Stay put," said a deep voice. "I'll let him out."

Eden looked over at the mound of sleeping bag and blankets that was Nevada. "I'm already up. Besides, I've done nothing but lie around since you got here three days ago." She rubbed her eyes and stretched again. "I'm like Baby—ready to prowl."

Nevada didn't bother to argue. He came out of the sleeping bag and got to his feet in an uninterrupted motion, took two long strides and opened the cabin door. Baby flowed outside like a shadow left over from the vanishing night. Nevada shut the door and turned back toward his sleeping bag.

Eden's breath came in with an audible rush when she opened her eyes once more. Nevada wore only black jeans, and all but one of the steel buttons were undone. Hints of golden light caressed him like a lover, emphasizing the shift and coil of powerful muscles beneath smooth skin. Black hair glowed and licked over his torso like dark flames. An odd feeling lanced through Eden, a hunger and a yearning that was unlike anything she had ever experienced.

When Nevada reached for his black flannel shirt and began putting it on, Eden wanted to protest. She also wanted to run her hands over Nevada, to test the strength and resilience of his muscles, to savor all the textures of his midnight hair with her palms and fingertips, to taste his lips, his cheeks, his eyelashes, his shoulders, to trace every velvet shadow on his body with the tip of her tongue....

"Eden? Are you all right?" Nevada stared into the shadows, wondering at the cause of Eden's unnatural stillness.

"Yes," she said faintly.

"You don't sound like it," he said as he rolled up his sleeves. "How does your chest feel? Still tight?"

"I'm fine."

"You won't be if you don't stay warm." Nevada crossed the cabin, knelt, and stuffed Eden back under the mound of covers. "You're shivering. Damn it, are you trying to get pneumonia?"

Eden shook her head. "Don't worry. I'm a long way from pneumonia."

"I knew you believed in fairy tales," he muttered, pulling the blankets up to Eden's chin. "Pneumonia is unpredictable. One minute you've got the flu or a cold and the next minute, *bang,* you're fighting for your life."

Memories sleeted through Eden, ripping away everything but the past. She tried to speak but had no voice. She swallowed and tried again.

"I know about pneumonia."

The resonances of certainty, grief and acceptance in Eden's voice made Nevada's hands pause over her blankets. He looked at her intently. In the increasing light of dawn her eyes were wide, shimmering with tears, unblinking, focused on something only she could see.

He caught a tear on his fingertip. It burned against his skin like a molten diamond.

"Eden," he said softly.

She let out her breath in a ragged sigh and blinked away the tears. "It's all right. It's just that sometimes…sometimes the memories…are stronger than other times."

"Yes," he said simply. "Sometimes they are."

Hazel eyes focused on Nevada. Eden smiled despite the traces of tears still shining on her eyelashes.

"The memories aren't sad, not completely," she said. "Just…bittersweet. Aurora was ten months old, and alive the way only a healthy baby can be. Tears and laughter, going full tilt one minute and sound asleep the next. Sweet little tornado. Her laughter made me think of bright orange poppies."

Eden smiled, remembering, and her smile was as real as her tears had been. Nevada's throat tightened around emotions he had not permitted himself to feel for too many years.

"How long ago," he asked, his voice low.

"Six years. Early in spring. I was sixteen, too old to be a child and not old enough to be anything else," Eden said, looking past Nevada, remembering another time, another place. "My sister, Aurora, was almost one. She got sick the way babies do, sniffles and short temper and endless fussing. Then she got an ear infection, then another cold, another infection, a cough, and each time she fussed less."

Eden hesitated before continuing in a low voice. "A late storm came down out of the Arctic, the temperature dropped seventy degrees and Aurora's breathing changed. We managed to get out on the radio to ask for help, but nothing could fly in that storm. All we could do was keep Aurora warm and pray that the storm broke in time."

Nevada closed his eyes for a moment, understanding all too well the feelings of helplessness and pain that Eden's family had endured. He had seen too many shattered families, shattered villages, shattered lands.

"I was the only one who didn't have a cold," Eden continued in a low voice, "so Aurora was sleeping with me. I was holding her when she died. I held her...for a long time."

The only sound was that of Nevada's big hands smoothing the blankets around Eden's shoulders as he watched her with an intensity that was almost tangible. He had no doubt of the depth and power of her grief. He could feel it beating silently around him, black velvet wings of sorrow and loss.

But he also had seen Eden smile, heard her laugh—and that, too, was genuine. Her joy in life was vivid and complex, generous and oddly serene. That was what had drawn him instantly to her—his absolute certainty that life was a hot golden cataract flowing through Eden, a fire that would burn against any darkness, any ice, any night.

Eden still smiled, although she knew that life was cruel and unpredictable, knew that it had betrayed joy and trust, leaving her to hold a dying child in her arms. She was even able to laugh.

"The ring on your necklace. It belonged to Aurora."

There was no question in Nevada's deep voice, but Eden answered anyway.

"Yes."

"Why."

Again it was not a question, not quite a plea, not fully a demand. Again Eden softly answered.

"I wear Aurora's ring to remind myself that love is never wasted, never futile."

Something stirred deep within Nevada, a part of him so long hidden that he believed it had died. The pain that came was shocking, making it impossible to breathe, much less to speak.

And he wanted to speak. He wanted to argue with Eden. He wanted it so fiercely that his hands clenched on the blankets. Yet he could find no words to counter Eden's certainty, no words to shake her serenity, nothing to equal her laughter; only a bleak, incoherent cry clawing at his soul, a cry of rage or fear or hope...or a wrenching blend of all three.

In a rush of barely controlled power, Nevada stood up and turned away from Eden. Silently she watched while he stirred the banked fire into life with a few harsh strokes, added wood, and walked to the sink. He dipped water from the bucket, primed the pump, and worked the long iron handle as savagely as though he were killing snakes. Water sped up from the hidden well and leaped out of the pump in a rushing crystal stream.

He filled three buckets, a kettle and the coffeepot before he released the pump handle. Buckets and kettle went to the hearth. The coffeepot went on the single-burner backpacking stove Eden had brought. Each move Nevada made was controlled, graceful despite the anger radiating from him like heat from the hearth.

Eden watched Nevada, reminded of the first cougar she had ever seen. It had been caged, and wild within that cage, raking with unsheathed claws at everything that came near.

What is it, Nevada? What did I say to make you so angry?

The question was asked only in the silence of Eden's mind, for she knew Nevada wouldn't answer if she spoke aloud.

After a few minutes Eden groped around in her sleeping bag, found her clothes, and dressed within the cocoon of blankets and bag. Even with prewarmed jeans and a turtleneck sweater, she shivered when she crawled out into the cold air of the cabin. She pushed her stockinged feet into her fleece-lined moccasins, pulled on her jacket and went outside.

The soft closing of the door was like a gunshot in the taut silence of the cabin. Nevada put one more piece of firewood on the flames and sat on his heels in front of the hearth, watching the renewed leap of fire with bleak green eyes. But it wasn't the flames he was seeing. It was Eden's tears, Eden's smile, Eden's lips, Eden's eyes admiring him, wanting him.

Nevada spread his hands before the fire, saw their fine trembling, and balled his fingers into fists. He wanted Eden. He wanted her until he shook with it.

A raw word tore through the silence.

"Other than that, how do you feel?" Eden asked dryly, closing the door behind her.

Nevada spun around and came to his feet with shocking speed, his body poised for defense or attack. He hadn't heard Eden open the door.

He hadn't heard her.

"I must be losing my edge," Nevada said, lowering his hands.

She shrugged and hung her jacket on a nearby nail. "More likely your subconscious figured out I'm no threat to you, so why spend energy staying on guard?"

"No threat," Nevada repeated. Abruptly he had an impulse to laugh that was more shocking to him than the fact that he had been too caught up in his own thoughts to hear the cabin door opening behind him. "Lady, the only threat that matters is the one you don't see coming. That's the one that gets you."

"I'm not big enough to 'get' you." Eden looked past Nevada. "Besides, you can read my mind."

"I can?"

"The buckets."

"What?" he asked, taken off guard once more. Nevada turned and looked at the buckets warming next to the fire as though he had never seen them. In some ways it was true. He had pumped water as a physical outlet, not because they needed three buckets plus a kettle of water warming by the fire. "The buckets make me a mind reader?"

"Sure. You knew I wanted to take a bath. Presto. Bathwater appears."

"Wrong. You're not well enough yet."

"Pucky."

Nevada blinked. "What?"

"Don't try to change the subject. I need a bath. This time you're not going to talk me out of it."

"I didn't talk you out of it last time," Nevada pointed out coolly. "I just said I wasn't going anywhere and you decided not to have a bath after all."

"Um. Well, this time you won't get away with it. If I don't wash my hair it's going to get up and walk off my head."

"Eden—" Nevada began.

"Nope," she interrupted. "No deal. I haven't run a fever for almost two days. I'm having a bath and that's all there is to it."

"What if I stay and watch?"

"I'll blush a lot, but I'll survive."

"You're playing with fire," he said flatly.

"People who are cold tend to do that."

Nevada shook his head in disbelief, hardly able to comprehend that someone as soft and vulnerable as Eden was ignoring the kind of warnings that had made grown men back off. "Has anyone ever mentioned that you're too stubborn for your own good?"

"Frequently. Gives me great faith in the powers of human observation."

Narrowed green eyes swept over Eden's slender body. "Oh, I'm an observant, noticing kind of man, as you pointed out. Right now I'm noticing how hard and tight your nipples get when they're cold. Do they get like that for a man's mouth, too?"

Eden's lips opened but no sound came out. She was too surprised to think coherently, much less speak.

"I've noticed your tongue, too," Nevada continued. "Quick and pink and clever. I'd like to feel it all over, everywhere, every last damned aching inch of me. But most of all I've noticed those long, long legs of yours. I want to be where they meet. I want to sink into you, all the way in, and I want to watch you while I do it. I want it so much I wake up sweating." His pale, crystalline eyes pinned Eden. "Still planning on taking a bath in front of me?"

"You're not—you can't—damn it, Nevada, you won't—"

Nevada hooked his thumbs in his belt loops and waited, watching Eden with eyes that missed nothing and concealed nothing of his response to what he saw.

Eden said something succinct and inelegant, glared at Nevada and stalked past him to the fire. Calmly Nevada joined her and added more wood, redoubling the flames.

"Scrambled eggs or oatmeal?" he asked as though nothing had happened.

"No," she said between her teeth. "Thank you."

"So polite."

"You ought to try it sometime. Works wonders in human relationships."

"I prefer honesty."

"Do you? Then try this." She flashed him a sideways look from brilliant hazel eyes. "I'm not angry because you want me. I'm angry because you *hate* wanting me. Why, Nevada? What is so awful about wanting me?"

"Not having you."

The breath, and much of the anger, went out of Eden in a long sigh. She started to speak, made a helpless gesture of appeal with her hands, and tried again.

"I won't say no to you, Nevada."

"Why? Do you go to bed with every man who wants you?"

"What do you think?"

"I think you're damned fussy about who touches you."

"I think you're right."

"So why me, Eden?"

When Eden opened her mouth to explain the complex, unexpected, seething, surprising mixture of emotions Nevada called out of her, the only words she could think of were very simple.

"I love you, Nevada."

His mouth flattened into a savage line. "That's what I was afraid you were telling yourself. Fairy tales. You can't accept that all there is between us is sex. I wanted you the instant I saw you. You wanted me the same way. Calling it love doesn't change what it is. Sex. Pure and simple and hot as hell."

"You can call it whatever you want."

"But you'll call it love, right?"

"Why do you care what I call it? I'm not asking you to lie to me about how you feel. When you get right down to it, I've never asked you for one damn thing but a bath!"

Nevada kept on talking as though Eden had never spoken. "Let me tell you what the real world is like, fairy-tale girl. The real world is Afghanistan, where you walk through a narrow mountain pass in single file with five handpicked men and arrive at your destination and look around and you're alone, nothing on your back trail but blood and silence. The real world is a place where you fight for what you believe in, and then find out that win or lose, the weak and helpless are still the first to die. The real world is a place where you know a hundred ways to kill a man and not one damned way to save a baby's life."

Eden tried to speak. It was futile. Nevada kept on talking, his eyes like splinters of ice, his voice emotionless, his words relentless, hammering on her, forcing her to hear.

"The real world is a place where you walk into villages with men whose wives and sisters and mothers and daughters have been murdered in ways you can't even imagine, villages where children are diseased and maimed by starvation, villages where babies are too weak to cry because they starved in the womb and their mothers have no milk and by the time you get to them, all you can do with your prayers and medicine and rage is hold those babies until they die and then you bury them and walk away, *just walk away,* because any man who cares for anything enough to be hurt by its loss is a fool."

"Nevada," Eden whispered, reaching for him, wanting to comfort him. "Nevada, I—"

Her words ended with a startled sound when his hands flashed out and pinned her wrists against her sides.

"Don't touch me, Eden," Nevada said in a low voice, but even as he spoke he was leaning down, coming closer to her, so close that all that lay between their mouths was the mingled heat of their breath. "I want you too much. I want you until I can't sleep, can't take a deep breath, can't look at my hands without seeing them on your body, can't—my God, I can't even lick my lips without wondering what you would taste like."

"Find out," Eden whispered against his lips. "Taste me, Nevada."

With a sound that was almost anguished, Nevada lowered his head the final fraction of an inch.

Eden's lips were soft, warm, undefended. They opened for Nevada without hesitation, yielding the secrets of her mouth to him at the first gliding touch of his tongue. Hot, generous, sweet, clean—he could not get enough of her. The changing taste and texture of her mouth lured him deeper and deeper until he could go no farther and yet he still wanted more, so much more. He was straining against her, shaking, tormented by all that he would not allow himself to take.

Then he realized that Eden was trembling, too, and her tears were hot against his lips. He tore his mouth from hers and stepped back, releasing her wrists as though they had burned him. When he licked his lips he tasted the salt of her tears. Something deep within him ached with a surprising pain.

He had tried to stay away from Eden because he had known that all he had to give her was tears. What he hadn't known was that he could still feel pain himself. The realization shocked him.

"Do you understand now?" Nevada asked in a soft voice, but there was nothing of softness in his eyes, his body, his certainty, his memories.

Eden was too shaken by Nevada's passion and his pain to do more than nod her head. At that instant she knew how he felt beyond any doubt or wishful misunderstanding. Her instincts had been right. Nevada was a winter man, his emotions frozen, and he was that way by choice, not accident. He had been stretched to the breaking point in Afghanistan. He had not broken.

And the price of remaining sane had been to walk away from his emotions. They were a weakness in a time and place where only the strongest and most fierce survived. Nevada Blackthorn had survived.

Warrior.

Eden had spoken only in the silence of her mind, yet Nevada's expression changed. He knew her too well, had known her instantly and wanted her with a violence equaled only by his refusal to acknowledge the possibility of love.

Sex, not love, Eden reminded herself, understanding now why Nevada had insisted on making the distinction ruthlessly clear.

Fairy tales. Fairy-tale girl.

Eyes closed, Eden interlaced her fingers to keep from reaching for Nevada in an offer of comfort and healing that he neither wanted nor would permit. Yet somehow she had to free her beautiful trapped cougar without getting ripped to pieces in the process.

If she could free him at all.

There was no guarantee of success. There was just his need and her love and the battle yet to be fought.

Win, lose or draw, she told herself bracingly.

No. It's win or lose, period. Nevada doesn't know any other way.

No second place. No truce. No genteel neutral ground between victory or defeat where two people could meet and shake hands and talk politely about things that didn't matter. Either they both won or they both lost. Whatever the outcome, Nevada would discover that he wasn't the only one willing to fight for what he believed in.

And what Eden believed in was love.

"Coffee's ready. Want some?" Nevada asked.

"Please," Eden said absently, still caught in the instant

she had first understood the risk and necessity of what she must do.

"Back to being polite, huh?" he asked. He crouched over the coffeepot and poured a fragrant stream of coffee into a mug.

Eden gave Nevada a sidelong glance from her place by the hearth and decided it was time to fire the opening shot of her undeclared war.

"Go to the devil, Nevada, but hand over my coffee first."

His mouth lifted at the left corner. Without looking at Eden he set the pot back on the burner and handed her the mug as he turned back to the fire.

"Guess I had that one coming," he said.

"And a few more besides. But I'm feeling generous."

Nevada turned and looked at Eden over his shoulder. "That was the second thing I noticed about you in West Fork. Your smile. Not a bit of calculation in it. Generous."

"My smile was the second thing, huh? So what was the first thing you noticed?"

"I'm a man," Nevada said dryly. "What do you think I noticed?"

"That I was wearing a quilted down jacket?" Eden suggested, her voice as dry as his.

"Yeah, something like that. Then you started walking. You move like a woman."

"Nevada, I *am* a woman."

He shot Eden a glittering green look before he turned back to the fire. "You were the wrong woman in the wrong place at the wrong time—and you walked right up to me."

"You had a beard."

"So did the bartender."

"I liked yours better. It looked sleek and healthy, a wonderful male pelt. I wanted to rub my cheek against it to see if it felt as good as it looked." Eden set aside the coffee mug, stretched and smiled to herself as she fired the second shot. "Then I found out it felt even better than it looked. When you kissed me, your beard was like a thick silk brush on my skin. I liked that, Nevada. It made me wonder what your beard would feel like on my neck, on my bare shoulders, on the inside of my wrists, between my—"

"You just can't stop pushing, can you?" Nevada interrupted roughly.

Eden finished stretching, lowered her arms, and let her fingertips idly brush Nevada's hair. "When you don't leave me any room to move, it's hard not to push."

Nevada hesitated in the act of dropping another piece of wood on the already vigorous fire. When he let go of the wood, there was a shower of sparks. Without a word he rotated the buckets, bringing a cool side to meet the increasing heat of the flames. He stretched out a long arm, picked up the mug of coffee and handed it to Eden again.

"Nervous?" he asked dryly.

"What?"

"You're petting me. That's what you do when you're nervous, isn't it? Pet the nearest thing?"

Eden realized that her fingertips had returned to ruffling Nevada's hair as though he were Baby. "Like I said. It's hard not to push or touch when you're being crowded."

"I didn't know I was crowding you," Nevada said, pinning her with a pale green glance. "In fact, I would have sworn it was the other way around."

For a moment Eden sipped coffee, gathering her scattered thoughts. She had fired the first two shots, yet she felt as though she had just stumbled into an ambush. The combination of passion and calculation in Nevada's eyes was unnerving. Obviously there was more to this kind of skirmish than she had thought. Maybe she would be better off doing as Nevada did—using the kind of honesty that could rock a man back on his heels.

"I'm not used to being told when I can track cats," Eden said, "or when I can take a bath, what I can eat, where I can—"

"You're sick," Nevada interrupted.

"I was sick. I'm well now. I have a very good appreciation of my own physical limits. Being raised in the Yukon does that for you. I'm fine, Nevada. So if you keep me locked up any longer, you'd better be prepared to deal with a major case of the rips."

"The rips?"

"Yeah. I'm like Baby. If I can't tear around outside, I'll tear around inside."

"The rips," Nevada repeated, shaking his head. "Honey, I've never met anyone like you."

"That makes us even," Eden said, watching him over the rim of the mug. "I've never met anyone like you, either. And I've never been kissed like that, heaven and hell and the rainbow burning between..."

She saw the sudden expansion of Nevada's pupils, heard the intake of his breath, sensed the hot leap of his blood.

"Was it like that for you, Nevada?"

For an electric instant Eden thought Nevada was going to pull her down to the hearth and kiss her again. Instead, he came to his feet in a lithe rush, stalked across the cabin, grabbed his jacket and opened the front door.

"I'm going to look for that cougar's den."

"Too much honesty, huh?" asked Eden. "Want me to go back to being polite? Or would you rather I just work off my excess energy by petting you?"

The door closed very softly behind Nevada.

"If Baby gets in your way, send him back to me," Eden called through the door. "I'll frolic with him, instead."

Nevada didn't answer.

Eden went to the window and looked out. Nevada was heading across the clearing with long, determined strides. An ecstatic Baby was leaping around him.

"I think, in military terminology, Nevada just executed a strategic disengagement," Eden said aloud. "Ordinary folks would call it a retreat."

Smiling, she tested the water in the nearest bucket and nodded approvingly. By the time she finished breakfast, the water would be warm enough for a bath.

Two hours later Eden was humming softly, feeling as clean as the sunlight itself. When she went outside to check on the bedding she had draped over the woodpile to air, warm air surrounded her. She shook out Nevada's sleeping bag and flipped it over to soak up more sunshine. The sheet she used to line her own bag was hanging from a rope strung between the cabin and a nearby tree. She touched the sheet. Nearly dry, but not quite. The lacy beige bras were still damp. The pairs of panties were almost dry, but not quite. She decided she could live without underwear for another hour. She went to check on her own bag, which was thrown over a bush in the clearing beyond the cabin. Warm air was everywhere, breathing spring into the day.

With the season's typical capriciousness, a chinook had arrived, sending the temperature soaring into the seventies. Meltwater trickled and glittered and shone everywhere. The sunlight itself was hot. The shade was crisp. The warm wind was a transparent river of wine. The air was rich with the scent of newly revealed earth. Every breath, every instant of being alive, was a sensual feast.

When a hidden bird sang, Eden stopped in the act of reaching for her sleeping bag and closed her eyes, absorbing the piercing, unexpected song with the same intense awareness with which she absorbed the sunlight itself. The bird repeated its call, notes rippling and soaring, transforming the day with music.

There was a rush of air, the near-silent brushing of feet against the ground, and a certainty that she was no longer alone. Eden opened her eyes and turned around.

"Hello, Baby," she said, rubbing the animal's fur, but it was Nevada she was looking at. In the sunlight he looked both dark and fierce, the power of him apparent in even his smallest movement. "Did you find what you were looking for?"

"I narrowed the search area. I'll try again after lunch. With this chinook, the snow is melting fast, even in sheltered places." Nevada's eyes noted the sheen of Eden's pale hair, the delicate color of her cheeks, the subtle radiance of her skin that only health could give. He closed his eyes for an instant, trying to still the hard rush of his blood. It was impossible. "Did you enjoy your bath?"

"Yes. I heated more water for you, in case you were interested."

"I am. Thank you."

Nevada's formality made Eden blink. "You're welcome. Yell when you're finished and I'll make lunch."

Nevada nodded, turned away and walked into the cabin without looking back. Sighing, Eden pulled her sleeping bag off the bush, shook out the warm folds and draped the bag over the bush once more.

Nevada's right. Warfare shouldn't be polite. It's worse that way.

Warfare didn't get any better when conducted over a meal. The hard salami and zesty mustard sandwiches Eden made lost their savor when eaten in stilted silence. She tried conversational gambits that ranged from outrageous to abstruse. Polite, dead-end answers were Nevada's only response.

Finally Eden looked at Baby, who was begging shamelessly at Nevada's knee, and said, "Bite him."

Baby gave his mistress a look of lupine disbelief.

"You heard me," Eden said. "First Nevada complains when I'm polite. Then he walks out on me when I'm honest. Then he uses politeness as a weapon against me. So make lunch out of him. Lord knows the man isn't good for anything else."

Baby ignored her. He rested his long muzzle once again on Nevada's forearm just beneath the rolled-up sleeve.

"Give the man some space, Baby," Eden said. "Can't you see he isn't interested? Quit begging."

Eden winced as her own words echoed in her mind. *Not bad advice. I think I'll take it myself.*

She stood up, opened the cabin door, looked at Baby and said, "Out."

Baby trotted outside, found a pool of deep shade and flopped down. Eden stowed the remaining food in the ice chest and went to stand by the open window, letting sunlight and warm spring wind wash over her.

Nevada finished his sandwich, drank some springwater and began packing his gear and stacking it near the door, ready to be carried to the truck. As the stack grew, Eden realized that Nevada was preparing to return to the ranch headquarters—and there was no guarantee that he would be back at Wildfire Canyon anytime in the future.

The realization sent a chill through Eden. When she had decided to fight the battle on Nevada's terms, she hadn't considered what she would do if he simply withdrew from the field, taking her heart with him and leaving her no chance to touch him in return.

Eden didn't know much about waging war.

Nevada did. He was very good at it.

CHAPTER NINE

NUMBLY EDEN BEGAN STUFFING A LIGHTWEIGHT down vest and windbreaker into her own backpack.

"Going somewhere?" Nevada asked, watching her intently.

"Cat hunting," Eden said, her voice carefully balanced within her aching throat. "It's something I'm good at. Obviously I'm not good at much else. Kissing, for one. Warfare, for another."

Nevada's eyes narrowed at the sadness Eden couldn't wholly conceal, but all he said was "I'll leave a cellular phone with you. Put it in your backpack."

"No, thank you."

"It isn't a request. It's a Rocking M rule. If you're in the backcountry alone, you carry a cellular phone in case you get into trouble. The coverage isn't perfect, but it's better than nothing."

"It didn't help you last week."

"The phone was in my saddlebag."

"Best place for it."

"Don't be pigheaded," Nevada said impatiently.

"Why not? It works for you."

Eden didn't bother to put on her backpack. She just hooked the straps over her arm as she reached for the front door. She barely had the door open when Nevada's hands shot over her shoulders and slammed the door shut again. His speed was literally breathtaking. The corded power of his bare forearms was a blunt statement of his superior strength. He was a warrior accustomed to fighting—and winning.

"I should let you go," Nevada said, his voice husky. "God help me, I tried to. Then I saw you standing in sunlight listening to a bird sing, and your smile was sad and sweet and so beautiful it damn near brought me to my knees."

Nevada's hands on the door became fists, then slowly relaxed once more, revealing the fine trembling in his fingers.

"Fairy-tale girl, all laughter and golden light," Nevada whispered against Eden. His lips brushed her hair, the curve of her ear, the warmth of her neck. "I'm worlds too hard for you, but I want you until my hands shake."

Silently Eden lifted her own hands, showing their trembling to Nevada. When he saw, he breathed a word that could have been either curse or prayer. She started to turn toward him, only to be pinned against the door by the full length of Nevada's powerful body.

"Think hard before you turn around," he said, his voice rough with the violence of his blood rushing. "I'm not offering you love and happily ever after." Slowly Nevada lowered his head, found the nape of Eden's neck, and bit her with exquisite care. "But when I'm finished, your hands won't be shaking anymore."

Even as the primitive caress shivered through Eden, she found herself freed, no hard masculine torso pinning her, no powerful arms confining her, nothing but the certainty that Nevada was standing barely a hand's breadth away, waiting for her answer. Slowly she let the backpack straps slide from her arm and turned toward him.

The look in Nevada's eyes made Eden's breath stop. With a muffled cry she reached for him even as he reached for her and lifted her, bringing her to his hungry mouth. She slid her arms around his neck and said his name in the instant before his kiss claimed her, taking from her the ability to talk, to think, to breathe.

Eden didn't care. All she wanted was to hold Nevada and to be held by him, to taste him and be tasted in turn, to feel the hardness and restraint of his body against hers. Her fingers smoothed the sleek pelt of his hair and beard before finding his powerful shoulders. Making soft, approving sounds, she kneaded the bunched muscles of his arms, glorying in Nevada's strength even as she gave him her own heat and the sweetness of her mouth in return.

Nevada took everything he wanted from the kiss and discovered that Eden had more to give, much more than he had ever found with any kiss, any woman. Eden's response to him was as loving and generous as summer, a pleasure that increased with each heartbeat, doubling and redoubling until he was focused only in the expanding, timeless instant of the kiss. Urgently he savored Eden's gift, tasting and caressing and enjoying her with slow movements of his tongue, luring her deeper and deeper into passion until her breathing was ragged and her arms were locked around him. Breathing harshly, swiftly, Nevada held on to Eden as though he expected her to be ripped from his arms at any instant.

Finally Nevada lifted his head and let Eden slide down his body, making no attempt to conceal the hard length of his arousal, shuddering openly with pleasure when her hips moved over his as he lowered her feet to the floor. Then he held her tightly, fiercely, while he fought for breath, for control, for the discipline of mind and body that he had learned at such great cost and had taken for granted for so many years.

"My God," Nevada said huskily.

He forced himself to loosen his arms from around Eden. One big hand stroked her hair as he let out his breath in an explosive hiss.

"Nevada?" Eden said, hugging him hard, afraid that he would turn away from her. "What's wrong?"

"Nothing. Everything. You surprised the hell out of me, Eden."

"I did?"

Nevada threaded his fingers through her pale, soft hair, tugging gently backward until Eden's face was turned up to his.

"Yes," he said simply. He caught her lower lip between his teeth, bit gently, and shuddered even as she did. "You wanted me."

Shivering, Eden whispered, "What?"

"I could taste it, feel it, see it. *You wanted me.*"

She watched Nevada with uncertain hazel eyes. "Is that wrong?"

He looked down at her, sensing her confusion as clearly as he had sensed the depth of her passion.

"No, it isn't wrong," Nevada said. "It's just…surprising. No woman has ever kissed me that way. No calculation, nothing held back, just a kiss as hot and honest as fire. Then I was kissing you the same way and you burned even hotter and so did I and it just kept on, hotter and brighter. I could have taken you right there, straight up. God knows I wanted to." A faint tremor rippled through his body. "It was a near thing."

Wide-eyed, still uncertain, Eden watched Nevada, trying to understand.

"You don't get it, do you?" he asked.

She shook her head.

"I didn't come up to Wildfire Canyon expecting to have sex with you," Nevada said bluntly. "In fact, I deliberately emptied out my pockets before I came up here so I wouldn't be tempted to touch you. Well, that didn't work, and now I have no way to keep from getting you pregnant. What about you? Can you protect yourself?"

Eden shook her head again.

Despite the hunger blazing in his eyes, Nevada's mouth kicked up at the left corner. "I didn't think so. You don't sleep with men much, do you?"

For the third time Eden's head moved in a silent negative.

"It's a good thing," he said, bending down to her mouth once more, "that there's more than one way to skin this particular cat."

"What?"

Nevada hesitated, lifted his head enough to see Eden's expression, and asked, "Just how experienced are you, fairy-tale girl?"

She bit her lip and looked at him rather warily. "Are we speaking of practical or intellectual experience?"

"Practical."

"Not much."

"How much is not much?"

"Not. Much."

Nevada whistled softly between his teeth, then said, "You're a virgin, aren't you?"

"That shouldn't matter," Eden said. "Every girl starts out that way."

"My God" was all Nevada could think of to say. He looked at Eden in a combination of disbelief and wonder.

"Don't worry," she said, exasperated. "Virginity isn't contagious."

"I'm not contagious, either," he shot back, "but that's not something you need to worry about."

"I don't understand."

"You're going to stay a virgin."

"But I don't want—"

Nevada kept talking. "You'll be a very experienced sort of virgin, but a virgin just the same."

"What does that mean?"

Nevada's big hands came up, framing Eden's face. He looked from her puzzled hazel eyes to her generous mouth. Her lips were still flushed with the kiss that had taught Nevada more than he thought he had left to learn about men and women and passion. He wondered what else he would learn, what he could teach, what discoveries awaited his exploration of his own private, passionate Eden.

The narrowed green blaze of Nevada's eyes as he watched her mouth made shimmers of sensation curl from Eden's breastbone to her knees. She felt like a tightly furled bud being discovered by the first, searching heat of spring's potent sun.

"Nevada," she whispered. "Aren't you going to kiss me?"

"Do you want to kiss me again?"

"Want?" Eden shivered and laughed softly, almost wildly, wondering how she could make Nevada understand feelings that were so new, so fierce, that she had no names for them. "When I grabbed your wrist to keep you from killing that cowboy in West Fork and you looked at me...you *saw* me, Nevada, all the way into me, and then you let me stop you, let me *see* you in return. Nevada," Eden breathed against his lips, standing on tiptoe, "Nevada, I was born for you and you were born for me. I want it all with you, everything, heaven and hell and the rainbow burning between."

With a low sound, Nevada bent and took Eden's mouth, giving her his own in return. When the warmth of her tongue touched his, Nevada's arms tightened, lifting her, bringing her whole body into the embrace. His hips moved slowly against her once, twice, and then he shuddered and eased her down until she was standing on her own feet once more. Holding her tightly, fighting to control his wild response, Nevada tried to end the kiss, but the pleasure of sliding his tongue into Eden's satin sweetness was too great to deny himself.

Just once more. Then I'll stop and catch my breath. Just once...

The hungry, gliding return of Nevada's tongue drew a soft moan from Eden. Slowly he took complete possession of her mouth once more, then began to retreat from her. But she didn't want the kiss to end. She needed more of his taste, his caresses, his elemental male passion. Instinctively her teeth closed on his tongue, silently demanding that he stay within her.

When Eden felt the response that ripped through Nevada at the unexpected caress of her teeth, she would have smiled, but his hands had shifted on her body, finding and stroking her breasts, sending burst after burst of pleasure through her. Her teeth released him as her breath came in with a sound of surprise and passion and she shuddered all the way to her core.

Hard, searching, hungry, Nevada's tongue claimed Eden once more, stroking the sultry softness of her mouth with rhythms of penetration and retreat. His hands moved over her breasts, long fingers stroking, kneading, teasing her until her nipples became a velvet hardness. When he plucked softly at them, the bursts of sensation that had been rippling through Eden merged into hot currents of pleasure that turned her bones to honey.

"Nevada, I can't stand up," Eden said raggedly as she clung to his arms, dizzy with the violence of her own response.

"Don't even try. I can hold you, Eden," Nevada said almost roughly, watching her, feeling her knees sag and at the same time feeling his own strength pouring through his body like a river of fire. "I could hold you in one hand. And I will, but not yet. There are other things I want to do first. A hundred of them. A thousand...oh, God, Eden, what are you doing to me?"

Eden opened her eyes, saw Nevada watching her, and wondered how she had ever thought his eyes bleak or cold. They were hot, burning, as hungry as his kiss had been.

"Put your arms around my neck," Nevada said, moving Eden's hands even as he spoke. "Hold on to me."

His hands moved once more, stroking her from hips to shoulders and back again, pressing her closer and closer to his body until she felt the urgency of his arousal. Her response was an instinctive, supple movement of her hips that dragged a groan from deep within him. His arms tightened, locking their bodies together while he moved against her once, twice, three times, and each time he promised himself it would be the last.

And each time it was not.

"Open your mouth and kiss me," Nevada said hoarsely, bending down to Eden. "I have to be inside you and that's the only way. *Kiss me.*"

Eden gave Nevada what he wanted, needing the urgent joining as much as he did. When the world shifted and spun beneath her feet she simply clung more tightly to him, her arms fierce around his neck. He held her close and hard even after he lowered her to his camp mattress and deepened the hungry melding of mouths. He wanted her with a force that he no longer questioned, for thought was impossible. It was all he could do to control himself.

After a long time Nevada shuddered and slowly, reluctantly, ended the kiss. He lifted his head and let breath hiss out between his teeth. Nothing had ever tempted him the way Eden did at that instant, lying warm and undefended in his arms, wanting him until she trembled with it.

"I should have taken that bath in ice water," Nevada said, his eyes closed and his voice rough with his own arousal. When his eyes opened he looked from Eden's mouth to the pulse beating in her throat and the taut nipples pressing up against the green cotton of her blouse. "But it wouldn't have done any good."

"It wouldn't?" Eden asked huskily. "I thought a cold bath always worked."

Nevada shook his head as he bent down to her breasts. "When you throw a bucket of water on a wildfire, all you get is steam."

His teeth closed delicately around one of her nipples, drawing a ragged gasp of surprise from Eden as pleasure streaked through her body, arching her against Nevada in sensual reflex.

"Wildfire," Nevada said thickly, arching into Eden in return. "Clean and beautiful and hotter than hell. Are you going to let me undress you or do you want to play it safe?"

"I'm always safe with you, Nevada. No matter what. I knew that the first time I saw you."

Thick, black lashes swept down, concealing the smoldering green of Nevada's eyes. Eden's hands stroked his hair, his beard, his mustache, and she smiled as she gently kissed him.

"Undress me, Nevada," she whispered, touching the tip of her tongue to his lips. "I've wanted to feel your beard on my skin for so long. I have to...feel you."

His hands moved from Eden's throat to her waist. Cloth fell away, revealing the creamy feminine curves of her breasts. Being bared to the waist was new to her. She blushed until she saw the look in Nevada's eyes. The passion and appreciation in his glance made her forget that she had never given herself in this way before.

The necklace with its tiny ring of braided gold gleamed softly against Eden's throat. Nevada bent and brushed the small ring with his lips, then pierced the golden circle with the tip of his tongue, touching the warm skin beneath. The intimacy of the instant made pain and pleasure twist deeply inside him, foretaste of what would happen if he let control slip from him.

Nevada knew he should stop now, leaving Eden as untouched as he had found her; and he knew he would not, could not walk away. Not yet. She was too beautiful, too warm, and he had been too long without warmth and beauty.

His hands moved, skimming the curves and peaks of Eden's bare breasts. She gasped as something deep within her shimmered and burst into fire. With a combination of hunger and anticipation, Nevada watched her rosy nipples tighten beneath his touch until they pouted and begged for his mouth. But he had seen Eden's first blush, sensed the instant of uncertainty when her breasts were bared to his eyes, his hands.

"I could hold you down and devour you," Nevada said huskily, aching to taste all the shades of pink and cream, to know all the feminine textures of Eden's body. "And you know it, don't you? Would you mind my mouth on you? Talk to me, Eden. I don't want to shock you or frighten you."

Eden tried to speak just as Nevada's fingertips delicately squeezed one pink crown. A shivering, hot sensation raced through her. She pressed his hands more closely to her breasts and looked into his eyes.

"I'm not frightened, Nevada. I know that you'll never use your strength against me, and that's all that matters."

Eden lifted one hand and ran her fingertips over Nevada's beard, over his mustache, over his lips, then dipped into the sultry heat of his mouth in a sensuous foray that made his breath break. She laughed softly at his surprise.

"As for shocking me," Eden whispered, "some of the thoughts I'm having right now just might shock *you*. I'm inexperienced, not frightened or repelled. Touch me however you want to. Teach me how you want to be touched. Because I want to touch you, Nevada. I want to give you what you want, what you need, everything you ever dreamed. I want...everything."

For long moments Nevada fought a pitched battle for self-control. Eden couldn't know what she was doing to him, what she was offering him, what he wanted so fiercely since he had seen her walking toward him in West Fork and heard summer call to him in a husky voice.

Eden was a gift he shouldn't take.

She was a gift he couldn't refuse.

"Eden..."

Nevada tried to say more. No words came that equaled his need. What did come was a silent vow that he would unwrap her gift gently, using the discipline learned in war to bring pleasure rather than pain to the woman who was watching him with all the colors of life in her eyes, all the passions of living in her voice, every emotion he had vowed never to feel whispering to him, promising him...everything.

Heaven and hell and the rainbow burning between.

Nevada curled his tongue around Eden's caressing finger, sucked, bit gently, and released her.

"Does that mean you won't mind if I take off your shoes and socks?" he asked softly.

Eden smiled.

With a swift motion Nevada shifted until he was kneeling at her feet. Before Eden could take a deep breath he had slipped off her shoes and slid his index fingers beneath the top of her socks, circling her ankles, stroking her, making her gasp at the unexpected sensitivity of her own skin. With a smooth movement he stripped her socks away, leaving her feet naked. He fitted a palm against the arch of each foot, rubbed slowly, and watched unexpected pleasure transform Eden's expression.

"You know my body better than I do," she said. "Your hands are so warm and hard. I love your hands, Nevada."

He turned and rubbed his beard against her instep, heard her breath break, felt her shiver. His teeth closed gently while the tip of his tongue drew a line of fire beneath her arch. Her toes curled and she made a breathless sound. Slowly he released her feet. His hands stroked from her ankles up the length of her legs and then on to the waistband of her jeans. There he stopped and looked into her eyes.

"Whatever you want," Eden said, huskily. "Just tell me what to do, Nevada. Tell me how to please you, too."

"Your trust..." Nevada's eyes closed, then opened brilliant with an emotion that was as great as his passion and as deep as his pain. "Fairy-tale girl, having you give yourself to me is more pleasure than I've ever known."

Nevada bent and brushed his mouth over Eden's lips, the tiny ring lying in the hollow of her throat, the taut velvet tips of her breasts. Soft sounds came from her, sighs like flames rippling higher as her jeans were smoothed caressingly down her body by Nevada's hard and gentle hands. When Eden realized that she was naked and he was looking at her, she trembled. He fitted his palm over her pale, soft triangle of curls and eased his long fingers between her legs, holding her in one hand, covering her vulnerable softness completely.

"It's all right," Nevada whispered against Eden's mouth. "You're not naked anymore."

His hand moved gently, rocking against flesh that was already humid, sensitized. Her breath broke, caught, broke again as something shimmered and burst softly, repeatedly, inside her, melting her against his hand. He felt the unmistakable heat of her response and groaned even as he searched through the hot curls.

"Kiss me, Eden. Let me inside you."

Eden parted her lips and felt the hot, gliding penetration of Nevada's tongue and his finger at the same time. The startled sound she made was transformed into a throaty cry of passion that he drank as he deepened the twin caresses, exploring and pleasuring her with the same slow movements. The repeated sensual forays sent more shimmering waves expanding through her, melting her around him.

All thought of shyness fled Eden, leaving her in the grip of enthralling passion. When Nevada's touch redoubled, filling her, Eden shivered and cried out. He drank that cry, too, and his caresses deepened as his thumb slid over the sleek hard nub of desire he had called from her softness.

Sensual lightning searched through every cell in Eden's body, drawing a surprised cry from her. Deliberately Nevada closed his teeth on her neck, both distracting her and paradoxically increasing the intensity of her body's response to the hot, intimate movements of his hand. His thumb returned again and again, spreading the liquid fire of her response, teasing her, inciting her, urging her higher and higher, drawing the sensual tension in her tighter and tighter until finally her breath stopped and pleasure burst, drenching her with sweet fire.

Gently Nevada withdrew his touch. He gathered Eden against himself and held her, trying to ignore the violence of his own unsatisfied need. It was impossible. Every breath he took was spiced with her fragrance, infused with her warmth, and the soft weight of her body against his made him burn.

After several minutes Eden sighed, stirred, and said softly, "You were right. My hands aren't shaking anymore." She kissed the base of Nevada's neck and felt the instant speeding of his pulse and the shiver that went through his body. "But yours still are."

"I'll live," he said tightly.

"I'm glad to hear that, because I'm going to need your help." She slid from Nevada's arms and went to work on the laces of his walking boots.

"Eden, what are you doing?"

"Taking off your boots."

"I can see that," he said roughly.

She smiled. "I thought you could." She pulled off one boot and sock, then the other. "Watch closely and you can see me taking off your jeans, too."

Nevada's hands flashed out, grabbing Eden's wrists as she reached for his waistband. Smoldering green eyes searched her face.

"You don't have to," he said.

"Would it shock you to know that I want to? You have a beautiful body, Nevada. Touching you would be like stroking a big cat, all steely muscle and satin pelt."

Nevada's eyes closed as he bit back a groan of need. The realization of how close he was to the limits of his self-control shocked him.

"Not now, Eden," he said roughly.

She leaned forward, bracing herself against Nevada's hard

torso. Her mouth sought his. When his lips refused to open, she ran the tip of her tongue across them.

"Yes, now," she breathed.

"You ask too much of me," Nevada said in a low, savage voice. "What happens if half a loaf isn't enough for me? What if I lose control and take you? I could get you pregnant!"

As Eden looked down the length of Nevada's body, her eyes changed, becoming a luminous golden green. "Yes, you certainly could."

The approval in Eden's voice was as seductive as the glide of her tongue over his lips had been. Nevada closed his eyes, no longer able to bear the sight of Eden kneeling naked by his side. He wanted her hands all over his skin, he wanted her mouth, he wanted her hot, silky body fitted to him.

Nevada didn't know he had released Eden's hands until he heard the first metal snap on his shirt open. The other snaps followed in slow succession, for Eden was enjoying each new bit of masculine territory that was revealed by the steady retreat of his black flannel shirt. Finally she tugged the shirttails free of his jeans and ran her hands almost greedily over his chest.

The pleasure Eden took in touching Nevada made the air wedge in his throat. She was smiling dreamily while her fingers kneaded through the wedge of black hair that began at his collarbone and narrowed to a finger's width just above his navel. When she smoothed her way back to Nevada's chest and bent to kiss him, her breasts swayed against him with soft invitation. She shivered as the cushion of hair on his chest teased her nipples to life once more.

"I'm new to this," Eden whispered, moving again, this

time deliberately, increasing the sweet friction of her breasts against Nevada's chest. "But I'm assuming that men and women like the same kind of touching." Her hands searched through the rough silk of his chest hair, seeking and finding the flat male nipples, teasing them into hard points. "If I'm wrong, let me know."

Nevada's breath hissed between his teeth as pleasure lanced through his body, tightening it as surely as the male nipples hardening beneath Eden's fingertips. This time when her tongue traced his lips, they opened hungrily, both accepting and demanding a deep mating of mouths. By the time the kiss ended, his skin was slick with a sultry sheen of passion and he was breathing much too hard.

Knowing he shouldn't, needing Eden too much to stop himself, Nevada lifted her astride his half-naked body and took the pink tip of one breast into his mouth. As he shaped her with the changing pressures of teeth and tongue, he felt the sudden arching of her back, the clenching of her thighs, and the secret rain of her passion. He groaned and pulled her more deeply into his mouth, loving her responsive flesh.

"I'm supposed to be—pleasuring you—not the other way around," Eden said, fighting for the breath that had deserted her without warning.

After a last, lingering love bite, Nevada released her breast and whispered, "Turning you on pleasures me."

Before Eden could answer, Nevada's mouth moved to her other breast. He licked its pink peak until Eden shivered and her nipple tightened in a rush that made her moan. His lips parted hungrily as he took all of her sweet flesh that he would into the heat and darkness of his mouth.

"It's dangerous, though," Nevada said finally, his voice thick.

He released Eden with a slow reluctance that was itself a caress. She trembled again, and again Nevada felt her hot, secret rain against his naked skin. He swore softly, shockingly, even as one hand traced her spine to the small of her back and from there down the warm cleft below until she gasped in pleasure once more.

"Too damned dangerous," he whispered.

"W-why?"

One of Nevada's hands flattened between Eden's shoulder blades, pressing her tightly against his chest, while his other hand explored the warmth that now lay open to his touch. Eden's breath went out in a moan as Nevada caressed the swollen, sultry flesh that had known only his touch. His fingertips glided inside, drawing forth more of Eden's secret rain.

Nevada's hand retreated, returned, caressed, and when Eden moaned, so did he. His hand retreated and there was a muted sound of metal buttons opening one at a time. Gently, inexorably, Nevada's hands eased Eden's weight farther down his body until the hard length of his arousal pressed up between her legs. Only the thickness of his underwear prevented the joining of their bodies.

The barrier was not nearly enough for safety.

"That's why it's dangerous," Nevada said savagely.

For a moment Eden couldn't answer. The elemental fitting of male against female had just taught her how much had been missing from her previous taste of passion. The realization was dizzying, like the heat spreading up in waves from between her thighs, wildfire melting her. Instinctively she moved her hips, rocking slowly, softly, hotly, getting as close as she could to the hard male flesh despite the barrier of cloth.

Nevada had meant to shock Eden from her passion with the blunt reminder of his arousal, but he was the one who was shocked. The melting response of Eden's body spread through the thin barrier between them as though nothing were there at all.

And then nothing was.

A sweep of his hands, a muscular twist of his body and Nevada lay naked between Eden's legs. She made a soft sound of discovery and approval at the new masculine territory he had given to her. He watched through narrowed green eyes while her fingertips caressed and traced hot satin skin, learning the contours of his hunger, capturing the single drop of passion he could not contain.

Eden lifted a fingertip to her lips, touched it to her tongue. "Now I know what life tastes like."

A groan was dragged out of the depths of Nevada's soul. His hands moved, lifting, seeking, finding, joining his body with Eden. He tried not to join with her completely. Then he saw that she was watching him take her and her eyes were like sunrise, burning away darkness, hungry for the day to come. Her name was torn from him and he pierced the veil of her innocence in a single incandescent instant.

Eden's breath unraveled as she accepted the transformation, taking all of Nevada until she was hot and sleek around him, fully alive and lush with the secret rain of her passion, and his name was a chant on her lips. As she bent to kiss him, the motion shifted her body around him, caressing him with silky urgency, calling to him in a communication far older and more potent than words.

"Don't move," Nevada said hoarsely.

"Why?" Eden breathed, moving, shivering, moving again, because she had never felt anything so perfect as being joined with the man she loved.

"I can't—control—"

Even as Nevada's voice broke he reached for Eden, drawing her mouth down to his, hungry for every bit of her. He rolled over swiftly, taking her with him, pinning her with his hips, making it impossible for her to move. Shaking with the violence of his restraint, Nevada began to withdraw from Eden.

But when only a last, tantalizing fraction joined them, Nevada found he couldn't force himself to leave Eden completely. Body rigid, he fought for the self-control that had been his only weapon and defense against life's treachery.

Eden's voice broke over Nevada's name. She shivered and whispered fragments of words, passionate sounds without meaning, pleading and demanding, knowing only that she must be completely joined with him again or die.

"Once more, fairy-tale girl," Nevada breathed against Eden's lips. "Just once."

Slowly he pressed into Eden again, filling her, feeling her cling to him with tiny, hot movements that were as involuntary as the wild beating of her heart. He withdrew even more slowly, and once again could not force himself to leave her entirely. Fists clenched, eyes tightly shut, skin gleaming with sweat, Nevada fought to make his body obey the demands of his mind.

Then Eden moaned and the wild, sensual rain of her release bathed Nevada in fire, burning through all possibility of control. With an anguished sound he thrust into her once more, filling her, giving himself to her with each elemental surge of his body until the gift was finally complete.

And then Nevada lay spent on Eden's breast, felt their hearts beating together, tasted their mingled breaths, and understood the full extent of his self-betrayal.

My God, how could I be such a fool?

The only answer was as bitter as it was true. The self-discipline that had been the very core of Nevada's survival had been breached at the same instant as the frail barrier of Eden's innocence. He could not have been more foolish. She could not have wounded him more savagely if she had slid a knife between his ribs into his heart.

Silently Nevada withdrew from Eden, dressed swiftly and walked away. With each step he prayed he would have the strength to build his defenses once more, and this time build them so high and so deep that he would never again be touched by the devastation of Eden's sweet and fatal fire.

CHAPTER TEN

AS ALWAYS WHEN BABY WAS AROUND, Eden woke up at dawn. As had become her habit in the past week, she looked automatically to the place where Nevada's bedroll had been.

It was empty.

It had been empty for seven days. She had no reason to believe it wouldn't always be empty. Nevada had made love to her, made her cry out with the pleasure and beauty of his touch—and then he had left without a word. He hadn't been back since.

Silently Eden asked the question that had been aching inside her every moment since she had awakened alone.

Why did you leave, Nevada? When I asked you why you hated wanting me, you told me it was because you didn't have me. Then we made love and you walked away as though nothing had happened. Why, Nevada? Didn't I please you?

Blinking back the tears that would do no good, Eden got up and quickly began preparing her breakfast. Her breath made silver-white plumes in the cabin's cold air. The chinook had been followed by a cold northern wind that had settled in as though it meant to stay until June. Last night a thin veil of snow had fallen once more over the land, making the ground glitter whitely.

"If that mama cougar has gone hunting, we'll find her tracks. Then I'll finally find her den. Right, Baby?" Eden asked, her voice husky from lack of use.

The big animal's ears pricked alertly at her first word. His yellow eyes had a gemlike clarity as they followed Eden's every motion until breakfast was eaten and the cabin was put in order.

"Ready to go tracking?"

Instantly Baby was on his feet, vibrating with eagerness. He pawed at the front door.

"I thought you would be. This time let's find something bigger than a bobcat."

Baby whined and pranced, understanding only that his favorite activity was about to begin.

Vowing to think only about cougars rather than the man who had touched her soul and then walked away as though nothing had happened, Eden opened the door and let Baby out. He shot across the clearing and raced into the sparse forest like a low-flying shadow.

Eden slipped on her backpack and walked quickly out into the light. The tracks Baby left were crisp, clear, and un-necessary. She knew where he was going—to the creek in the bottom of a ravine, and up the opposite slope to the base of the big fir tree where the cougar had first been spotted.

The cat had managed to elude her trackers since the wild chase two weeks ago.

While looking for the mama cougar, Eden had found the tracks of two other cougars, photographed them, logged them, and followed them as far as possible. One of the cougars had been a young cat searching for territory that was unoccupied by other cougars. The boundary markers left by resident cougars had discouraged the young cat, pushing it along until it was beyond the boundaries of Eden's study area.

The second cougar whose tracks Eden had found was apparently a permanent resident, but it didn't have a den, which meant that it wasn't a female with cubs. Cougars without cubs covered as much as thirty miles in a day. Following such animals was very difficult, even when Baby's nose was thrown into the effort. In bad weather, tracking cats without radio collars was impossible.

Eden had pinned her hopes on Nevada's belief that the "big tree cougar" was a mama. The fact that the cat had vanished for the past two weeks was encouraging rather than discouraging. It probably meant that the fir tree was more toward the edge of the cougar's territory than in its center, and the cubs were keeping her close to home. But a mama cougar nursing cubs had to eat to keep up her own strength, which meant she had to go out and hunt. Hunting cats left tracks, especially in freshly fallen snow.

When Eden reached the big tree, Baby was casting about for fresh scent. When he found none, he looked to Eden. She whistled. Baby shot off along the shoulder of the rise, quartering a new area. She followed his progress, whistling or calling occasional instructions, communicating with him in a code that the two of them had worked out over years of hunting together.

Three hours later and seven miles distant from the big tree, Baby struck fresh tracks. His howl electrified the silent land. Instantly Eden whistled for Baby to return to her. He obeyed on the run, mouth wide, pink tongue lolling, laughing up at her when he found her.

At Eden's signal, Baby fell in step at her left heel. So long as Baby hadn't been penned up for days, he was more than happy to collaborate on the hunt. In the past week, he had gotten plenty of exercise. Eden had spent as little time as possible within the cabin, for it was haunted by Nevada's absence.

A few minutes later Eden was studying the tracks Baby had found. They were indeed fresh. More important, they had been left by the cougar Baby had once treed. The slightly oversize toe on the cat's left front paw was unmistakable. Eagerly Eden followed the tracks, moving quickly. The forest thinned even more, giving way to a boulder-strewn, south-facing slope. The tracks suddenly became very close together, almost overlapping. Abruptly the tracks dug in hard and deep—and vanished.

Eden paced off the length of empty snow until the tracks began again and whistled soft approval.

"Thirty-three feet in a single bound. Not bad for a young female."

Through binoculars, Eden scanned the landscape immediately in front of her. The wind gusted, shifting and swirling down the slope, blowing from her back rather than across her face.

Suddenly Baby threw back his head and howled.

"Quiet," Eden said without putting down the glasses.

Baby yapped and danced.

"Heel."

Baby heeled. And whined very softly.

"Settle down, Baby," Eden said impatiently, still scanning the landscape. "What's gotten into you?"

"Me."

The sound of Nevada's deep voice made Eden spin around and stare in disbelief. The first thing she noticed was that Nevada had a rifle slung across his back. The second thing she noticed was his eyes. They were as cold as the wind, as dispassionate as the sky, and full of shadows so bleak they made Eden want to cry out in pain.

"There was a decent tracking snow," Nevada said, "so Luke sent me back up here to help you."

Like his eyes, his voice lacked emotion.

"Sent you," Eden repeated. "I see."

She turned back and began scanning the landscape with a composure that was pure desperation. Her heart was beating much too hard, too fast, and her hands would have shaken if she hadn't gripped the binoculars until her knuckles showed white.

Luke sent me. Sent me. Sent me.

The words echoed in Eden's mind, slicing into her. Nevada couldn't have made it clearer that he hadn't sought her out for any reason other than a direct order from the owner of the Rocking M.

"Tell Luke thank-you, but it's not necessary," Eden said when she could trust her voice once more. "Baby and I do our best work alone."

"Luke didn't ask if you needed me. He told me to check on you."

"You have. I'm fine."

Narrowly Nevada surveyed the straight line of Eden's back. He heard her words, but he couldn't accept them. Her voice belonged to a stranger, flat where Eden's had been vibrant, thin where hers had been rich.

"You don't sound fine," he said.

She said nothing more.

Nevada swore beneath his breath. He walked silently up to Eden, not wanting to get any closer to her but unable to stop himself. As he moved, his body was tight with the conflict that had been tearing him apart since his self-control had broken and he had taken and surrendered to Eden in the same passionate instant.

"Damn it, I didn't want it to be this way," Nevada said harshly. "I didn't want you to be hurt."

Eden lowered the glasses. They were useless anyway, for she was crying too hard to see anything but her own tears.

"Is that why you left without so much as a word to me?" she asked. "To keep from hurting me?"

"What was I supposed to do, tell you fairy tales about love? I won't lie to you, fairy-tale girl. You knew it when you came to me at the cabin and burned me alive."

Abruptly Nevada stopped speaking. Memories of Eden's incandescent sensuality were lightning strokes of pain that scored him repeatedly, giving him no peace, ripping through new defenses and old, scoring across the unhealed past, threatening to touch him as he had vowed never to be touched again.

And he fought his hunger as he had never fought anything except death itself. Wanting, not wanting, fighting himself and her, trapped in an agonizing vise, Nevada turned Eden to face him and saw the silver glitter of her tears.

"Don't you understand?" Nevada whispered savagely. *"I can't be what you want me to be."*

She closed her eyes. "A man who believes in love."

"Yes," he said flatly. His hard thumbs tilted up her face to his and his fingers trembled against her skin. "I told Luke I wouldn't come up here. He told me I could take his orders or I could pack up and leave the Rocking M. I packed, but I couldn't let you run me off the only home I have, so I came up here knowing I would hurt you all over again."

"Nevada," Eden whispered, reaching to him.

"No! I don't want to hurt you again, but it will happen just the same unless you stop asking me to kiss you every time you look at my mouth, stop asking me to touch you every time you look at my hands, stop asking..." Nevada's eyes closed, then opened once more, clear and hard and cold. "I would sell my soul not to want you, Eden, but the devil took my soul a long time ago and I want you like hell burning."

As Eden looked at Nevada's silver-green eyes, a chill moved over her. He was a wild animal caught in a trap...and she was that trap. The knowledge was in his eyes, shadows and bleakness, watchfulness and calculation and fear, and most of all in his pain, an agony that drew Nevada's mouth into a hard line.

His pain was as real as the unsheathed claws of his honesty.

Eden took a deep, shaking breath and acknowledged the truth. "I understand. You won't love me. I can't help loving you. Too bad, how sad, and all of that. Meanwhile, the earth turns and the seasons change and babies are born and some die and there's not a damn thing we can do about that, either."

"Eden…"

She waited, hoping in spite of herself.

"Eden, I…" Nevada made an odd, almost helpless gesture with his hand.

After a few more moments Eden smiled with the bittersweet acceptance that she had learned after Aurora's death.

"It's all right, Nevada. I was warned going in, and several other times along the way, and that's more than we usually get out of life. You don't have to love me. I'm yours without it, if you want me. And even if you don't."

Nevada's jaw tightened against the pain of Eden's acceptance of what he was and was not. "That's not…" he began, then his throat constricted again, taking away his ability to speak.

"Fair?" she suggested.

Eden's smile was as sad and enigmatic as her changing hazel eyes. Nevada looked away, unable to bear what he was doing to her.

"I thought you didn't believe in fairy tales, warrior."

"I don't."

"Then don't talk to me about 'fair.' If life were fair, my sister would have celebrated her sixth birthday today. But life isn't and she didn't and wailing about it won't change one damned thing."

Nevada looked back slowly. His eyes were intent, fierce. "You really mean that."

"I always say what I mean. It's a failing of mine."

"You don't believe in fairy tales, but you do believe in love," he said, unable to understand. "Knowing what life truly is, you still allow yourself to love." He hesitated, not wanting to hurt Eden any more but unable to stop himself from asking, "How can you?"

Eden looked into the untamed depths of Nevada's eyes and saw a curiosity that was as great as his wariness, as intense as his passion...a wolf circling closer and closer to the beckoning campfire, pulled toward the flames against his deepest instinct of self-preservation, enthralled by the radiant possibilities of fire.

"How can I do anything else?" Eden said simply. "Man is the animal that wrote Ecclesiastes and still laughed, still loved, still lived. Not just survival, Nevada. *Living.*"

Silence stretched, stretched, then was broken by a harsh word. Nevada pointed off to the right, where a deer had left tracks along the margin of the open forest.

"Follow those tracks, Eden. They'll tell you all you need to know about the true nature of *living.*"

Without a word Eden signaled for Baby to heel and began following the deer tracks, knowing what she would find. The mama cougar was alive, which meant that other life must die to sustain the cat's own life. It had always been that way. It always would be. Life fed. It was the very thing that distinguished life from death.

The deer tracks ended in a turmoil of snow and muddy earth. Cougar tracks led away. The cat had been walking easily despite the limp burden of the deer clenched in its jaws and the hooved feet dragging across the snow.

"A quick, clean kill," Eden said calmly, reading the tracks. "There's nothing surprising in that. Cougars are among the most efficient predators on earth. All you have to do is watch them move and you know that they're supremely adapted for the hunt and the kill."

She waited, but Nevada said nothing. Taking a deep breath, she turned and confronted the warrior she loved.

"In moose country," she continued, "a cougar will routinely stalk and kill moose that weigh five or even eight times as much as the cat does. Sometimes the moose wins and the cougar is injured. Cats are very tough. It takes them a long time and a horrifying amount of pain before they finally die. When it comes to death, nature is much more cruel to predators than predators are to their own prey."

Nevada simply watched Eden with bleak eyes, saying nothing.

"And man is the only predator who can see into the future," Eden continued in a soft, relentless voice. "Man knows that he, too, will die. That's the crucial difference between us and cougars. Yet, even knowing that we'll die, mankind is capable of creating as well as destroying, of loving as well as hating, of true living as well as sheer animal survival. Violent death is only a part of human reality, and not even the most important part at that."

"And I suppose that love is?" he asked sardonically.

"Yes." Without realizing it, Eden raised her hand to the open collar of her jacket. She touched her throat, reassured by the familiar presence of Aurora's ring. "Love is never wasted," Eden whispered. "Never. But it can hurt like nothing else on earth."

Nevada watched Eden with narrowed eyes, wanting to argue with her, to shake her from her foolish belief in love; yet the words died unspoken, for Eden's pain was very real and not foolish at all.

Saying nothing more, Eden turned away from Nevada, lifted the binoculars, and searched the landscape until she found the place where the cougar had dragged the deer. She examined the remains of the cougar's meal with the eyes of a wildlife biologist rather than those of a woman who loved deer as well as cougars. Usually cats ate their fill, raked debris over the remains and walked off to nap nearby, returning to feed until the carcass was consumed or the remains disturbed by other predators. A careful survey with the glasses allowed Eden to pick up the cougar's tracks without coming close enough to alert the wary animal when it returned to feed.

"Baby. Heel."

The big wolf came to Eden's side instantly, eyes alert, his whole being intent upon the woman who had rescued him from an agonizing steel trap despite his own best attempts to savage the very hands that were helping him. Gently, firmly, Eden's fingers wrapped around Baby's muzzle in a command for silence.

The change that went over the wolf was indescribable. It was as though he had been standing in shadow and then stepped out into the sun. Past experience told Baby that the command to be quiet meant that the object of the hunt was probably close by, and the wolf was a predator from the tip of his erect ears down to the black pads of his feet. Walking as though on springs, Baby followed Eden in a wide semi-circle around the deer carcass. When he came across the fresh cat tracks, he bristled but made not one sound.

For a mile they followed the tracks. Nevada followed Eden as silently as the wolf did. The cougar's tracks led up a long, shallow rise where trees offered only sparse cover, if any at all. Where the snow had melted through, a distinct green blush covered the ground. Despite the intermittent snow squalls, spring wasn't going to be denied.

Partway up the slope it became obvious that if the cougar—or the cougar's den—was on the far side, Nevada and Eden would be spotted as soon as their heads cleared the rise. Eden didn't want to panic the cat, perhaps sending it on a search for a new den for its cubs. All she wanted to do was find the cougar's tracks and follow them to the den, where she could watch the cat from a distance so as not to disturb the animal.

Frowning, Eden tested wind direction with a wet finger-tip. She tested again and shrugged. The wind was weak, but unpredictable. Thankfully, scent wasn't nearly the problem it would have been if she had been tracking wolves. Cougars depended on their eyes and ears rather than their noses.

Eden stopped, looked at the gentle slope rising ahead of her, and sighed. It would be a cold, wet and sometimes muddy crawl, but there was no help for it if she hoped to get to the top without giving away her presence. She slipped out of her backpack, but before she set it aside, Nevada went past her like a black wraith. He had removed his hat and backpack but had kept his rifle.

Crouching, taking advantage of every scrap of cover, crawling on hands and knees and finally on his stomach, Nevada went up the slope with a speed and silence that sent a shiver over Eden. He moved like a cougar—confident, soundless, graceful, and potentially deadly.

Let me tell you what the real world is like, fairy-tale girl...you walk through a narrow mountain pass in single file with five handpicked men and arrive at your destination and look around and you're alone, nothing on the back trail but blood and silence.

Nevada eased up behind the cover of a bush, slowly pulled his binoculars out of his jacket, and began quartering the slope below. The cougar's tracks continued, zigzagging across a boulder field where ancient trees had fallen like jackstraws. The tracks vanished. They didn't reappear anywhere on the new snow beyond.

Patiently Nevada scanned the boulders, looking for several big stones canted together to create a sheltered hollow, or for an uprooted tree, or for any irregularity in the land that would provide a den for a mama cougar and her cubs. Finally he spotted a collection of boulders with an opening at their base where a tree had blown down and created a small cave between the uprooted tree and the rocks. In the darkness of the hollow lay a long, tawny shadow.

Nevada focused the glasses and found himself looking at the white muzzle, wheat-colored cheeks and sleek black facial markings of an adult female cougar. There was no doubt about the cat's sex, for she was lying on her side while three spotted cubs nursed enthusiastically.

Slowly Nevada put down the glasses and looked until he spotted the den once more. He memorized landmarks, cover, approaches, and the general lie of the land with the thoroughness of a man whose life had depended on knowing just such information in the past. When he was satisfied that he could find the den again, he retreated down the slope as swiftly and silently as he had gone up it.

Eden waited for him at the bottom, a silent question in her eyes. He nodded and slid his hand up along her cheek, holding her while he bent down until he could speak directly against her ear. Although there was little chance of the cat's hearing them, Nevada knew that voices carried an astonishing distance in the snowy silence.

"She's denned up about two hundred feet beyond the far side of the rise," he said softly. "She has three cubs."

A shiver coursed through Eden's body, but it came from the touch of Nevada's hand rather than from the news about the mama cougar.

"Did she sense you?" Eden asked, her voice low and soft.

"No." Nevada lowered his hand. "She's still sleeping off her meal. I doubt that she'll be out and about before sunset. Maybe not even then."

"Do you have a clear field of view from the ridge?"

"Pretty good. It would be even better from there," he said, pointing to a spot farther along the crest, "but that's the way she went from her kill to the den. I didn't figure you wanted to leave tracks there."

"Not until she's finished with the deer," Eden agreed.

Eden tried to think about possible hiding places, places to build a blind for observation, places where the cougar wouldn't be likely to find them and become alarmed; but all she could think about at that instant was how close Nevada was, and how much closer he had been seven days ago.

Motionless, Nevada watched Eden's changing hazel eyes and the delicate pressure of her teeth against her lower lip and the fiddling of her fingers over his jacket hem while she thought about other things. If she had been aware of her actions, Nevada would have been angry. But he knew she wasn't aware of what she was doing. Unfortunately, that knowledge did nothing to counter the sudden hard rush of his blood when her hand brushed against his jeans. He captured her fingers and placed them on his beard.

"If you have to pet me while you think, keep it above the waist."

Eden flushed. "I didn't mean—"

"I know," Nevada interrupted tightly. "You weren't thinking about what you were doing. But I was. I like being petted by you. I like it way too much. The ground is cold and hard and wet, but I wouldn't care, and after a few minutes you wouldn't, either. The mama cougar might get kind of curious, though. You make such wild sounds when I'm buried in you."

Eden's color deepened to scarlet.

"Don't," Nevada said in a husky voice, knowing he shouldn't speak but unable to help himself. "I like hearing you, feeling you, smelling you, tasting you. I liked it too damn much. You were a virgin, but you took all of me and shivered with pleasure..." He let breath rush out between his teeth in a hissing curse. "I came up here for cougars, not sex. So get on up that slope and watch your mama cat, fairy-tale girl. I'll circle around and reconnoiter the far side."

Nevada turned and walked off, heading away from the rise, moving with the easy, powerful stride that was as much a part of him as his pale green eyes. Eden watched him for a full minute before she took a ragged breath, turned around and went up the rise, following the tracks Nevada had made.

I came up here for cougars, not sex.

The words hurt, but he had no more meant to hurt her than she had meant for her absentminded fidgeting to arouse him.

You wouldn't have gotten sex from me, Nevada Black-

*thorn. You never have. You never will. What I gave you was
love, not sex, and somewhere deep inside your stubborn
warrior soul you know it.*

Don't you?

There was no answer but the one implicit in the nickname
Nevada had given to her.

Fairy-tale girl.

CHAPTER ELEVEN

SWEARING UNDER HIS BREATH, NEVADA lay beneath a sky so black no stars could be seen and listened to the thunder rumbling and churning overhead. He had eaten meals with Eden since he had returned to Wildfire Canyon, but he had slept outside the cabin—much to Baby's delight. Tonight, however, the wolf had shown the innate good sense of a wild animal; at the first cannonade of thunder, Baby had gone to scratch at the cabin door. Curling up to sleep on a few feet of comfortable snow was one thing. Sleeping beneath a barrage of hail mixed with slush was quite another. A wolf had no compunctions about grabbing whatever shelter was available.

Grimly Nevada wished that spring would just settle down and get the job done rather than teetering from snowstorm to chinook and back again, turning sky and ground into a battlefield that was spectacular when viewed from a snug shelter, and a real pain in the butt otherwise.

Quit whining, Nevada told himself as hail hammered down, breaching the uncertain shelter beneath the evergreen where he had dragged his sleeping bag when the storm first had awakened him. *You've been a lot more uncomfortable and survived just fine.*

Yeah, but I wasn't lying thirty feet from Eden, watching her shadow move across curtains while she took her nightly bath, watching her and imagining...too damn much.

That was hours ago. She's asleep by now. You should be, too.

Nevada rolled over, scrunched down in the sleeping bag and pulled the waterproof tarp over his head. He tried to ignore the icy fingers of slush that found every possible entrance into his sleeping bag. It was difficult. Each time he thought he had defended every bit of exposed territory, the storm discovered another opening. Sleep was impossible.

So was controlling a mind that was as unruly as the storm. Nevada found himself wondering if Eden had stood outside the cabin after dinner and watched his own shadow on the curtains while he had his turn with soap and washrag. Then he wondered if the storm made Eden nervous. If it did, maybe she would like something more interesting than a wolf to keep her hands busy.

Lightning shattered the night into a billion brilliant shards. Thunder followed like a falling mountain, flattening everything in its path. Overhead, Nevada's meager shelter tossed and moaned while evergreen branches shed hail, slush and ice water over him in endless, unpredictable streams. The tarp turned aside some of the storm, but not nearly enough.

What would you call a commando who slept in ice water

when there was a warm, safe shelter nearby? Nevada asked himself tauntingly.

A bloody damned fool.

Then I guess you're a bloody damned fool, aren't you? Or are you afraid Eden will creep up on you and ravish you while you sleep?

More likely she'll cut my throat. Since I told her I didn't come up here for sex, she's done everything but climb trees to avoid touching me.

And you're grateful for that, right?

Yeah, right. I'm grateful as all hell on fire.

Nevada wished he could lie to himself convincingly, but that kind of lying wasn't a survival trait, and if Nevada was good at anything, it was surviving.

Sure you are, mocked the voice inside his head. *That's why you're lying out here slowly turning into a Popsicle. Some survivor. You don't even have enough sense to come in out of the rain.*

Branches bent in a gust of wind that lifted a corner of the tarp just in time to let ice water gush over the back of Nevada's undefended neck. With a savage word he shot to his feet, grabbed the tarp and the damp sleeping bag, and stalked up to the cabin.

The door opened before he could raise his fist to knock.

"There's a towel by the fire," Eden said, turning away from Nevada even as she spoke.

With eyes that reflected the leap of flames he watched her retreat. He knew she was making no effort to be sexy yet the motion of her hips beneath the clinging scarlet of her ski underwear was so feminine that it loosened his knees.

Lightning bleached the interior of the cabin in the instant

before Nevada closed the door. Baby lay sleeping soundly in the coldest part of the cabin. The wolf didn't even lift his head at Nevada's entrance.

"Go back to sleep," Nevada said, watching Eden retreat.

If Eden said anything in response, it was lost in a crash of thunder. Nevada watched from the corner of his eye as she slid gracefully into the soft folds of her bedding. He peeled off his black T-shirt and grabbed the towel. The terry cloth was warm against his chilled skin. The knowledge that Eden had deliberately heated the towel by the fire in case he came in out of the storm made the brush of the cloth even more pleasurable on his skin. The thought of having Eden's sweet, warm hands on his body instead of the towel made blood rush heavily. His hands clenched on the towel as he fought his response to Eden.

Stop thinking about it.

Right. And while I'm at it, I'll stop breathing, too.

Nevada's hands went to the buttons of his cold, damp jeans. He hesitated, remembering that he had nothing on but clammy denim, then shrugged and resumed undressing. He doubted that Eden was watching him. Even if she was, she had seen him dead naked once before and hadn't fainted at the sight.

A memory exploded in Nevada with a force so great it nearly sent him to his knees—Eden warm across his thighs, touching him intimately, cherishing his hunger, tasting him, whispering of life itself.

Savagely Nevada whipped off his damp jeans, wadded them up and fired them across the cabin. The soft thump of cloth against wood couldn't conceal the sound of the sudden rush of air through Eden's lips when she saw his profile outlined by firelight and knew beyond doubt the hunger raging in him.

"Nevada…" Her husky whisper shivered like firelight in the silence.

Slowly Nevada turned toward Eden. Fighting himself every second, losing every second, Nevada began walking over the cold wooden floor, pulled against his will one slow step at a time until at last he stood by the edge of Eden's mattress, breathing deeply, trying to stop the fine trembling of his hands. He could not. As though driven by a whip, he closed his eyes and sank to his knees. His hands became fists on the powerful, clenched muscles of his thighs.

A moment later Nevada sensed movement, heard the small sounds of cloth rubbing over cloth as the bedding shifted, and then felt Eden's breath rush warmly over his fists. Light kisses touched his hands, gentling him even as the caresses seared him to the bone. With a ragged sound of pain and pleasure he unclenched his fingers and reached for Eden.

As she came to her knees before him, he eased his fingers deeply into the fragrant silk of her hair, tipped her face up to his hungry lips and locked their mouths in a searing kiss. It wasn't enough. No matter how wild, how sweet, how deep, he couldn't get close enough to her with just a kiss. He couldn't touch her completely. He couldn't bathe in her fire.

"Eden," Nevada said hoarsely, tightening his hands in her hair. "Eden…let me…"

"Yes," she whispered, not even waiting to find out what he was asking of her.

A shudder rippled through Nevada. His eyes opened.

They smoldered with reflected flames as he looked at Eden kneeling in front of him, watching him, wanting him.

"Lift your arms, fairy-tale girl," Nevada said huskily.

As Eden raised her arms, the graceful motion reminded Nevada of the shadows he had seen on the curtains as she bathed. His hands slid from her hair down to the hem of her soft ski top, and then beneath. Watching her at every instant, he slowly eased the scarlet top up her body until the cloth was at her elbows and her breasts were completely bare. Abandoning the cloth still tangled around her elbows, he stroked her upper arms and shoulders, caressing the sensitive skin of her inner arm.

"When I saw your shadow moving while you bathed," Nevada said, bending down to Eden's breasts, "I was so damned jealous of the washcloth I thought I would go crazy. I wanted to be the one rubbing over you, getting you wet, making your skin shine in the firelight."

The satin heat of Nevada's mouth rubbed warmth and dampness over first one of Eden's breasts, then the other, making her tremble. When she would have cast aside her top and lowered her arms to hold him, he moved swiftly, holding her as she had been with her back elegantly arched and her breasts utterly defenseless against his mouth. His tongue circled one nipple, his teeth gently raked, and she gasped with pleasure. Before she could catch her breath, he was softly, completely devouring her.

The sweet, changing pressures of Nevada's mouth on her breasts sent fire streaming through her blood. Eden shivered and his name broke on her lips. His answer was the renewed tugging of his mouth, the sweet stabbing of his tongue, pleasure gathering and bursting until she cried out and he made a low sound of satisfaction and triumph. For long, shivering minutes he pleasured her, holding her suspended between firelight and his hungry mouth. When he finally lifted his head, her breasts were taut, flushed, full, and they shone in the firelight.

Nevada looked at Eden for a long time, memorizing the picture her breasts made. Then his burning glance moved down her body and he shivered with an eagerness he had never known and could barely control. When he spoke his voice was thick, rasping, as caressing as his hungry mouth had been.

"Stand up, fairy-tale girl."

Eden made a sound that was halfway between a laugh and a protest. "I can't."

With a quick motion Nevada swept off Eden's top, freeing her arms. His warm hands slid down her body and his shoulder muscles bunched as he lifted Eden to her feet.

"Brace your hands on my shoulders," he said.

Eden obeyed. Moments later she felt her long ski underwear sliding down her legs, leaving her naked but for the soft scarlet cloth pooled at her ankles. Nevada's hair gleamed blackly as he lifted her right foot free of the cloth, caressed the high arch lovingly with his fingertips and brushed a kiss over her inner thigh. Slowly he released her foot as he rubbed his beard against the warmth and resilience of her thigh. When he reached for her other foot, his beard smoothed over her flesh once more.

"I love your beard," Eden said with a broken sigh of pleasure.

"I'm glad."

Nevada's voice was like his beard, a soft, silken rasp of sensation that made Eden melt. She shivered again as he lifted her other foot, slid off the last of the cloth, caressed her foot and released it.

"Do you like this, too?" he asked.

Eden felt the brush of his beard against her inner thigh, the hot touch of his tongue, and the sweet heat of his lips. For long moments Nevada's mouth moved over her thighs, sliding higher, shifting her subtly, parting her legs a bit more with each gentle kiss. The sight of his dark head against the creamy smoothness of her own skin sent rippling sensations throughout Eden's body, echoing of the supple dance of firelight.

"Nevada?"

Her husky whisper sent a tremor through Nevada. The kiss he was giving her changed, becoming a claiming that was just short of pain and simultaneously a pleasure so intense that it made her moan. Eden gasped. For an instant he froze, afraid that he had hurt her; then he felt the melting heat of her response. His hand shifted, skimming the burning gold delta at the apex of her thighs, seeking her softness, finding it, sliding into her with a caress that made her gasp.

The sight of Nevada touching her so intimately made passion and embarrassment twist hotly through Eden. She pushed against his shoulders, silently asking to be released. It was like pushing against sun-warmed stone. His fingers skimmed her again, gliding in and withdrawing slowly, dragging a ragged moan of pleasure from her that was both his name and a protest. Slowly his head turned up to her until she could see the blazing silver green of his eyes.

"Did I hurt you?" Nevada asked huskily.

Eden shook her head and started to speak, but seeing his mouth so close to her hungry flesh scattered her thoughts.

"Watching you—you were looking at me—watching me while you—" Her voice broke on a sensual shudder that she couldn't control.

"Did it embarrass you?" Nevada asked.

She nodded and whispered, "A little."

"Any other objections?"

She bit her lips and shook her head.

"Did you like it?" he asked softly.

"Yes," Eden said, her voice low. "I liked it so much I—"

Her voice shattered into a moan as Nevada stole once more into the shadowed softness only he had ever touched.

"Then close your eyes, fairy-tale girl," he said, gently biting the soft skin of her belly, "or what you're going to see will make you blush to the soles of your perfect feet."

"I don't understand," she whispered.

"Neither do I," Nevada admitted, brushing his bearded cheek against the hot golden curls that so tempted him. "I've never wanted a woman the way I want you. I want all of you. Everything. Every way there is."

His hand moved again, gliding up between Eden's smooth thighs, silently asking that she open herself to his caresses. The slow advance and retreat of his touch tantalized her, making her hungry for more. Compelled by Nevada's gentle seduction of her senses, she shifted her stance with each of his caresses until she was trembling and breathing brokenly, her eyes heavy lidded, almost closed, and her body was open to whatever caress he wanted to give.

The touch of Nevada's tongue astonished and unraveled Eden in the same wild instant. His name was torn from her lips as her nails dug into the flexed power of his shoulders. His response to the sensuous bite of her fingernails was a low sound of pleasure and hunger and anticipation. His big hands shifted quickly and closed around her hips until he held her in a passionate vise. Unerringly his mouth found the satin nub his caresses had teased from her softness. With a tenderness that was all the more shattering for its restraint, he caught her delicately between his teeth, holding her hotly captive while his caressing tongue stripped away all thought of embarrassment or inhibition.

Eden shuddered heavily and made a ragged sound of surprise and pleasure, holding on to Nevada for balance as her own deserted her. The steamy intimacy of Nevada's mouth was a delicious assault against which she had no defense. Nor did she want any, for she trusted the warrior who held her within his grasp, his elemental male sensuality a lesson and a lure to her own feminine response. A searing spiral of sensation whirled around her, driving her higher and higher with each caress until she twisted like fire within Nevada's grasp.

And like fire, Eden burned.

The wild, broken sounds of her ecstasy shivered through Nevada. He caressed her again and again, hungry to hear more of her pleasure, unwilling to release the softness and passionate response of the woman he had only begun to explore. Reluctantly he lowered Eden to the bedding, but even then he could not release her, not completely. His hand curled possessively around the golden nest of curls as he kissed her navel, her breasts, the pulse beating frantically in her neck.

Eden tried to speak but could not. Nevada's palm was against her violently sensitive flesh, rubbing lightly, pressing, and a long finger was dipping into her as though he were sipping her secrets one by one. His name came from her throat in a husky moan as ecstasy speared through her unexpectedly once more, convulsing her secretly—but she had no secrets from Nevada anymore. He was inside her, sipping at her, touching her delicately, sharing her pleasure, watching her. His caress redoubled, deepened, and so did her response.

"Nevada?" Eden whispered, not understanding why he still withheld himself from the passion he had brought to her.

But Nevada understood. "That was one way, fairy-tale girl. This is another." His voice was low, dark, and he spoke without looking away from the picture made by his hand and the smooth, creamy curves of Eden's body. "I want them all. Every last one. There's no tomorrow, no yesterday. There's only the night and the storm and the fire, you and me and…this."

Nevada's hand had moved again, taking the world from beneath her body, sending her spinning. She gasped his name and was rewarded by another hot caress.

"Look at me," Eden said huskily.

"I am. I never knew a woman could be so beautiful."

Nevada bent down and traced her satin nub with the tip of his tongue. The sight of him caressing her so intimately sent shock waves through Eden's mind and body. She felt cherished, threatened, protected, wanton, a woman locked within storm and fire and night, and the essence of all three was the warrior with the haunted silver-green eyes and gentle hands.

"I love you," Eden said raggedly. "I love you so much I can't—"

Ecstasy burst, breaking her voice.

"I don't want love," Nevada said, his voice as dark as the

shadows pooled in his eyes. With a swift, powerful movement he lay between her legs, poised at the very entrance to the inviting Eden he had made his own. "All I want is *this*. But I shouldn't take you. Unprotected. Undefended." A harsh shudder went the length of his body as he fought against himself, against her. *"Damn you, Eden, you're tearing me apart."*

"Take me," Eden whispered, reaching for Nevada, touching the hot, hard flesh that she desired, loving all of him. "And I'll take you, all of you, lover and warrior and man, everything you want to give, every way there is, no recriminations and no regrets. That's what love is, Nevada, and I'll love you until I die."

With a tearing sound that was both pain and pleasure, Nevada thrust into Eden's silken warmth, joining with her in a union that was both savage and sublime. When he could go no deeper he held himself completely still but for the shudders that racked him as his untamed hunger sought to escape the restraints of his discipline.

Eden wrapped herself around Nevada and held him, feeling each tremor of need that tugged at his control. Her fingertips probed through his hair and then down the rigid muscles of his back and hips, wanting to touch all of him at once, to surround him with loving warmth.

When Eden's slender fingers discovered the shadow cleft between his lean hips and the tight, shockingly sensitive flesh below, Nevada's whole body jerked. Making soft sounds of discovery and pleasure, Eden explored the changing textures of his need. Groaning, Nevada drove even more deeply into her, all defenses stripped away, held lovingly in the palm of Eden's hand.

With a new understanding she felt the primal, shivering pulses of Nevada's release, heard her name breaking again and again on his lips, and whispered her own love against his open mouth. After the last tremors finally faded, Eden felt Nevada's body shift. Remembering the time when he had made love to her and then walked away without a word, she tightened her arms around him.

"Don't leave me," she whispered. "Not yet."

"I won't." Nevada made a harsh sound. "I can't."

She looked into his eyes and saw the savage leap of reflected fire. Before she could speak, he was talking again, his voice raw.

"You asked for all of me. I hope you meant it, fairy-tale girl, because you're going to get what you asked for. Every damn bit of it, everything I have to give."

Nevada's lean hips moved and Eden's breath rushed in at the sensations streaking up from their joined bodies.

"I just had you," Nevada said harshly, his voice as savage as his eyes, "and I'm ready for you again. That's why I walked out on you before. I knew I would take you again and again until finally I didn't even have the strength to lick my lips—*and then I would still want you.* It's never been like that for me with a woman. You're in my blood like fever and my body is on fire. I'm going to do the same thing to you that you're doing to me, fairy-tale girl. I'm going to burn you alive."

Nevada bent and took Eden's mouth, opening it with a quick twist of his head, searching her softness even as he pinned her beneath the hard weight of his body. One powerful arm slipped beneath her hips, pulling her even closer, holding her so tightly that he could feel her bones beneath her soft flesh and she could feel his. Then he began moving, driving into her, taking all of her again and again, hot skin sliding against hot skin until the sweet friction ignited her soft flesh with an intensity that shocked her.

She called his name wildly and saw his eyes blaze with response. He rocked hard against her and then harder still, fanning the passionate fire, driving into her until sweat gleamed on both their bodies and she cried out as ecstasy raked her with incandescent claws.

And still there was no end, no peace, no safety, for he was still moving inside her in a rhythm as relentless as it was savage, driving her higher and yet higher until Eden felt as though she were going to die, as though she had been ripped from one world and thrust into another and in this one she was on fire. With a wrenching moan she arched into Nevada, burning fiercely, needing even more of him, telling him what she needed with words that also burned.

"You're feeling it now, aren't you?" Nevada said darkly as his teeth scored Eden's ear. "This is what you did to me the first time I saw you, before I ever even touched you, a burning all the way to the marrow of my bones. And then I had you and still it wasn't enough, it's never enough, because there's always more and it's always just out of reach, a rainbow on fire against a black sky, untouchable and so damned perfect it tears at your soul until you bleed but it doesn't make any difference because your blood is on fire, too, and you just keep burning."

Twisting, burning, caught between heaven and hell, hearing Nevada's dark voice and fiery words, Eden fought for the embrace, for the fulfillment she knew blazed just beyond her reach. Nevada bent down to her, holding her motionless while he caught her mouth with his own. She drank his wild hunger, matched it, demanded more and yet more of him until he drove into her, pinning her beneath him, grinding against her as though he would become a part of her or die.

Impaled on ecstasy, consumed by wildfire, Eden would have screamed but she had no breath, no voice, no being. She felt Nevada shuddering beneath rapture's savage blows, heard him cry out as though in torment, but she could not help him for she was him and he was her and together they were the rainbow stretched between heaven and hell, burning.

When the searing fire finally released Eden, she lay spent beneath Nevada, stunned by the passion that had consumed both of them, feeling their bodies fight for breath, for reality. When their breathing finally slowed, Nevada eased himself from Eden's body, caught her face between his hands and looked down into the many colors of her dazed hazel eyes.

"All the colors of life," Nevada whispered, brushing Eden's lips with his own.

As one person, they felt his heartbeat deepen as he quickened against her body once more.

"Nevada?" Eden whispered.

"I can't stop it. I don't even want to try. It's as new to me as it is to you. Fairy-tale girl, all sweet golden fire," he whispered. "Burn with me, fairy-tale girl."

Gently Nevada joined his mouth with Eden's, caressing her sweetly, drinking her with the slow, shared rhythms of remembered hunger and release. The kiss was like his heartbeat, deep and unhurried, certain. Urgency was a distant echo, pleasure a shimmering companion, and their breath whispered as softly as flames in the hearth.

The kiss ended as gently as it had begun, drawing a murmured protest from Eden, for she didn't want it to end. Nevada's lips brushed hers once more, stilling her with a gentle caress that promised things he had no words to say, only a certainty whispering deep inside him, shimmering with pleasures as yet untouched, unknown, unnamed, waiting for them, ecstasy burning as softly as his kisses.

The brush of Nevada's lips closed Eden's eyelids. She sighed as the moist tip of his tongue traced her eyelashes, her hairline, her temples, and his breath caressed her sensitive skin. His words sank gently into her as his teeth and tongue caressed her earlobes, the soft line of her neck, the hollow of her throat, tasting her, sipping her, discovering her. His mouth moved slowly from her shoulders to her fingertips, her breasts, her belly, then down her long legs to the soles of her feet.

Nevada was a warmth moving over Eden, his caresses telling her that she was more beautiful than life, more perfect than fire. The velvet warmth of his tongue was heightened by tiny bites so gentle they made her softly moan. When he knelt between her legs, touched her, cherished her, she wept and gave him what he asked for, opening for him like a flower. He whispered her name and her beauty against her skin, asking for yet another gift, and she gave him that, too, softly bathing him in her fire.

With a gentleness that made Eden tremble, Nevada kissed her, slid his hands beneath her knees and slowly raised her legs, moving them apart with soft pressures and whispered words. Then he lifted his head and looked into Eden's eyes, asking that she trust him in this as she had trusted him in so much already.

The contrast between the heavenly gentleness of Nevada's hands and the shadowy hell in his eyes tore at Eden's heart. She trembled and gave her body to his keeping, heard her name wrapped in the dark velvet of his voice as he gently curled her legs back upon her, leaving nothing secret from him.

There was no embarrassment in Eden this time when Nevada looked at her, kissed her once, twice, and then brought himself to her undefended gate, watching the union as he pressed into her. The taking was so gentle, so slow, his eyes so black, so wild, that Eden unraveled in shivering ecstasy. She saw her undoing echoed in the shudder that rippled through Nevada, but his slow claiming of her softness did not speed up in the least. He took Eden the way dawn takes the night, moment by moment, breath by breath, leaving nothing unclaimed, nothing hidden.

And when he filled her, all of her, sealing their bodies while she watched, she softly moaned at the completion. Tiny convulsions stole through her to him as she shimmered and burst soundlessly into fire. He rocked slowly against her, his movements as gentle and overwhelming as her body unraveling, bathing him in soft flames, rocking, rocking, and she wept and still ecstasy came to her, repeatedly, and each time the gentle rocking, rocking of Nevada's body breathed life into her once more.

And still he rocked gently, filling her, bathing in her fire as they gave themselves to one another in secret molten pulses, burning away the world, leaving only their interlocked bodies and an incandescent ecstasy that had no ending, only beginnings, renewing and consuming and burning until finally they fell asleep, still intimately joined, their interlocked bodies gleaming in the firelight.

Yet even in sleep, Eden wept, for she had seen the darkness in Nevada's eyes and knew she would wake alone.

CHAPTER TWELVE

BABY FOUND NEVADA'S TRACKS AT THE base of the ridge that overlooked the cougar's den. The realization that Nevada had been so close to Eden and hadn't so much as said hello drove black splinters of pain into her. Even as Eden looked frantically around, hoping to find Nevada, she knew it would be futile. If he had wanted to talk to her, he would have. He hadn't. He had been very careful not to alert her to his presence, avoiding the keen edge of Baby's senses.

Eden looked at Nevada's tracks and fought not to cry out with loneliness. It had been two weeks since Nevada had come in from one kind of storm, only to create another in the cabin's firelit intimacy. The memories of being joined with Nevada haunted Eden, bringing tears to her eyes even as her body shivered with remembered ecstasy. Blindly she looked at the indentations Nevada's boots had left in the newly fertile earth, then tilted her head back and called into the wind.

"Nevada! Nevada, can't you hear me? I love you!"

Nothing answered. Nothing would. Nevada was gone.

For the first time Eden admitted to herself that her warrior would not come to her again. Her love had not been able to heal Nevada. Even worse, her repeated offerings of love had undermined the peace of mind he had won at such terrible cost in the burned-out villages of Afghanistan.

The real world is a place where all you can do with your prayers and medicine and rage is hold the babies until they die and then bury them and walk away, just walk away, because any man who cares for anything enough to be hurt by its loss is a fool.

Nevada had taken his emotions, locked them up and walked away, forgetting even the existence of a key.

It had worked. Nevada had survived where other men had died. He had stayed sane where other men had gone mad. He had kept control of himself where other men had become savages.

Then Eden had come to the dark warrior, offering love to heal him, offering herself in ways he couldn't refuse, stripping him of the control that was all that had kept him whole.

I'd give my soul not to want you, Eden.

Yet even when cornered, torn apart, wild with the pain of Eden's temptation, even then Nevada had not turned on her, had not defended himself against her with his superior strength and savage skill. Instead, he had given her ecstasy.

In return, she had given him a new taste of old agony. She would die remembering the wild darkness in his eyes and the extraordinary gentleness of his hands.

"Warrior," Eden whispered, trembling, "I'm sorry. I

didn't know what I was doing to you. I didn't think what the cost would be if I couldn't heal you."

Eden heard her own words and for the first time understood her own naive arrogance—she had thought herself capable of healing a man she couldn't even make smile. As the instant of understanding came, agony went through her as deeply as ecstasy had, hammer blows of pain twisting through her mind and body, driving her to her knees. With a low sound she bent her head and held on to herself.

The pain, Nevada. My God, the pain.

I would give my soul…

After a long time Eden straightened and slowly stood up. Despite the tears that would not stop falling, she walked back to the cabin. There was no reason to stay there any longer, no excuse. Her preliminary survey was complete, her notes were in order, everything was ready to be handed over to others who would decide whether to continue the research at Wildfire Canyon.

She should have left a week ago, but she had stayed on, making excuses about unfinished work, watching the horizon, hoping and praying and hungering for the man she loved. Now nothing remained but to take the advice of the warrior who knew how to survive.

Walk away, just walk away.

Eden began packing up her belongings and stowing them in the truck. Baby watched her with total alertness, yellow eyes intent, sensing that something was wrong. Eden spoke to him quietly from time to time, but never slowed the pace of her movements until the cabin lay empty again, no trace of her presence but the ashes cold in the hearth.

Without a backward look, Eden drove away from

Wildfire Canyon, never hesitating until she came to a Y in the dirt track. The left-hand road led to West Fork. The other led to the Rocking M's ranch house.

Eden's mind chose the left-hand fork. Her hands chose the right.

When Eden drove the truck into the ranch house's broad, graveled front drive, there was only one vehicle parked between the house and the barn. She got out of the truck and started to close the door. Baby shot by her in a fluid leap. Once free, he made no attempt to run off. He simply stood and watched her with an unwavering yellow glance that told her he would resist being separated from his mistress. The wolf didn't know what was wrong; he simply knew that something was.

"Heel," Eden said softly.

Baby condensed at her heel like a black shadow.

The sun was almost hot in the ranch yard. Flowers bloomed vividly in the beds that ran along the porch. Their bright colors and soft petals spoke eloquently of winter's surrender to spring.

Eden knocked on the door. A feminine voice answered from the second story.

"Door's open. There's coffee in the kitchen. I'll be with you as soon as I get Logan dried off."

Eden hesitated, then opened the door and walked into the living room. Two playpens stood along the wall beneath a whimsical, hand-carved mobile featuring spurs and branding irons. One playpen was empty. The other held a child dressed in pink who looked about a year old. She was fussing in the manner of a baby who had been awakened too early.

"Sit," Eden said quietly to her wolf. "Stay."

The wolf obeyed, content as long as Eden was within his sight.

Drawn by the little girl's muted fussing, Eden went and stood by the playpen.

"Hello, little angel," she said gently. "I'm sorry I woke you up."

Carolina stopped grumping, looked at the stranger and held her arms out in the confident demand of a well-loved child. Eden bent over and lifted the little girl into her arms. The compact warmth and sleepy resilience of Carolina's body brought back an avalanche of memories of another small person, another compact bundle of warmth, and laughter like a field of poppies in the sun.

Holding Carolina, rocking slowly, humming softly, Eden closed her eyes and prayed that Nevada had given her his child to love.

"I'm Diana Blackthorn," a voice said from behind Eden. "From the looks of that great black beast watching you, you must be Eden Summers."

"His name is Baby," Eden said, turning around and looking at the small woman with the intense blue eyes. "He won't hurt you. But if you're worried, I'll—"

"No problem," Diana interrupted, looking curiously at the motionless wolf. "I've been dying to see Baby ever since Nevada mentioned him."

Eden looked from Carolina to Diana and back again. "She's yours, isn't she," Eden said quietly. "You both have eyes like slices of sapphire."

"Carolina's half mine," Diana agreed, smiling. "Thanks for soothing her. Once she gets going, she's hard to stop. She has the deep-running passion of a Blackthorn."

Eden couldn't conceal the bittersweet shaft of pain lancing through her at Diana's words, but all she said was "Is Luke MacKenzie here?"

"No. He and Carla won't be back until dinner. Mariah and Cash won't be here at all. They've moved into Cortez until the twins are born."

"Is your husband Tennessee Blackthorn, the Rocking M's ramrod?"

"Yes, but he's out working the lease lands on the other side of MacKenzie Ridge. He won't be back until well after sundown. But Nevada should be back within the hour. Perhaps he could help you?"

Eden closed her eyes for an instant, then shook her head very slowly and smoothed her cheek against Carolina's shiny black hair.

"Here," Diana said, looking at Eden's pale face and drawn mouth, "let me take Carolina. She's getting heavier every day. Pretty soon we'll need a crane to lift her."

Reluctantly Eden gave the sleeping child back, shifting Carolina's limp weight with an expertise that hadn't faded in the years since Aurora had died.

"You know how to handle babies," Diana said, bending over and tucking Carolina beneath a fluffy quilt in the playpen. "Do you have children of your own?"

"No, but years ago I had a younger sister. She was just Carolina's size...."

Something in Eden's voice caught at Diana's emotions. She turned and saw the sadness in Eden's eyes.

"Would you pass a message along to Luke MacKenzie?" Eden asked, looking away.

"Of course."

"I've finished the preliminary survey of the cougars in and around Wildfire Canyon. There are two full-time resident cats. One is a mother with three cubs. The other is a young male. I've found absolutely no indication that the cougars are feeding on anything but natural prey."

Diana let out a long sigh and smiled. "That's good news. The Rocking M women really didn't want our men to have to hunt down those cougars. The men weren't happy about the prospect, either, but they would have done it to protect the calves."

Eden felt cold at the thought of Nevada having to kill the mama cougar. Nevada had known too much of death and violence, not enough of love and life.

"I'm glad the mama cougar lives on Rocking M land," Eden said after a moment. "She'll be safe here."

"God, yes. Nevada watches over her like a mother hen. I've been trying to get him to take me to see the cubs, but he's worried about disturbing her before the cubs are old enough to leave the den."

"She's a good mother," Eden said. "All three of her cubs are lively and strong. When she calls to them, she makes the most beautiful fluting sounds...."

Eden closed her eyes and touched the golden chain and the tiny ring lying in the hollow of her throat.

"You look tired, and it's a long way from here to anywhere else," Diana said. "Why don't you stay for dinner and then overnight? Luke and Ten would love to talk to you about the Rocking M's cats."

"Nevada can answer their questions."

"Thanks," Diana said dryly, "but I'd just as soon Ten didn't take on his brother right now. Carla feels the same way about Luke. Nevada never was an outgoing kind of man, but in the past few weeks he's set new records. He's shut down, sealed up, and his eyes are enough to give your wolf pause. Frankly, Ten and I were kind of hoping you would show up here. Anyone else who tries to reach Nevada will get their head handed to them."

Slowly Eden shook her head.

"Don't misunderstand me," Diana said quickly, touching Eden's arm. "Nevada is a good man. A woman wouldn't have to worry about her safety with him. He would never hurt you physically. He's capable of great gentleness, too. You should see him with Carla's new baby. It's enough to make me cry."

"I know," Eden whispered.

"Then why won't you stay and talk to him?"

"Because he doesn't want to talk to me."

There was no mistaking the pain in Eden's voice, in her expression, in the fine trembling of her fingers as she reached up and unfastened the gold chain from around her neck. Carefully she looped the chain on the curve of the Rocking M brand. The gold glistened like sunlight caught in the mobile's changing lines.

"Eden?"

"Tell Luke that the university will send him a copy of my report, including photographs of the cougars' tracks and sketches of the boundaries of their territories," Eden said, her voice husky. "And tell him thank-you from the bottom of my heart. Too many ranchers simply would have killed the cats out of suspicion and mistrust and ignorance."

Eden turned and walked quickly to the door. At a single small movement of her hand, Baby rose. With the silence of smoke, the wolf followed Eden outdoors. Behind them the chain and its tiny braided gold ring shimmered and shone above the sleeping Blackthorn child.

WHEN NEVADA CAME IN THE front door of the ranch house, his first stop was always the playpens. They were empty, which meant that the "Rocking M Monsters" were getting their bedtime baths. Disappointed at having missed a chance to play with Carolina and Logan, Nevada took off his black Stetson, snapped it against his thigh, and tugged the hat back into place on his head.

"Need any help?" Nevada called up the stairs.

"So far, so good," Carla called back. "Coffee's ready in the kitchen."

Nevada poured himself a mug of coffee and went back to the living room, bothered by something he couldn't name. Eyes narrowed, he looked around while the squeals of a child splashing enthusiastically in the bath drifted down the stairs. Though nothing seemed obviously out of place in the living room, something kept nagging at Nevada just beneath the threshold of conscious thought, telling him that all was *not* as it seemed.

Stirred by the passage of Nevada's restless body, the mobiles moved. A shimmer of gold caught his eye. He turned and walked closer. An instant later he recognized the chain and the tiny braided ring he had last seen nestled in the hollow of Eden's throat. Nevada's breath stopped as his heart contracted in his chest.

I wear Aurora's ring to remind myself that love is never wasted, never futile.

Shards of past conversations sliced through him, making him bleed with a pain he had vowed never to feel.

I love you, Nevada.

That's what I was afraid you were telling yourself. Fairy tales. You can't accept that all there is between us is sex. Pure and simple and hot as hell.

With great care Nevada freed the delicate chain from the mobile.

I'm worlds too hard for you, but I want you until my hands shake.

Now I know what life tastes like.

Eden's fingertips brushing him, her husky voice whispering, words burning into his soul and the tiny ring gleaming as light caressed the intertwined strands of gold.

I'm not offering you love and happily ever after. I can't be what you want me to be.

Hazel eyes luminous, alive with all the colors of life, watching him, loving him.

Love is never wasted. Never. But it can hurt like nothing else on earth.

Heaven and hell and the rainbow burning between.

I would sell my soul not to want you.

Fairy-tale girl, all laughter and golden light.

But no longer.

He had stripped her of laughter as surely as he had stripped her of innocence. She had loved him; he had denied that love was possible. He had left her without a word of hope...and now she no longer wore the chain and its tiny gold ring.

She hadn't been able to teach him to believe in love, but he had been able to teach her to believe in despair.

Nevada made the low sound of a man who has just taken a body blow. He hadn't meant to destroy anything at all, much less something as rare and beautiful as Eden. Yet he had destroyed just the same. The proof was lying in his hand, a dead child's ring and a living woman's endless loss.

For a long time Nevada stood motionless, staring into space, seeing nothing, not even his own tears.

THE LONG WIND BLEW, SWEEPING DOWN out of the distant mountains, bringing restlessness to the mixed evergreen forest. A river ran pale with glacial melt, brawling through the wide, flat valley down to the sea. Everywhere there was the subdued frenzy of life that has only a short growing season and a whole new generation to raise.

Eden sat in the small log cabin that had been her parents' first Alaskan home and now was hers. Although the early June day was vibrant with sunlight and wind, she wasn't out searching for lynx across the fertile green land. The changes in her body had made her sleepy, slightly nauseated, lacking any ambition other than to sit in the sun and remind herself that tears were wasted. If she could have gone back and lived again the weeks in Colorado, she would have changed nothing that was within her power to change.

And if Eden were haunted by memories of a warrior's unsmiling green eyes and gentle, passionate hands, then so be it. She would not change that, either. Nevada had given her more of beauty and ecstasy than she had ever dreamed of having. The fact that the pain of her loss was greater, too, than she had imagined possible, was something she would just have to live through as she had lived through the loss of Aurora, enduring until the bitter and the sweet were inextricably mixed, each defining and refining the other until they became a seamless, beautiful whole.

Baby sat near Eden's feet, looking through the screen door toward the uninhabited land. His long black ears were erect, his narrow muzzle tipped into the cool rush of air, his yellow eyes gleaming.

Without warning he came to his feet in a lithe rush, drank the wind, and tipped back his head in a howl. The eerie, primal sound froze Eden. She heard that particular howl from Baby only when she returned to him after a long absence. But she hadn't been absent. Her body had been present all the time, if not her heart and mind.

Perhaps Mark had returned early from his stint in the oil fields.

Eden sighed and stood up. As she opened the screen door, a man stepped from the willows sheltering the path to the cabin. His shoulders were wide and his walk was as easy as that of a cougar prowling. The world tipped and spun dizzily, forcing Eden to hang on to the door frame or fall.

It can't be. Nevada.

Baby leaped through the open door and hit the ground running and yapping, nearly walking on the sky in delight. Nevada caught the wolf in midleap, spun around, and sent Baby flying off in another direction. The wolf turned nimbly and launched himself at the man again in a game that the two of them had created in a land thousands of miles distant.

Numbly Eden watched wolf and warrior play, wondering if she were dreaming…or if she had simply gone mad.

When the first exuberance of Baby's greeting was quenched, Nevada looked toward the cabin door. A single glance at Eden's blank face told him that the mistress wasn't nearly as happy to see him as her wolf had been.

"Hello, Eden. You look…"

Nevada's voice died. He had no words to describe how Eden looked to him. Nor could he describe his hunger to hold her warmth and laughter within his arms once more.

"How did you find me?" she asked finally.

"It took some doing. I had to lean on some folks at the university pretty hard before they gave me any help."

Nevada's light green eyes searched Eden's face, noting each sign of change, but most of all he saw the darkness of her eyes, a darkness she tried to conceal by looking away.

"Don't," he said softly.

"What?"

"Don't look away from me."

"I can't—I—seeing you—"

Eden laced her fingers together and looked at Nevada and felt as though she were being torn apart.

I'd give my soul not to want you.

She knew how Nevada felt, now. Too late.

She tried to take a deep, steadying breath, but no matter how much air she took in, it wasn't enough. The world was spinning too quickly, she was off balance, no center, nothing stable, nothing but the longing for Nevada that would not end.

"Eden!"

Nevada caught Eden as her knees gave away, carried her into the cabin and set her gently on the bed. The pallor of her skin made him want to cry out in protest. Her lashes stirred, then opened to reveal eyes that were darker than he remembered. She started to sit up.

"No," he said, catching Eden's shoulders gently, pressing her back into the bed, brushing his lips over her forehead, her cheek. "Just lie still, fairy-tale girl."

Nevada's glance went over Eden like hands, noting everything. His nostrils flared, drinking in the subtle change in her scent. His whole body went still. He lifted his head and looked into her eyes.

"You're pregnant," he said flatly. "I knew it. Damn those university bureaucrats! I should have been here weeks ago!" He cursed once, savagely. "Is everything all right?"

"Yes."

"Bull. You fainted."

"Shock, not pregnancy." Eden closed her eyes, unable to bear Nevada's scrutiny. "I never expected to see you again. It was like having someone come back from the dead."

"Why didn't you tell me?"

"That I'm pregnant?"

Nevada nodded curtly.

"And make you feel even more trapped than you did in Wildfire Canyon?" Eden shook her head and opened her eyes. "I can't bear watching your pain. I can't heal it. I can only make it worse. I won't do that, Nevada." Not wanting to, unable to stop herself, she lifted her hand and touched the coarse silk of his beard. "Don't worry, warrior. I'll be a good mother to our child."

"But you don't think I'll be a good father."

"In every way but one, you would be a marvelous father."

Nevada waited, watching Eden with hooded eyes.

"Children need love," she whispered. "You don't believe in it."

"Neither do you, now. I took that from you as surely as I took your innocence."

Eden stared at Nevada. "What do you mean?"

He reached into his shirt pocket and brought out a golden chain and tiny braided ring.

"You told me that you wore this to remind you that love was never wasted, never futile. *And then you left it behind.*"

"I didn't need Aurora's ring anymore. My reminder was alive within me. Your baby, Nevada. My baby. Our baby. A child of the love you don't believe in. But I understand why, now. If you allowed yourself to feel emotion, you would be vulnerable again. Your emotions run strong and hard and so very deep. Your ability to feel could destroy you. It nearly did. So you walked away from feeling, from emotion, from love."

"Eden, I…" Nevada's throat closed.

She smiled sadly. "It's all right, warrior. If I weren't pregnant, I would have done the same thing you did. Walked away from feeling, shed my pain like a snake shedding skin, and walked away, just walked away. Then I held Carolina and remembered little Aurora's laughter and I prayed that I was pregnant. And I am. Thank you for that, Nevada. Thank you for allowing your control to slip that much."

Eden's husky voice made Nevada's throat close around emotions he no longer could deny. Silently he bent down and fastened the gold chain around Eden's neck once more. The metal was warm from his body, almost weightless. He kissed the tiny gold ring where it lay in the soft hollow of her throat, then gathered Eden close and held her, simply held her, fighting for the self-control that always slipped away when he was close to Eden.

"Do you want to live here or on the Rocking M after we're married?" Nevada asked without lifting his face from the warm curve of Eden's neck.

The subtle rasp in his voice was like a cat's tongue licking over Eden's nerves. The temptation he offered was dizzying, almost overwhelming.

"No," she breathed.

"Then where?"

"No. Just no."

"Why?"

"Don't. Please, don't. If I weren't pregnant, you wouldn't be talking about marriage."

"Are you sure of that?" Nevada asked softly.

"I'm sure I can't bear to watch your eyes turn bleaker each time we make love," Eden said with desperate calm. "I'm sure I can't bear being something you don't want yet can't refuse." She closed her eyes but couldn't prevent her tears from falling as she whispered, "I can't heal you but I can set you free. Walk away, warrior, just walk away."

Eden felt Nevada stir, sitting up, moving away from her. It was what she knew must be, yet even knowing it she had to bite back a cry of pain.

The feel of Nevada's lips against Eden's left hand was like a soft brand burning her. She made a tiny sound of protest, but couldn't free her hand. Something smooth and warm slid over her third finger.

"Open your eyes," Nevada said, brushing away Eden's tears with his kisses.

When Eden opened her eyes she saw gold gleaming on her ring finger, a circle of braided metal that was exactly like the tiny ring lying in the hollow of her throat. Silently Nevada held out his left hand. On his hard palm a third ring gleamed, golden braids intertwined.

"If you believe I can love," he said, "put the ring on me."

Eden looked into his eyes for a long moment, remembering the instant when she had caught his wrist in the bar and seen both the darkness and the light that was Nevada.

Slowly she picked up the golden ring, kissed it and slid it onto his finger, whispering her love against his palm. Nevada kissed her ring in return, lifted his head, and looked into the eyes that saw so deeply into him, accepting him for what he was, loving him despite the darkness he had known.

Her love was like stepping into the sun, a blazing joy transforming him as surely as pain once had.

"Nevada…?"

Eden's breath stopped, for she had seen nothing more beautiful than her dark warrior's smile, a smile to make angels weep. With trembling fingers she touched Nevada's lips. His hard and gentle hands framed her face, holding her, seeing the reflection of his newfound freedom in her radiant hazel eyes.

"You are my life, my soul, everything I wanted and feared I would never have," Nevada whispered, bending down to Eden. "Fairy-tale girl, I love you."